Susan Frances was born in Surrey, England and went to Godalming Grammar School. As a child, she was fascinated by her grandfather's stories of their Devon family, which later inspired her to research her family history and write *No One Must Know*, the first book in The Chiddleigh Saga. She lives with her husband in Devon, close to the Ashetyne village in her book.

Visit Susan online at www.susanfrances.co.uk
and follow her on Twitter @SusanFrances18

NO ONE
MUST KNOW

BOOK 1
OF THE CHIDDLEIGH SAGA

Susan Frances

This edition 2021
First published in Great Britain by Susan Frances Wheeler.
Copyright © Susan Frances Wheeler 2021
Susan Frances asserts the moral right to be identified as the author of this work.
A catalogue record for this book is available from the British Library.

ISBN: 978-1-3999-0110-9

Printed and bound in Great Britain by Severn, Gloucester.

Cover Design: Dante Masuri
Typesetting: Bill Wheeler

I owe thanks to my husband, Bill, for his support, encouragement and book formatting skills.
I also thank my friend and fellow author, Jude Austin, for all her hard work and for giving me the benefit of her literary experience.

Without either of you, I would still be on Chapter 1.

CHAPTER 1

1st May 1330

Joan de Conteigh twirled, the soft folds of pale blue fabric rippling around her ankles. She preferred pale yellow, her favourite colour, but her mother insisted her wedding kirtle be blue for purity. She held out an arm, admiring the close-fitting sleeves, and ran her hands along the seams hugging her waist. It had been worth the wait whilst the maid tied the laces down her back. It was the finest dress she had worn, and now she felt like a lady. But why couldn't she be beautiful like Mama, who was tall and elegant with skin the colour of milk, instead of short with freckles?

Would Sir John like her? Pray God he would, but she'd never met him.

'You look beautiful,' said her mother, Edith. 'Fifteen birth dates and ready to be a Lady of the Manor. Are you nervous?'

The butterflies were still dancing in her stomach. Was that nerves or excitement? 'A little.'

'I have something for you.' Edith carefully opened the purse on her belt. Her face glowing with pride, she reverently held out her hands. A small gold cross set with a sparkling red jewel nestled in her palms. 'It belonged to my mother.'

Her first piece of real jewellery. 'It's beautiful,' Joan said, her eyes as bright as the jewel. 'Can I wear it today?'

'Of course, as I did on my wedding day. And as your daughter will on hers.'

Joan blushed. She knew her duty as a wife but didn't like to think about it. She touched the cross at her throat. 'I shall treasure it always. Thank you, Mama.'

'Now, how do I look?' Edith stood back. Her dress was similar but in a darker shade of blue to deceive bad spirits and keep the newly married couple safe.

'Comely, Mama, most comely. Give me a twirl. How I wish I had one of those new looking glasses, then I could see myself. Just imagine! Do you think they work?'

'I'm sure I don't know, nor do I like the idea of such trickery —'

'Are you two ready?' Her father's short stocky frame filled the doorway. He ran a finger inside the collar of his new jupon jacket and pushed a long sleeve up his arm. 'It's five miles to Ashetyne, and we must be there by the midday bell.'

Ready? Joan's stomach lurched. She'd been looking forward to this moment for so long, but now it was here, she wasn't so sure. Her maid stepped forward, the surcoat draped over her arms.

This was it, then. There was no going back. Joan clipped her maiden's veil in place. Strange to think she'd never wear it again, for once she was married, she would have the married woman's linen wimple.

Before stepping outside, she took a last glance around the hall; at the sheepskins on the floor, the battered old stool she'd always loved and her Pa's favourite chair. She breathed in her last smell of candle wax and rushes.

It was a comforting old room and the only home she had known.

'Joan! Come on, we've a long way to go and we'll be late.'

With a lump in her throat, she lifted her skirts and closed the door softly behind her.

Edith was already seated in the wagon, tapping her fingers on the rail. Usually pulled by an ox, the cart was crudely made of wood with two solid timber wheels. Joan hoped Sir John wouldn't think it too poor. Her cousin's wedding wagon had been very grand, but Papa had said that he was just a farmer and couldn't afford one like that. He had made a canopy, though, and covered it with goat skins in case it rained. And she supposed the bunches of flowers adorning the poles and sides added something. She smiled thinly. Papa had tried, and although it wasn't exactly fit for Queen Phillippa, it was fine enough.

Sitting opposite her mother, Joan gripped the bench as the wagon jolted forward. She hated goodbyes and promised herself that she wouldn't cry or look back, but her home called to her as they left the yard, and she had to have just one last look. She stared at the little stone farmhouse as it blurred and diminished to a speck in the distance. Her knuckles white, she swallowed.

The track stretched ahead. Her mouth was dry as a bone, but there was nothing to drink. Thank the Lord she hadn't been able to eat, for now she felt sick to her stomach.

Lady Joan de Chiddleigh of Court Barton Manor. She ran the title around in her head a few times. It sounded very grand.

The cart dropped into a deep rut, almost bumping her off the bench. She gripped harder. The horse strained, the wheels lurched clear and rolled on, clicking on each rotation. Click, click, click.

When were they going to get there? She counted the clicks but soon got bored. The Forest of Dartmoor loomed high to her left, mysteriously dark and forbidding. She shivered. It didn't look as friendly as the green rolling fields of home.

They passed an untidy scattering of cruck houses, sitting squat like a row of upturned boats with tiny doorways and a mop of thatch reeds for the roof. A boy and a girl ran out and stood barefoot, in thin ragged tunics and stared with open mouths. Presumably, they belonged to the Chiddleigh estate and would soon be her peasants. The small girl waved and smiled. Joan lifted her hand to wave back but hesitated. The Lady of the Manor wouldn't acknowledge her peasants, would she? She tucked her hand under her and turned her eyes to the front. There was so much to remember.

They stopped at the top of a steep hill. She looked up to the sun. It was directly overhead. On cue, the church bell rang. It was midday, and the journey had gone too fast. She needed more time; time to compose herself, time to give her mother one last hug. She fought to clear her thoughts, and her hands felt clammy.

'We're nearly there. I'm walking with the horse to help him down the hill. We don't want the wagon running away with us. That would make an entrance!'

Papa was trying to lighten the mood, but he sounded false, and fumbled as he took hold of the bridle. Mama was straightening her sleeves and fiddling with the amethyst pendant at her throat. They were as nervous as she was.

They made it safely to the bottom, turned a bend, and splashed through the ford. Joan could see the square grey tower of the church above the high hedges and leaned forward to get a better view. Crowds of people lined the way, spilling on to the track in front of them. As she passed, the men removed their caps and the women curtsied. She'd had no idea it was going to be like this. What was it Mama said? Hold your head high, stand tall, walk slowly and don't forget to smile. How could she smile, when all she wanted to do was run away and hide? And the wretched butterflies refused to stop dancing in her stomach.

She ran her fingers through her long chestnut hair. She should have listened to Mama and worn it in sensible braids looped neatly behind her ears. But her hair was her best feature and it was the last time she could wear it loose in public. Once she was a married woman, her hair would have to be coiled or braided under a wimple.

As they approached the centre of the village, the buzz of excitement fell silent and the crowd inched forward. Never again would she mock the poor caged wretches in the market freak shows. The wagon stopped in front of the church. Every eye was boring into her, and somewhere amongst all those people was Sir John.

Her mother stepped daintily from the wagon and nodded to her. She was waiting to see her daughter make her first grand entrance. Everyone was waiting.

Her legs trembling, Joan took a deep breath. Slowly, pretend they're not there. Carefully, she lifted her skirts and turned to take the steps. Holding on to the sides, she felt with her foot for the first step. Breathing again, she went to take the next.

She heard fabric rip and froze, mortified. Her sigh fell from her heart to her feet. It was only a little tear; maybe no one would notice.

Below her, Mama coughed discretely. Joan knew they were watching, she didn't need reminding. Grabbing her skirts in her fist she took the final step and with a wriggle of her hips, straightened her gown.

She didn't dare turn around. Rubbing her hands together and avoiding the reproach that was sure to be in her mother's eyes, she kept her back turned from the crowd and stared at the ground as Mama fastened a ring of apple blossom on her head, the sweet scent filling the air around her. Her mother stepped back and nodded as if to say, go on, what are you waiting for?

Joan tilted her chin, forced the corners of her mouth into a smile, and with her heart thumping through the fabric of her dress, turned and faced her people.

A young man stepped forward. 'Good morrow, I am Sir John de Chiddleigh.' He inclined his head. 'I pray you had a good journey.'

Many times, she had tried to imagine what he looked like, and now he was here and she daren't look at him. If he repulsed her, she'd never keep it from her face and everyone would see, but he was looking at her. His eyes slowly took in every inch of her from the top of her head to her toes. It was an uncomfortable moment and she dare not move. Dear God, let him like what he sees.

She dipped a curtsey and felt the colour flood to her cheeks.

'The priest is waiting,' Sir John said.

As Joan felt the touch of his hand on her elbow, she focused on the rich fabric of his cote-hardie, hanging in luxurious folds to his knees. Out of the corner of her eye, she caught a glint from a large gold buckle on his shoulder.

He steered her the few steps to their positions in front of the old oak church door. Standing on his left, she only came to his shoulder. His very proximity made her feel more like a little girl than his new lady. She'd give anything for a goblet of wine.

He was looking at her again, she could feel it. She kept her eyes focused on the punch-holed pattern on her new shoes.

The priest cleared his throat and began the service, but his words floated over her. With every word, her childhood was slipping away and taking her closer to womanhood, an exciting but frightening place she didn't understand.

'Sir John de Chiddleigh, wilt thou take Joan de Conteigh, here present, for thy lawful wife, according to the rite of our Holy Mother the Church?'

'I will,' Sir John replied in a loud confident manner.

There was a slight pause. Reluctantly, she lifted her gaze.

The priest nodded and continued. 'Joan de Conteigh, wilt thou take Sir John de Chiddleigh, here present, for thy lawful husband, according to the rite of our Holy Mother the Church?'

'I will.' Hoping the quiver in her voice didn't show, she stole a glance across to her mother for reassurance, but Mama was dabbing her eyes with a kerchief and didn't notice.

Joan desperately wanted to steal a glance at her husband but didn't have the courage. Out of the corner of her eye, she could see that he had fair, straight hair cut in the latest fashion to the shoulder, but that was all she could make out without staring at his face, and she daren't do that.

She felt his touch for the first time as he joined her right hand with his. His fingers were long, slender and cool to the touch. It was her first contact with her husband, and a hot flush spread from her neck to her cheeks. Mortified, and praying no one noticed, she stumbled through the rest of her pledge.

The priest sprinkled them with holy water before blessing the bride's ring.

'Let us pray. Bless, O Lord, this ring, which we bless in Thy name, that she who shall wear it, keeping the faith unto her spouse, may abide in Thy peace and in obedience to Thy will, and ever live in mutual love. Through Christ our Lord.'

The priest sprinkled the ring with holy water in the form of a cross and passed it to Sir John. She held out her hand and tried to stop the trembling as he placed the ring on her finger. Forcing herself not to look at it, she bit her lip and focused on the black shape of the priest in front of her.

'With this ring, I thee wed and I plight unto thee my troth,' Sir John promised.

It was her turn. She placed a matching ring on his finger and repeated the oath in a quiet voice.

She was now Lady de Chiddleigh, and she didn't feel any different.

The priest opened the church door. Sir John led her forward into the church for the nuptial mass. Before she crossed the threshold, she glanced over her shoulder and smiled at her parents. Turning back, she raised her head and walked forward to begin the next chapter of her life.

CHAPTER 2

Sir John stood at the high table with his hands behind
his back, his head held high as he surveyed his guests
below him. His high set jaw gave him a determined look
and he obviously took care of his appearance, for his
hair was clean beneath his feathered hat and his beard
neatly trimmed. His deep blue cote-hardie was laced
down to his waist and gathered by a leather belt
adorned with blue and red jewels and clasped with an
imposing gold buckle. He was fair indeed, but he was
so adult, and the hall was massive, much bigger than
any she had been in before.

Tall, grey stone walls towered above her to rows of
arched oak beams spanning the width, now festooned
with garlands of greenery. The roof was high and
thickly thatched. Set in the thickness of the walls were
four small arch windows on each side, interspersed
with flaming torches, set in iron sconces, their brilliant
yellow flames sending pools of light up the walls and
across the floor. Two lines of dark oak trestle tables and
benches ran the length of the hall from just below her
to the pair of solid oak doors at the far end.

This was now her hall and it was magnificent. As she
sat to Sir John's right, what little confidence she had

deserted her. This was his world. Could it ever be hers?

At home, they didn't have a high table, and she'd never even been to such a grand occasion before. The most important guests, the men dressed in bright jupons or tunics with their ladies in brilliant coloured gowns and sparkling jewels, sat closest to the high table, going down in rank to the peasants by the draughty doors, in their more muted greys and coarse green cloth.

And, dear God, they were all staring at her. She fidgeted. Would Sir John say something and rescue her? He was facing forward and seemed unaware. She must remember to smile, so she did, but focused her eyes on the doors. Why had she made such a fool of herself getting off that wagon, and God only knew why she'd curtseyed! Her cheeks flamed at the memory, making her feel hot and uncomfortable. All these important nobles probably thought her an up-country young maid not fit to be a lady, and right now that was exactly how she felt.

Joan dropped her eyes to her lap and dreamed she was galloping across the fields at home, just her and her pony, Mead. But she had to get used to this; after all, she was the Lady of the Manor and should act like one.

Straightening her back, she lifted her chin and forced herself to look up but she still couldn't face them. Instead, she stared at the far wall and thought of Mead.

The priest gave prayers of thanks and, as the enticing smells of the feast to come drifted around them, everyone dipped their fingers into the water bowls. The first line of servants placed pewter platters loaded with roasted quail, goose, and chicken, and platters of lamb stuffed with rosemary and beef stewed with saffron on

16

the tables. A second line of servants quickly followed, carrying earthenware dishes piled high with cabbage, carrots, and beans. Young boys brought willow baskets filled with loaves of white bread to accompany the salted fish. Finally, there were dishes of sweet custards, and fruits and almonds coated in honey, all beautifully garnished with blossom flowers and rose petals.

Never had she seen such dishes before and her stomach rumbled. The people switched their attention from her to the food and she let go of the folds of her gown, which she'd scrunched tightly in her hands.

A fatherly looking man with grey hair sitting on her right smiled at her. She stifled a giggle, for he had an extraordinarily long straight nose.

'Prithee, my lady, I am Carac de Perceux, Sir John's bailiff. I thought the service went well.'

'Yes,' She didn't remember much about it and ought to make conversation, but her mind was blank. To her annoyance, heat rose up her neck and her cheeks burned.

He leaned in towards her. 'If it helps, pretend to be a lady until you feel like one. No one will ever know.'

He had a kind face and she smiled gratefully back. Taking his advice, she reached forward to take a bowl of beans, but his soft hand on her arm stopped her. 'It is customary to use a knife and take a slice of meat first. Then take a spoonful or two from the accompanying dishes. It is quite acceptable to return for more.'

Her cheeks burned once more. She knew that. What must he think of her?

'And if you would like more wine, hold up your goblet,' he demonstrated, 'and one of the servants will fill it for you. If they don't attend quickly enough, I find that turning around and giving them a hard stare always has the desired effect.'

The side of his eyes creased into fine lines as he smiled.

Whether it was the food, having Carac next to her, or simply the wine, she didn't know, but for the first time that day, her stomach stopped churning and she began to relax. She tapped her foot in time with the troubadours' music and, along with everyone else, joined in their songs and laughed at their stories. From time to time, she cast a look at Sir John, but he didn't notice. He seemed very aloof, which was disheartening, but perhaps that was the correct way to behave in front of his peasants. Or maybe he didn't enjoy such entertainments. She hoped that wasn't true. It would be very dull to be married to someone with no sense of fun.

Perhaps he was just not interested in her. She shrank at the idea. That would be much worse.

Later, when the dessert dishes lay empty, and the guests had opened their belts a notch or two, she was captivated by the acrobats tumbling across the floor and at the jugglers tossing lighted torches high into the air; three, four, and five at a time to the delighted applause from their audience. Never had she been to so fine a banquet or enjoyed herself so much. If this was how life as Lady de Chiddleigh was going to be, she was looking forward to it.

The excitement of the entertainment died down, boys replenished the dwindling candles and men started to clear the tables and move them back to the sides of the hall. Some guests drifted off, but the troubadours returned and played their pipes and lyres. The dancing was about to begin and she loved dancing. But there was still the cloud nudging at the back of her mind. The evening was passing too fast and the time would soon come when—she put a hand to her stomach to quell the knot inside. As a wife, it was her duty but…

Joan shook her head ever so slightly. She wouldn't let the thought spoil the evening. She gave herself a quick check; her hair was still in place and she hadn't spilt any food down her front. Excitement building, she waited for Sir John to ask her to dance, but he was staring at a group of men at the far end of the hall. His jaw was tight, his face hard as stone. He'd been aloof earlier and now he seemed angry. Was it those men that had caused his ire, or was it her fault? Maybe he was a moody type of person. Her uncle Edward was like that, and she never knew how to behave or talk to him for knowing how he would respond. Such a husband would be difficult to live with. Maybe her appearance displeased him. That would be awful. Perhaps she had made a mistake and embarrassed him. She didn't think she had.

'I trust you enjoyed the entertainments,' Carac broke into her thoughts.

'I did, and the music is very good. I should love to dance.'

Carac gave her a thin smile. 'I couldn't presume, my lady. You must wait for Sir John to accompany you.'

'I didn't mean…' Her face burned again. 'The peasants are enjoying themselves. They dance with such abandon. I don't know where they get their energy from,' she said quickly.

'Indeed, and it's good for them to have a break from their work and forget their troubles. They labour long hours and have a hard life.' Carac's foot tapped in rhythm to the music.

'Yet they seem so happy. Look at that young girl with the long dark hair in the grey kirtle. Her feet are so light, she hasn't left the floor for the last three dances.'

'That's Annie, the kitchen maid, I believe.'

Sir John continued to stare at the group of young men now huddled by the large tun barrels of ale. They were dressed and held themselves like nobles, but their clothes were dishevelled and dirty. One — a dark, burly man with a thick unkempt beard — suddenly threw back his head with a raucous laugh, spilling his drink down his front and on to the floor.

'Who's that man over there? Is he one of the local nobles?' she asked.

Carac stopped tapping and shifted in his seat. 'That is Sir John's cousin, Aldred de Chiddleigh. With him are his brother and some of his friends, I imagine.'

'I'm surprised he's not here on the high table. I'd like to meet him.'

'It wouldn't be wise.'

'Why ever not? He's family.'

Carac put his two hands together as though in prayer and rested two fingers on his lips. After a pause, he held up her goblet to the boy behind. 'More wine, my lady?'

Curious, Joan thought. Sir John wasn't pleased to see them, and now Carac was evading her questions.

'The dance has finished,' she said. 'Now is a perfect time. Will you introduce me?'

She made to stand, but Carac put a firm hand on her arm. 'Sir John wouldn't like it. Maybe I should explain.' He lowered his voice and leaned close. 'By rights, Aldred and his brother, who's the one standing next to him, shouldn't be here. They are the proverbial 'black sheep' of the family. They weren't invited, and they are not welcome. This is not the place to discuss such matters, but I know Sir John will be livid they're here.'

Did her husband have a temper? 'Is that why he

seems so tense?'

A wry smile played around Carac's lips. He leaned closer, almost whispering in her ear. 'Partly, but Sir John never enjoys such occasions with his peasants. Now, if you'll excuse me, my lady.'

Joan sipped her wine thoughtfully. She shouldn't discuss her husband with her bailiff, even if she did like him. Carac had dealt with her mistakes kindly and was easy to talk to, but why wouldn't he tell her about Aldred and his brother? Sir John looked her way, stupidly making her flustered. Pray God, he wasn't going to lead her to the bedchamber now.

'We ought to dance.' He stood and offered his hand.

He wasn't exactly smiling. It was as though he were performing a duty rather than a pleasure, but she still sighed with relief.

In the circle of dancers, Sir John took care to stand with the nobles and not with the common peasants. Everyone joined hands and the piper began to play. For the first time, she didn't blush when Sir John took her hand, but proudly held her head high. Two gentle steps to the right, a swing of her leg, and two steps to the left. Into the centre and out, three claps, and begin again. She knew this dance. He didn't bother to clap and as the piper increased the tempo and everyone laughed as they tried to keep up, he didn't join in with their merriment. After only two dances, and with a straight face, he returned her to her seat.

Joan was just beginning to enjoy herself, so what had she done to be sitting back at the high table when everyone else was still dancing? She'd held herself well and remembered all the steps. Perhaps he was a dull person. She hoped not, for she could never respect such a man. But it didn't matter what she thought; she was his lady and must never forget that. It was her duty to do his bidding. That might be difficult at times, for — as Mama was always telling her — she was too strong-minded for a girl.

She almost pouted, but then remembered where she was. Maybe Carac would offer to dance with her, but with his precise manner and serious face, he didn't look like the dancing type either. With trepidation and mounting nerves, she wondered when Sir John would lead her out of the hall. Leaning forward, she tried to catch her Mama's eye, but Mama was talking with one of the guests. Smiling bravely, Joan watched her husband laughing and conversing with the wealthy landowners and swallowed the knowledge that he hadn't talked or laughed with her like that.

As Mama was always telling her, she was fortunate to be in such a match. Their family was untitled, but Sir John's father, Sir James de Chiddleigh, had approached her parents. She was under no illusion, though. It wasn't her that he wanted for his son; it was her Papa's rich grass pastures in the north of the shire. The de Conteigh lands were only three leagues from the port of Bristol, which would give him easier access to exports for his wool, something he didn't have. By the time Sir James made his offer of a marriage contract, she was the only surviving child out of three daughters and two sons, and Mama was past child-bearing age, making Joan the sole heir.

Carac was mingling with the guests and she lost sight of Sir John. She searched the faces, but he seemed to have disappeared. He must come back to her! She would die of shame if he didn't.

Candles sputtered in the sconces, their dying shadows lengthening across the floor as their thick smell filled the air. Joan watched the boys snuff them out with long iron candle hoods and replace them. The butterflies in her stomach were back and she drank more wine, listening to the guests' voices growing louder. Enviously, she watched them dance with more abandon and heard their laughter filling the hall.

'It's time we left.' Sir John towered over her. His face was pale and his voice strained.

The time had come.

A moment ago, she'd been bored sitting in her seat, but now it felt like a nice safe place to be. She wasn't ready. She focussed on a few wine spots on his surcoat — she could do with some more wine — and ran her hands down her sides. 'The celebrations aren't over. Couldn't we have just one more dance?'

'I've had enough of it. Leave them to enjoy themselves as they wish. It's time to go.' He looked down on her, his eyes commanding her will.

Where was Mama? Mama would understand and persuade Sir John to wait. Desperately, she looked along the table for help, but her mother just gave her the smallest of nods and a thin, knowing smile.

She had no choice; her lord was waiting. Gripping the table, Joan stood. Taking extra care to hold her gown so as not to trip, she lifted her chin and walked at his side down the long, long length of the hall as every eye pierced her back.

The hall door closed with a final clunk behind her.

She was on her own.

His authority.

Her duty.

CHAPTER 3

The minstrels returned to their places, and folks put down their ale cups and took to the floor for more dancing. This was the lord's wedding, after all.

Cook had kept Annie working days and night for this feast, and she wasn't going to waste a moment. Having eaten more than she should, she was going to dance the night away. She loved dancing; unlike her friend, Mary, who was still sitting next to her with her hands held primly in her lap.

Annie felt sorry for Mary, who was plain with freckles and not nearly as pretty as she herself was. Mary was two summers older than her; maybe that was why she was so sensible. But Mary had never been much fun. She would never cross the seven stones by the mill in case she slipped and tore her skirts; unlike Annie, who didn't care whether her clothes were torn or not.

They'd been friends since the good Lord had seen fit to take Annie's Ma one harsh winter. She didn't remember her, being only three summers old at the time, but from what Pa told her, Annie thought her Ma would have loved the wedding.

Annie fiddled with the purse hanging from her belt,

watching the dancers and scanning the crowd to catch the eye of a likely lad. 'I loved the new lady's gown. I wish I had one like that. She doesn't look much older than us. I wonder what's she's like?' She smiled through her lashes at a lanky lad from across the hall who was looking her way.

'Like all of her kind, I expect,' answered Mary. 'Haughty and above the likes of us. He hardly said a word to her all evening, did you notice? And they didn't dance for long. Perhaps he doesn't think her fair, or she already hates him. He's so miserable, I wouldn't want him for a husband.'

'Neither would I.'

'What's your brother up to?' Mary asked suddenly as she adjusted her veil and took a sip of ale.

'Where?'

'There, with his hood up and scuttling out the hall with young Roger like a pair of naughty rabbits.'

'I'm sure I don't know or care. Peter's always into something. Come on, I'm not sitting around for these cloth-head lads. Let's dance!'

Small and agile, Annie flew across the floor, loving the feel of her long dark hair flying around her as she twirled her way through dance after dance. Ignoring the frowns of the older dancers, she lifted her skirts so the lads caught a glimpse of her legs as she kicked them higher and higher and flashed a smile when she saw them staring.

'Whew! I'm hot.' She flopped down on the bench and reached for another drink. 'I've never had so much fun!'

'You be careful. Go easy on that ale,' said Mary. 'And you should be wearing your headscarf in public!'

'A few cups won't hurt me.' Annie put down the cup,

blinking. The room was blurring a little.

'You dancing?'

Startled, Annie looked into the dark brown eyes of a broad-shouldered young man standing in front of her. He had a thick dark beard and even darker, thicker hair sitting like thatch on his head. He was older than the village lads and wearing the red tabard of a noble. He wasn't the most handsome in the room, but fancy such a man choosing her above all the noble lasses here! Annie's face broke into her prettiest smile as she recognized him as Aldred de Chiddleigh, a distant relative of Sir John. 'Of course I'm dancing!'

All the lads told her she was the prettiest maid in the village and the best dancer. She'd show this high-born man how a peasant girl could dance. As the tempo picked up, she spun and twirled, throwing back her head, exposing her white throat, her small neat breasts straining against the bodice of her kirtle. The lads always noticed that. She looked teasingly into his hungry eyes, her loose skirts whirling as she spun round and round to the music. She may not be the brightest lass in the kitchen, but this would give those maids something to talk about.

After three dances, she flopped breathless to her seat, fanning herself with her hand. 'Did you see me?' she asked Mary.

'Everyone saw you, and you should be ashamed of yourself, showing your legs and flirting like that!' Mary remonstrated, frowning at Annie.

'What do you mean? I'm only having a bit of fun.'

Mary raised her eyebrows. 'You do know who that is, don't you?'

'Of course I do. He's Aldred.'

'Aldred de Chiddleigh, no less, and if you know what's good for you, you'll stay away from the likes of him and his brother. That whole branch of the family's trouble.'

Annie pouted. 'You're always telling me what to do! You're just like Cook with Annie do this, and Annie do that! I'm not a cloth-head; I can make up my own mind. Anyway, I like him and I'm having fun.' She crossed her arms tightly across her chest.

Aldred was on the other side of the hall with his group of friends, keeping watchful eyes on her over his cup. Pretending not to notice, Annie trilled a laugh and twisted a lock of hair around her fingers. He'd be back, she was sure of it.

The minstrels resumed their playing, and Aldred put down his ale and headed towards her just as she'd hoped he would. Her heart racing, she drained her cup and straightening her skirts.

'Want some more?' he said.

She giggled with false modesty and, with a challenging look to Mary, took his hand.

This time as they danced, the turns started making her dizzy, and when the music slowed, the room kept spinning and she started to feel sick. She knew she should stop and sit awhile, but if she did, what would Aldred think of her? So she kept smiling and forced herself to dance. She threw a glance to the minstrels, pray God the piper would stop soon. Her legs felt weak and she couldn't kick them high if she'd wanted to.

To her relief, the piper soon took a break, but Aldred didn't take her back to Mary. Instead, he put his arm around her waist and rejoined his friends, and Annie didn't like to protest. Their faces blurred in front of her, but she smiled and laughed as their voices faded in and out and the room spun faster and faster. The air was thick with the smell of candle wax and smoke, and her dress felt tight against her chest. The room was so hot that she could hardly breathe, and the stink of stale sweat from Aldred and his friends was making her gag. She had to get out or she'd disgrace herself and vomit where she stood.

'I need to find Mary.' Her voice sounded distant.

Aldred didn't reply but just held her firmly. Annie tried to twist away but his hold was too strong. She couldn't wait any longer; if he didn't let her go now, she'd be sick all over him.

'Let me go. I want to find Mary.' She slapped at his hand and heard him laugh as his fingers tickled her waist.

'You don't want to go yet. Have another drink.' He tickled her again, making her squirm.

'She's a funny colour. Looks like she's going to part with her feast,' said a voice.

'Let her go; she's not worth it. We don't want a scene,' said another.

'All she needs is a bit of fresh air,' said Aldred, running a finger down the side of Annie's face. 'Come on. You'll feel better, I promise.'

'Then you'll take me back to Mary?'

'Of course.'

He was a noble and he'd promised. What harm could it do?

A twig snapped. Annie didn't move. Steps, heavy steps coming close. She clutched the linen across her front and curled tighter into the base of the tree. Holding her breath, she screwed her eyes tight shut and pressed her hands against her face as the steps came closer, crashing through the undergrowth. She curled even tighter, her heart thumping so loudly, she was sure he would hear her.

The steps stopped, and Annie held her breath. Silence.

A hand touched her shoulder, and she opened her mouth and screamed and screamed and screamed.

She was rocking in the darkness. She was a little girl in her mother's arms, safe and secure. The familiar smell of horse – her Pa's smell – wrapped around her like a warm blanket.

'Lass,' was all he said and like a river bursting its banks, she sobbed as she snuggled into the comfort of her Pa's bear-like arms.

'My God, I'll kill whoever did this to her.' That was her brother, Peter, his rough hands gently stroking her hair. 'Our little Annie,' he whispered.

'Lass, who was it?' Her Pa's voice unusually soft and gentle.

She couldn't. If she said his name, it would make it real again and she couldn't bear that.

'Ye must tell us,' Peter said. 'Ye'll feel better if you do.'

Her big brother. He was always right, but oh, the shame! She couldn't bear to see it in his eyes. Swallowing, she wiped her face on her sleeve.

'I'm sorry. I'm so sorry. It was Al-Aldred, Aldred de Chiddleigh. He promised and I thought he was nice,' she said it so quietly she could hardly hear it.

'A noble. I should have guessed.' Peter spat the words, his mouth stretched into a thin hard line. Swiftly, he pulled the hood over his head, drew his

knife from his belt, and without a word, ran into
the woods.

CHAPTER 4

Joan opened her eyes, glanced around and remembered where she was. She stretched out an arm, but the other side of the mattress was empty and cold. Had she displeased him so very much? She'd done what her mother told her. She'd let him take her. True, she'd screwed her eyes tight and bit her lip, but it hadn't been so very bad. It had all been over very quickly, for which she was grateful, but her new husband hadn't spoken a word; he'd simply turned his back on her and was soon snoring.

Was that usual? She didn't know. She sighed. She supposed she'd get used to it.

Joan sat up and hugged her knees. This was her new bedchamber. She'd been too nervous to notice much last night and with only a small candle it was too dark to see. The room was small with no openings and the roof so low that she could touch the thatch if she stretched her arm. She wrinkled her nose; the place smelt damp. There were two wooden shelves in the corner holding last night's candle, a jug, a small earthenware bowl, and willow baskets. A three-legged stool sat close by, and a shallow drainage channel ran down the middle of the earth floor. She'd seen rooms like this before. Not so long ago, animals had been stabled where the Lord and Lady of the Manor now slept.

It was disappointing. She'd imagined something far more luxurious. At home, she'd slept in the main hall close to the hearth, where it was warm and airy. She shivered; even for May, it felt chilly.

Maybe Sir John – no, John – had thought he'd let her sleep late and was planning to meet with her later, maybe over a goblet of wine this evening. That would be nice. She'd take extra care with her appearance and dab some herb water on her wrists. She'd smile – Mama said she had a lovely smile – and she'd talk to him and make him laugh. Then, pray God, he'd like her more.

Joan sighed. What was she supposed to do until then? Where was her maid? She must have one, but Sir John hadn't mentioned it. Slipping a long linen smock over her head, she opened the door and poked her head into the cross-passage outside.

There was no maid in sight. Should she call out? The pair of solid oak doors to the hall opposite was closed, and she could hardly leave her bedchamber wearing nothing but her under-smock. She retreated to her room and looked longingly at her trunk of clothes. She very much wanted to wear one of her new kirtles on her first morning, but there was no way she could fasten the laces down her back without a maid. It would have to be a less-fashionable kirtle without laces and gathered at her waist with a belt.

Joan sighed, took out a woollen green kirtle and slipped it over her head. She could wear one of her new sleeveless surcoats over the top. After some deliberation, she chose one of cream linen. Without a maid, it would be difficult to braid and coil her hair, so she made a long braid down one side and tied a linen kerchief over her brow, and then picked up her wimple. She'd practised wearing it a few times at home and quite liked it. Draping the long linen rectangle over her head, she wrapped one end loosely around her neck, then pinned it at the side of her kerchief. Putting on her felt slippers, she stood tall. She was as ready as she could be.

Pausing in the cross-passage, she ran her fingers over the finely carved oak leaves and flowers in the wooden panels on the pair of doors that led into the only other room in the house: the main hall. Feeling very alone, she inched open the doors and stepped inside.

The wedding decorations had already been taken down, making the room seem larger and more intimidating. The high table where she'd sat had been moved to the centre of the room and set out with pewter trays and candles. At the far end on the right-hand side was an impressive chimney, its cavernous hearth glowing red with burning embers. Placed squarely a few feet away stood a solid wooden table, where a short plump woman was working. Her cheeks were almost as red as the fire, her face screwed with effort as she fiercely ground grains in a bowl. Now and then, she paused, blew out her cheeks and wiped the sweat from her brow with the back of her wrist before bending to her task once more.

She must be Cook, the woman Joan had most feared meeting, looking every bit as forbidding as she had imagined. Cook was the most important servant in any manor house, the only servant who spoke directly with the lady. Somehow, Joan had to find the courage to speak to this woman, and, despite Mama's teachings, she knew little of the ways of the kitchen. Suddenly, she didn't feel like anything to eat and stood motionless by the door, uncertain of what to do.

Always look confident, even if you don't feel it. Her mother's words ran across her mind. Cook glanced up, acknowledged her presence with a nod, and quickly bent her head to her task again.

She'd been seen. Painfully aware of the tread of her short steps on the flagstones, she approached the table.

Show an interest. Mama's voice nudged her.

'My lady.' Cook dropped her eyes, dipped a respectful curtsey and stood there, waiting.

Joan's hands were sweating so she put them behind her back. Her throat felt dry but she had to say something.

'I'm surprised you only have one kitchen maid.' Her voice sounded weak.

'I have two maids, my lady, and lower maids, but Annie hasn't shown up today. Poorly, I expect.'

'I see.' As the lady, perhaps she was expected to say more, but her mind was blank. She stood there feeling like the village fool.

There is no need to be afraid of your cook, Mama had said. All cooks love to show off their skills. Get her talking about her best dishes. 'Cook, tell me about some of your dishes,' she said with a confidence she didn't feel.

Mama was right, because Cook talked at length about her special recipes and methods of cooking that Joan had never heard of. She stood there, smiling and listening and praying that Cook wouldn't ask her opinion on anything, for she wouldn't know what to say.

'And the herbs?' She'd picked a few herbs with her

cousin Eleanor and Mama sometimes. Herbs would be a safe subject. Joan picked over a pile of green-grey leaves. 'What do you use this marjoram for?'

Cook hesitated. 'That's rosemary, my lady, and I use it with lamb.'

Joan's cheeks flamed to the colour of the embers. What a cloth-head Cook must think her! 'Of...course.'

Cook fiddled with her cap and wiped her hands down the sides of her apron. 'Black beans, my lady,' she said quickly, grabbing a fistful out of the nearest basket and holding them out in the palm of her hand. 'The best around. I only use the best.'

'I'm sure you do,' said Joan. She picked out a few from Cook's slightly trembling hand.

Awkwardly, the two women stood either side of the table. As the Lady of the Manor, Joan supposed she should be the one to end this. 'I'll leave you to it, then.'

'Yes, my lady.'

Aware of the rustle of her skirts and the tread of her slippers, Joan walked slowly down the long length of the hall. Opening the door, she glanced back. Cook had her two hands on the table, her head bent between them. Surely she hadn't been nervous to meet a fifteen-year-old new mistress?

As soon as the door was closed, she sagged against the passage wall. Pray God, she was glad it was over. That wretched herb! She knew it was rosemary, it was one of the few things she did know, so why had she said marjoram? Returning to her bedchamber, Joan idly picked up her bone comb and rearranged her hair into two braids. Tying the last ribbon, she heard Cook's hushed voice in the passageway. Putting down her comb, Joan strained her ears.

'Now you get in there, Agnes, my girl. Her ladyship's first day and you not there. You deserve the back end of her tongue! You pray she doesn't tell Sir John.'

The girl said something Joan couldn't catch. A few seconds later, there was a soft knock on the door, and a thin looking girl with lank brown hair stepped timidly inside and bobbed a shy curtsey. 'Forgive me, my lady. I didn't know you were awake. I...I should have been here. I'm Agnes, your maid.'

Agnes didn't look much older than she was, and from the way the girl was scrunching her apron in tightly clenched fists, her eyes flitting everywhere except to Joan, she was terrified. It made Joan feel a little uncomfortable. Surely she wasn't so fearsome?

'It doesn't matter,' she said. 'Tomorrow I'll call when I'm ready.'

The girl nodded but didn't move.

'You can go, Agnes.' It was easier to give orders to a girl her own age.

The girl curtseyed again and rushed out the door. Everyone seemed so scared of her. Joan supposed she would have to get used to it, but it did feel strange. She should have asked Agnes to stay and help her change, but she hadn't thought of it and didn't like to call the girl back.

She finished her hair. What now? There was always her work basket. She sniffed; it wasn't her favourite pastime, but with nothing else to do, it was a safe choice.

Joan returned to the hall and, ignoring Cook's glances, settled herself in a chair under a window. She wasn't in the mood for needlework, but found the purse she was attempting to embroider. The servants scuttled to and fro, their eyes darting across to her. Selecting another thread from her basket, Joan tried to ignore them, but the silence was palpable, broken only by Cook crashing her pots and the maids' chopping knives working furiously on the wooden table.

As Lady of the Manor, Joan had every right to be there, but she certainly didn't feel like it. On the other side of the hall, the maids bent their heads close together and spoke in hushed whispers. She couldn't hear what they were saying, but by the way they kept glancing across, they were talking about her.

She'd lost the thread of her needle again. Licking the end, she tried to rethread it, but her hands were shaking too badly. It was no good. She pushed the work crossly back into her basket, stood up and, with as much dignity as she could muster, walked the length of the hall to the safety of the doors.

No sooner had the heavy iron latch clicked into place than she heard an explosion of giggles from the other side. Mortified, she clamped her hands over her ears, fled to her bedchamber, slammed the door behind her and threw herself down on to the bed.

Joan seldom cried, but she hadn't felt so miserable since the day she found her puppy drowned in the water trough. She hated this place with its vast cold hall and stifling bedchamber and she hated the maids with their wagging tongues. No one liked her. Even her own husband ignored her. She didn't know what to say or how to behave. She didn't want to be a lady anymore. Her mother should never have abandoned her. It wasn't fair!

Picking up her head cushion, she hurled it across the room, biting back the urge to scream. If the maids heard, they would laugh even more.

She lay back on the mattress and must have fallen asleep because the next thing she knew, it was dark and her stomach was rumbling. She had missed the midday meal. The sounds of the servants emptying pails and the swish of the besom on the floor meant that they were finishing their work for the day. Had Sir John come back when she was asleep? If so, she hoped he didn't think her idle.

Joan sat up and hugged her knees. How she missed home with the welcoming sheepskins on the settles. The maids were friendly, and Betty the cook always had a ready smile and spare oatie cake for her. The place was warm and comfortable; not like here where she wasn't wanted. Right now, Papa would be out with the sheep somewhere and Mama would probably be inside, tending to some domestic matter. What she would give to be there!

She could pack her things and run away. Her heart skipped a beat and then crashed. Mama would only send her straight back to do her duty, and she'd never be able to face any of them again. Somehow she had to be strong because, for better or worse, she was the Lady of the Manor. Like it or not, she was there to stay.

Three days later, Joan woke to a cold bed once again. Stretching her arms, she sat up and let out a long sad sigh. It was becoming her morning ritual, and she was fed up with being on her own all the time. She hadn't dared sit in the hall and endure the maids' ridicule again, and she couldn't face another day of hiding in her bedchamber like a timid mouse. She had to get out or she'd go mad. Throwing back the sheet and woollen blankets, she called across the passage for Agnes. Even her maid was the silent type, saying no more than she had to.

Agnes came in and went to the little table by the wall to prepare the washbowl and cloth. Gently, she wiped Joan's face and arms and applied primrose lotion to her skin. Joan loved the smell of it and ran her hands over her arms, marvelling at how soft they felt.

Agnes put the bowl to one side, and Joan clenched her teeth as the maid picked up a large wooden comb and began to untangle her long thick waves of hair. When the comb stuck in a knot, she wanted to cry out but bit her lip and said nothing. She wasn't going to look weak and feeble, it would give the maids something else to laugh about. Relieved when it was over, she relaxed as Agnes began plaiting the hair into braids, carefully tucking in cloves as she worked. When she'd finished, she gave a nod of satisfaction and picked up the stockings and linen tapes.

Joan remained seated, holding out each leg in turn as Agnes tied a linen tape around the top of each stocking, then stood and raised her arms for Agnes to drop the linen smock over her shoulders. She wished the girl would hurry up. Now she had made up her mind, she was impatient to get outside.

But Agnes always worked slowly. Regally, she picked up the green kirtle and slipped it over Joan's head. Dutifully, Joan turned around and with growing impatience, waited while Agnes tied the laces down her back. She put on her belt herself, tying on her purse

and eating knife, and waited for Agnes to slip the
surcoat over her head. Finally, she put on her wimple
and leather shoes. Neither spoke, and Joan was
relieved when the ordeal was over for another morning.

Putting her hand on the latch, she paused. Cook and
the laughing maids were on the other side, but her
stomach was growling.

She was being silly. She had to eat. She took a deep
breath and turned the handle.

'This bread tastes like grit! You, girl, bring some
fresh,' Sir John's command bounced off the walls as he
tossed a chunk of bread across the table with disgust.

Joan was shocked at his behaviour but relieved to see
him. The maids wouldn't be so off-hand with him beside
her. The youngest scurried across, bobbed a curtsey,
timidly replaced the basket of bread, and scurried back.

'John, I'm so pleased to see you. I—'

He looked at her over his goblet with piercing grey
eyes. 'It's my lord in front of the servants,' he said,
making her feel small.

He didn't need to shout. Quickly, she glanced over
her shoulder at the maids. 'I'm sorry, I didn't know,' she
said, taking a seat opposite. 'What are you doing
today?' she asked brightly.

For an awful moment, she thought he was going to
ignore her, but then he scraped back his stool and stood
up, towering over her. 'I'm riding out to see my bailiff
and I'm late.' He threw down his cloth on the table.

'I love riding! Can I come with you?'

A wry smile played across his lips as though she had
said something ridiculous. 'I prefer not. Why don't you
talk to Cook or something? I must go.'

With a sinking heart, she watched him leave. She

could have gone with him but he didn't want her, he'd made that very clear. Did he dislike her so much?

The kitchen was very quiet. Deliberately, Joan kept her head down. That way, she wouldn't have to see the maids. She nibbled at a small piece of bread, but somehow she'd lost her appetite. She didn't notice the young kitchen maid until the girl suddenly appeared at her shoulder.

'Cook asks as how was the bread, m'lady, and would you like it changed?' she said with a sweet smile and curtsey.

The irony wasn't wasted on Joan. Who did these maids think they were, giggling behind their hands like that? She may be new to her role, but she was still the lady and not there to be made a fool of!

Joan bit her lip. Slowly, she ripped the chunk of bread in two. Placing her hands flat on the table, she stood, her stool scraping the flagstones. Raising her chin, she forced her trembling legs to take the few short steps to Cook's table and waited.

Cook raised her head and wiped her hands on her apron. 'How can I help, my lady?'

'You asked if I wanted the bread changed.' She spoke slowly and carefully with a haughty tone she'd heard Mama use when chiding her maids.

'I didn't ask, my lady.'

'Oh. Well, it was well-baked and very good, and no, I don't want it changed, thank you.'

One of the maids turned away, her shoulders shaking. Cook flicked a cloth over her head. 'You, get on with your work! I'll deal with you later.'

Joan was sure that she would, but she was the Lady of the Manor and if her life was to be tolerable, this was

41

one battle she had to win on her own. Her mother's voice echoed again in her ear: Be confident and assert your position early. You may need to be firm. Remember, you are The Lady and the servants are there to do your bidding.

She lifted her chin a little higher. 'Still only three kitchen maids? Where's the other one? Annie, isn't it?' she said, praying her voice sounded stronger than she felt.

'She's not shown up for the last three days, my lady.'

'Why not? Her place is here with the others.' Clenching and unclenching her hands, she shot the maids a superior look. 'Send one of the maids to enquire.'

Cook pursed her lips and frowned.

Please God, don't let her defy me, Joan prayed. She wouldn't know what to do if she did.

'Yes, my lady.'

'And you maids can all work late to make up the time.' That told them. Pleasingly, their faces fell. Nonchalantly, Joan picked up some herbs and sniffed them.

'Is there anything else, my lady?' Cook's voice cut as sharp as her knife.

Joan's stomach was still rumbling. She took an apple from the dish and with a tilt of her chin and a haughty stare at the maids as she passed, walked as slowly as she dared out of the hall with her head held high. On the other side of the door, she let out a long breath, wiped her hands down the sides of her surcoat and suppressed a giggle. She'd done it!

She almost skipped outside to the yard. It was a beautiful day, the smell of wild daffodils and apple blossom drifting in the sunshine. Maybe this place wasn't so bad after all. Swinging her legs, she sat on the wall and took a large bite out of her apple.

The manor house was built in two parts, with a covered passageway separating the high thatched hall on one side and the low thatched animal shelter, now her bedchamber, on the other. The walls were grey stone, typical of the Devonshire long houses she'd seen as she travelled across the shire for her wedding. Dull and cold in appearance, they weren't so warm and welcoming as her own home, built from local cream sandstone. Maybe that was why everyone was so surly. Tilting her head to one side, she wondered if she could grow honeysuckle on the front, like the one Papa had planted. It would certainly brighten it up a bit and she'd smell the sweet scent every time she came home.

She turned round to the Great Barn opposite. It was twice the size of the house, with dirty brown cob walls made from mud and straw and upright planks of oak, giving it a striped effect. Stepping inside, she glanced upwards to huge curved timbers forming arches high over her head and supporting a steeply pitched thatch roof. No doubt livestock and corn would be stored here in the dark months, just as Papa did at home.

To the left of the Great Barn, there were linhays – open-fronted wagon sheds – which held little interest, and a dairy. In the corner was a walled track. She couldn't see where it went. Curious and with nothing better to do, she tossed her core over the wall and decided to explore.

The moment she stepped down the track, she could smell the answer and she smiled. It was the smell of horses and leather and that meant the stables were nearby.

It would be good to see her pony, Mead, and it was just the day for a ride. Sir John had told her to stay in, but she'd spoken to Cook as he told her to, and if he could go out and about as he pleased, why couldn't she? She was the Lady of the Manor, after all.

Mead put her head over the door, pricked her ears and whinnied. A lump formed in Joan's throat and, picking up her skirts, she ran towards her.

'At least you're pleased to see me,' she whispered, stroking the familiar soft grey muzzle. 'I hope the other horses are more welcoming than my husband.'

The sound of a besom swishing on the cobbles behind her made her spin round. A short, broad old man with a weather-beaten face was vigorously sweeping the ground, his thick hands gripping the handle tightly. Pray God he hadn't heard her.

Putting on her 'Lady of the Manor' voice, she faced him. 'And you are?'

The man stopped sweeping mid-stroke and respectfully pulled down the hood of his tunic. 'Will, my lady. Head stableman.'

'I thought I'd go for a ride this morning.'

'I'll fetch the saddle, my lady. Who's going with you?'

She laughed. 'No one! I'm riding out on my own.'

Will nervously ran his fingers through his hair and didn't move.

'Is there a problem?'

His lips moved but he hesitated. 'Prithee, m'lady, but I don't think Sir John would like it. You going out on your own, I mean.' He studied the floor, his fingers clutching the handle of the broom. 'Being the Lady of the Manor an' all,' he added nervously.

Joan bit her lip, furiously controlling her frustration. Was there nothing she could do without seeking her husband's permission? Well, he was away and what he didn't know wouldn't hurt him. She was going for a ride whether he or this—this head stableman wanted her to or not.

'I said I am going for a ride. Saddle her up.' She used the same hard voice that had worked for her earlier.

Will gave the slightest of shrugs, nodded, and obediently disappeared into the harness room.

Cantering beside the long edge of a field, Joan felt the cool wind on her face and listened to the satisfying sound of Mead's hooves beating the grass. She threw back her head and laughed with pure joy. What a relief to be away from the place and be free! She hadn't felt so happy since before her wedding.

She heard another set of hooves pounding behind her and glanced back. A man on a black horse was following her. Alarmed, she took a firmer hold on the reins and threw another glance over her shoulder. Mead was no match for such a fine animal, but she kicked her on anyway. The pony surged into a gallop even as the sound of the following horse's hooves grew louder. Whoever it was, he was gaining ground.

Joan gripped her reins and threw another glance behind. The rider was close enough for her to recognise now and she grinned. So her husband did have a sense of fun after all! Well, if it was a race he wanted, he could have it. Giggling to herself, she leaned forward, pressed both heels hard into her pony's sides, and urged her faster.

'Joan! Stop!'

She heard Sir John's voice but chose to ignore it. She was a good rider, and now was her chance to impress him. Mead was breathing hard and Sir John was right on her tail, but again Joan urged the pony on. She hadn't had so much fun in a long while! The end of the field, bounded by a stone bank and thick hedge loomed towards her at an alarming rate. It was high, but she'd cleared as much before. Shortening her reins, she squared Mead ready to jump. As the pony lifted her front legs, Joan leaned forward, but a dark shadow drew alongside and Sir John leaned over. Grabbing hold of the reins, he pulled her to a sudden stop in a shower of dust.

It was so unexpected, Joan almost went straight over Mead's head but managed to hold on, ending up with her arms clutched around the pony's neck. Pushing herself back into the saddle, she rounded on Sir John. 'What a muxy, dangerous thing to do! You could have killed us!'

'Why didn't you stop? You must have heard me shouting.' The steel-cold anger in his eyes made her flinch.

'No, I didn't,' she lied. 'I thought you wanted a race.'

'Why would I want a race, woman? And just what do you think you're doing? Have you no sense of propriety?'

In just a few words, he had ruined her wonderful day. He wasn't having fun, she had displeased him, but— woman? Papa had never spoken to Mama like that. She was the Lady of the Manor. Hadn't she dealt with the maids? Tugging hard on her reins, she snatched them out of his hands.

'I am simply enjoying a ride. There's no harm in that.'

'There is every harm. May I remind you that you are now Lady de Chiddleigh and not some farmer's daughter? I can't have you galloping around the place on your own. Suppose someone saw you? Look at you, with your wimple askew and your skirts covered in dirt! God's bones, have you no thought to my position?' His eyes were no longer those of a warm and welcoming lover, but cold and alien.

Not some farmer's daughter! The de Conteighs were well respected, at least in their own circle.

'So as the lady, what am I supposed to do all day?' She adjusted the wretched wimple, straightening it back into place.

'Whatever it is ladies do; stitching or some such. I don't know. But you do not go galloping around on your own. I shall have to find a suitable companion for you.' He sighed. 'I haven't time to take you back to the manor now. Carac will be waiting. I suppose you'll have to come with me. Try to keep up.' Without a backward glance, he set off at a rapid canter.

And so I shall, Joan thought.

She pushed Mead to her limits and, when Sir John slowed Baron to a walk, she was close behind him although her pony was now blowing hard and lathered with sweat. There was no way she was going to stay demurely behind, so she trotted up alongside. The tightness of his jaw told her that he was still annoyed.

Remember, my daughter, men are such vain creatures. In times of trouble, pander to his vanity. Easy for Mama to say but how?

'Is this all your land?' She plucked the question out of the air.

Sir John stopped his horse and regarded her curiously as though nothing had happened. What a moody person he was, angry one moment and calm the next; something Joan tucked away to the back of her mind.

'You can see almost the entire estate from up here,' Sir John replied. 'The Chiddleigh lands from the line of those trees eight miles to the north, to the low hills of Ashetyne lands, twenty miles to the south. And see that church tower in the distance?' He pointed. 'That's Holdesworthe in the east, about fifteen miles from here. My land goes to within a league of it and stretches west around the Forest of Dartmoor for another twenty miles.'

She followed his gaze and then looked closer, along the green veins of hedge-lined tracks threading their way through the red earth fields and on to the grey stone tower of Ashetyne church. There, beyond the village and nestled in the wooded valley was the grey roof of Court Barton, her manorial home.

'I've waited seventeen years for this, ever since my father died. Now I'm twenty-three, all this is mine at last, and I shall make it the best estate in all of Devonshire. The Chiddleigh lands are mine, but the Ashetyne lands, I manage for the Earl of Barcombe. It's a long story.'

He was talking to her! No, it was more than that, he was confiding in her, as a husband to his wife. He didn't dislike her, at least not for the moment.

'Please tell me,' she said.

'Well, if you're interested —' She could almost see his chest swell with pride.

'Oh, I am.' She looked deeply into his eyes and gave

him her most beguiling smile.

'Well, in 1310, the Earl of Barcombe and other nobles tried to oppose the weak King Edward II. They were frustrated with his lack of leadership. I'm not sure of all the details, I was only a little boy and it was before my time.' He smiled as he warmed to his subject. 'My father, Sir James, supported the Earl. As it turned out, the rebellion failed, but the Earl rewarded those who had stood by him, and he gave my father the management of Ashetyne.'

'And now you run it. That's makes you a large landowner and an important person in these parts.' Pander to his vanity.

'Yes I do, and yes it does.' He visibly straightened in his saddle.

'You said your father died when you were six. What about your mother?'

'My mother? I never really knew her.' His voice was evasive and his jaw set firm. 'Enough of all this. We must move on.' He gathered his reins, his eyes cold once more.

What was she to make of that? And she'd been doing so well.

CHAPTER 5

Carac de Perceux looked out of his small window. He couldn't see much through the opaque horn glass, but it let in light and kept out the draughts. He could see that the sun was already in the first quarter. Impatiently, he paced backwards and forward across the stone floor of his hall. Conscious of his height, he bent his head a little forward and clasped his arms neatly behind his back. He was looking forward to this meeting but couldn't quite quell the little niggle in the back of his mind. He'd had control of the estate for many years, but now Sir John was the rightful lord, things might change. Sir John could be impulsive, even headstrong if he got an idea into his head. Carac would have to keep a close eye on his young lord.

He tutted. Sir John should be here by now. He straightened the goose quills on the table, moved a parchment that was just a little out of line, and nodded with satisfaction. Everything was accounted for and in its proper place just as it should be.

Horses' hooves clattered to a stop outside. In two long strides, Carac threw open his door. Sir John had said nothing about bringing Lady Joan. She appeared a little flushed but he greeted her cordially with a bow.

'God save you, my lady, Sir John.'

'And God save you, Carac. I thought Joan should come along. She needs to get an idea of things.' Sir John threw a casual leg over his horse's neck and slid to the ground.

That seemed a little premature, but maybe it boded well that Sir John was aware. 'Yes, yes, of course. Come along in, I've some ale and wine waiting. The boy will take your horses. Boy!'

Ushering them inside, Carac offered Joan a seat at the long table facing the window. He was proud of his home and had spent a lot of time and money getting it just as he liked. The room was smaller than the hall in Court Barton with the same kind of vaulted roof, and felt bright and airy. The chimney and hearth were similar too, but, unlike Court Barton, there were wooden stairs next to the chimney leading up to another floor that spanned half the roof. The cob walls were limed to a smooth creamy white and adorned by two large tapestries that had been worked in vivid wools, silks and gold thread. One depicted the May Day celebration with maids dancing around a maypole and groups of women gathering blossom. The other was a hunting scene with men in brightly coloured tunics and hoods holding long staffs tipped with sharp iron points surrounding a ferocious boar. Both tapestries had cost Carac a fortune and were his most prized possessions. In the far wall, two long narrow openings let in shafts of light, landing in pools on the floor.

'Take a seat, John.' Carac settled himself in his usual high backed chair at the far end of the table, moved his pot of ink a little closer and checked over the parchments neatly lined up in front of him. 'We should make a start, but before we do, perhaps Joan — may I call you Joan?'

Joan nodded, giving him a beguiling smile and making Carac think that Sir John was a lucky man.

'Joan, I expect you'd like to know a little about the background to all this.' Carac spread his hands over the parchments.

'John told me something of the history on our way over.'

Sir John cleared his throat. 'But what I didn't tell you is that Carac taught me everything I know. When my father died, Carac was appointed bailiff to run both the Chiddleigh and Ashetyne lands until I became the lord in my own right. He's still my bailiff, and we have big plans for the future. That's why I'm here.'

Carac laughed. 'Well, I don't know about teaching you everything, but we've been waiting a long time for this day.' He turned the parchment round. 'This is an outline map of the estates. And this,' he put a finger on the map, 'is the fulling mill in the valley below Court Barton where we make the felt cloth.' He poured some wine and offered her a goblet. It was best to give Lady Joan something to do, or the poor woman would be bored out of her mind. 'Why don't you take a look and familiarise yourself with the lands while John and I make a start?'

'I've had word from the Bishop that he wants to buy more large timbers for the building of the new nave at Exeter Cathedral,' said Sir John.

'That is good news. We're felling too many mature oaks though. I know we've talked about this before, but I still say that we should reduce our supplies of large oaks for shipbuilding and concentrate on the rebuilding of the cathedral. The bishop pays well, eventually.' Carac tasted his wine and nodded in approval. Changing wine merchants had been the right decision.

'I know, and having thought about it, I agree. Are you still happy about expanding our coppicing program instead?' said Sir John.

'Indeed, and I've located seven areas that we can work in yearly cycles. Joan, can we take a look at the map for a moment?'

'Why coppicing?' Joan asked.

'By cutting one area every year, it will give us ongoing materials for making hurdles, wattles for buildings, stakes, firewood, poles, and all sorts of other things,' Sir John explained.

'And we can sell any surplus,' Carac added.

'What about sheep?' Joan asked. 'My father keeps a lot of sheep.'

'Now, sheep are an exciting part of our plans,' Carac answered. 'The market for exporting raw wool has been all over the place during the past few years, what with the King stopping exports one day, changing his mind the next and then imposing taxes on top of that. We don't know what will happen from one season to the next. It is most frustrating.'

'The money now is in exporting good-quality cloth. So we're going to dig a second leat to drain some of the water from the river to the mill, just below the manor house along here.' Sir John ran his finger over the map. 'And we shall build a much larger waterwheel and install looms. Hence we shall need more sheep that will graze on the lush water meadows, because good grass produces a longer fuller fleece, and that's better for weaving.'

'Do you intend to use dyes on your new cloth?' Joan asked.

'Blue and yellow mostly, they're the easiest and most usual.'

'If you want the best cloth to sell at the best prices, wouldn't it be better to use unusual dyes, the ones no one else is using?'

Carac raised an eyebrow. Sir John's new lady may be young, but she was clever.

Sir John waved a dismissive hand. 'I don't think we need to go to all those lengths. Better to stick to what we know.'

'I'm not so sure,' Carac said. 'I think Joan might have something. Do you know of such matters?' he asked her.

'I'm no expert, but my father always said that if he ever got into cloth making, he would copy the Flanders merchants. Their cloth always fetches the best prices, not just because of the quality but because it's red.'

Sir John gave her a hard look. 'Everyone knows about the Flanders cloth, but we can't make the red. It's difficult and we don't know how.'

'Then why don't we learn?'

'I don't know where to begin, and we've enough to do for now.' Sir John sighed and returned his attention to the map.

'I could try,' she said.

Carac smiled to himself. Lady Joan certainly was persistent. Sir John might have met his match. Maybe he'd been worrying over nothing.

Someone banged on the door. Carac raised his eyebrows questioningly, but Sir John shrugged his shoulders.

Another, louder knock. Whoever it was, they were impatient. Carac left Sir John and Joan peering over the map and went to answer it.

'Excuse me, Sire, but is Sir John with you? I've an urgent message for him.' An untidy looking lad stood on his threshold, his cheeks flaming and brow glistening with sweat.

Carac looked over his shoulder. 'John! A message for you.'

'M'lord.' The lad lowered his hood and bowed. 'A body's been found by the river, and the priest said to say it's no accident.'

'No accident?' Sir John echoed. 'Is he sure?'

'That's what he said, m'lord.'

'Do you know who it is?'

The lad studied his feet. 'They saying – as it's Aldred de Chiddleigh, m'lord.'

'My cousin?'

Keeping his eyes fixed to the ground, the lad shuffled his feet and mumbled a few words.

'Speak up, you moxy peasant!' Sir John ordered. 'Is it my cousin or not?'

The young lad nervously cleared his throat. 'Yes, my lord. He was—he was stabbed in the chest. They've taken him to the church.'

'God's teeth. This had better be true or it'll be the worse for you, my lad.'

'John, you must make haste,' Carac interspersed. 'Boy! Boy, saddle Sir John's horse, he's leaving now. And you, lad, see to your own horse; you've ridden him hard. When he's rested, you can escort the Lady Joan back to Court Barton.'

'Come over to the manor in a few weeks, and we'll

speak again then.' Sir John threw himself into the saddle, spun his horse around and galloped off in a cloud of dust.

'Is it true?' Joan asked, as Carac closed the door behind him.

'I don't know. But I could do with some more of that wine.'

CHAPTER 6

Five days had passed since the wedding, and Annie knew she should have been back at work in the kitchen. Cook would be going mad, and the other maids would have to do her share of the work. She felt awful about that, but she was so drained and confused that she couldn't face them. It was bad enough seeing the condemnation in her Pa's eyes every time he walked in.

The day after it happened, he'd been sympathetic. He'd even suggested she stay home that day and said he'd make excuses for her, but when he'd come home that night, he'd been a different person.

He'd sat on his stool, holding her in his stare. He'd questioned her, accused her, and chastised her for her sin in lying with a man out of wedlock. His harsh outpourings had sent her reeling with shame and now he'd gone quiet. She didn't know which was worse; his ranting or his silence.

She felt dirty and invaded, as though it wasn't her body anymore, and she had a persistent sick feeling in her stomach. Many times, when Pa and Peter were out, she stood in the middle of the cottage and wrapped her arms around herself, trying to squeeze Aldred out of her until she hurt. She dreaded going outside, where every rustle made her heart stop, and when she took the pail to the stream, his face was in the water sneering back at her.

Night time was the worst. When the men were asleep and snoring under their wool blankets, she stared into the emptiness of the dark cottage, reliving the events of that evening. The sounds of the minstrels' pipes and lyre, her laughter as she threw back her head at something Aldred said, the endless dancing showing her legs and the ale. She cringed with embarrassment. Why had she drunk so much? Why hadn't she listened to Mary? Why had she been a silly show-off with her stupid pride hoping everyone was watching, when she was just making a fool of herself.

When she could bear it no more, she curled into a ball and screwed her eyes tight shut until they hurt. It didn't help; the memories refused to go away. When sleep finally came, she woke in a cold sweat, Aldred's leering face just inches from her own.

Pa was right. She'd brought this on herself. She was glad Aldred was dead, but was that thought a sin too? Dear God, she didn't know what to think anymore.

Hearing the familiar click of the latch, she tensed and turned her back to the door for fear of seeing her Pa's silent look of disdain once again.

'The whole village is talking,' he said, bending his head to get through the low door and lowering his hood. He let the door slam shut behind him, sending shadows across the tiny room as the taper's flame quivered in the sudden draught. 'Gossipin' about ye, girl, and your giddy ways.'

Annie fought back her tears and prayed he wasn't going to rant at her again.

'And there's some say as how ye, lad, killed Aldred.' His words came unevenly between deep breaths as he stood in the middle of the dirt floor in his worn tunic and muddy boots.

'And there's some say it was the tinkers, camped in the water meadows that time,' said Peter, his eyes on his Pa.

'Ye went after him. What really happened? I'm your Pa, and I've a right to know.' He sat down hard on the little three-legged stool and clutched his chest. 'I've seen your hands, bruised and swollen. Don't take me for a fool, my lad. Tell me the truth. Ye beat him, didn't ye? And then what?' His voice growing louder with every word.

'I don't know!' Peter banged his fist down furiously on the table, making Annie jump.

'He's dead, isn't he? Who killed him? Tell me that.' Her Pa leapt up, threw back his stool, and stood not a pace from Peter as man to man they eyed each other fiercely.

Annie put her hands over her ears. She hated it when they quarrelled. 'Don't fight! Please don't fight!'

'Keep quiet, girl. It's ye who's brought this on us.' Peter jabbed an angry finger at her.

It was true. Silenced and ashamed, she slumped to the floor.

Her Pa ran his fingers through his grey hair. He took a slow deep breath, righted his stool and slowly sat down. 'She's right, lad. Like the good priest tells us, no good ever comes from kin fightin'. Sit down and tell me how it was, but honest now.'

They had stopped their shouting, and Annie ventured to raise her head. Peter sat cross-legged on the ground by the hearth, facing his father.

'I told ye, Pa. I left ye with Annie and thought Aldred was goin' home, so I headed for the track by the river. I was right, because I saw him just ahead of me. I followed him to the small clearing by the deep pool where the women wash clothes. He was so drunk, he never heard me comin'. Aldred's a big bloke, so I jumped him from behind and surprised him with a few hard punches. He groaned and thrashed his arms some but was too drunk to hit me. I punched him again and again until his knees buckled and he fell to the ground. I stood over him, ready, but he didn't move. I swear to God he was still breathing. On my soul, I never drew my knife and I didn't kill him.'

Annie looked hard at her brother. She wanted to believe him, but Peter was strong, and everyone in the village knew of his quick temper.

Her Pa turned on her. 'This is all your doin'. You've been a trial to me ever since your Ma died, God rest her soul, and now ye've got the whole village talking. Ye've sinned against God, that's what ye've done, and with Sir John's cousin of all people! Do ye want to spend eternity in hell? Ye'd better get yourself down to see Father Peter pretty quick and confess, or ye won't be settin' foot inside any church again. And then the tongues will really start to wag.'

Annie shivered at the thought of the hellfire licking her feet. Folks would turn their backs when she walked the lane, and the kitchen maids would snigger behind their hands. Pa was right, but she didn't know how she could ever be brave enough to admit such a sin to Father Peter.

'I tried to stop him.' She stared at the floor, her voice barely above a whisper. 'I tried to stop him, but he was too strong.'

'Go easy, Pa. It's not all her fault. She tried to stop him, and he's a big bloke, I know.'

Peter flexed his swollen hands.

'That won't count if folks get to hear of it. Sir John'll throw us out, and then where'll we be? I've worked hard so ye can have your apprenticeship, just as your Ma wanted. One day, ye'll be a free man. Now ye could lose all that.' Her Pa's face burned red and the veins on his neck stood out as he glared at Annie again. 'Ye never think, do you, girl? Well, I tell ye this: I won't let your shame ruin us. We keep this our secret. We say nothin' – and I mean nothin' – to anyone, not even Mary, and not to the Sheriff when he starts askin' questions, and he will. Do ye understand me, girl?'

Annie swallowed. She'd never seen her Pa so angry, and she'd never seen a Sheriff either, let alone lied to one. What would happen if he caught her in a lie? He might send her to Lyndeford Gaol. Dear God, she couldn't go there.

'And I'll tell ye sommat else: it's time ye were wed. A husband would settle you down.'

Her head shot up. 'No! No, I couldn't, not after…'

'Not now, girl; these things need plannin'. After harvest, I reckon. I've a mind to the miller.'

'Geoffrey? He's so old! Please, Pa, not Geoffrey!' Geoffrey had lines on his face, his belly sagged with age and he had grey hair, what there was of it. The thought of Geoffrey coming at her like Aldred—Annie shook her head. No. Never.

'He's not that old!' her Pa answered. 'He's younger than me. Think on, girl. A miller's an important person. Ye'd live in a proper stone cottage, instead of a draughty cruck hovel like this. As a miller's wife, ye'd be safe and respected. Ye could do a lot worse, and it's more than ye deserve.'

Pa didn't understand. Annie couldn't marry anyone now, not ever, but it was what maids did and, God help her, she was in no position to argue.

CHAPTER 7

Joan rode alongside Sir John to Ashetyne for Sunday morning Mass. It was their first service together, and Agnes had seemed more bothered about her lady's appearance than the lady herself was. The maid had spent forever binding her braids with green linen strips to match her kirtle. But Agnes was right, because all those eyes would be staring at her again. One day, Joan hoped they might find something else to stare at.

Sir John's blank face was giving nothing away. It was so hard to read his moods, unless his eyes turned steely grey like iron and then she knew she'd done something to anger him. The day they'd visited Carac, he'd been like a different person. His eyes lit up as he spoke proudly of his family history and explained his plans. His ambitions excited her and Carac seemed impressed with her suggestion for a red dye. She'd lain awake for nights thinking about it and already had a list of roots and plants to try. Her role had a purpose and she'd thought that it was the start of how their lives would be together.

But she'd been wrong and now things were as they'd been before, with Sir John leaving early, returning late and saying little. She hadn't embarrassed him in front of Carac; she'd taken a genuine and, yes, a learned interest. And as much as she wanted to, she'd resisted riding on her own.

So why was he so aloof again? She didn't understand. Maybe if she could get him talking about the estate again she could mention her ideas for the dyes.

'Have you made a start on choosing the timbers for the bishop?' she asked.

'Not yet. Why do you ask?'

'I was just wondering, after what you said to Carac the other day.'

'We will soon, but it's nothing for you to worry about.'

'But I'm interested, and I've been thinking about the red dye. I've got some ideas —' Was that boredom on his face?

'I told you, it's not a good idea.'

'Carac seemed to think it was.'

'Carac is not the Lord. I am. And I say that we are not wasting time on it. Don't get the wrong idea. The only reason you were there was because I didn't have time to take you home. Carac and I manage very well on our own. As a woman, your job is to be my lady and run the house, and not to meddle in my affairs.'

'I wasn't meddling,' Joan protested. 'I just thought —'

'Well, don't,' he interrupted.

Just because she was a woman and his lady, it seemed that was to be her lot. Damn the man, sitting on his fine black horse and dressed in his fashionable jupon and hose. He couldn't see beyond his title. She was more than capable of mixing dyes. It would be fun, give her something to do and put coins in the coffer chest if she could get it right. 'Well, as a woman, if I'm to be confined to being the lady of the house and not allowed to have a part in running the estate, have you had any more thoughts about a companion for me?'

Sir John frowned at her. 'What?'

'A companion, remember? We spoke about it. I hardly ever see you, we never talk, and I've nothing to do all day. I like to be busy, that's why I thought I could have a go with the red dye.'

He turned those cold eyes on her. 'No, I haven't. And right now, I've more important things on my mind.'

'It's important to me, and I am your lady.' Even to her, the words sounded petulant.

Sir John sighed and reined his horse to a halt. 'God's teeth, woman; I have a murder on my hands and I'm waiting for the Sheriff to arrive. I had a very unpleasant encounter with my Uncle Boren over Aldred's body stinking out the church, and, on top of all that, Carac and I are trying to get work started on our new ideas. There's haymaking coming up in June and then the harvest, and you're pestering me with some muxy idea of using a dye we don't know how to make and demanding I find a companion to stop you from being bored!'

The firm set of his jaw, the irritation in his voice and those cold eyes all told her that she was being a nuisance and that she shouldn't be bothering him with such trivialities. She was his lady and it should be enough, hadn't he just said so?

But it wasn't enough. If she couldn't make him see that, she would go mad, and this short ride to church together might be her only chance for a while. 'I do get bored sitting and sewing. I know it's a small matter for you, but it's a very big matter for me. I should have thought that, busy as you are, I do feature somewhere on your list.'

'Well, if you appreciate how busy I am, you will also appreciate that right now, you feature somewhere near the bottom.'

She winced. She was his wife, it was her duty to do his bidding, she knew all that, but surely she deserved a little more? She didn't want much but he always had the final word. It seemed she couldn't even breathe without his permission. It wasn't fair.

'Then there is an obvious solution, my lord. You are busy, and I am not. I shall find my own companion and save you the trouble!'

The words were out of her mouth before she could stop them. She had defied him, the one thing her mother told her never to do. Well, it was too late now; she'd done it. She'd even enjoyed it.

Not daring to look at him or wait for the consequences, she kicked her pony forward, leaving him behind.

CHAPTER 8

All through Mass, Joan had been dreading the ride home. Sir John was all smiles for Father Peter, but once he was out of sight, his jaw tightened and he kept his eyes fixed firmly ahead. She hadn't meant to oppose his will, but he'd pushed her into saying those things.

In strained silence, she gathered her reins and settled into the saddle. Turning right from the church, she heard the ripple of the ford behind her and saw a path opposite her following the river. A little way ahead, the grey thatch of a high roof poked its head above the trees. It must be the corn mill, for she could hear the regular creak of a wheel as the water fell from the paddles into the pool below with a gentle splash.

It was the first time she'd been to the village since her wedding, and she'd been so nervous at the time that she hadn't noticed it. She smiled as they rode sedately past the cottages but followed Sir John's example and ignored the peasants who stood aside, caps in hand. Still, he said nothing to her.

The smell of woodsmoke hung low from thin plumes of smoke coming from the cottages. Sitting long and low with their thatched roofs almost touching the ground, they hugged the sides of the lane in black and white stripes of wood and white cob. Some had a small door in the middle and an opening to one side that was covered with sacking to keep out the weather. Further along the lane, stone cottages with shutters reminded her of home, and for a moment she longed to be back there. She didn't know any of the people who lived here. Would she ever know them?

They rode passed the inn and the pillory opposite, the high wooden bars hanging empty. A grass lane curved off to her right. Joan wondered where it went and would have liked to have taken it, but Sir John was in no mood for a pleasure ride.

In silence, they trotted up the hill out of the village and on to Court Barton. When she turned into the yard, Sir John stayed on the track, stating that he was going out for the rest of the day and – with a strong hint of sarcasm – that he trusted she would find something to do. An angry outburst would have been better, since at least that would have shown that he cared, but instead, he was just leaving her again. Well, in his vexed mood, she wouldn't want to be with him anyway.

She watched him ride out of sight, sighed and handed her pony to the stable boy. It was the Sabbath and the place was almost deserted. The day stretched ahead until the evening meal. What was she supposed to do? She promised Mama she would write.

Dear Mama

I am writing as promised and to put your mind at rest for I am well and settled although Court Barton is not as warm and friendly as home. There are times when I long to be back with you and Papa sitting around the hearth. I expect I shall get used to it here although whether I shall ever think of it as home, I cannot yet say.

I confess I don't know what to make of my husband. He is very moody and I never know how to take him. Sometimes, he is warm towards me but at other times he is so very cold and forbidding it chills me to look at him. He seems a very aloof sort of person and I am disappointed that I see so little of him. He seldom speaks to me unless he is boasting about his estate, and on the few occasions when he has spoken, he has proved to be very curt and demeaning. I wonder how he sees me or even if he cares that I am here at all. Is it because I am so much younger than he?

She chewed the end of her cane quill. Should she tell her mother about her outburst? No, she'd leave that part out; Mama would only remind her to think before she spoke, as she had on so many occasions. She dipped the end of her quill into the ink pot and continued to write.

John is always busy with estate matters and isn't interested in my opinions and doesn't want me to get involved. Does he think me still a child? He says that my place is to be his lady and to run the home and I am not to go riding or walking alone and he seems to think I should be content with that. Does he take me for a fool? I shall go mad if all I am to do is sit in the hall and sew every day.

Are all husbands like this? Please give me your valued advice for I don't remember Papa behaving in such a manner.

John has mentioned finding me a companion. Perhaps he plans for us to visit other landowners in Devonshire and I shall make some friends. I do hope so for it is hard to be alone day after day with no one to talk to or spend time with and I confess to being lonely.

Don't be alarmed, dear Mama, for I am not so very unhappy and did enjoy a morning with John and his bailiff, Carac de Perceux.

She wouldn't say how she got to be there. That was another incident best forgotten.

Did you meet with Carac at the wedding? He seems a kind and wise man and has known John for many years. I think he is one of the few people John talks and listens to.

She stopped and frowned. She'd like to mention her ideas for the red dye but she didn't want Mama to think her too bold.

I have met Cook and am warming to her, although the maids are very silly.

But what am I thinking? God save us, but John's cousin, Aldred, was found murdered by the river. It is dreadful of course, and pray be reassured, such an incident has never occurred before and I am quite safe. But I wonder who did it and why? Did you meet Aldred at the wedding? I know John doesn't like him and have a feeling there are matters concerning John's family I have yet to learn. Nothing sinister, I'm sure, but I am curious.

Please write as soon as you can. If you see my cousin Eleanor, tell her I miss her and give her God's speed. Give my respects to Papa and tell him I am trying my best to be a dutiful daughter and wife and hope his back is better.

Your dutiful daughter,

Joan

Feeling better for venting her thoughts, Joan folded the parchment neatly into thirds. Taking a small key from her purse, she unlocked her casket and removed a small piece of red wax and her seal. Having warmed the wax over the candle, she watched it drip over the folds of her letter, then pressed her seal firmly into the soft wax to secure the edges of the parchment. She smiled. It always delighted her to see the imprint of a woman, supposedly herself, now embossed in the wax, and especially her signature around the edge: Fidelis autem Deus. Faithful to God.

Idly, Joan wandered outside. The sun had hardly reached midday, and she kicked a stone across the yard with the side of her shoe. She'd said that she would find her own companion, but the truth of it was that she didn't know anyone to ask. If only she could ride out, but someone was bound to see her and tell Sir John.

But it was the Lord's day. There'd be no peasants tending the fields or working in the mill, and if she was careful not to be seen she could go for a walk. Besides, she should exercise. Exercise kept the bad humours away; everyone knew that.

Excited at her daring plan, Joan deliberately ignored the orchards that Sir John had reluctantly given her permission to walk in, and instead followed the path in the opposite direction, down the lane and away from the house. She glanced back once, but everywhere was quiet.

When the mill was within sight, Joan tucked behind a tree and waited. The millwheel stood idle, and the only sound was the steady gurgle of the water in the leat. She was alone. Ignoring the bridge, she picked up her skirts and jumped on to a large boulder in the river. With a smile, she leapt to the next and the next until she was on the other side. Dropping her skirts, she giggled. She and Eleanor used to play that game all the time when they were little.

The path climbed sharply ahead of her, spiralling against the wooded hill. It was steeper than she thought, and by the time she reached the top, she had to stand to recover her breath. Picking her way through a tangle of undergrowth beneath tall beech trees, she caught her arm on a thorn, swore and rubbed the dot of blood with some spit. It would be nice to sit a while, and at the very edge of the hill, she saw a small clearing dappled with sunlight. A fallen tree provided the perfect place but someone was there before her.

The small figure stood up, spun around and straightened her kirtle in a fluster.

'My lady, prithee, I'm not working today, I'm just-'

'It's alright. It's Annie, isn't it?' Joan stepped closer.

'Yes, my lady.' The maid curtsied and stood awkwardly before her.

'So what are you doing up here?'

'I just wanted to be on my own, to think and to spin.' Annie held up her drop spindle by way of explanation.

'Think about what? You can tell me, you know.' The girl certainly seemed troubled about something.

Annie hesitated. 'Nothing much. I've just upset my Pa, that's all. I often come here. I love the quiet. You can see right over the valley to the moor and watch the buzzards.'

Joan walked to the edge. In the distance, purple shadows floated against the greys and greens of the high moor. On the skyline, the tors jutted ragged and proud, and in the valley below, buzzards circled lazily upwards on the warm air currents, mewing their mournful cries.

'I can understand why you come here. It's magical.

This tree has fallen here, just for us.' Joan brushed away some surface dirt, sat down, and patted the space next to her.

Annie fiddled with the edge of her apron, keeping her eyes down. 'I couldn't, my lady. I'm just a kitchen maid and, well, it wouldn't be right.'

'Oh, come on, sit down. To tell you the truth, I'm not supposed to be this far from the house on my own. Sir John likes me to stay in the fields closer to home. Still, I'm not on my own now, am I? I have you, so that's alright.'

'My lady, I don't know —'

'How old are you, Annie?'

'I'm fifteen summers, my lady.'

'So am I! Shall I tell you a secret?'

'Oh, no, please don't! I have enough secrets —'

'Well, I shall anyway,' Joan interrupted. 'I don't always want to be the Lady of the Manor. I know I haven't been one for very long, but there's no one to talk to and nothing to do. I miss Mama and my cousin, Eleanor. Eleanor's a little younger than me and lives on a farm, like Papa's. Sometimes, when her family visited, we'd go for walks or ride out together. And I was always outside with the animals. The sheep were the best, especially the lambs in springtime.' She looked at the far distance. 'They were lovely times, and I miss all that. I miss being me.'

'But you have everything. Your fine clothes, you don't have to work and do as Cook tells you, or have a Pa and a brother to look after. You can just do as you please. I wish I could do that. Oh!' Annie's hands flew to her mouth. 'Oh, my lady, pray forgive me. I forgot myself. I shouldn't have spoken ...'

'It's alright, really it is. It's because of who I am that no one talks to me.' Joan patted the space next to her again. 'Please sit down. I'd love to chat. Just two fifteen-year-old girls together.'

'I must go. I'm late.' Annie ruffled her surcoat and tied the spindle to her belt.

Joan stood up swiftly. She had just found someone to talk to and she wasn't going to let her go now. She was shorter than Annie, but she stood straight with her chin held high.

'Annie, as your Lady of the Manor, I order you to sit next to me and keep me company!'

Annie stopped, wide-eyed, and took a small involuntary step back.

'There's nothing to be afraid of.' The thought of a girl her own age being frightened of her made Joan giggle.

Annie smiled, then started to giggle with her.

'That's better. Come on, Annie, sit down. For the time we're here, you're to call me Joan. Not Lady, just Joan.' Joan held up her hand. 'Let's enjoy just being us. You start and tell me all about yourself.' She stretched out her legs, crossing them at the ankles just like Sir John. It was a very unladylike fashion, but it felt wonderful.

Annie began shyly, but, as she spoke of her brother and how her family had worked on the estate for three generations, she relaxed and seemed to forget who she was talking to.

Joan liked Annie. Some of her tales were quite funny, particularly the time she hid up a tree so her Papa couldn't find her to do her chores. She'd have done the same.

The sun moved into the third quarter and the afternoon

bell tolled from the village church. Reluctantly, Joan stood up and shook out her skirts. The time had gone so quickly, but now she had to return to the manor and be the lady again.

'I'm so glad I met you,' she said.

'It'll feel strange going back to the manor with you as the lady and me as your kitchen maid.'

'It will, but you mustn't tell anyone. It'll be our secret. We can meet here. From now on, this will be our place. It'll be fun!' Joan was already looking forward to their next chat.

'I'd like to...if you think it's alright.'

'Of course it's alright; and, Annie, it's so lovely to have you as my friend.'

If you took away all the trappings, Joan thought, they were really very alike.

CHAPTER 9

Annie and Joan agreed on a secret signal: if Annie put the pestle and mortar on the end of the top shelf in the kitchen, Joan knew that Annie would be free later that day, Sometimes, she'd catch Annie's eye without the other maids seeing, and they'd both turn away to hide their giggles. When Cook sent Annie out to pick herbs in the meadows, Joan would grab her shoes and rush out to join her.

Being with Annie gave her the freedom she longed for. She could be herself and forget about being the lady and all that went with it. Annie talked to her just like a normal person, and Joan loved that. Their meetings were something exciting to look forward to, and the secrecy made it extra special.

A few weeks later, Joan hurried over to their log and flopped down next to Annie, dropping her basket at their feet. 'Look! I've brought some oatie cakes from the kitchen and two apples and — ' she rummaged deep into the basket — 'some salted pork. We can have a picnic!' Proudly, she laid out her spread and waited for Annie's squeals of delight.

But Annie didn't even look.

'Are you alright?' Joan asked.

'It's Pa. He keeps talking of marrying me off. He says a husband will stop me from being such a cloth-head.' Annie sniffed and used the edge of her apron to wipe her nose. 'I can't. I just can't. I know I'm silly and not a good daughter. I've sinned and brought shame on them, I know that and I feel so guilty—'

'I'm sure you haven't, and all girls must wed some time. Dry your eyes, it's not that bad.'

Annie stared at the ground once more. 'Pa says that if Ma was alive I'd be a better daughter.'

'Well, if Sir John's mother was around, maybe he would be a better husband.' Joan bit her lip. She felt traitorous and didn't even know if it was true.

'What do you mean?' Annie perked up.

'Forget it. I shouldn't have said anything.'

'Come on, I'm your friend. I won't tell anyone.'

'Promise?'

Annie nodded.

'Well, Sir John can be so uncaring. He hardly ever talks to me, and I never even get a hug. Mama and Papa used to hug each other all the time. I thought that's how it was for all married people. I don't think John knows how to show his feelings, if he's even got any. And he's so mean. He won't let me ride out on my own. He said he'd find a companion for me but he hasn't. I just want him to notice me once in a while. Is that too much to ask?'

She felt better for getting it off her chest, but maybe she shouldn't have said anything. These things should be private between man and wife and particularly between the Lord and Lady. What if Annie let it slip to the kitchen maids? Then Cook would know and soon the whole village. Sir John would get to hear about it and might send her home in disgrace. Then what? She could already hear Mama's scolding tones. 'You won't say anything, will you?'

'Of course not. And I don't think it's too much to ask, but then what do I know? What I do know is that men can be horrid and vicious. They don't have to worry about the sin and shame they put on a girl. They don't have to live with the guilt. I hate them and I shall run away rather than let Pa marry me off.'

Annie's eyes narrowed, her mouth was tight, and Joan had never heard her voice so vehement. For a moment, she thought Annie was going to burst into tears. 'No matter how you feel, you mustn't run away, where would you go?'

Annie stared miserably at the ground. 'I don't know. Somewhere.'

'Promise me you won't. You could end up in all sorts of trouble, and you're the only friend I've got. I'd miss you so much. Annie?'

Annie shrugged and ran her hands over her face as if to wipe her troubles away. 'Don't worry, I won't do anything silly. Now give me one of those oatie cakes.'

'I've got something better than that to cheer you up.' Joan delved back into the basket. 'It's for you; a token of my friendship. You must keep it forever and ever and then we'll always be friends.' She held out a small folded piece of pale pink silk. 'It's a kerchief. I made it myself. The stitching's not very good, but I hope you like it.'

Softly, Annie ran her fingers over the small silk square. 'I've never felt anything so fine. It's beautiful. Thank you. I shall keep it safe and treasure it always.' She dropped her head again. 'But I haven't got anything to give you.'

'Don't be silly, I have you for my best friend, and that's better than anything.'

'I know I'm only a maid and you're the lady, but I love seeing you and hearing your tales. Your life's so different and that makes it exciting. We'll always be friends, won't we?'

Annie was right; their lives were very different, and many a time when Sir John made her feel miserable with his cold face, Joan envied Annie and her simple peasant life. 'Haven't I just said so? Now cheer up and eat your cake.'

Annie managed a smile.

'That's better. I don't like to see you so sad. Tell me, what do you know about the Chiddleighs?' Joan polished an apple on her skirt and, satisfied she could see her face in it, took a good bite and continued. 'I know John's father died when he was six, but when I asked him about his mother, he went quiet and wouldn't talk about her.'

'I don't know. Maybe she was ill, or maybe—' Annie's eyes shone with the possibility— 'maybe the demons got to her and she went mad and they locked her up in the tower! They do that you know, in the noble families.'

'Oh, don't say that. I couldn't bear it if there's mad blood in the family. No, I'm sure you're wrong.' Joan took another bite of her apple. 'What about Aldred? Carac said the two sides of the family haven't spoken for years. You must have heard the gossip—'

Annie's head shot up. 'I don't know anything about Aldred! Why should I?'

The sudden change of her mood stung like a slap around her face. 'I just thought that as a peas—'

'As a peasant, I would know. Well, I don't, and anyway

it's time I went.' Annie stood up and furiously shook her skirts.

Joan winced. Her and her big mouth. Didn't Mama always say it would get her into trouble? It was an awful thing for her to have said, but it had just slipped out. 'I'm sorry, I didn't mean—Can we meet again tomorrow?' she called to Annie's disappearing back.

'I suppose so.'

Pray God Annie would come. Joan didn't know what she'd do without her now.

CHAPTER 10

Joan let the sewing drop in her lap. She'd never finish the wretched purse. She hadn't meant to upset Annie this afternoon; the words had just slipped out. Maybe she could make it up to her somehow.

The sound of horse's hooves and Sir John's voice in the yard interrupted her thoughts. Pleased for the excuse, she stuffed her work into her basket and watched him stride across the hall. There was no hardness of jaw or fierce look in his eye, so she could relax. Sir John took his seat next to the hearth, helped himself to wine from the flagon and smacked his lips in appreciation.

'You're early. What a lovely surprise,' Joan said.

'Baron was fresh, so I galloped most of the way home. I met a messenger on the High Drovers road with good news indeed. The Sheriff should be with us by the end of the week to investigate Aldred's murder. I can't tell you what a relief it is to get on with the matter.' He held out his hand to her and smiled. 'Come here.'

Delighted with the unusual gesture, she took his hand and went to him.

'Maybe I've been a little harsh, but I've a lot on my mind. I meant what I said about estate matters, but when all this Aldred business is over, I promise I will find you a companion.'

His eyes were unusually soft, perhaps he did care for her. Now was the perfect opportunity to tell him about her idea. 'And pray, forgive me. I sometimes speak without thinking. It is wrong of me.' She smiled and dropped her eyes demurely. 'About my companion; I have an idea—'

'Tell me later. First...' He stood up and, still warmly holding her hand, led her to the bedchamber.

Later, as she lay in his arms, she smiled at his contented face as he stroked her hair. He could be so gentle and loving when he wanted to be. If only she saw more of this side of him.

Well, maybe she would. She'd tell him her idea and please him even more.

'I've been thinking,' she said, running a finger down his chest. 'I can save you the trouble of finding me a companion, for I have found someone.'

'That was very clever of you. Who is she?' He twisted a long curl of her hair absently around his fingers.

'Annie,'

'Annie who?'

'Annie. You know, Will the stableman's daughter.'

Sir John threw back his head and laughed. 'For a moment there I thought you said, Will's daughter. So tell me, who is this Annie?'

There was a flicker of foreboding but she'd said it now. 'That's who she is. Annie, Will's daughter.'

Sir John shifted away, his head resting on his elbow with a puzzled frown on his brow.

'You see, I was out walking and met her,' Joan explained, the words coming all in a rush. 'It all happened by accident, but the point is, she's my age and she's very good company. We're much alike and I thought she'd make an ideal companion —'

His smile faded and the warmth in his eyes turned cold. She'd got it wrong.

'Don't be ridiculous! You're not at all alike. I can't believe I'm hearing this.' He sat up and stared at her.

'But I like her and —'

'Don't be such a nun-nuzzling jade. She's a kitchen maid and you are my Lady. I can't believe you can seriously suggest such a thing. It's out of the question.'

She'd spoiled everything. Sir John was cold and displeased with her again. All thoughts of picking flowers with Annie over the fields, sitting in the sun idling away the time and teaching her to ride, vanished in a heartbeat.

'I know Annie's a kitchen maid and it's not usual, but if she were spared her kitchen work, I can show her how to be a proper companion. I'll teach her to stitch silk, play cards, and ride. She'll learn and she'll be perfect.'

'I don't know what is expected in untitled families like yours, but I can tell you that Annie will never be perfect.'

Joan sat up and stared back. 'How dare you say that! I'll have you know that the Conteighs are well respected in their circle. If my family is so beneath you, I wonder why you kept to the marriage contract at all. But then, with only me to inherit, isn't that why the Chiddleighs agreed to the marriage in the first place?'

'In exchange for a title,' he muttered, just loud enough for her to hear.

'As you say, but as your Lady of the Manor, perhaps I should live in a proper manor house!' she retorted.

'What do you mean, a proper manor house?' Sir John demanded. 'What's wrong with it?'

'What's wrong with it? It wasn't so many years ago that the cattle slept where we do! Carac's house is more of a manor house than ours. My untitled father's farmhouse is more of a manor house than ours.' She paused, her eyes flashing triumphantly. 'Court Barton is nothing more than a hovel!'

'A hovel!' He flung himself angrily off the mattress and grabbed his clothes. 'There is nothing wrong with Court Barton,' he said, struggling with his hose. 'I had the whole place cleaned out for you, and now you say it's a hovel!' He snatched up his tunic and pulled it roughly over his head. 'I'll have you know that my father had that chimney built when chimneys were hardly heard of!' Struggling, he turned his tunic the right way round. 'This place was good enough for him, so I'm sorry if it's not good enough for you.' Furiously, he tugged his belt tightly around his waist, cursing as the buckle refused to clasp. 'Annie will never be your companion, and I forbid you to talk to her. Do I make myself clear?' He thrust his feet into his boots. 'I shall be away on estate matters. I don't know when I shall be back.' He stormed out, banging the door behind him.

Joan listened to his feet stomping across the yard. He was heading for the stables. When she could no longer hear the crunch on the cobbles, she clenched her fist into a tight ball and punched it hard into the mattress. God's teeth, there was no talking to the man!

She lay back on her bed and put her hands behind her head. Sir John was mean and cold-hearted, and she wouldn't waste any more tears on him. She hated him.

I forbid you to talk to her.

Did he indeed? Well, if she couldn't have Annie as a companion, she'd have her as a friend, whether he forbade it or not. She'd have to be careful, though. No more picking herbs in the meadows or sitting on the grassy riverbank for prying eyes to see. From now on, they would only meet in their secret place on the log.

Joan drew up her knees and hugged them. He was her lord and she was wrong to disobey him but doing so made it more special. It would be a part of her he knew nothing about, her secret. Let him think he controlled her, but this was one thing he'd never even know about. And, with a warm feeling, she grinned.

CHAPTER 11

'Carac!' Sir John's voice blasted around the hall. 'Carac! Where are you, man?'

Carac laid his new tabard neatly on the top of his trunk and hurried down the stairs. Sir John was pacing the hall, his face black as thunder.

'Good morrow, John. What ails you?'

'Women! That's what ails me.'

'Ah,' said Carac, his eyebrows raised just a fraction. 'Come and sit down and I'll pour us some wine.'

'I tell you; I was reasonable, I was understanding, and what did I get? Some muxy-headed idea about having our kitchen maid as her companion, that's what!'

Carac's peace was shattered; there would be no rescuing it now. He tutted to himself. His records would have to wait, but it was most annoying. He handed Sir John a goblet of wine. 'I see, but—'

Sir John took a long swig and rushed on. 'She says she's bored. Bored! She's got her sewing; isn't that what women do all day? And then she says that Court Barton isn't good enough for her and that it's no more than a hovel. A hovel!' He gulped his wine and banged the empty goblet back on the table.

Slowly, Carac refilled it. Best to let him get it out of

his system. There would be no reasoning with him until he did.

'I don't know why I got married in the first place.'

'For the same reason all men in your position get married: for land and an heir,' Carac said with an ironic smile.

'Yes, well, I didn't think she'd be this much trouble.' Sir John fidgeted in his chair, his fingers drumming on the wooden arm.

'I concede it is difficult for you. You never had any role models. Your father died early and your mother —'

'My mother was never there!' Sir John snapped back.

This was a delicate subject, so Carac chose his words carefully. 'Your mother had to be the woman she was.'

'She was the death of my father —'

Carac kept his voice smooth. 'And I was going to say that it left you with me: a dry old bailiff doing his best.' He poured the last of the wine into Sir John's goblet. 'Anyway, there's no point dwelling on the past. I'll fetch more wine and you can tell me what's happened.'

Passing his table, Carac looked ruefully at the scrolls that were laid in a precise pile next to the row of quills. He nudged the last one into a perfect line and nodded. Now it was straight. Returning to his seat, he put his hands together, rested his chin on his fingertips and listened, giving the odd, 'Yes, I see,' or a thoughtful, 'Perchance...'

When Sir John finished talking and his fingers were still, Carac picked up his goblet, rose from his chair and began slowly pacing the room. He thought better if he paced. With his head down and a little hunched, he took long thoughtful strides.

'I was right, wasn't I?' Sir John broke the silence.

Carac stopped his pacing. 'In some ways, yes, I think you were. But I have to say, Joan does have a point about the house. Maybe you should consider a little updating, as I have.' He swept his arm proudly around his hall and, before Sir John could argue, resumed his seat and continued. 'Of course, you're right about Annie. She's totally unsuitable, but did you try to find a companion?'

Sir John shifted in his seat. 'As I tried to explain to Joan, I have the Aldred business to deal with, and what with the Sheriff coming and work on the estate, I didn't have time. You know how it is.'

Carac had some sympathy for Joan; he knew exactly how selfish Sir John could be. 'John, I've watched you grow up and I know you. You can be stubborn and maybe you should spare some time to —'

'But I'm the Lord —'

'Hear me out.' Carac held up his hand. 'She's still young and needs time to adjust, but she's no fool, and it seems to me she needs more than just sitting and sewing. Why not let her try making a red dye? Think of the profits if she succeeded.' He might as well try to get something useful out of his wasted morning.

'I bet you didn't have all this trouble with your wife,' Sir John muttered.

'Margaret? Ah, now there was a woman. She was a gentle soul, very calm and controlled.' Carac smiled at the fond memory. 'Don't misunderstand me; Margaret and I didn't always agree.' How could he explain? 'Look, you understand horses. Think of Joan as a chestnut filly. She's fiery and with a lot to learn. She needs firm but gentle handling.'

'I thought she'd know how to do things and just

get on with it.'

'Well, that's my advice.' Carac glanced longingly at his scrolls, bored with this conversation. He'd done what he could.

'The dye is a ridiculous idea. If the Guild members can't make it, how is a woman going to? But you're right about the old home. It does need some rebuilding.'

'I didn't mean rebuilding exactly, just a few improvements. Your hall is perfectly acceptable, just hang a tapestry here and there, lighten the walls, that sort of thing. No need to do too much.'

Sir John was gazing around the room and oh Lord, Carac had seen that gleam of excitement in his eyes before.

'No, it needs more than that. You're right, Court Barton does not reflect my growing status. It's old and shabby. I mean, what will the wealthy and influential people of the shire think when they visit?' Sir John's eyes roamed to the upper level. 'Take that upstairs of yours. I believe it's the new idea, isn't it? I can't have my bailiff outdoing me, can I?' He laughed lightly. 'If you've got an upper room, then as Lord, I should have one too.'

Carac's heart sank. It was said in jest, but Sir John meant it, whatever it cost.

'No, not one. I'll have two, one at each end of the hall, and instead of spanning half the width, mine will span the whole width with an opening overlooking the front. And I'll have horn glass. What do you think? Impressive?' Sir John was now standing in the centre of the hall, grinning and sweeping a hand majestically round.

It would certainly be expensive, and Carac kicked

himself for mentioning it. He should have known Sir John would get carried away. It would take every penny in the coffers and more, and he'd be the one left trying to balance the figures. Now he had to find a way to rein in his impulsive young Lord and maybe his Lady as well.

'Have you any idea what all that will cost?'

'I don't suppose it will be cheap, but that's not the point. Anyway, we're getting more sheep. That means more wool, and with the new waterwheel and larger mill, we'll have more cloth and that means more profit. I'm sure that'll cover it.' Sir John leaned close and peered at the tapestries. 'Where did you get these? I've never really noticed them before. They're rather fine. I can imagine one or two larger ones like these hanging in my hall.'

'You'll want to wait until the new mill is running and we know how much money it's making before you do anything.'

Sir John spun on his heel to face him. 'Whatever for? No, we'll start straight away.'

'But is that wise?'

'You don't seem to understand. I need a manor house befitting my status —'

'But surely —' Carac tried again.

'No, Carac. My mind is made up.'

Carac shook his head. That glint of over-excitement was still in Sir John's eyes along with the set line of his jaw. He'd seen it before and knew it was futile to argue. Once Sir John had an idea fixed in his mind, there was no stopping him. As a boy, Sir John would stand in front of him with tightly crossed arms, listening to what he had to say, and then simply ignore every word and go off and do what he wanted. Only a few years ago, there had been the fiasco of the new track over the hill. The woodsmen knew it couldn't be done, the soil was too thin and the granite too hard. A dozen men had wasted over a year digging with shovels and chiselling the stone before Sir John had finally abandoned the idea.

'If that's what you want—'

'It is, and I'm glad you agree. Another exciting new project for the estate! I can't wait to get started, can you?' Sir John said, rubbing his hands.

Yes, Carac thought. Yes, I can.

CHAPTER 12

Annie woke with a start. It was dark, but something or someone was shuffling about. She lay still, trying to make it out. It was over there in the corner, too big for a rat.

The shape moved slowly across the floor. Annie shrank back, screwing her eyes shut, and pulled the woollen blanket over her head. It was Aldred, she knew; he was coming for her again.

No. He was dead.

Soft footsteps crept to the door and the latch clicked open. Cautiously, Annie lowered her blanket and peeped through her fingers.

Peter! What was he up to? He'd been very quiet, even sullen, recently. Hastily, she threw her smock and kirtle over her head and grabbed her belt, tying it as she followed him out of the cottage.

A thin slit of yellow lined the moors and the early mist lay on the ground like a soft cloud. Annie wrapped her shawl around her and glanced back to the safety of the cottage. Peter was already running down the hill. If she didn't go now, she'd lose him. She tightened her lips and started to follow. At the bottom of the hill, he crossed the fields and disappeared into the woods.

Annie stopped at the edge of the trees and gazed up at the tall trunks, their branches lost in the dark. Nothing moved.

This was where he'd dragged her. She glanced nervously behind. She could just make out Peter's shape in the depths. She called his name but her voice bounced back. If he was running away, she'd never forgive herself. She had no choice. Crossing herself, she picked up her skirts and entered the woods.

She mustn't lose sight of him. Her heart thumping wildly, every part of her as tight as rope, she took her first step. The silent darkness swallowed her and the damp chill air closed in. Trees loomed out of the mist like ghosts watching her every move. An early wood pigeon slapped its wings together as it took off from a nearby branch, making her jump out of her skin and her heart leap through her chest. She stopped and wiped her hair away from her eyes, tight for signs of any movement. Aldred was dead.

She had lost sight of Peter.

Pray God, don't let me be lost. Sweating, she quickened her step along the path that twisted and turned through the dense undergrowth. Every snap of a twig, every rustle in the trees chilled her. Forcing herself not to look back, she clasped her shawl tighter across her chest and hurried on. Peter must be ahead; if she kept going, she'd find him and would be saved.

The path straightened ahead of her and early shafts of light striped the ground. Thank God, she was nearly out! Breaking into a run, she reached the end of the woods and stood at the edge of a meadow.

Panting, she watched Peter run to the far end of the meadow and turn left. He was heading for the river.

Picking up her skirts once more, Annie chased after him. Running along the river path, she caught sight of him again. He'd stopped at the wash pool, the place where Aldred's body had been found by the women coming to do their washing. What was Peter doing here? She crept closer, failed to see the treacherous bramble in her path and tripped, falling flat on her face in the dirt.

Peter was over her immediately, his fist clenched just inches from her face.

'Don't! Peter, it's me!' She cringed back, covering her face with her hands.

His arm froze in mid-air for a moment, then dropped to his side. 'Ye numbskull! What in God's teeth are ye doing here?'

Annie scrambled to her feet and dusted herself down. 'I saw you leave. What with the sheriff coming and all, I thought you were running away. And I don't want you to.' She added lamely.

'Well, I'm not, so ye'd better get back before Pa misses ye. I'm in enough trouble because of—' He broke off.

'Go on, say it. Because of you. That's what you were going to say, isn't it?'

'Yes—no—look, just go home!'

'I can't, not on my own. It's dark in there and I'm scared. What are you doing here, anyway?'

Peter sighed and scratched his head. 'I'm looking for something.' Squatting down, he frantically ran his hands through the long grass.

'Can I help?'

'Annie, go home. I don't have time for this. I've to be at the forge soon. The reeves brought in the scythes yesterday and it's my job to hone and repair them ready for the haymaking.' He glanced up. The sun was already rising.

'What are you looking for?'

'I'm lookin' for a knife, if ye must know. But don't ye dare tell.'

'A knife?'

'It's not what ye think. I made it for Roger. He was supposed to pay me for it on the day of the wedding but he didn't have the money. So I put it back on my belt and I've lost it somewhere.' He moved closer to the bank, continuing his search through the reeds.

'I thought apprentices weren't allowed to make and sell things. Does John Forge know?'

'No, he doesn't and don't ye tell. I made it after I'd finished for the day. I told him I was workin' on pieces to present to the Guild at the end of my term. If he finds out, I'll lose my apprenticeship.'

'So why'd you do it?'

'Annie! If ye must stand there, help me look for it. It's a small plain iron knife with a short crosspiece.' He waded into the shallows of the river, turning over rocks and feeling his hands over the bed.

'So why'd you make it?' She cast about under the trees.

'I just wanted a few coins in my purse. Pa gets everything I earn. It was just a bit of ale money, a drink with the lads, that's all.'

'Well, I can't find it, and I don't understand why you're so worked up about it.'

He stood up, water dripping from his tunic. 'I have to find it. This is where I fought Aldred and where the village women found him. Maybe that knife was used to kill him. I don't know, but don't ye see? If someone finds it here and it's got blood on it and it's traced back to me, what do ye think the Sheriff will make of that? I'll be on my way to Gibbet Hill quicker than a rabbit out of a hole!'

Had Peter killed Aldred? Of course he hadn't. He couldn't have. But he did have a temper, and everyone had been drinking that night. Was he so drunk that he didn't remember, or was he lying? Annie didn't know, but he was her brother and it was her fault that they were here now.

The stripes of light looked wider. The sun was almost up. It was such a pretty place, and yet this was where Aldred had been murdered. She shuddered, but she wasn't sorry.

'I won't tell, but I'm dreading the Sheriff. He'll know I'm lying, I just know he will,' she said.

Peter's head shot up. 'Just stick to what we agreed with Pa.'

'Don't worry, I won't say anything. Promise. I'm sure Roger won't either; about the knife, I mean. Anyway, I think you're safe, because it's not here. Can we go now? This place gives me the shivers.'

The sun was up, and Peter wasn't the only one who had to get to work. They should both be going. He waded out of the water and they set off for the village, each with their own thoughts.

CHAPTER 13

Pacing anxiously outside the inn, Annie could hear the mumble of voices inside as folks waited for their turn to talk to the sheriff.

What would he ask her? She should be tired, for she'd tossed and turned all night thinking about it, but her nerves were so tight that she could run to Oakwolde and back without pausing for breath. Every time the door opened, her stomach lurched. She fiddled with her veil and straightened her skirts for the umpteenth time, Peter's words echoing in her mind.

It wasn't so much what she must say as what she mustn't; she mustn't tell of her secret friendship with Lady Joan, and she definitely mustn't say what happened that night. Well, that would be easy enough; she couldn't bear to even think of her shame, let alone speak of it. And now she had the added secret of that stupid knife Peter had lost. She wished she'd never followed him.

A pink, bald head poked round the door. Rheumy eyes looked up and down the lane and rested on her. This was it. Taking a breath, she was as ready as she could be. She stepped forward, but the head disappeared behind the door. Good Lord, when would it be over?

The bell tolled. It was already the first quarter, and the longer she waited, the more nervous she felt, and the more nervous she felt, the more muddled she got about what she was supposed to say.

The bald head reappeared. 'Annie, daughter of Will the head stableman!'

Annie swallowed, trying to moisten her dry mouth. Her mind went blank, taking all her practise with it.

Don't panic, keep calm, she told herself. Shaking all over, she followed the bald head into the inn, through the group of folks and into a storeroom at the back.

The musky smell was so overpowering in the room that she reeled, and it was so dark, she could see nothing. As her eyes adjusted to the gloom, she made out a long table in front of her with three men sitting behind it, their faces shadowed in the light of two thick candles. The large man in the middle, she didn't know and didn't like the look of. His bulk spilt over the sides of his chair and the laces of his jupon stretched tight across his chest. He nibbled his fingernails, which were bitten low and black with dirt. He must be the sheriff. Sir John sat to his right, his legs outstretched under the table. She didn't like him either. Carac was on the left with his parchments laid out and a quill already poised in his hand. Carac was alright.

Annie felt so small. She'd never dared speak to Sir John before, let alone a sheriff. The sheriff pointed with a thick finger to the stool placed squarely before them, so she perched awkwardly. She tried to smile thinly at Carac, but his head was bent, ready to write.

The sheriff stopped biting his nails, his eyes narrowing to slits. As he stared at her, she shrank inside and looked away.

'So, girl, tell us what you know,' he said.

'I-I don't know anything, Sire.'

'Don't give me that! You were at the wedding festivities that evening, weren't you? Tell us what you saw.' His booming voice ricocheted around the walls of the tiny room.

She shrivelled a little further and whispered, 'I didn't see anything, Sire. Truly, I didn't.'

'Don't mumble! Speak up; I can't hear you. You danced with Aldred, didn't you?' The jowls of the sheriff's cheeks wobbled as he leaned forward.

Words jumbled inside her head as she squirmed before such an important man. There was no use denying it; plenty of people had seen her. She'd made sure of that. 'Yes. Yes, I did, Sire.' She hated the way her voice trembled.

'And?'

'And that was all, Sire.'

'Who else was Aldred with?'

His stare was relentless and, try as she might, she couldn't look away. 'He was with his brother Gilbert and a few friends, I think, Sire.' Now her voice was no more than a squeak.

'Anyone else? What were they doing? Come on, girl, I haven't got all day!' His hand slapped the table.

She jumped and hot tears sprang to the backs of her eyes. 'They were drinking, Sire.'

'And you were with them. Spend a lot of time together, did you? Get a little drunk, did you?' The sheriff leered at her, showing a row of small yellow teeth.

'No, Sire,' she lied.

He slammed down his fist down on the table. 'Don't

lie to me! Others saw you.'

What was she supposed to say? Think. 'I...may have been a little merry, Sire.'

'So what did you do?'

'I danced and went home.' As she told the lie, the heat crept up her neck and over her face until it burned. He'd see that and know she was lying. She twisted the folds of her tunic. Dear God, let this be over soon!

He leaned back, his hands in his lap and sighed. 'What do you know about a knife?' His voice was now so quiet she could hardly hear it.

Don't say anything about the knife. She repeated Peter's words over and over to herself.

'What knife, Sire?' She tore her eyes away and focused on a flickering candle flame.

'Don't play the innocent with me, girl! The knife Peter, your brother, made for Roger.'

God's teeth, how did he know about that? What was she supposed to say now?

'Oh yes, we know all about that. Roger told me. Now you tell me.'

So Roger had told on Peter. How could he?

The Sheriff stood, placed both hands flat on the table and leaned close. She shrank back from the heat of his stale breath and the ferocious glare of his narrow eyes. For a moment, she was back at the wall with Aldred. 'Tell me! It'll be worse for you if you don't. Did Peter still have the knife that night?'

Did he? Annie bit her lip but couldn't stop the tears trickling down her cheeks. She wished he'd sit down. The sheriff was scaring her, his face blurring with images of Aldred's, and now she was so confused that she didn't know what she was supposed to say anymore. Slowly, she gave the smallest of nods.

'And where is it now? Does Peter still have it?'

She was beaten. 'He lost it,' she whispered.

'Where? Do you know?'

She bowed her head. In the silence, Carac's quill scratched across the parchment. She mustn't say. She'd promised.

'We have someone who saw you and Peter coming from the river path to the village ford early one morning. The interesting thing is that Peter was soaked. Now, why was that? Go for an early swim, did he?' The sheriff glanced at his two companions and chuckled at his own joke.

This man knew everything. Who had seen them? She didn't remember anybody else being there.

'Tell me! What were you doing on the same path where Aldred was murdered?' He was just inches from her and he slapped the table.

She winced. What should she do? They'd been seen. 'Peter was looking for the knife.' Her shoulders sagged in misery.

'Thank you.' The sheriff sat back down. He stretched his legs out in front of him but kept her in his sight, like a cat watching a mouse.

'Shall I tell you what I think?' he said. 'I think that you danced with Aldred and got drunk. I think that Aldred was getting too friendly, your brother saw that and didn't like it. I also think that when Aldred went home, Peter followed him. I might even think that he killed him with the knife he made for Roger.'

'No! No, he didn't. Peter couldn't kill anyone. He just got into a fight, that's all —'

'We're getting somewhere at last,' the sheriff said out

of the side of his mouth to Sir John. 'They close ranks, you know. Don't want to talk. But they always do in the end. They let something slip, and then —' he swiped the air with his hand as though snatching an insect— 'I have 'em!' He returned his attention to Annie, his voice now silky smooth. 'And where was this fight?'

'By the deep pool,' she sobbed.

'Thank you.' The sheriff was practically purring with satisfaction. 'You may go.' He dismissed her with a nonchalant wave of his hand.

Her eyes darted to each man in turn. Carac nodded and she fled, the stool crashing to the floor behind her. Blinded by tears, she rushed through the inn and didn't stop running until she was across the ford and clear of the village. With her heart pounding in her throat, she leaned over a stone wall and put her head on her arms.

What had she done?

CHAPTER 14

'But you must help me! You're the Lady of the Manor;
you can do anything.' Annie was squeezing Joan's
hands, begging her. 'The sheriff thinks Peter did it.
He's sent for the coroner to see if there's a case to put
to the circuit judge. Please speak to Sir John. He'll
listen to you.'

Joan shifted uncomfortably on the log. If only that
were true. She could hardly plead a case for Annie's
brother when Sir John had come home two days ago,
rubbing his hands in glee, saying the sheriff was a fine
fellow and they'd got their man.

'I'm not sure what I can do. The matter's out of
John's hands now.' She avoided Annie's pleading eyes.

'Please, Joan. I don't like asking, but I feel so guilty
and I have to do something. Peter's lost his job because
of this, and we can't survive without his money. Pa's
that worried he's getting his chest pains again.'

'Why has Peter lost his job? It's not as if he's been
found guilty.'

'Because of the knife he made. Peter said when he
went to work next day, John Forge was waiting for
him. He didn't even get through the door. John said
he'd trusted him, but Peter had lied and stolen from

him. He said he was more upset about the lies than the knife. He was very sorry but needed time to think on. Peter said he'd have felt better if John had ranted and raved as he deserved.'

'It's not your fault. You mustn't blame yourself,' said Joan. Why did she feel so guilty?

'Yes, it is. I promised I wouldn't say anything but I couldn't help it. That horrible sheriff made me, and if I hadn't been so stupid—the fight, Peter losing his job, Pa being ill again, and now folks thinking Peter's a thief and a murderer. It's all my fault.'

Joan sighed. God knew, she wanted to help, but Annie didn't understand. She assumed that Joan had some sway over Sir John by virtue of being his wife, but the truth was that he'd no more listen to her over this than he had the red dye. There was nothing she could do. She put an arm around Annie's shoulders. 'Cheer up. I'm sure things will get better.'

Annie shrugged her off. 'Please speak to him. You're the only hope I've got.'

The more Annie pleaded with those big brown eyes, the worse Joan felt. 'I'd love to, you know that, but I don't know if I can. I'll send food from the kitchen to make up for Peter's money. Would that help?'

'It's not your charity I want; it's your influence. Being highborn, you don't know what it's like for the rest of us. There's one law for your lot and another for us. Peter didn't do it, I know he didn't.' Annie stood with her hands on her hips, her troubled eyes flashing accusingly. 'I thought you were my friend. Where I come from, friends stick together.'

Annie was right, Joan thought. She didn't know what it was like to be a peasant. She didn't want them to fall out over this, and she wanted to help, yet she couldn't see how.

'I'm your friend,' she said at last. 'I can't promise anything, but I will try.'

Annie relaxed a little; that was all she'd wanted to hear. 'I knew you wouldn't let me down.'

Joan smiled, but somehow, she felt as though she had betrayed her only friend.

CHAPTER 15

The hall of Court Barton was packed. Annie elbowed her way nearer to the front and stretched up on tiptoe, craning her neck to see. The coroner was already seated at the high table. He had a long serious face and a brown mole on his chin. As he leaned forward, he revealed a shining bald patch. If it hadn't been for his immaculate tabard and jewelled shoulder buckle, Annie thought that he resembled a monk more than a coroner. He sat there with an air of authority and looked like a reasonable man; unlike the sheriff on his right. That man was wearing the same stained jupon and, as he scratched his ear, his fingernails were still black. Sir John was next to him, looking bored and with his legs stretched out in his usual arrogant manner.

It seemed the entire estate had turned up and the noise of the excited crowd vexed Annie. They were behaving as though they were at a bear-baiting. This was her brother's life at stake, and some of them were supposed to be his friends!

Pa was standing by the wall with Malcolm. He waved for her to join them but, as she was about to push her way through, the coroner lifted his head, and a hush descended on the room.

'Peter, the stableman's son, step forward.'

Her pulse raced. Please God that Joan had put in a word for him! Annie scanned the room frantically but couldn't see her.

Peter took his place in front of the table. He looked pale and scared but held his head high. That morning, he'd been sick outside the cottage. Annie felt like being sick herself.

'You are Peter, apprentice to John Forge, is that correct?' the coroner began.

'I was, Sire. I mean, John let me go.'

'John Forge dismissed you from your apprenticeship. Is that what you're trying to say?'

'Yes, Sire.' Peter's voice sounded sad and he dropped his head.

The coroner's quill scratched quickly across the parchment. 'You told the Sheriff that you fought with Aldred that night. Was that in the same place where his body was found?'

'Yes, Sire, but—'

'And you also said that you left him alive. Is that correct?'

'Yes, Sire. Ye must believe me. It was just a fight.' Peter's voice was stronger now as he looked the coroner in the eye.

The coroner glanced through the sheriff's scrolls. 'A fight about what?'

'It was nothin'. He owed me a little money from a dice game, that's all.'

Annie held her breath. Would the coroner believe him? The sheriff coughed, his breath making candles gutter.

'Do you have debts?' he demanded.

'Debts, Sire? No.'

'I'm just wondering why getting this little bit of money was so important that you left the marriage party to follow Aldred through the woods to the river. Couldn't you have talked to him in the barn? And if you don't have debts, as you say, then why were you stealing from your employer to make knives to sell? You were risking your apprenticeship, which you have now lost.'

'It was only one knife, Sire. I just wanted a little ale money. Roger asked me as a favour; he couldn't afford John Forge's price.' Peter's voice was now wavering.

The coroner put down his quill and sat forward with his hands clasped together in front of him. 'Did you steal the contents of Aldred's purse?'

'No, Sire, I did not.' Peter threw down the words like a challenge.

Stay calm, Peter. The room was so hot. Annie fanned her face with her hand and tried to catch Peter's eye, but the coroner was already moving on.

'The sheriff has noted that some people saw tinkers camped in the water meadows. Did you see anyone that night?'

'No, Sire. It was very dark.'

'I believe Malcolm saw you early one morning coming from the river path, totally soaked. Can you explain that?'

'I'd got up early, before work, to look for the knife I made for Roger. I'd lost it and thought it must have come off my belt in the fight.'

'And had it?'

'No, Sire. I couldn't find it. I still can't.'

That was true, but what did the coroner think? Annie could read nothing in his face.

'Hm. I may want to speak to you again. You may step down.'

It seemed to have gone well, Annie thought, but she still didn't know if the coroner believed her brother or not.

Annie stayed for the rest of the hearing and prayed she wouldn't be called upon to speak. She dreaded the thought of everyone watching her, especially if she had to lie again. Every time the coroner told someone they could step down, a part of her inside knotted, waiting for him to call her name, but he didn't. Peter wasn't called again but many folks were. As she listened to what they said, her feelings swung from soaring hope one moment to despair the next. It seemed everyone had different thoughts about that night. To her shame, a few mentioned her drunken behaviour with Aldred, and she bowed her head, wishing she could disappear forever. By the end of the day, she felt like she had been pulled in every direction like a piece of cloth stretched on tenterhooks for drying.

She didn't want to go back for the second day but was told she had to, in case the coroner wanted to question her. Thank God, he didn't, and at midday he adjourned the proceedings for dinner, stating that he would reconvene the hearing with his findings at the third quarter bell.

The Great Barn was packed. Folks clamoured around the free platters of bread and cheese and poured numerous jugs of ale as if they were at the May Day celebrations instead of a trial. Annie sat with Peter on the floor watching them enjoy their day out. The coroner, Sir John and the Sheriff sat together at one end away from the likes of them and occasionally the sheriff's raucous laugh rose above the general din.

'Glad that's over. The coroner seems a fair man, I'm sure he believes me.' Peter picked at his bread. 'And did ye hear what Cyril said? He said that I'm the most God-fearing fellow in the village. That must mean something.'

He was putting on a brave front, but he was rushing his words and twisting his ale cup round and round in his hand. Deep down, he wasn't as sure as he was making out. Annie didn't dare to remind him of the other witnesses who had mentioned his fiery temper.

The coroner stood and wiped his mouth. The sheriff got to his feet, rubbed his stomach and belched. It was time for the coroner's findings. The crowd moved to the doors, pushing and elbowing in their efforts to reach the hall first and get the best view.

Annie smiled at Peter and patted his shoulder. 'Best go,' she said still smiling but inside she was empty and suddenly wanted a pee. She couldn't squat in the barn; she'd have to go outside.

By the time she got back to the hall, there was hardly space to stand, but her Pa was just ahead. Pushing her way rudely past two women, she squeezed in beside him. Feeling her Pa so close beside her was a comfort. Peter was already standing next to the coroner's table. He looked pale, his mouth was tight and he kept rubbing behind his ears, like he always did when he was worried.

The coroner entered the hall, and the room fell silent as all heads turned in his direction. Folks removed their caps or lowered their hoods and paved a way as he swept past, his leather boots hitting the stone slabs with each authoritative stride. Annie watched him settle in his seat and gripped her Pa's arm.

The coroner shuffled his parchments, looked up and cleared his throat. 'I have finished the proceedings and reached my conclusion. This is a confusing case. We have a fight between Peter and Aldred. Peter claims that this was over a small debt from a dice game, and that Aldred was alive when he left him. There are no witnesses to prove this. Aldred was stabbed many times but the murder weapon has never been found.

'That brings me to the question of the knife Peter made for Roger and lost. I ask myself: why was Peter so secretive and desperate to find it? Was it just because he had violated the terms of his apprenticeship? Or was it because it placed him at the scene of the murder? Peter was making and selling knives behind his master's back for money. He said he has no debts but does he? Is that why Aldred was robbed?'

The coroner paused. The only sound in the room was the door creaking on its hinges. No one moved. Annie dug her nails into her Pa's arm, crossed herself, shut her eyes, and prayed. Dear God, let Peter be found innocent. Dear God, let Peter be —

The coroner cleared his throat and continued. 'There are still questions to be answered, but based on everything I have heard, I consider there is enough doubt for a circuit judge to decide. My judgement is that Peter be arrested on the charge of robbery and the murder of Aldred de Chiddleigh.'

In the deathly hush, his words swirled in Annie's head. Her mind went numb. He'd got it wrong. Peter was innocent.

'I told ye the truth! I thought ye'd see!' Peter yelled,

his face red and contorted with anger. 'It's him and him!' He pointed to the sheriff and Sir John. 'They've twisted my words!'

The crowd murmured and started to fidget as her Pa's voice raged beside her. 'Ye can't do this. My boy didn't do it!' Again and again he shouted, as Peter screamed his innocence. Folks turned their heads, their murmurs growing louder. An anonymous voice from the back shouted his support, and then it was joined by another and another, until the hall was filled with an undiscerning din of cries and shouts.

'Men! Take the prisoner!' The sheriff's harsh voice carried across the mayhem.

Sir John stood and held up his hands. 'Be quiet! I order you to be quiet!' No one was listening as his command mixed with the melee of voices.

Peter was no prisoner, but as Annie was about to call out, she was wrenched from her Pa's arm as the crowd surged forward. She tried to look back, but she was caught amid a sea of brown and grey tunics and jostled in the crush. Everything was happening so fast. All around her, men were raising their arms, shaking their fists and screaming in her ears. A warm glob of spittle landed on the back of her neck, and she couldn't free her arm to wipe it off. The crowd pushed nearer to the front, where two men held Peter with his arms behind his back. He was struggling and kicking, swearing and cursing, but they were too strong and held him fast. Annie heard her own voice but her pleas were drowned by the noise. Squashed in on all sides and unable to reach Peter, she buried her face in her hands.

'Silence, or I'll have you all arrested!' The coroner banged the table with his fist.

The voices dwindled to a murmur and finally silence. Peter stopped struggling and the coroner inclined his head. 'And that he be taken to Lyndeford Gaol—'

'No, Sire, not there! I beg of ye! I'll die in there, please, Sire!' Peter's face drained to white, and the fear in his eyes ripped Annie into guilty shreds.

'—to Lyndeford Gaol to await trial! When is the circuit judge due?' Ignoring a shuffling in the crowd, the coroner turned to the sheriff.

'Eh, autumn or early winter, I believe.'

'Men, take the prisoner away.'

'This isn't fair!' Peter screamed. 'I didn't do it! Let me go! Pa, please!'

Somewhere behind her, her Pa shouted, but his voice was hoarse and anyway, it was too late. The guards hauled Peter down the length of the hall, the crowd parting in resigned stillness to let them through. Annie felt so guilty she couldn't bear to look at anyone. She screwed her eyes tight and put her hands over her ears to block out his terrified cries as her innocent brother was dragged outside.

Would he survive to forgive her?

CHAPTER 16

Joan quickly left the hearing and stood outside as the guards hustled Peter into a waiting wagon and tied his hands and bound his ankles with rope. Could she have done anything? She'd hardly seen Sir John in the past two weeks to speak to, and he was so cold-hearted it wouldn't have made any difference if she had, but she wished now that she'd tried.

Annie pushed her way through the crowd, ran over to the wagon and reached up to touch her brother. They held each other's gaze, and, as the wagon moved off, Annie ran alongside until she could no longer keep up. Left behind, she stood still in the middle of the track with her shoulders down and her arms hung limp at her sides, until the wagon carrying her brother to Lyndeford Gaol disappeared round the bend.

Annie looked so lost, making Joan want to reach out and comfort her as a friend should, but the crowd was spilling out from the hall and it would look odd.

'I'm sorry,' she said as Annie brushed past. Annie paused but didn't respond and disappeared into the throng, leaving Joan hollow with guilt.

Sir John turned in his saddle. 'Well, thank the Lord that's over. I thought it would never end. Now we can get back to important matters. I was thinking about things during the trial. Our first job, Carac, is to get those oaks loaded and on their way to Exeter for the Bishop's new nave. The second is to get the route for the new leat marked out.'

'How can you be so callous?' Joan demanded. Did her husband have no feelings at all? 'You've just sent one of your people to gaol, probably to swing on the end of a rope on Gibbet Hill and you're talking as though nothing's happened!'

'My dear woman, it is the way of such things. And I didn't send him; the coroner did. He was very thorough, I thought.'

'I am not a child, John. I do understand such matters. I agree that the coroner was thorough, but I didn't like the sheriff. He slept through most of the proceedings,' she said.

'The coroner was just as he should be: organised, efficient and authoritative,' said Carac with a nod of his head.

'I'm surprised the coroner found the case against Peter —' Joan began.

'I'm not,' Sir John interrupted. 'You've only got to look at him to see he's guilty. He deceived his master and stole from him, and that's enough by itself for him to swing or lose a hand. And why was he so certain he'd lost that knife where Aldred was found?'

'He wasn't certain, and I suspect he looked everywhere for it. I'm not convinced he's guilty and I thought the sheriff most unprofessional,' Carac argued. 'He's behaved like a lubber and a bully from the start. He had no real evidence against anyone but his mind was set on Peter. I'm only sorry I didn't have a chance to say something to the coroner about him. I will write to him though.'

'No, you won't! You're my bailiff and it would put me in a very embarrassing position. I was part of those proceedings too, don't forget. The sheriff was right and the coroner agreed. All we have to do now is wait for the circuit judge to come in the autumn and convict him.'

Joan listened with growing alarm. Annie was right: there was one law for nobles and another for peasants. As unfeeling as ever, Sir John saw everything in black and white, but it wasn't always that clear. Annie was so sure that her brother was innocent, Joan wasn't convinced of Peter's guilt either, and now it seemed that Carac had his doubts too.

Guilt twisted in her gut. She should have talked to Sir John, as Annie had begged her to. Maybe she could do something now to make up for it.

'How will the family manage without Peter?' she asked.

Sir John looked at her from under raised eyebrows. 'Whatever do you mean?'

'They'll miss his earnings. Our peasants struggle to survive in the best of times. Without him, Will and his family will find it even harder.'

'He should have thought of that before he did it.' Sir John's acerbic tones cut through her, but she bit her lip.

'We could help them.'

'Whatever for?' Sir John demanded. 'They're peasants. They're nothing. I make the rules and they obey. That's the way it is. That's the way it's always been. I'm not here to support them when things get tough. If I did that, I'd end up as poor as they are.'

'Joan's right, John. You do have some responsibilities, you know. You must see that if the peasants are starving for lack of coins or poor harvest and suffering because they can't repair their hovels, they won't work so well.'

Good old Carac. Joan could have kissed him for his support.

'I don't believe I'm hearing this again. Peasants are different from us. They think differently – if they even think at all – and they don't feel things in the same way as we do. And I do uphold my responsibilities: pannage rights, gleanings, harvest feasts, not to mention other costly festivals. But that's where it ends.'

Carac sighed. 'I'll never persuade you, will I?'

'No, you won't. Now let's ride on. This whole affair has taken far too long and I'm sure you've things to do, as I have.'

Carac raised his eyebrows to Joan as they cantered on to keep up with Sir John's disappearing back.

CHAPTER 17

It was the last day of June. Joan picked a large stem of cow parsley and put it in her apron with the rest. She glanced up at the clear sky and breathed in the fresh air. Thank God, for the first time in three weeks, the rain had finally stopped. She shielded her eyes from the sun, it felt so good to have the warmth on her face again, and with God's will, the hay might yet be saved. The sound of approaching hooves disturbed her peace.

'John!' Waving her hand in a wide circle over her head, she gathered her skirts and ran towards the yard, spilling her flowers as she went.

Sir John threw a careless leg over the front of the saddle and slipped to the ground, threw back his hood and slowly removed his leather gauntlets, one finger at a time.

'I'm so glad you're home,' Joan said.

'It's good to be home. It's a long ride to the hazel woods. There's good news from the Bishop. He's delighted with the oaks and wants more.'

'That's wonderful! How are things after the rains?'

'May was too dry to start the first ploughing, and now the oxen can't pull the ploughs through the heavy ground. We should be going over the ground with the scratch ploughs and harrowing by now. Carac's got the men marking out the coppicing areas though, so we can start cutting this winter.'

He was actually talking to her as an adult. His face was soft and his voice kind. It was a shame she didn't see more of this side to him. She allowed herself a brief smile.

'Maybe we could ride out there one day and you could show me,' she ventured. 'I'd love to see.'

'Perhaps, but I do have something to show you now. Come with me.'

Curious, Joan quickened her steps to match his, dodging the puddles as he walked briskly down the lane, the feather in his hat bobbing with every stride. The wildflower meadow in the orchards was flattened, but hopefully the cornflowers and poppies would recover. Otherwise, there'd be no seeds for the healer's sleeping tonic and less nectar for honey. That would mean an irritable Cook to deal with and little mead for the winter.

'Up there.' Sir John pointed to the top of a steep field on their right.

Reaching the top, they stood under a small copse of beech trees.

'What do you see below us?' he asked.

Joan shaded her eyes against the sun. 'The village over there, the river, and I can just make out the mill and Court Barton below.'

'Exactly, Court Barton. I am Lord of all this and one day, we shall be counted amongst the highest in the shire.' His gaze swept around the view and came to rest on her.

'Soon, we shall be entertaining important people.

You'll have new kirtles, surcoats, and wimples made from the finest linens and silk and embroidered with gold thread. Gold, green emeralds and blue sapphires will adorn your neck and fingers. And as promised, I have taken steps to find you a suitable companion.'

She still didn't understand him. Where did all this come from, and didn't she have enough clothes already? He obviously didn't think so. And as for a companion, she thought he'd forgotten.

'There doesn't seem to be anyone suitable in these parts, so I've sent word to your mother, asking for help. There must be a family friend or relative somewhere.'

'It's a long way to come and it'll take weeks before we hear anything,' Joan protested. 'What do I do in the meantime?'

He lifted her chin and gently kissed her. 'Be patient,' he said.

Joan didn't know about that. Patience wasn't her strong point, and he was talking down to her again. It was beginning to get irritating, but she let it pass rather than spoil his mellow mood. 'Have you thought any more about the red dye? I'd like to get started, but I need madder roots.' She gauged his reaction, but there was no hint of the set jaw or steely eyes.

'I haven't. Ask me again when I'm not so busy.'

All he had to do was get a few men to dig up some roots and clear a bit of ground. She needed to get the madder planted soon because the roots needed time to grow before harvesting next autumn. She bit her lip. At least he hadn't said no.

Joan sat with him in the shade of the trees watching the ploughmen working in the field next to the orchard. Sitting high on the hill and looking down, they seemed very small. They were struggling to hold the heavy wooden plough to the furrow as the two goaders leading the oxen hauled on the ropes, encouraging the beasts through the thick red mud. It was slow work. Would the ploughing be finished by the end of the month, ready for the sowers? It would be a poor harvest if it wasn't.

In the grass meadow, two maids came out of a wattle pen in the corner. One balanced a jug on her head, the other fastened the pen shut and carried a wooden bowl. They'd been milking sheep and were heading for the dairy.

Joan could have sat there all day watching the comings and goings. In the background, Sir John was talking about extensions and improvements to their home. This was a rare intimate moment, and it would be foolish to miss it. Joan switched her attention back to him.

'We shall have an upstairs bedchamber and another for guests. Fine tapestries on the walls, silver dishes in place of pewter – all the best houses have silver – and new candle holders with only the best beeswax candles.' He turned and smiled warmly. 'A manor to be proud of and one that visitors will envy.'

Joan liked this side of her husband. What a pity she didn't see more of it. Of course, the new gowns, jewellery and building were all exciting, but being and talking together meant more to her than anything he could buy.

CHAPTER 18

Joan didn't understand why, but Sir John was like a different person. He was still away during most of the day, but when he was with her, he seemed more aware, somehow. He'd changed after the coroner had finished his hearing, as though some huge weight had been lifted from his shoulders. His step was lighter, he walked taller, and she'd even heard him whistling across the yard. It was a long time since he'd done that. Maybe he'd been more worried than she'd realised. Whether Sir John had liked Aldred or not, he was still his cousin. If one of her cousins had been murdered, Joan knew that she'd have been upset for weeks. Perhaps it was the anticipation of the building works; he was certainly excited about those.

Sir John still had his moments, though. Like the other day, when she'd asked him again about Aldred and his family. He'd frozen, his eyes deepening to a cold iron grey, and refused to speak of it. Then suddenly, he'd got up and left. She hated it when he did that. When he came to her that night, his breath stank of wine and he'd fallen off her in a drunken stupor.

Work on the estate was frantic. The sound of sheep in the close fields disturbed her at night, and she wished the men would get on with shearing and move them back to the high grazings. Piles of stinking sludge cleared from the ditches littered every lane, and she covered her ears against the raucous cries of the gulls following the ploughmen from dawn to dusk. Despite all this, it was a relief to see the workers in the fields again. Along with everyone else, Joan prayed that the dry weather would hold.

God was listening and by the end of July, the tall grass in the fields swayed in gentle green waves, the seed heads fluffy and ripe for cutting.

On the first day of haymaking, just after the first quarter bell, Joan picked up her willow basket and hurried down to the first field. The men were working in a line across the field, swinging their scythes in long sweeping arcs before them, singing as they worked.

Finding a pleasant spot at the edge of the field with few thistles and a thick hedge to lean against, Joan spread her blanket and settled down to wait for the midday break. She'd had the maids pack a picnic and couldn't wait to see Annie. She hadn't seen her since the coroner's hearing and had so much to tell her.

When the sun was at its highest, the reeve stopped work. The men removed their leather mitts and sat in small groups waiting for the women and children to bring the baskets of bread and cheese and flagons of cider.

Joan scanned the group as they entered the field but, disappointingly, Annie wasn't with them. Maybe she'd come along later. It was a perfect day and with nothing else to do, she watched the men swinging their scythes, now followed by the women and children, who tossed the cut grass high with their pitchforks and then tidied it in rows to dry in the warm sunshine.

Joan lazed back until she was in shade. The peasants would work until the moon was high and then, exhausted, they would say their farewells and wearily make their way home to sink into a deep sleep until the following dawn, when they would do it all again. How they kept going day after day, she didn't know. She certainly didn't envy them.

Joan returned to the fields the next day and the next, but Annie still didn't come. By the fourth day, the hay was dry and the women worked along the lines, gathering the sweet-smelling grass into small beehive-shaped ricks. She was getting worried, and even Cook didn't know where Annie was.

On the fifth day, teams of men methodically pitched the ricks on to wagons to take to the barns for winter storage. Sir John's hay was nearly gathered and whilst the workers were taking a rest before moving to the communal fields, Joan saw Annie sitting on her own by the wagons. At last, she could tell her the news. Grabbing her basket with a flutter of excitement, she hurried towards her.

The oxen stood dozing in the heat, lazily swishing their tails to flick away the troublesome flies. Keeping to the shade, Annie sat back against one of the wagon wheels. She was exhausted and wanted time alone to think. She had a lot to think about.

'At last, I've found you!'

Annie groaned inwardly. She wasn't in the mood for chatter. Reluctantly, she opened her eyes, shielding them against the glare of the sun. Joan was hurrying towards her, skirts in one hand, basket swinging in the other.

'I've been worried. You look awful. Are you alright?'
Joan settled herself beside her.

'Bit poorly, that's all.'

'I've been looking for you. I'm sorry about the hearing. I did try.' Joan blushed as she spoke, knowing the lie for what it was.

'It's alright.'

'I'm so glad we're away from the others. I've got loads to tell you. Oh, I'm so excited, I don't know where to begin!' Busily, she unpacked the contents of her basket. 'Do you want some bread and cheese?'

This was going to be a long session. Annie shook her head, resigned to letting her friend chatter on. Joan broke off a large chunk of cheese and took an enthusiastic bite. 'Firstly, John's being so wonderful. I'm not sure why and I really don't care. It's just so nice when he's like this,' she enthused, taking another bite.

'That's good.'

'It is, and I can't tell you.' Joan's words rolled together in her haste. 'He has plans, big plans. John says that with all the improvements to the estate, we shall need a manor house to reflect our growing status. He wants us to entertain important landowners, so of course, I shall have new clothes and jewellery.'

'Of course,' Annie muttered under her breath. This was Joan the Lady talking. Well, she was welcome to her fancy clothes and jewellery. She might have all that, but she'd still have to put up with Sir John.

Joan hurried on. 'And guess what? He's going to build upstairs! We're to have a bedchamber going the whole width of the hall with an opening to the front, with horn glass and shutters to keep out the winter winds and rain. The hall chimney will be inside keeping

125

it snug and warm. Imagine it!'

Annie could imagine it only too well in contrast to her own home: a one-room cruck house. Its thin draughty walls were made from sticks and mud, the floor was dirt covered with a bit of straw when they could spare it, and there was a central hearth with a hole in the roof for the smoke. On a windy day, more smoke was blown back into the room than went out of it.

'Sounds lovely,' she said in a monotone.

'There'll be wooden stairs in the corner of the hall to reach it. And that's not all; another set of steps will lead to a similar chamber at the other end. I don't know what will happen to our present bedchamber, another spare for visitors, I suppose. Oh, I'm so excited, I could burst!'

Joan paused for breath and took hold of Annie's hands. 'But that's not the best bit. I haven't told anyone this.' She lowered her voice conspiratorially. 'Not even John.'

At that, Annie sat up, now faintly interested.

'Don't say anything,' Joan instructed her, 'but I am with child. I've been feeling so weary of late and a bit queasy, not sick or anything, but I've missed two of my courses so I must be...' Her eyes sparkled and her cheeks flushed.

Annie had never seen her look so happy, but the news only made her feel worse. She wished Joan hadn't told her, but somehow, she forced a smile and hugged her friend.

'...I know I should tell John first, but as my special friend, I wanted you to be the first to know. I'm so happy—Annie? Annie, what's wrong? What have I said?'

It wasn't fair. Annie had been trying so hard to put that

night behind her, forcing a smile on her face as she went about her duties, joining in with the maids' japes as though nothing had happened. Then, what with Peter going to gaol and now her latest problem, she couldn't pretend anymore. She just wasn't strong enough.

A tear trickled down her cheek. 'It all sounds so wonderful and ...you're so happy and...' She buried her face in her hands.

'Annie, whatever is it? I'm your friend. You can tell me. Is it Peter? Is that it?'

'No, it's not that. Not just that, I mean.'

'Well, what then? Please tell me.'

Annie gulped back a sob. 'It's all such a mess and it's all my fault.'

'What is? Annie, look at me. I'm your friend. Maybe I can help.'

Maybe she could. Joan was cleverer than she was and always made things seem better. It was what Annie loved about her. She sniffed a few times, then wiped her nose with her sleeve. She'd thought many times about when and how she would tell Joan of her shame, and she would have to tell her; she couldn't hide her secret forever. Now was as good a time as any, and she'd feel better sharing it. Joan would understand and be the one person she could turn to when others turned their backs. After all, they were special friends.

'If I do, you must promise that you won't tell a soul,' she said.

'Of course I promise. Now, what is it?'

'On your soul?' Annie pressed.

'Yes, yes, of course.'

Annie took a deep breath. 'Well, everything you've just said, about being tired and all that? That's how

I feel. It's why I haven't been on the fields. I've missed three —'

Her voice faded to nothing as she saw the horror in Joan's eyes. Saw her special friend move away from her.

'You can't be.' Joan's voice was hoarse with shock. 'You — oh, Annie, what have you done?'

'Yes, I can be. And I haven't done anything.'

'But before wedlock? That's a grave sin against God. The shame, folks will talk, you'll be shunned. Annie, how could you? Whatever were you thinking?'

Where were Joan's open arms of comfort and the understanding words? One look at her face was enough to see how appalled she was. She shouldn't have told her. 'I wasn't thinking anything. I didn't want to do anything. He made me. As my friend, I thought you'd understand.'

'I am, I do — but Annie — I mean, before wedlock.'

'You're shocked. I can see it on your face. It's what everyone will think of me, but I thought you'd be different.'

'Of course I'm shocked, and I am different. I'm your friend. So tell me, who was it? I promise I won't tell anyone.'

Joan wasn't being the loving friend she needed. She was no different than the maids; eager for gossip, wanting all the details, and if Annie knew anything at all about her, Joan wouldn't let it rest. And Joan was the Lady of the Manor, so Annie couldn't very well tell her to mind her own muxy business. Maybe she'd help her. God knows, she needed it.

'Aldred. It was Aldred de Chiddleigh, if you must know.' Flustered, Annie stood up, clipped her coif back into place and put her hands on her hips. 'It was Aldred. On the night of your wedding. I'd drunk too much, but it was a party wasn't it? He found me, forced me.' Avoiding Joan's eyes, she irritably shook bits of hay from her skirts.

'Aldred?' Joan shook her head. 'No. I don't believe you.'

'As God's my witness, it's the truth.' Annie crossed herself.

'I'm so sorry. Really I am. But even if he did...you know, you've still sinned grievously against God. Nothing can change that.'

'No, it can't.'

There she sat, the Lady of the Manor; secure, happy and respected. Her skin was blooming like a healthy pink rose, her eyes were shining and her hair shone like burnished copper in the sunlight. The news of her baby would be celebrated. While here Annie stood, a nobody, her hair dishevelled, sweat stains under her arms, her clothes as dirty as she felt. There'd be no celebrations for her.

'It's alright for you, but it's different for me. I thought you'd understand, but you don't.' The words slipped out. It wasn't Joan's fault. It was the difference between them. Annie dropped her hands. 'The truth is, I'm frightened. What's going to happen to me?'

Joan didn't answer.

'You'll still be my friend, won't you?' Annie whispered. 'I don't know what I'd do without you.' Joan couldn't desert her, not now of all times. They were friends, weren't they? 'Joan? You will, won't you? I need you.'

Joan hesitated and spoke to the field. 'We'll always be friends, you know that. But I'm Sir John's wife and

Lady of the Manor. I can't ignore my position, and I can't go against the will of God, can I?'

Joan wasn't going to help her. Annie felt as if someone had dumped cold water on her. She was just a peasant and had been a fool to think otherwise. 'No, I suppose you can't. I see that now.'

'Annie, please understand.' Joan swallowed. 'I'll help you if I can, but...maybe we shouldn't meet anymore. Just for a while. You do see that, don't you?'

It was at that moment Annie knew there would be no comforting arms, no words of sympathy and no more friendship. She was on her own and she'd never felt so let down in her life. Joan, her closest friend was disowning her, and it hurt. Joan the girl would stand by her, but she'd been a cloth-head to think Joan the Lady would.

Well, she was damned if she would show her feelings! She may have been a peasant, but even peasants had their pride. Annie raised her chin and forced herself to look at Joan.

'I understand. But remember: you swore on your soul not to repeat this!' she said.

'I won't forget.'

'Reeve's calling, I've to get back to work. Farewell, my lady.' Annie, as a dutiful maid, dipped a curtsey and, turning her back to hide her tears, walked resolutely back to work.

CHAPTER 19

Joan rested her chin on her hand, watching the rain and counting the puddles in the yard. Sir John couldn't be much longer. She watched a small figure scuttle into the dairy. She'd know that walk anywhere. Her hand went up to wave, but she stopped herself. She mustn't, not now she knew.

It wasn't fair, but what could she do? She was caught between her position and God on one hand and her secret friendship with a kitchen maid on the other. She'd never forget the disappointment on Annie's face. Annie had looked so vulnerable when she'd walked bravely away, trying not to cry.

It was the curtsey that really got to her. And the worst of it was, Joan missed her. Did Annie miss her too, or was she so hurt she never wanted to speak to her again?

And now she was about to tell Sir John he was going to be a father, while at the back of all her excitement was a pang of guilt that refused to go away.

Later that afternoon, Joan watched Sir John's face as the torches cast changing shadows across his cheeks and brow. She hadn't waited for him to take off his hat and, as he reached out for some wine, the feather tickled her nose. He put the goblet to his lips and took a hearty draft. His eyes creased into white lines at the corners, his jaw relaxed and his mouth spread into a rare broad smile. He opened his arms and she stepped into them.

'A son! I am to have a son!' He rested his chin on the top of her head.

'The child might be a girl...' She looked into his eyes, feeling his arms close around her waist.

'No, this child is a son. I just know it. He'll grow tall and handsome, just like his father.' He grinned, and she gave him a playful slap on his arm. 'I shall teach him everything I know, and together we'll make our estate the biggest and the best in the whole of Devonshire. I can't quite believe it.'

'You had better believe it, for this child will be born sometime in February. So, my lord, you had better get those builders working, because I intend to have this child in my new bedchamber.'

'And so you shall.'

'Lady Joan?' Her maid's voice came through the door.

'Not now, Agnes,' Joan said over her shoulder.

'Prithee, my lady, but I'm to tell you that the harvest is gathered.'

She sighed. 'Tell the reeve we'll be along soon.'

'Yes, my lady.'

'They're waiting for us. You'd better wear this.' Sir John carefully placed a thick green mantel around her shoulders.

'It's September and still warm outside. I won't need that.'

'From now on, you must look after my son, and I shall make sure that you do. Now wear it.' He fastened the gold brooch at her shoulder.

'Yes, my lord.' She dipped a mock curtsey, and, laughing, they left the manor house.

Crossing the stubble field, their long purple shadows stretched in front of them. Some men leaned on their scythes while others sat on the ground. Women held tired children in their arms and young lads played chase.

'I understand that the harvest is safely gathered?' said Sir John.

'Yes, my lord.' The reeve stepped forward and bowed. 'Both your harvest and our communal harvest are in, and it's better than we hoped. Not a full yield but about two thirds, Sire.'

'Good news indeed.' Sir John turned to face his people. 'Before the last sheaf is presented, I have an announcement to make.' He drew Joan protectively close.

She knew what he was about to say. There was warmth and pride in his eyes. Finally, she was his true lady, and it felt wonderful. She stared at the brooch at his shoulder, for fear of seeing Annie amongst the crowd.

'You won't be seeing so much of Lady Joan in the months to come.' His voice carried clearly through the quiet evening air. 'Because, praise God,' he paused for effect, 'she is with child. I am to have a son and heir.' For the first time in his life, he smiled at his people as he waited for the cheering to die down.

Annie wouldn't be cheering. Joan lifted her chin and stared at crows flying amongst distant ash trees.

'Reeve, bring forth the last sheaf,' Sir John said. 'Who is to make the harvest doll?'

'Isobel has the honour, Sire.'

A short elderly woman in a green woollen kirtle and brown shawl stepped forward, her grey hair neatly tied back with a precious green ribbon. Keeping her head bowed and her hands clasped at her chest, she curtseyed.

'Your fellow villagers have bestowed a great honour on you,' Sir John said. 'Make a good corn doll from this last sheaf to guard our harvest stores over the dark months and bring us a fruitful harvest next year.' Then, looking over the crowd before him, he raised his voice. 'Tomorrow night, we shall have the Harvest festival. All food and drink will come from the manor, and Isobel will present the corn doll.' Men threw their caps in the air and the people cheered. He held up his hand to quieten them. 'Now go home, and tomorrow decorate the village and manor with boughs and greenery for the evening celebrations. Pray to God, for we have much to be thankful for.'

Joan would pray, and she'd ask God to ease her guilt and help Annie.

The following evening, just before the sun slipped behind the high moors, Joan stood at the high table with Sir John as folks gathered in the hall. The grin hadn't left his face since she'd told him. She hoped it never would.

The room quietened to a hush as Isobel began her long walk down the length of the hall, carrying her precious corn doll proudly in front of her. Her hands trembling, she lay her creation in front of Sir John, curtseyed and took a small pace back.

The body of the doll was shaped from plaits made from the longest stalks of wheat. Five shorter sprays, still with their ears intact, were woven through them and splayed out in the shape of a star. From the centre, a twist of wheat formed an intricate loop of corn ears. It was the best doll Joan had seen in many a year.

'Reeve, take this Harvest Doll to the Great Barn to guard over our grain during the dark months to come, and let us all give thanks to God for such a good harvest and the coming of my son.' Sir John paused, looked fondly at Joan, and raised his goblet. 'Let the celebrations begin!'

Joan sat tall and tilted her chin as she looked down on her people. If only her mother were here now. She'd be so proud. How she would smile, just as she did when Joan was a little girl and made a daisy ring to wear on her head like a crown. She'd drape Mama's huge fur mantel around her shoulders and push her tiny child feet into the very toes of her velvet slippers and shuffle up and down on the stone floor of their hall, her head held high. She was Queen Philippa of England. Mama would smile. 'You'll never be Queen of England,' she'd say, 'but one day, God willing, you will be a Lady of the Manor.'

And here she was, a real lady and carrying Sir John's heir. She felt cherished and cared for by her lord, and she had her new house to look forward to. Everything was just perfect.

Her gaze met Annie's. Well, nearly perfect. It wasn't surprising that Annie looked a shadow of her former self; she must be scared out of her wits. She was in the worst position any lass, noble or peasant, could be in. If only Joan could meet with her, she'd soon put a smile on that face.

For a moment Annie's eyes narrowed and unnerved her

with such a stare of—was it accusation? Joan's cheeks burned and she looked away, giving Sir John one of her most loving smiles and placed her hand on his.

CHAPTER 20

The following day, Annie sat on the dirt floor of the cottage. Going to the celebrations with Mary and Ellyn had been a mistake. She'd thought that having a dance again would cheer her up, but it had only made her feel worse. The last time she was with Mary like that was at Lady Joan's wedding, and she wouldn't dwell on that.

Geoffrey Miller asking Mary to dance hadn't helped. Annie hadn't really wanted to dance with him; it was just that she was far prettier than Mary and was always the first to be asked, and she was a better dancer too. But as Ellyn said, they made a nice couple. No matter what her Pa wanted, she would never marry Geoffrey or anyone else. And one day, she would be back on that dance floor, her feet flying to the beat. One day.

Sir John had sat at his high table, dressed in his fine silk jupon, looking down on everyone. She bet that jupon cost more than her Pa would see in his lifetime. Sir John had never liked her. Well, she didn't much like him with his hard eyes and noble ways. She didn't know how Joan could stand being his wife. She'd looked almost as arrogant as he did with her baby in her belly, her chin held high and all dressed in her fine yellow kirtle and surcoat with her hair beautifully braided and jewels at her throat. She wasn't the Joan she knew, the young girl who sat with her on the log sharing stories, giggling and skipping across the meadows in the summer sunshine. Joan the girl had been much nicer than Joan the Lady.

Joan saw her alright, but turned away as if she hadn't. How she wished she'd never told her. Thank the good Lord for Mary's Ma, Ellyn the healer. She didn't miss much and had let her weep on her shoulder.

Ellyn was right. She was what she was, and Joan was what she was, and there was no use pretending otherwise. From now on, she'd stay with her own kind.

Annie glanced around the cottage. They needed more sticks for the hearth, but she was too tired and couldn't stop crying. Some days at work, she just wanted to throw the dirty pots back at Cook and scream and scream.

She bit her tongue, picked up the wooden pails and trudged to the well, turning the thick wooden handle until she heard the distant splash of the pail hitting the water in the depths below. Then she hauled on the handle until her arms burned, only to lug the heavy pails of water back to the kitchen ready to start scrubbing the next pile of pots until her hands were red and raw.

She ran her hands over her small bump. She'd start showing soon and then what? She hated whatever was growing inside her and she hated Aldred.

An acrid smell hit her nose and she sniffed. God's teeth, the bread! Annie grabbed it from the hot hearthstones, scorching her fingers, and flung it across the floor. She left it in the dirt and sat crying.

When it was almost dark, her Pa came home and leaned in the doorway. He looked as worn out as she

138

felt. His face was heavily lined with dark circles under his eyes, and nowadays, he always came in clutching his chest after the long walk up the hill.

'You'll wear yourself out,' Annie said. 'Can't someone else take Peter's food? It's four miles to the gaol and back. After a day's work, it's too much, Pa.'

She spooned some thin vegetable stew into a bowl. He deserved better. She should have pulled more carrots and picked some beans, but at the time she couldn't be bothered. She'd do better tomorrow.

He took the piece of blackened bread and eyed it with suspicion.

'Sorry, I left it on the stones too long,' she said.

He sighed, chewed on the charred bread and put the bowl of stew to his lips.

'Shall I ask Malcolm if he'll take our swine to the woods for pannage? That'll save you a job.'

'No use, lass. I haven't the fees.' He blew steadily on his stew.

'We must get them on the acorns or they won't fatten, and then we won't have enough meat for the winter.'

'Ye tell Sir John that. No fees, no usin' his woods.' He chewed on the hard bread, dropping a few crumbs which got lost amongst his beard.

'Should have put the geese on the fields to glean the loose grain after the harvest, but I can't get them to the fields. Don't suppose ye can and follow to pick up after?'

The thought of walking across the stubble fields after a day's work, her back bent, handpicking what few grains of wheat the geese had missed, made her want to cry. His haggard face and tired eyes were pleading with her. The little grain she collected could make all the difference come the winter months.

She looked at the bowl of watery stew and the burnt bread and nodded. 'I'll do what I can.'

'There's the communal strip to look after too. Peter used to do that.' His voice trailed off.

Wearily, she picked up the little wooden bowls and took them outside to the stream to wash. She'd have to tell Pa soon, although how she was going to do that, she had no idea. He'd go mad. He might even throw her out. As if she didn't have enough to worry about. She didn't know which was worse, her guilt or her tiredness.

Standing up, she stretched and put a hand to her aching back and wiped her brow with her apron. Someone was coming along the path. It looked like — she squinted, yes, God's teeth, it was Ellyn and she didn't miss much. She shook out the front of her skirts and apron and quickly grabbed the pots and held them in front of her.

Ellyn was a short, round woman with rosy apple cheeks and a mass of fair, wiry curls that bounced on her head as she took quick short steps. In the crook of one arm, she balanced a large willow basket on her hip, making her lean a little to one side as she walked. Her cottage was just a furlong or two beyond theirs, and Annie loved her like a mother. It was Ellyn who'd stepped in to help when her Ma had died and had been like a mother to her ever since. But today, she was too tired for idle chat.

'Annie, hail, I haven't seen you for a while. How fare you?' Ellyn stopped by the weathered wattle fence and hitched her basket further on to her hip.

'I'm well, thank you. On your way home?'

'I am, and I'm that worn out. I've been to Malcolm's

place with some of my borage and rose tonic. Said he was feeling tired after the harvest. You look a bit tired yourself,' she said, peering closer.

'No, I'm fine.' Annie forced a bright smile on her face.

'Are you sure you don't want some tonic? I might have another jar in here somewhere.' Ellyn began rummaging to the depths of her basket.

'No, no, I'm not a bit tired. Really, I'm not.'

'Well, if you're sure.' Ellyn frowned and stared at the pots Annie was holding.

'I'm well. No need to worry.' Annie shifted uncomfortably. Surely Ellyn didn't suspect anything?

'Hmm. Well, if you say so, but I might have something at home that'll do you some good. I'll drop it by next time I'm passing. Can't stand here chatting, better make haste. Those boys of mine always want feedin'.' And with a thoughtful look and a wave, Ellyn continued on her way.

Annie looked down at her front, something she did every day. Ellyn couldn't suspect, her belly wasn't that big yet. But it wouldn't be long before it was, and what would she do then?

CHAPTER 21

Carac stood by the mill wall, his hands together, his fingertips to his mouth, and stared. No matter which way he looked at it, it wasn't going to work.

'Have the new men started yet?' Sir John asked, as he picked his way along the path to join Carac.

'Yes, but are you sure that hiring men is the right thing to do?'

'Of course it is. All the big landowners are doing it.'

'That doesn't mean we have to.'

'Carac.' Sir John put an arm around his shoulders. 'We have to move with the times. Think about it. No small patch to build their hovels and scratch out a few vegetables. No communal grazing and crops and fewer men to drink their way through festivals and saint's days—do you know how many barrels of ale and cider they got through at harvest?'

'Actually, I do.'

'I thought you might. Then you'll know what I mean.'

Carac raised an eyebrow. He wasn't sure that he did, but he let it pass. 'I've asked you here, John, because we have a problem. The new leat cannot run straight from the river to the mill. Over there, the granite rock sits much deeper than we thought, and we can't cut through. The only way I see to solve the problem is to divert around. We'll have to cut more timbers for shoring. That will take another two or more weeks and mean more wages for your hired labourers. Now, if we use our own peasants —'

'We use hired labour. As we speak, drovers are walking the lanes with another two hundred sheep for us. Next year we'll have more lambs and more wool for the mill. Don't worry, that'll pay for it.'

Carac sighed. When Sir John was in this mood, there was no point in reasoning with him.

'And don't forget, it's the harvest market soon. Are the shepherds sorting the ewes and ram lambs to sell?' said Sir John.

Of course they were, Carac thought irritably. 'I spoke to them yesterday, and it's all in hand.'

'Good. I want to buy some new rams. Any thoughts of the type?'

'We already have good Dartmoor Whiteface sheep, but I think we should try a couple of Blackface from the northern shires. I hear they're very hardy, and by crossing the breeds we should get a longer fibre that will be perfect for quality cloth making.' Carac had done his homework.

'Good, we'll do that. And the timbers for the waterwheel?'

'All organised, just as we planned.'

'As always, you have everything under control. Anything else?'

There was, but persuading Sir John wasn't going to be easy. If only he were more like his father. Carc had always hoped that one day he would see a glimpse of the old Lord, Sir James, in Sir John, but he realised now that he never would. Sir James had been so reasonable, so patient with a rational sense of forward-thinking. He understood and looked after his workers and held their respect; not just because of his title, but because of the man he was. But that was all before that business with Hilde.

'There is one thing,' said Carac. 'It's the building on the house. I've spoken to a few merchants and builders, and what you want will empty the coffers and more. Building an upstairs chamber is quite new. Skilled carpenters and stonemasons will have to come from Exeter and will demand top wages. They'll need strong poles, boards and timbers. The work will take weeks, maybe months, to finish. The materials alone will be hugely expensive; stones from the quarry will have to be brought here in carts and on mules, not to mention the horned glass for the openings. I strongly advise that you wait until we have money from the cloth sales next year.' He scrutinised Sir John's blank face. Had he got the message?

'You know your trouble? You worry about money too much. Joan wants to have my son in the new bedchamber. And that is what she shall have.'

Clearly, he hadn't. Carac sighed. 'Put bluntly, John, you don't have the funds. Can't you at least use shutters and forget the glass? Explain to her. I'm sure she'll understand.' If he got the chance, he'd mention it to her himself. He couldn't rely on Sir John to do it.

'Carac!' Sir John shook his shoulder. 'It's not just about Joan. I need to entertain influential landowners and I can't do it in the house as it is. It does not befit my status. You said so yourself.'

'I suggested a few minor improvements—'

'No, my mind is made up. Arrange for the builders to

start work and order what they need.'

Carac had tried, but Sir John had been as impetuous as always. Once he fixed an idea in his head, there would be no stopping him, regardless of the consequences.

That was all very well, but how was he going to pay for it?

CHAPTER 22

Annie got off her knees and crossed herself. It was three long months since the coroner sent Peter to Lyndeford gaol and she hadn't seen him since. The cottage was so empty without him.

When the circuit judge arrived two days ago, the village was buzzing with the news, and folks looked for any excuse to be at the trial. Today was expected to be the last day. Annie hadn't been before – she'd suffered too many knowing looks and whispers behind hands and hadn't wanted to invite more – but Peter would be there today. She had to give him her support.

The sheriff would be there too, with his piggy eyes. Annie shuddered. She wasn't looking forward to seeing him again.

Peter was innocent. She was sure of that, but what if the judge found him guilty? He'd send Peter to the gallows – that didn't bear thinking about – and how would they manage without him? Pa was getting too old to work all day and do his share at the communal fields and she couldn't push a plough, especially now. They wouldn't have enough grain for the winter and then they'd starve.

Annie shook her head. She was being a cloth-head.

Any numbskull could see that Peter hadn't done it. Her brother would soon be home.

Wrapping a large shawl loosely around her shoulders and making sure it covered her growing bump, she picked up the ridiculous basket, holding it high in front of her. The hateful bulge was growing daily and – even loosening her belt – she couldn't hide it forever. Then what? She had to tell Pa soon.

Every day, she said to herself that she would do it that evening. She would put extra carrots in the stew just as he liked, and when he'd finished his meal but before he got too sleepy, she would kneel in front of him and say the words, It is God's will and I am with child.

Just eight little words, but every time she saw his tired, worry-lined face, they stuck in her throat. Another evening would go by, and she'd tell herself that she'd be braver tomorrow, but she never was.

It was no good thinking about that now; she must get to the hall. Had she remembered the little sack-wrapped parcel? She checked in her basket. Yes, it was there. She'd made some oatie cakes for Peter as a present. They were pale and flat compared to the ones Joan used to bring to their log – God's teeth, how long ago that seemed – but she was sure he'd be pleased.

Annie peered through the wall of grey tunics packing the hall and elbowed her way through to her Pa sitting close to the front.

The high table was in its usual place but in the centre sat the circuit judge, a thin stern-looking man with thick eyebrows too large for his face. He wore a rich red houppelande with long slits in the sides showing a

147

linen undertunic with a gold brooch on his shoulder. Sir John was there and the sheriff on his left, just as she remembered him. She looked away.

The doors opened. The crowd stopped talking, turned and made way for the gaoler and his charge who clung to his shoulder, his legs barely moving, his feet dragging behind.

'The prisoner, Sire,' he said, dropping his hood and bowing before the judge.

Annie leaned forward and glanced at her Pa who was frowning. She stared back at the pile of human rags gripping the table for support. His face was haggard with dull eyes staring out from deeply sunken sockets. His legs were so thin they belonged on a crow, and the skin under the arms sagged like an old maid's.

They must have got it wrong. Or perhaps the judge had other business with this man before it was Peter's turn.

'Can he stand?' The judge leaned forward, peering under his brows.

'Don't think so, Sire.'

'Try him.'

The gaoler propped his burden between the bench and table but he slumped like a sack of corn.

'Well, sit him down then.'

Hastily, the gaoler manoeuvered the prisoner onto the bench and pushed him down. He swayed to one side. The gaoler grabbed his shoulders and pulled him straight, giving him a final shove. The prisoner lifted his head and gazed uncertainly around the room, and then he stared straight at Annie with dead eyes.

Annie gasped. Dear God, it was Peter, but what had they done to him?

The judge cleared his throat and leaned back. 'I've read the coroner's reports and heard all the evidence. Now, prisoner, it's your turn. What do you have to say for yourself?' He picked up his quill, poised.

Peter turned away, his lifeless eyes leaving Annie.

The judge spoke a little louder. 'Well? What have you to say?'

'I—I don't know, Sire. I can't think.'

'Do you know where you are and who I am?'

Peter looked around vacantly and blinked.

'You are in the main hall of the manor house. I am the circuit judge and you are accused of the robbery and murder of Aldred de Chiddleigh. Do you understand?' He said his words slowly and loudly.

Peter nodded.

The judge ruffled the folds of his clothing. 'Good. This is your chance to give your account of what happened. You fought with Aldred that night and...?'

'Yes, Sire, I remember that.'

'Why did you fight with him?'

'I—I don't know. I...'

Annie looked desperately around and dug her nails into her hands. This wasn't fair! Peter was in no state to remember anything! He hardly even knew where he was. He was stumbling over his words, and he never did that.

'I-I think it was an old quarrel, nothin' really, Sire.'

The judge frowned, dipped his quill into the inkpot and began to write. Heart racing, Annie looked at her Pa, who was pressing his lips together so hard they were white, his hands opening and closing into tight fists. Surely, Pa, someone, anyone, would do something?

The judge paused, the quill's scratching stopped. The

149

hall was silent. 'Is that it? Is there nothing more you want to say?'

Annie wanted to say something but her voice stuck in her throat. Her shame, maybe losing their home, none of it mattered now.

'No, nothin', Sire.'

'Peter!' She didn't know where it came from, but her voice echoed around the hall.

Her Pa grabbed her arm. 'Be quiet, girl. You'll make things worse.'

'But—'

The judge swivelled his head, his authoritative eyes chilling her to silence. Her words were still in her mouth but nothing came out. Slowly, he turned back to Peter.

'Not much for me to go on, is it?'

'Pa, you must do something,' she whispered, clutching his arm.

For a moment she thought he hadn't heard, then in a voice so full of pain and desperation, he bellowed from the depths of his soul. 'Peter! It's your Pa. Tell him.'

Two hands gripped his shoulders from behind.

'Be quiet, Will, you're not helping!' Malcolm hissed into his ear.

'Silence! I will have order in my court. One more interruption and you will all be removed.' The judge's commanding voice bounced off the walls.

No one moved. Annie could feel the hope draining out, leaving her weak and empty inside. The judge wasn't going to listen. There was nothing they could do to save him. She stared miserably at the floor.

'I have heard all the evidence and the defence from the prisoner. I am now ready to declare my verdict.'

This couldn't be it. She screwed her eyes tight and prayed.

'Peter, son of Will, the head stableman and villein, under the Lordship of Sir John de Chiddleigh of the manor of Court Barton and Ashetyne, I now pronounce that —'

'No!' A deep plaintive voice shattered the silence. 'No, Sire, I beg of you, this is my son.' Will shook off Malcolm's grip and faced the judge, twisting his cap between his two hands. 'Look at him, Sire. He can't defend himself. We can all see that.' He turned to the people but they kept their eyes firmly down. 'This isn't fair —'

'I will decide what is and what isn't fair. Now sit down.'

'But —'

Malcolm gently put his hands on Will's shoulders and pressed him back into his seat. There was nothing they could do. As always, they were in the hands of their betters.

'As I was saying, I have heard all the evidence —'

'I must speak!' A voice came from the back of the hall.

A murmur went through the crowd and everyone turned. Annie turned with them but couldn't see who had spoken.

'Silence! The hearing is over. Now sit down or I shall clear the room.'

Carac approached the table. Leaning forward, he spoke in Sir John's ear who in turn spoke to the judge. The two silently regarded each other for a moment, then the judge nodded and Carac returned to his seat. What was that all about?

The judge adjusted the high collar at his neck and cleared his throat. 'It is true, that even after I have heard the final evidence from the prisoner, that until my

151

verdict is declared, you do still have the right to speak.'
He glared at Carac who inclined his head.

Pray God for Carac. She shifted the weight of her
basket on to her hip.

'Say what you must.'

There was a shuffle at the back of the hall as a man
got to his feet and glanced nervously around. 'Sire, I am
John Forge, the blacksmith. I did give my evidence
earlier but that was before the prisoner came in. Will's
right, Peter can't speak for himself. He deserves a fair
hearing.' He cast his gaze around the crowd, but no one
moved. Annie caught his eye. Go on, she mouthed.

'Sire, I've known Peter since the day he was born.
He's my apprentice and I can tell you that he is an
honest and hardworking young man. He would never
rob anyone—'

'He made Roger's knife using your tools and
materials. That doesn't sound very honest to me,' the
sheriff cut in and a titter rippled through the crowd.

'Sire, he's young. He just wanted a few extra coins in
his purse. I swear my soul to God that he's no robber
and no murderer. He's a good, God-fearing lad. We
don't have any real evidence against him. We don't
know whose knife killed Aldred, and there are no
witnesses to the fight. If Peter is guilty of anything, it
must be murder by stealth, self-defence. And that
means he goes free.'

'I am well aware of the law, but I shall note your
words.' The judge reached for his quill.

As John Forge spoke, a murmur of approval
gathered momentum around him. The mood in the
crowd was changing and, at last, they were supporting
their own. A lump came to Annie's throat. John Forge

had said what the crowd hadn't dared to say, but now they nodded in agreement, slapped him and Will on the back and voiced their support loud enough to reach the judge's ears. Their excitement spread. Annie beamed and jumped up and down trying to catch Peter's eye, but he still looked dazed.

'Thank you, John Forge. Of course, the opinion of the people is important, and I shall take that into account when considering my judgement. I need time to reflect. Tomorrow is the start of the harvest fayre. I shall adjourn my verdict until the day after that.'

Annie breathed again. Peter still had a chance.

CHAPTER 23

Carac kept as much as possible to the sides of the narrow street as he edged his way through the throng of people. In one careful stride, he stepped over the midden, a narrow channel running down the centre. His eyes watered from the stench of human faeces, rotting foodstuffs and any waste folks cared to throw in. He reached for his kerchief and pressed it close to his long nose.

It was the first day of the Okewolde Harvest Fayre, and the town heaved with people from far and wide. Buyers pushed their way to the stalls, anxious to get the best bargains; women stood amongst the clutter, their woven baskets at their feet, full of eggs, fruit and vegetables. Chickens squawked in their wicker cages, flapping their wings and shedding feathers in a chaos of white and brown on the ground. Mongers set out their goods where they stood, and hawkers shouted their wares over the din.

As Carac passed a bakery, the angry baker, well known for adding dust to his dough, argued with the weights inspector, protesting his innocence. Not wanting to linger, Carac fought his way to the end of the street, where he took a deep breath of cleaner air. It was quieter here, although there was no escaping the noise and bustle of the market completely.

'Pies! Fat meaty pies! The best in Oakwolde! Buy a pie, Sire, only—'

'No, thank you.' Carac quickly dodged the seller and kept walking. He was never sure what went into the pies, and he valued his constitution too much to take the risk. He passed the cock-fighting ring, surrounded by a thick circle of rowdy men, their ruddy faces already showing the effects of too much ale. The more they drank, the more wagers they lost, and soon they would be fighting between themselves. Carac hurried to the town square.

Lining the sides of the square, merchants from Europe stood behind stacked wooden barrels of wine, alongside traders displaying fine silks or spices from the eastern lands. The puppeteer was setting up his show next to the dancing bear, who eyed the nearby jugglers with suspicion.

Crossing the main square and leaving the dice tables behind, Carac made his way towards the livestock pens grouped around the water trough at the far end. The auctioneer was moving to the last pen with a remaining straggle of yeomen farmers, still hopeful for a deal.

Joan was standing at the back of the group, watching the last of the sales. Avoiding an old woman with her basket of flowers, Carac joined her.

'Carac, hail! Did you see? Our Barton sheep did well against the rest here. They fetched good prices.'

'Indeed, I was most gratified. I've just organised a wagon for our new rams.'

'You're travelling them? They must be special,' she said.

'I don't want them losing condition on the long walk

155

back. What do you think of them?'

'They're quite strange. Much smaller than ours but handsome with their black faces and ears.' She leaned over and pushed her fingers deep into the wool. 'The fleece is longer and straighter than our Whiteface breed.'

'Isn't it? Let's hope it will give us the cloth we want.'

'It might dye well.' Joan glanced over her shoulder. Sir John was standing a little way away, talking to someone. She lowered her voice. 'What I need is a small area of ground cleared to plant some madder plants. I can't harvest the roots until next autumn, and with the baby coming...' she patted her bump. 'I don't need many to get started. Do you think you could get a couple of the men to do that for me? I've asked John, but he's always too busy to listen.'

'It would give me great pleasure. I have high hopes that a red cloth would prove most profitable, and we may need that if you are determined to birth your child in the new bedchamber.'

'I'm not determined exactly, although I did say it would be nice. I had no idea costs were an issue. John never said anything. I don't want to cause any problems if we can't afford it.' She bit her lip.

Carac smiled. It seemed that Joan wasn't the extravagant spender he'd feared. 'Don't worry. I just thought you should know.'

'I'm glad you told me. I saw Will earlier. He was outside the inn looking a little worse for wear, and there were a couple of rough lads loitering nearby. I think they're purse thieves. Can you tell the men to take Will back on the wagon?'

'Leave it to me.' He raised his voice. 'John, I'll just see

the wagon on its way and join you in the inn. Are we still meeting the judge and sheriff?'

'Yes, and tell the men to go slowly. I don't want any broken legs before those rams get home.' Sir John turned back, engrossed in his conversation.

'Are you joining us?' Carac asked.

Joan leaned close and lowered her voice. 'Not if I can help it. I find the sheriff quite odious. I shall amuse myself browsing the stalls.'

'It seems we are of like minds. I'll see to the wagon. Until later, then.' He bowed and watched her thread her way through the crowds.

Joan wasn't what Carac would think of as beautiful, but there was something alluring about the way small lines formed around her eyes when she smiled. He would have liked to have accompanied her and postponed the pomposity of the sheriff's company. The man may be in his third term of office, but why the nobles kept voting him in was beyond Carac's comprehension. The sheriff was a self-opinionated fool who cared nothing for justice, only for the prestige and remuneration of office. And, in Carac's opinion, there were far too many like him. Old Sir James would be looking down from heaven in despair. He'd been the High Sheriff of Devonshire for three terms, and, during those six years, he'd considered every case with fairness and due diligence. Sir James always hoped that his son would one day follow in his footsteps, but Sir John wasn't interested, at least not yet. Carac prayed he never would be. Sir John was too impetuous and far too gullible to make a good sheriff, but he was also ambitious. If the idea ever occurred to him, Carac would have to find a way to persuade him otherwise.

Carac liked his daily routine and sitting by his hearth of a winters evening. His place was on the estate, keeping his eye on things, and particularly on the coffers. He didn't want to be travelling all over the shire as Sheriff John's scradlee.

With the rams loaded on the wagon, Carac gave the men orders to find Will. The midday bell tolled over the town, but he wasn't hungry. He'd take a look at the dice tables. Not that he'd gamble; that was for fools and knaves.

Carac stood at the back of a small crowd where three tinkers were playing. The big burly one was winning. With a greedy grin on his face, he swept up the dice in his grubby fist, throwing them down in triumph, sending them clattering across the board.

A man wearing a large flat hat shouldered his way to the front, blocking Carac's view. Normally, he'd walk away, but there was something odd about the tinker he couldn't quite make out. Squeezing his way to the side, he watched the tinker move his hand across the table.

There! He watched more closely. Again and again, the hand scooped up the die and sent them rolling across the table.

Could it be—but how? Carac stared again to make sure. If he were right, that meant—with his heart quickening, he pushed his way back through the crowd, missed bumping into the pie-man by a whisker and ran to the inn.

Sir John, the judge and the sheriff were seated in the far corner, the sheriff's voice rising above the rest. In three long strides, Carac was beside Sir John and, leaning over, whispered in his ear.

Sir John turned, looking as surprised as he felt. 'Are you sure?'

'As sure as I can be. But we must make haste before they leave.'

'Is anything wrong?' The judge creased his bushy eyebrows together and peered over his goblet.

'Carac wants us to take a look at some tinkers playing dice.'

Carac glanced over his shoulder and lowered his voice. 'I'd rather not say too much here, but I think...'

'We'd better take a look.' The judge drained the last of his wine, smacked his lips appreciatively, and as the one in command, led them out of the inn.

Carac stopped a little way from the dice table and prayed he was right. He was going to look like the village fool if he wasn't. The tinker was still there, rolling the die and scooping up his winnings.

His heart pumping wildly, Carac stared hard again at the tinker to make sure. There was no mistake. He smiled to himself, he wasn't often wrong.

'Watch the tinker on the far side,' he said behind his hand to the judge. 'And regard the ring on his little finger.'

The tinker picked up the die and threw them across the table as before, a gold ring catching the light as he did so.

'Is it possible, Sir John?' said the judge.

'I don't see how. There are only two such rings in existence. One was worn by my father and passed to me.' He held up his hand to show them. 'The other was given to his brother, my uncle Boren; but his eldest son, Aldred, always wore it.'

The three men exchanged glances.

'When you identified Aldred's body, was he still wearing his ring?' said the judge.

Sir John hesitated. 'I'm not sure, but no, I don't think he was.'

Carac said nothing. Sir John had been very agitated about the murder because he hadn't known what to do and had bluffed his way through, just wanting to get the whole business put into the hands of the sheriff. He doubted whether the ring or any missing jewellery even occurred to him.

'There was nothing in the documents about a missing ring. Did you mention it to the sheriff?'

'We noted the missing ring as part of the robbery,' the sheriff said smoothly. 'I can't think how the coroner missed it in the records.'

Carac raised an eyebrow. That lying toad. He'd scribed the records himself, and there had been no mention of any missing ring.

'I think we should take a closer look at this ring.' The judge pushed the men in front of him aside. 'You, tinker, put your hands on the table.'

At the sound of authority, one or two in the crowd dropped their heads and slunk away. Two of the tinkers held out their hands. The third looked frantically round and turned to run, but the sheriff was standing behind him, his large frame blocking the way. Quickly, he grasped the tinker's wrist in a firm grip. 'Now, show us your hands, you miserable peasant,' he growled.

Carac wasn't keen on the sheriff, but sometimes his crude methods were very efficient.

Sir John snatched hold of the tinker's hand and wrenched off the ring. He held it up to the light, scrutinising it. Then taking off his own ring, he placed the two side by side on the table. 'These rings are both Chiddleigh rings. This one — ' he indicated with his finger— 'is mine, and this one—' he put the ring in the palm of his hand— 'belonged to my cousin, Aldred.'

A crowd was gathering. This was better entertainment than the dice or the wretched dwarf in a cage.

'Where did you get the ring?' The sheriff pushed his face just inches from the tinker, making him flinch. 'Well?'

The tinker screwed his eyes shut and winced but said nothing.

'Not yet, sheriff. You there, take off his belt and put it on the table.' The judge directed a man with arms as thick as oak trees.

As soon as the belt hit the table Sir John grabbed it and emptied the purse. A few coins fell out but there was nothing else.

'That's my knife. What's it doing there?' A thin voice piped up from the crowd.

Every head turned to a wiry young lad standing a little way back and who was pointing to a small black knife still attached to the tinker's belt.

The tinker made to snatch it back, but the sheriff was too quick and slammed down hard on his hand.

'It's my knife!' the tinker yelled. 'I've 'ad it fer years!'

The judge beckoned the lad forward. 'What's your name, boy?'

The lad made to step back, his eyes darting nervously.

'There's nothing to be afraid of. Come forward.'

The lad didn't move, then someone behind him shoved him in the back, sending him sprawling at the feet of the judge. The crowd laughed as he picked himself up, glancing around like a frightened hare.

'Tell the judge your name,' said Carac, helping him to his feet. He knew Roger. He was a simple but harmless lad.

161

'Roger, Sire,' he said, twisting the cap in his hands.

'Well, Roger, take the knife off the belt and take a good look at it,' said the judge.

Roger did as he was told and turned the knife over carefully, just as he had on the evening of the wedding. It was a bodkin, a small, sharply-pointed dagger.

'What makes you so sure that this is yours?'

'The oak leaves, Sire, Peter etched those, just as I asked him to, see?'

'That don't mean nothing,' the tinker sneered. 'Plenty of knives 'ave patterns.'

'This is important, Roger. Are you certain that it's yours?'

Roger ran his thumb underneath the short crossguard and smiled. 'Oh yes, Sire. It has Peter's mark. A 'P' under the bar, just here.'

'Let me see.' The judge looked closely at the knife. 'He's right. There is a 'P'. It seems as though we have found the mysterious missing knife.' He turned to the tinker. 'Where did you get this?'

'I'm not saying nothing.'

'Sheriff, I want you to question all three of them and get to the truth of the matter.'

The sheriff puffed out his chest with due ceremony. 'I arrest you on suspicion of the robbery and murder of Aldred de Chiddleigh. You men —' he pointed to three strong men from the crowd — 'take them to the Guild Hall for questioning.'

Carac watched them go. That numbskull of a sheriff had got it wrong. By chance, he had saved Peter from the hangman's noose. It was most satisfying.

CHAPTER 24

Annie stood in the half-light of the hearth, her skirts raised, her hands resting on her swollen belly.

Please, God, make it go away.

She didn't hear the latch or her Pa's steps. It was the rasps of his heavy breathing that made her look up. She hadn't expected him back from the market so soon. He stood in the doorway, one arm supporting himself against the frame. His gaze travelled from her bump, to her eyes for a moment, and back down to the bump.

She couldn't face him. She dropped her skirts and hung her head, waiting for his rage to hit her, but it didn't come.

How long they stayed like that, she had no idea, but it seemed like a lifetime.

'Tell me it's not true. Annie, tell me...' he said.

Annie raised her head. Her Pa was still staring at her bump, his face pale and fixed, and she bit back her tears of shame, unable to speak.

Her Pa's face slowly twisted into a contorted grimace as his skin turned deathly grey and he staggered forward, clutching his chest. She couldn't move and stared in horror as his legs buckled and he made a grab for the stool. He crashed to the floor on his side, groaning and holding his chest, eyes rolling back in his tortured face. And still, she couldn't move.

'Hold my hand, girl,' he gasped, stretching his arm to her.

Annie crouched down and took his hand, pressing it to her cheek. His fingers curled around, clinging to hers.

'Tell me I'm wrong...tell me it's not true. God help us...' He fought to sit up, his voice rasping between heavy breaths.

She couldn't, she just couldn't. Not like this. Dear God, what was happening?

'I'll fetch Ellyn—' She tried to stand, but he clutched her hand with such force it hurt.

'Stay with me, girl.' His frightened eyes fixed on hers.

She wanted to run but how could she? She'd caused this, and suppose God took him while she was gone? She'd never forgive herself.

So she stayed as he tightened his grip and fought for every painful breath, his chest heaving, his face straining with the effort. Beads of sweat broke on his brow and trickled down his cheeks.

She knew she was losing him when his fingers slipped from her hand and his breathing slowed to shallow rasps. 'Don't leave me, Pa! Dear God, don't take him, please don't take him!'

His fingers tightened one last time as they bit into her hand. 'Annie, my little An...' His eyes never left her, his chest heaved violently, and with a final hideous gasp, he lay still. His fingers went limp, his eyes rolled back and his head fell to one side.

'No!' She buried her face in her Pa's chest and wailed her grief from the very depths of her being. He couldn't leave her on her own. He was all she had left.

The embers died to ash, and the taper burned out with a final splutter, but still Annie sat there, staring into her Pa's lifeless face and praying for him to come back. She'd let him down and he'd wanted her to stay, so she did, and prayed for his soul and forgiveness until she drifted into a troubled sleep.

Pa was reaching out to her, his face red and contracted as his soul was being sucked into the flames of eternal hell. She cried out to him, the heat burning her skin as she stretched to reach him, but every time she touched the ends of his fingers, he slipped a little further into the abyss until, with a final cry, he slid into the black depths forever.

She woke in a cold sweat, the sound of his screams still ringing in her ears. Slowly, she turned her head. Pa was lying on the floor beside her. His skin was pale and waxy, his mouth gaped open and his eyes stared like a fish. That wasn't her Pa. It was horrible. She looked away.

She should have told him before. It wasn't right for him to learn of it like that. Now the Lord had taken him, and it was her fault. Trembling, she leaned forward, touched his cheek and recoiled. It was clammy and cold.

But she had to do this for him. Summoning her inner strength, she prayed and leaned forward again. She squeezed her eyes tightly shut and, with shaking fingers, gently closed his eyes to rest his soul.

She felt sick, she had to get out. Ellyn, she must find Ellyn, she'd know what to do. Grabbing her shawl, she paused and looked at him.

'I'll be back soon,' she said, gently closing the door.

CHAPTER 25

Annie never remembered how she got to Ellyn's door, but when Ellyn opened it, she collapsed gratefully into her arms.

'My child, whatever's the matter? Come in, come on in.' Ellyn mothered her close and took her inside. 'Out the way, you two.' She made to kick her two young sons out of the way. 'Make some space for the poor girl. Here, lass, sit down with me and Mary.'

Mary raised her eyes to her mother, but Ellyn shrugged.

'It's alright now, lass. You have a good cry and then you can tell me all about it. Mary, pour Annie a cup of my calming clover tonic, that'll help.'

At that moment, Annie didn't know what to do, what to think or how she felt, except for one terrible truth.

'It's my fault,' she said. 'It's all my fault.'

'What is, lass? You can tell old Ellyn.' Ellyn snuggled her into her ample bosom, just as she did when she was a little girl. Annie had to tell her, but how?

'Nothing's that bad,' said Mary. 'You can tell us.'

Annie shot her a fierce look. 'You don't understand,' she said. 'You just don't understand,' she repeated in a whisper to herself.

'Now look, lass,' said Ellyn. 'We're your friends, and

we want to help, but we can't if you won't tell us what's wrong.'

None of this was real. 'It's Pa. It's my Pa—'

'Annie, what about your Pa?'

Annie sat up and studied her hands in her lap. What could she say? That she had sinned, that her Pa knew and had died because of it? She sniffed back her tears. Ellyn was waiting with that mother-knows-best look on her face. She couldn't leave her Pa on the floor, she had to tell her.

'I was at home and Pa came in, and-and he saw me. He wasn't supposed to but he did. He saw me and he knew. And then he…he groaned and…'

'What do you mean, He saw you?' asked Mary.

Her eyes dropped to her bump. 'I've done a terrible thing and was praying that He'd make it go away. Pa came home and saw me…and he knew. I should have told him but I didn't and now…'

'Annie, are you trying to say that you're with child?' Ellyn asked.

She couldn't. She couldn't lift her head and see her shame in Ellyn's eyes. Ever so slightly, she nodded. 'Pa cried out and fell to the floor. I meant to tell him, really I did, but I was so ashamed and I didn't know how. If I had, he'd be alright, wouldn't he?'

Ellyn folded her arms around her. 'It's nothing I didn't suspect,' she said.

'You knew?' said Mary.

'Not for certain, but I had me doubts. I am the healer. But 'nough said about that for now.'

Annie felt better now she'd said it. She was a child again, lying safely in Ellyn's arms, soothed by the feel of her hands stroking her hair and the gentle rocking as if she were a baby. Everything would be alright now. Ellyn would take care of her.

'How was your Pa when you left him?'

'He's gone, Ellyn. The Lord's taken him and it's my fault.'

'Are you sure?' said Mary.

'Of course I'm sure! I killed him, didn't I?'

'Now Annie, I'm going to get my herbs and things and go over to see your Pa. You boys, make yourself useful for a change and run for Father Peter. Tell him to make haste and go to Will's place. Mary, you stay here and make sure Annie finishes that tonic and then give her another one.'

'What about the verdict?' Annie said.

'Plenty of time for that. Judge's not starting 'til the third quarter.'

CHAPTER 26

When Annie awoke, her head was pounding. Sleepily opening one eye, she took in the grey embers in the hearth, two stools neatly lined up against the opposite wall and a wooden shelf crammed with jars, their reed stoppers poking out like miniature hayricks. Bunches of dried marigolds, wild thyme and other herbs she didn't know the names of hung from makeshift hooks along the walls. She knew it well; it was Ellyn's cottage. She must have fallen asleep after drinking that tonic.

The events of the previous day flooded back, crushing her to nothing. Her Pa, her poor Pa. Why did God have to take him like that? Was He punishing her for her sin and for not telling Pa? She didn't know and anyway, it didn't matter. She hadn't told him, and now he was gone.

Annie turned her head, and wished she hadn't as the pounding beat through her like John Forge's hammer. Must have been that tonic. The cottage was empty, quiet.

The verdict! Had Ellyn and Mary gone without her? No, they wouldn't do that.

Wide awake, she rushed to the door and glanced up. A milky sun hid behind wisps of high cloud. It was between midday and the third quarter. She wasn't too late.

The pounding in her poor head continued. When Pa had the ale on him, he dunked his head in a pail of water. He said it cleared his head. She could hear him saying it as if he was standing behind her. She turned but he wasn't there. What she'd give to have those last days again and tell him, then he'd still be here.

She found a pail by the door and went to the stream. 'I hope you're right, Pa,' she said and plunged her head into the pail. The ice-cold water took her breath away but she dunked her head again and again as if doing penance. When her ears were numb and her cheeks tingling, she shook her head and dried her hair with her skirts. Surprisingly, the banging in her head was now just a thump, and she did feel better.

She glanced up again. Ellyn should be back by now. Father Peter had a long walk from the church to her Pa, and Ellyn had to bind Pa in the winding sheets. If she wasn't back soon, Annie would go to the hall on her own. No matter what had happened or how she felt, Pa would want her to be there, and she wasn't going to let him down again.

Ellyn scampered up the path in a flurry of basket and shawl, her red cheeks glowing with the effort. 'I got back as fast as I could! Father Peter took ages to get there; I'd almost finished the winding cloths by the time he arrived. Your Pa's at rest now, lass. I just need a quick something and we'll go.'

Annie could imagine him lying on the floor now bound in the strips of white cloth. She crossed herself and fought back the sting in her eyes. At least now he was properly seen to, and the Priest had spoken over him.

They arrived at the hall just as the third quarter bell struck. They were the last to arrive, and the hall was so packed they had to squeeze in at the back. Annie stood squashed between Ellyn and Mary, still wearing her over-sized shawl. The man in front of her turned and scowled as her basket dug into his back.

The judge was in his usual place at the high table with Sir John on one side and the sheriff on the other. Three men stood to their right. She didn't know who they were or why they were there, but, by the state of their clothes, they were a rough-looking lot. The one on the end looked the oldest; a large bulk of a man with a tight little mouth almost lost amongst a thick wiry grey beard which came to a ragged point at his chest. He stared defiantly at the crowd through eyes that were too close together. Her Pa had always said that was a sure sign of a rogue. The one next to him was taller, thinner, and chewing his nails. She couldn't see his face as he stared at his boots. The last one in the line was no more than a skinny lad. His grubby brown tunic hung off his shoulders as though it were once on the shoulders of an older brother. There was nothing defiant about him; he was white and shaking.

Peter was back on his bench, but looking a little brighter. Annie wished that she did. The hammering in her head had eased, but her stomach still churned, and she was squeezed in so tightly that she could hardly breathe. She hadn't eaten since a piece of rye bread and a small bowl of potage yesterday, and she felt empty and sick.

The judge shuffled his papers and looked up, bringing the hall to a hush. 'Sheriff, have you a report following yesterday's questioning of the three tinkers?'

Tinkers? Annie thought. What were they doing here?

The sheriff puffed out his chest. 'I do!' With due ceremony, he passed the parchment over. The judge took his time to read it, then gazed out at the staring faces below and cleared his throat.

'Thank you, sheriff. I shall now read out your account.'

Every eye in the room was on him, and the room was so silent that Annie could hear her heart beating in her chest. She looked nervously at Ellyn, who patted her arm and gave her an encouraging smile.

'These three tinkers — the father, Sadon, the oldest son, Matt, and the youngest son, Cedric — were sitting around their campfire. They heard shouting down by the river so went to see what was happening. When they got there, the man we know to be Aldred was lying on the ground, not moving. They saw a gold ring on his finger and the bulging purse on his belt. Matt took the ring and Sadon cut the purse —'

'There was another man when we got there! We said that! He was running away through the trees!' Sadon shouted.

So Peter had been seen. Annie glanced anxiously at him, but his face was blank. She shifted her basket, tightened her shawl and craned her neck to see around a large pair of shoulders in front of her.

'That Aldred had blood all over him —' Matt added.

'Quiet! You had your chance yesterday with the sheriff.' The judge found his place again and continued to read. 'As Sadon cut the purse, Aldred stirred and, realising he was being robbed, went for his knife to defend himself —'

'That's a lie! Like we said, he'd been knifed in his side when we got there.' Sadon yelled.

He was lying. Annie was sure of it. He had to be lying, trying to shift the blame on Peter. The room was stifling, her armpits were wet and her forehead uncomfortably damp. Her heart was thumping so loudly she thought it would burst.

'Sadon pocketed the purse and they reached for their knives. There was a fight, and Aldred was killed.'

'That's not true! None of it's true!' Sadon raged like a bull. He thrust his arm angrily at the sheriff. 'You're a liar! You know what we said. Just 'cos we're travellin' tinkers, you're blamin' us.' He made to step forward, but a sheriff's man shoved him back.

Annie's stomach twisted in knots. She wanted to wipe her clammy hands on her skirts, but she was too squashed to move. A trickle of sweat ran down her back, and she could feel hot breath on her neck from the man behind her.

'So now you're saying that Aldred was already dead when you arrived?'

'He couldn't have been,' Annie whispered to Ellyn and gripped her arm. Ellyn's face was pale and tight. She gave just a hint of a nod.

'Yes, Sire, I swear. He was on his side and we didn't know at first. Then I rolled him over, and we saw the blood. He wasn't breathing, and we was scared. I sees a knife on the grass and, thinking it's mine, grabs it. Then we run like the devil's chasing us back to camp. Matt yells to pack up and he's already stamping out the fire. We're out of there, I can tell you. And that's it, Sire. That's what happened, on my soul to God.'

'But the knife you picked up wasn't yours, was it?'

'No, but we was that scared. We just wanted to get away 'fore the devil took us. Next morning, I realised

173

but as Matt said, one knife's much the same as another.'

'Only they weren't the same, were they? Because the one you picked up had Peter's mark on it.'

'He,' the tinker pointed to Peter, 'must 'ave dropped it after he killed him.'

That damned knife. Annie mouth was dry as chaff, her head felt light, and the room was starting to spin. She clung to Ellyn and prayed the trial would end, but the tinker was still talking.

'Sire, I beg you. That's how it was, honest. We took his coins and that, but he was already dead. I swears it. We didn't kill him; he did.' Sadon's blazing eyes turned on Peter, and he thrust out his arm. 'He was the one we saw running away.'

The crowd shuffled their feet, muttering among themselves as Annie fidgeted with her shawl. Peter was innocent and the tinker was lying, anyone could see that.

The judge raised his hand and the crowd come back to silence like an obedient cur. 'This is an interesting situation. If the tinker is telling the truth, then it appears Peter was lying and he must have killed Aldred, as the tinker claims. But if Peter is telling the truth, then the tinker is lying and they must have killed him. Either story could be true.'

He paused and, in the deathly silence, Annie could feel every beat of her heart. Was he going to condemn all of them? She gripped her basket so tightly the willow bite into her hands.

The judge continued. 'I have no reason to doubt the word of my honourable sheriff.' He cast his eyes around the room before resting on Peter.

No! Peter didn't do it. Annie felt the blood drain from her face.

The judge held his gaze. A candle flickered its last breath with a splut. Slowly, he turned his stare to the tinkers.

'I find the three tinkers equally guilty of the robbery and murder of Aldred de Chiddleigh. You will be taken to Gibbet Hill and be hanged, your bodies left to rot as a warning to others. Take them away.'

Then the room erupted around her. Men were throwing their caps in the air, shouting and cheering. She was being pushed and shoved from all sides. Mary was crying and jumping up and down. She shouted something in her ear, but Annie couldn't make out what it was. Ellyn was laughing and gave her a huge hug, then took her face between her two hands and squeezed it like a soft plum.

Annie's eyes watered. All she could think was that Peter was free, and her Pa wasn't there to see it.

CHAPTER 27

The birds had only just started singing, and already the queue of sorrowful looking peasants stretched from the hall door at Court Barton, across the yard and down the lane. It was the same every year. Folks wanted to pay their dues early and get on with their work. Otherwise, they'd still be toiling when the moon was up.

Inside the hall, Carac turned from the window and took his seat behind the table, his records in neat piles and his set of quills lined up in a precise row in front of him. It was the 29th of September, Michaelmas Day, and he loathed it.

Every year, he sat behind this table from sun up to sun down as men came before him, their tales of hardship etched on their faces. A few lied, and he didn't blame them. He knew these people and saw the filth and makeshift hovels they lived in. He witnessed their struggle to survive and knew that many would be starving by February. When Carac thought of his own privileged life, Michaelmas Day made him feel a little uncomfortable.

Sir John was such a stickler about his dues, it was a pity he wasn't so strict on his spending. Their plans had not come cheap, and now Sir John was spending even more on building for the house. After coins were counted, Carac intended to draw up a spending plan, then sit down with Sir John and try and make him see sense. He sighed. It wouldn't be easy.

He glanced to either side of him. 'Are we ready?'

The reeves nodded.

'Then let's open the doors and make a start,' he said and picked up his quill.

'Look at the queue.' Sir John stood by the trough in his yard, smiling broadly. 'The coffers will be full by nightfall.'

He was almost rubbing his hands together, Joan thought. He had no mind for the peasants struggling to pay. He didn't see their ragged clothes or bare feet. Sometimes, she wondered if he had any feelings at all.

It was the same after the trial. He had no thought for the tinkers. Guilty or not, they were going to a grim death. He had seemed distant and snapped when she tried to discuss it, saying that Aldred had got what he deserved and he was glad it was all over. There were times when she just didn't understand him.

'I'm not sure I should let you ride,' he said.

'But you promised. I've been looking forward to it. Carac's taken over the hall, and you said we might as well keep out of his way and go riding.'

'I know I did, but in your condition, I'm not sure you should. You've got my son to look after.'

'It is not your son! It is our child! And I've months to go yet.' Joan almost stamped her foot. He was becoming impossible. He'd told Cook not to serve her any sweet fruits because it would give the baby bad humours, although goodness knows why he thought that. It hadn't stopped her; she'd sneaked out and eaten them anyway. Then he'd insisted that she retire to her bedchamber every afternoon and had even ordered Agnes to sit with her, to make sure she obeyed.

Joan hadn't listened to that either. As soon as Sir John was out, she'd simply dismissed her maid and done what she wanted to do. And now, she wasn't allowed to go riding. She might as well just lie on her bed and wait for it to happen.

'I cannot live like a hermit,' she told him.

She waited for the hard expression that always followed when she challenged him. Only a few months ago, the cold eyes and the firm jaw would have intimidated her, but not anymore. She was no longer a child. She was a Lady of the Manor and soon to be a mother.

'I am quite capable of making my own decisions. I shall know when I need to rest and when to stop riding. I don't need all this fuss.'

'I'm just trying to look after my son's interests, and yours too, of course. I insist that this will be the last time you ride out, and that we go no faster than a walk. I shall have Mead turned away to the far fields. From now on, you ride in the wagon.'

A jolting on the hard boards of a wagon with their solid wheels jumping in and out of ruts would probably do her more harm than any horse. 'You're impossible! But no matter, I shall walk. I've heard tell that exercise is good for a woman with child. You can't stop me doing that.'

'Will! Where are you?' Sir John yelled.

'Will is no longer with us,' Joan reminded him. 'God rest his soul. Poor Annie—'

'Poor Annie? What's she got to do with it? I'm the one left to find a new head stableman.'

'John! May God forgive you! That's a terrible thing to say. I don't think you've any idea how hard it is for people like Annie. There's just her and Peter now. They work, they still have the communal strip to tend, they give extra days of work to us while tending their crops and fowl and maintaining their home.' Having said it, Joan realised that she'd been so wrapped up in her excitement of the baby, she'd pushed thoughts of Annie to the back of her mind, and now she felt awful.

'Home? Don't you mean hovel?'

'No, I mean home. It's not much, but it's all they have. I don't know how they will manage. Can't you forego their dues this year?'

'No, I can't! If I start doing that, they'll all be making excuses. Anyway, they won't have the hovel soon. I shall need it for the new head stableman.'

Joan was appalled. 'You can't throw them out! They've just lost their Pa. Where will they go? You can't, you just can't.'

'I don't see why no. It's the usual way. Will has gone, Peter is apprenticed, and kitchen maids like Annie are easy to replace. That hovel is for my head stableman. In fact, I'll go and see the reeve about it now. And don't saddle that damn palfrey of an animal yourself; wait for me!'

He was so callous, Joan thought. He didn't have a kind bone in his body and really didn't care what happened to his peasants. Poor Annie and Peter; they'd been through so much. The man was a cold-hearted monster, but this was no time to lose her temper. She needed to think clearly. Joan bit her lip then went to fetch the saddle.

Where was he? She waited in the yard, tapping her foot furiously on the cobbles.

'Prithee, my lady.' A young maid approached and bobbed a nervous curtsy.

'What is it?'

'A messenger has arrived, my lady. I was told to give you this.' The girl held out a parchment.

A letter! This was something very special. Joan recognised the wax seal immediately and carefully prised it open, taking care not to tear the precious parchment. She leaned against the wall, savouring the moment.

My dearest daughter,

Your father and I are delighted to hear that you are with child. How I wish I could be with you, but the winter tracks will be impassable. Maybe I can persuade your father to leave the farm in the summer for a few weeks and come to see you. You know what he is like and I make no promises.

I was dismayed to receive Sir John's concern regarding your friendship with the kitchen maid. What were you thinking? Was I lacking in my lessons to you? I truly believe that I instructed you well. Are you so lonely? I agree with your husband and, if he hasn't already brought you to your senses, I say this to you that this friendship must stop. Can you not see how it demeans your position as Lady of the Manor, and more importantly, embarrasses your husband? There, I have said my piece, and I hope and pray that by the time you read this, the matter will be finished.

Now I have good news for you.

Your cousin Eleanor is to be your companion. She will leave her home in Dorsetshire and journey to you just as soon as the tracks are passable. I fear she will not be with you for the birthing, but take heart, and look forward to the day she arrives.

Now, at this precious time I advise you thus;

Have daily visits from your healer and insist she rubs in a daily application of lavender...

...I pray to God for the safe delivery of a healthy boy child. Send word on this as soon as you are able.

Edith de Conteigh

Joan read the letter again. What was she supposed to do now? She knew her duties only too well, she didn't need reminding. Her mother was treating her like a child. She was fully aware of her position, and she'd told Annie they couldn't meet. But Annie was still her friend; she missed her, and Joan had said that she would help her if she could. That was important too.

But Eleanor was coming! Darling cousin, what fun they used to have. They'd ride together again, though she'd have to find Eleanor a suitable mount. They'd have picnics — Eleanor liked her food — and when it was wet they could play Nine Men's Morris. Eleanor always beat her at that. She'd ask Sir John to buy a board and pieces for her. She couldn't wait. Her life was so full of promise; the baby, the house, and now Eleanor!

But first, she had something else to do.

Sir John was coming at last. Joan put her letter safely in her purse.

'That's all seen to, but Baron's cast a shoe. The lads are taking him to the forge, but our ride is off. I'll busy myself here until after midday, then I'm riding to the woods to check on the coppicing.'

This could work very well. 'Just this once, I could ride on my own. It is my last ride for a while.' She smiled prettily.

'In your condition, it's out of the question. No; as I said, I'll have Mead turned away. Can't you walk or something?'

She hadn't expected him to agree, but it had been worth a try. She'd have to walk, but it was too far to get there and back by midday, and if she was out for too long, Sir John would ask awkward questions.

'I'll go this afternoon. I'm far too excited now!' she lied. 'I've just had word from Mama. My cousin Eleanor is coming in the spring as my companion, and then I can ride as much as I want.'

'Good, good.' He wasn't listening; he was already walking away.

Joan couldn't settle and kept going to the window but there was no sign of the lads with Baron. She needed Sir John gone. The midday bell tolled and, with little appetite, she picked at her meal. The sun was moving to the third quarter before she heard hooves on the cobbles outside and rushed to the window. At last, the lads were back with Baron, and Sir John was already in the yard, ready to leave. Wrapping her wimple over her head, Joan grabbed her mantle and the outdoor shoes she'd put ready and hurried out the door.

Deliberately slowing her pace, she made herself stroll across the yard.

'I shall be back later. Don't go too far,' Sir John said, from where he was already in the saddle.

'I won't.' Joan smiled sweetly and watched until he

was safely along the lane and out of sight, then she picked up her skirts and walked briskly out of the yard. She'd heard tell from Agnes that Annie and Peter were staying with Ellyn. She hoped Agnes was right, because she didn't have time to go to both cottages.

Her legs ached and she was exhausted by the time Ellyn's cottage came into view, low and squat on the skyline. She stood to catch her breath. She never realised how hard it was going to be; it wasn't so long ago that she'd have taken this path in her stride. Her breathing shallower, she put a hand protectively over her bump. This child had better not tarry coming into this world. She pressed on; it wasn't much farther now.

Ellyn's cottage was a typical cruck house, sitting like an upturned boat made of sticks, straw and mud, with a thick reed thatch on the top like an unruly mop of hair. Fronds of bracken poked out here and there where someone had hurriedly tried to patch up the holes. There was a crude square opening cut out on one side, with a threadbare square of sacking hanging over it and a wooden door at the end. Joan remembered seeing such places from the wagon on her way to her wedding. How long ago that seemed.

She knocked on the door. There was no sound from within. She knocked again. There had to be someone in.

The door opened a crack and Annie peered round. Her eyes rounded in surprise then, slowly, she opened the door.

Joan was shocked. Annie's face was haggard, like a crinkled old maid. Her eyes were red, and her shoulders drooped.

'I heard about Will and came to pay my respects. I'm sorry, but it's been a long walk. Can I come in and sit down?'

'My lady.' Annie stepped to one side, lowered her head and dipped a curtsey.

Joan wasn't very tall but even she had to bend a little to get through the door. She'd never been inside a cruck house before. It was very dark.

Annie lit a taper candle and brought a stout stool towards the hearth. Joan dutifully sat and glanced around. The place wasn't very big. Ten or twelve good paces in length and about six wide. The curved walls met together at the top and were tied with nettle twine to a long pole running along the length. There was a roundish hole cut through the thatch in the middle of the roof and above the hearth to let out the smoke. She wondered if the roof ever caught fire.

Bunches of dried herbs hung from every conceivable space and a shelf was crammed with pots and jars. Draughts of air wisped around her legs from gaps in the walls but the air still smelt stale. Joan wrinkled her nose. It was a mixture of dung, smoke, potage, and herbs.

A couple of hens scratched in the dirt floor. Annie shooed them outside but their wet droppings littered the floor.

Joan knew peasant homes were poor, but she'd never thought they'd be quite this bad. How could anyone live like this? She thought of her own home and her new bedchamber being built. She ran a hand down the fabric of her new surcoat and suddenly felt out of place in her fine clothes and new leather shoes. Consciously, she tucked her feet under the stool and drew her mantle round her.

'Peter's asleep and the others are out. Would you like something to drink? I've got some of Ellyn's elderberry water. It's very good.' Annie held her hands behind her back like a maid and was avoiding her eyes.

Joan hadn't noticed Peter, but now she looked and saw someone lying on a very thin straw mattress at the end of the room. There was only one other mattress, which was next to him, and was even thinner.

'No, thank you. Can we go outside? I wouldn't want to wake him.' In truth, the rank air was making her feel queasy.

They went outside and stood by the vegetable plot, a little way from the door. The last of the beans hung limp on their stalks, their leaves turning yellow. A chicken scratched in the soil amongst the carrots. No doubt she'd found a way in through the wattle fence which was leaning and in need of repair.

'It's good about Peter, isn't it? You must be so pleased, and I'm sorry about your Pa. He was a good man.'

Annie's chin wobbled and her face crumpled.

'Oh Annie, come here. It's so good to see you again.' Joan opened her arms and Annie wept on her shoulder. 'I'm sorry. At haymaking, when you told me, I am so sorry.'

Annie nodded. 'I've missed you, but I do understand. You're like two people: Joan my friend, and Joan the lady.'

'That's just what I was thinking. I've missed you too, but I'm here now.'

'I've tried so hard to be strong, and I thought I was winning. But then, Pa...'

'Don't cry,' Joan said. 'He wouldn't want that, would he? He'd want to see his lively cheerful girl. You know he would.'

185

Annie nodded, sniffed, and wiped her eyes with the back of the hands. 'Pa knew. Just when I thought I might cope, he saw...this.' She looked down at her obvious bump. 'That's what killed him. It's my fault, and I can't live with it, I just can't. I'm not strong enough.'

Joan took a step back and gripped Annie's shoulders. 'Yes, you are. You're the strongest person I know. So you keep your chin up and stay strong, promise me?'

Anne nodded but her chin wobbled. Joan held her again. Some friend she was; she should have been there for her all along.

Over Annie's shoulder, she saw Ellyn coming up the path towards them. 'Ellyn's coming. The fewer people who know I've come here, the better. If John found out, he'd probably banish me to the house forever.'

Ellyn had just passed the hawthorn tree and had nearly reached them.

'Can we trust her?' Joan asked.

'Of course.'

'Good. Now listen to me. I'll always be your friend, even if I can't always show it. I said I'd help if I could, and that's why I'm here. Ellyn!'

'My lady.' Ellyn dipped a courtesy, but her manner was stiff.

'I'm sorry to hear about Will. Sir John doesn't know I'm here. I trust I can count on your secrecy. He'll be home soon, so I haven't got long. I've come to warn you that Sir John is putting his new head stableman in Will's cottage and has already instructed the reeve. You must go over there and take what you can. I'm truly sorry, but there's nothing I can do to stop it.'

Ellyn crossed her arms and pursed her lips. 'Obliged, my lady, I'm sure. 'Tis the way of things, I know, but don't mean it's proper.'

They stood in awkward silence. Annie stared at the ground while Ellyn held her head proudly. Joan was trying to help, but she thought that these folks could be so stubborn at times.

'Yes, well, I wanted you to know. It's getting late and it's a long walk back. I must go if I'm to be home before Sir John.' She pulled her mantle around her. 'Take care, Annie, and don't forget, stay strong. I'll help when I can.'

CHAPTER 28

My Dearest Eleanor,

I am so excited, I just had to write to you. Yesterday, I received a letter from Mama with the news that you are to be my companion! How I wish you could come now, and I long for the day when I can see you again, but I shall try and be patient. I don't know how I shall manage, for I am so thrilled I think I shall burst!

I have been desperate for a companion, for in truth there are times when I am quite lonely, and, dearest cousin, I can think of no better person than you. We shall have such fun together as we used to when we were little. We shall walk and ride and have picnics by the river. You will adore Cook's oatie cakes; they are simply the best I have ever tasted.

I know that you will love it here but don't be alarmed by the starkness of the high moors as you approach, for the country here is quite charming once you get used to it.

I am sure Aunt Philippa has told you that I am with child, and I would that you were here for the birth, but just think what pleasure we shall have watching him grow. John is convinced it will be a boy, and I pray he is right for I have no wish to disappoint him.

I can't wait to see you again and pray God keep you safe.

Your loving cousin,

Joan

CHAPTER 29

Annie tucked herself into the far end of Ellyn's cottage where the two curved sides of the walls came together in a point. It wasn't the most comfortable place, but it was as far out of the way as she could get in the crowded cruck house.

Too much had happened. The guilt over Pa's death hung over her like a cloud, along with the shame of her secret to Ellyn and Mary and the excitement of the verdict. Her head swam with it all, so she looked on from the relative peace of her corner. It seemed the only thing to do.

More than that; she was hiding. At the time, it felt good to talk, but now she wished she hadn't. Now they knew, she felt even more shame and guilt.

Ellyn carefully wrapped a thick wad of sacking around the sides of a heavy iron pot and lifted it off the embers. She poured some steaming potage into a wooden bowl and took it to Peter. 'Here we are. Have some of this,' she said, sitting down beside him clutching the bowl in her lap. She spooned some up, blew on it, and held it to his lips. 'I'll soon have you up and about again.'

'Thanks. I don't know what we'd have done if you

hadn't taken us in. What with Pa an' all.'

Ellyn waved his comment away and put a hand to his forehead. 'It's no more than any folks would do. You're a bit cold. Come on, get some more of this inside you, it'll warm you up.' She glanced across at Annie. 'Would you like some?'

The smell of it was making her heave. 'No thanks,'

'You've got to eat. I know you've just lost your Pa but you can't just sit there. You've got the baby to think of—'

'Ellyn!' Peter, she mouthed jerking her head towards him.

'Well, I'm sorry, but he has to know sometime. I'm pleased to have you both here, but God's teeth, I've enough to do! There's water needed and eggs to collect, and I promised Isobel I'd look in. How about if you sit here with Peter, so I can get on?'

Reluctant to leave her sanctuary, Annie took Ellyn's place and, holding the bowl in her lap like Ellyn, put her arm around Peter's back and offered the spoon to his lips. His colour was already returning. He seemed a little stronger, and he wasn't sleeping so much. He must have heard, but she didn't want to talk about it.

She refilled the spoon. Ellyn was right; he'd know soon enough anyway. She scooped up the last of the potage and put the empty bowl on the floor.

'You can have some more later. You're only to have a little at a time. Would you like me to rub some balm on your ankles like Ellyn does?'

Annie went to the shelf and brought back the small brown jar of Ellyn's primrose balm. Taking a small amount in her hands, she slowly massaged the creamy lotion into Peter's sore ankles, round and round, until it seeped into the skin to work its magic.

'I thought ye were, but I didn't like to say anything,' he said.

Her hand paused in mid-stroke, then she continued her large, slow, hypnotic circles. She dared not look and see the shame in his eyes, the same look she'd seen in Lady Joan's. Her hands didn't stop moving, round and round.

'Was it that night, when Aldred...'

She nodded. Round and round. She'd have to tell him, but how many more times would she have to admit it?

When she'd finished, she put the reed stopper back into the top of the jar, returned it to its place on the shelf and sat quietly back down beside him.

'You're not ashamed of me, are you?' she asked, daring to raise her eyes. There was no scorn on his face; just pity.

Peter shook his head. 'I don't hold with all that. Things 'appen sometimes and none of us knows why. I know what the priest tells us, but it's easy for him and his like. He's a free man in his fancy stone cottage, not like us, ruled by the whims of Sir John who doesn't give God's balls what happens to us. We have to live by our wits to survive, ye know that.' His mouth tightened. 'All the nobles think they're better than us, but they're not. Not in my eyes. They're arrogant, selfish and cold-hearted with no mind to anyone or anything but themselves and their dues. That Aldred was one of them, and he was an animal to take advantage of a lowly maid. So, no, lass. I'm not ashamed of ye, but many will be.'

'Thank you.' She rested her hand on his. Dear Peter. How could she have doubted him? 'Something troubles me: what was it like in Lyndeford Gaol?'

191

'Ye don't want to hear about that.'

'Yes, I do. I need to. When the gaoler dumped you in front of the judge like a sack of corn, I didn't believe it was you at first. Then you looked at me, and I felt so guilty.'

'Ye mustn't. The sheriff and Sir John sent me there, not ye.'

He could say what he liked, but if she hadn't been such a fool dancing and flirting with Aldred that night, he would never have got into the fight and lost his knife. Then he wouldn't have gone to gaol. He could have died in there, very nearly did, and none of it would have happened if it hadn't been for her.

'Please,' she begged. 'It might help.'

'I don't see how. If ye really want to know, I'll tell ye, but it will make grim listenin'.' He struggled to sit up, but his arms were still weak. Annie helped him and put her scrunched up shawl behind him as support.

'When I saw the gaol, I'd never been so scared in my life. I'd seen it before, of course, but knowin' I wasn't going to walk on by made it different. It stood square and forbiddin' on top of the hill, like it was waitin' for its next victim. The very greyness of it chilled me to the bone. I remember turnin' to take a look at the moor behind me. I thought it would be the last time I'd see it.

'The men carried me, one holdin' my shoulders, the other my feet, and they hauled me up the steep steps. We went down a narrow dark corridor. It smelt stale, and I remember thinkin' how cold it was and lookin' at the damp glistenin' on the stone walls. We stopped in front of a small door with a square iron grid. The gaoler ground his key in the lock, I got used to that sound.

'They dumped me on the floor. It was so dark I

couldn't see a thing. They untied the ropes on my legs and sat me up, then dragged me back against the wall so hard, the stones bit into my back. I saw the shackles bolted to the floor and panicked. I fought, but it was no use; they'd done it before. One held my legs down while the other fixed a shackle to each ankle. I was helpless and so scared. They did the same with my arms, fixing a thick metal band to my wrists, attached by a chain to the wall.

'One of them kicked me in the legs, and they went out and slammed the door behind them. I heard the grate of the bolt, the grind of the key in the lock, and the bang of the wooden bar being brought down from outside.

'It was so final. The dark and the walls seemed to close in on me. I've never felt so terrified and alone. I tugged at the chains, although I knew it was useless, and banged my fist hard down on to the floor. It hurt but strangely, I enjoyed the pain. I still had fight in me then.' He smiled ruefully and stared at the floor.

'There was one small arrow-slit opening in the end wall, letting in a narrow band of light, it wasn't much but enough for my eyes to accustom to the surrounding gloom. The cell was half the size of this room with a very low ceiling and an arrow slit in the wall to let the light in. I thought it was just for me, but there were two sets of shackles on the opposite wall and another set next to me. There was a wooden pail nearby. I peered in but the stink made me gag. I couldn't imagine four of us in that tiny space. There was another pail on my left. I was more careful lookin' into that one, but it was full of brackish water. I thought of the brook behind the cottage and the taste of the sweet clear water gurglin' over the stones. I longed to be there but fought back the tears. Later on, I didn't bother.

'At first, I was beside myself with anger with the sheriff and Sir John, but mostly with the coroner. Many times in those early days, I shouted at the top of my voice until I was hoarse. I trusted you! I thought you'd see. I suppose I did it to prove I was still alive and to hear a voice, even if it was my own. I can't tell you how cheated I felt. I'd never been helpless before, and believe me, it's not a good feeling.

'I'm not ashamed to admit that I used to weep. Then the violent anger would burst and I would scream and scream out again. That's how it was, over and over like a millwheel. In my blackest moments, I used to think about the prisoners who'd sat where I was and wondered what they'd done and what happened to them. There were times when I swear I could hear their plaintive voices in the stones. Mostly, I wondered if they'd died there.

'I thought I'd never get out. I strained at my hated chains, pullin' against them time after time until my wrists bled and I could pull no more.

'The only way I knew it was mornin' was when the gaoler pushed a small bowl of watered potage and a small piece of black bread by my side. That was all I got each day.'

Annie had heard tales of the gaol but hearing it from her brother made it worse. How did he survive? She stared at her lap; he very nearly hadn't. 'Didn't you get Pa's food? He made himself ill walking over there most days after work.'

'I did wonder, but no. I expect the gaoler had it. In the beginnin', the hunger wasn't so bad. I don't know when it started but the gnawing grew into a constant pain that twisted so hard it made me feel sick. I could think of nothin' but food. Ma's goose on the spit at Christmas mostly, roastin' 'til the skin turned crisp and brown, the fat running down the sides as it melted and hissed on the hot embers. It was so real, I thought I was going mad. The heart-wrenching smell of bread baking on the stones around the hearth was the other one that turned me into a snivelling numbskull. When I could bear it no longer, I lashed out and screamed until my throat hurt and my empty guts twisted even more.

'As the days past, I became weaker. I felt so low I didn't care. Sometimes, I really believed I was back in the forge. I could feel the warmth of the coals, smell the smoke and hear the sizzle of a hot shoe on a horse's hoof. Then the gloom and rank smell of the cell would close in. That was the worst. I thought I would never see the forge again and I was going to die in there. There were times when I prayed for it. I used to let the tears run down my face, and do you know what? I didn't care.'

She had done that to him, and now tears were running down her face, and she didn't care either.

CHAPTER 30

It was hard to believe, Annie thought, but it was the truth. They were burying her Pa.

Standing in the village cemetery, she clung to Ellyn's arm and stared into the newly dug hole. Soon, the men would carry her Pa from the church. The place was eerily silent. Sir John had refused a bell, just as he'd refused to grant Pa's friends time off for the funeral, so there were just the two of them. It wouldn't have taken long, Pa would have liked it, and it meant so much to them all but their lord had the Devil's heart in him. Right now, she wished the Devil would take him down to hell where he belonged.

Peter's words went round in her head. The worst of it was that not once had he blamed her. And she deserved to be blamed.

The sound of feet crunched on the gravel path. They were coming with him now. They couldn't afford a coffin, so it was just her Pa's body somewhere inside those tightly bound winding sheets. Annie knew she should cry, but she had no tears left.

The priest stepped forward and began to read. She bowed her head. Pa never had the last rites. There hadn't been time, but he'd been a good, God-fearing man. Surely, the Lord wouldn't let his soul go to Purgatory. Remembering her nightmare, Annie prayed harder.

Slowly, the men lowered her Pa into the hole. Annie took a step forward and threw in a handful of soil. She didn't know why. It was just what people did. The clump hit the white cloth and shattered into tiny pieces like breadcrumbs.

It was over.

Annie looked up to the heavens. It didn't seem much for a man's life. Here one day, then put in the ground and gone the next as though he'd never existed. Ellyn squeezed her arm and heads together, they walked away.

Annie felt drained and numb from the funeral. Now she couldn't believe what she'd seen. She was too tired to be angry and slumped in her corner. Ellyn dropped her shawl on the floor instead of neatly folding it and putting it in its rightful place on the shelf as she usually did. Mary stopped stirring the potage, the two boys stopped their game of chase around the hearth and Peter sat up.

'What it is?' he asked.

'There was nothing there.' Ellyn's blank face stared vacantly at her shawl.

'What do ye mean, nothin' there?' Peter demanded.

'We were too late. After the burial, Annie and me went to your Pa's place. But when we got there, it was like I said, there was nothing there. The cottage was empty. All gone. They took the lot, even the fowls.' Ellyn sat on a stool and shook her head.

'Who took it, Ma?' asked Mary lifting the pot on to the stones.

'Who do you think? Sir John, that's who.' Ellyn's eyes flashed white. 'Get me some of my borage water, Mary, for God's sake! I need something.' Absently, she picked up her shawl and clutched it.

Annie had never seen Ellyn like this. She was always so in control, and now she seemed as lost as she felt.

'When we got there, a wagon was stopped outside, all loaded up. The reeve came out the cottage with three men. He was very sorry an' all that, but they were only obeying Sir John's orders. They were that embarrassed, none of them could look me in the eye.' Ellyn sipped her borage drink.

'But why?' said Mary, tucking her grey skirts away from the embers.

'Sir John has taken his dues. That's why,' said Peter out of the gloom.

'You'll have nothing to go back to,' said Mary.

'We won't be going back,' Annie said quietly. 'Sir John already has someone doing Pa's work and he'll move in.'

'He can't do that!' Mary protested.

'I'm afraid he can, lass,' said Ellyn.

'And he has,' said Peter. 'By God's balls, I hate those muxy Chiddleighs. Sorry, Ellyn.' He quickly crossed himself. 'What more can they do to us? First, Aldred takes Annie, leaving her with child. Then Sir John sits back and lets me rot in gaol, not carin' if I'm guilty or not. And now, after all the years of good loyal service, he can't even wait for Pa to be buried before taking what little we had. I tell ye, Ellyn: one day I'll get even with him if it's the last thing I do.'

'Here, lad,' said Ellyn, handing him her drink. 'Don't make yourself bad. There's nothing the likes of you or me can do.'

'So you know about Annie then?' said Mary.

'Yes,' Peter wheezed.

'You said it was Aldred. I didn't know that.'

Annie sighed. Her secret was out. It was a relief in a way, but Mary's probing eyes were waiting for more. She might as well tell her; Mary wouldn't rest until she knew. 'It was the night of the wedding. Aldred dragged me into the woods and made me — I didn't want to, you have to believe me! Pa and Peter found me. It was what the fight was about.'

'And all this time, you've been keeping it to yourself? I'm your friend. Why didn't you tell me?' Mary wrapped her arms around her. 'I'd have understood.'

Dear, kind Mary. Annie felt awful about the way she'd ignored her. 'I wanted to, but I was so ashamed, and Pa said I mustn't tell anyone.'

'Listen to me, Annie,' Ellyn said. 'A baby out of wedlock, no matter how it comes about, is a most dreadful sin against God. Doesn't the priest say so? But as the healer, I've seen many a young lass's life ruined. Disowned by folks and sometimes forced out by her kin, or the whole family made to leave if the Lord of the Manor gets to hear of it, to end up goodness knows where. Now I know I shouldn't say this, and may God forgive me —' Ellyn crossed herself— 'but in cases like yours, I don't see how that's right. It wasn't your fault. Surely the good Lord above understands that?'

'Folks won't understand. We've lost our home and got nowhere to go. I got no work and a baby comin'. It's not fair.'

'If you're poor, it's never fair. It's the Lords and their like who do as they please,' Peter retorted, his eyes full of hate.

199

'Well, I'm not ashamed of you, Annie, and you can both stay here with us,' Mary announced. 'Can't they, Ma?'

Annie felt hope stir inside her. If only they could, just for while. 'But what about the baby? I'm already big and folks will know.'

'You'll have to stay out of sight 'til after it's born,' said Ellyn.

'And then what?'

'I don't know.' Ellyn ran her fingers through her tangle of wiry curls. 'I'm too tired for all this now. Things have a way of sorting themselves, and happen something will turn up, but for the life of me, I don't know what. One thing I do know: no one outside of these walls must ever know the truth. It stays between the four of us.'

'The four of us and Lady Joan,' Annie said from her corner.

Later that evening, as Mary was dishing out the bean stew, they heard voices outside. Surely Sir John hadn't come to take more of their things or worse? Had he found out about her condition and they were coming to throw her out? No. Joan would never tell, Annie was sure of that.

Ellyn wiped her hands on her apron, straightened her skirts and went purposefully to the door. 'Yes?' she said with her hands on her hips.

Behind her, Annie shrank against the wall, hiding behind her shawl. She sat still as a mouse and held her breath. Maybe the men wouldn't see her.

'Got some things from the manor.' That was Cedric, a young stable lad. 'The saints are smiling on you, that's for sure. Luke, give us a hand, me stomach's growling and I want to get home 'fore those brothers of mine eat me meal.'

Mary frowned at Annie, who shrugged. She had no idea what was going on either, but at least they weren't coming for her.

Cedric and Luke heaved in a thickly filled new straw mattress and dumped it on the floor. It was so large they had to bend it double to drag it through the tiny door. 'There's three more on the cart.' Cedric tutted and wiped his brow with the back of his hand.

Annie had never seen such a thick bed, and the linen looked new.

'Give me a hand, Mary,' said Ellyn, dragging the old ones across the dirt floor to the door. 'These'll come in handy for the fowls.'

'Are these really for us?' Mary bounced on one end and squeezed the side.

'Happen so. Come on, get them over there. I can't walk over me own floor, they're so big.' Ellyn shooed her off.

Cedric and his mate struggled in with two huge baskets. Annie's jaw dropped, and Mary's eyes were so wide she thought she would have a turn.

'That's the lot.' Cedric wiped his hands together. 'Don't know what you've done to please his Lordship, but wish I'd done it.'

Annie hugged her knees and smiled as Ellyn and Mary pounced on the baskets. It wasn't his Lordship.

'A jar of pickled cabbage.' Mary put it carefully on the floor. 'Another jar of pickled cabbage, and look, raisins!'

'Now there's something the likes of us don't see,' said Ellyn, plunging her hands into the basket. Her eyes grew larger as more jars were added to the ones already on the floor. Pickles, a jar of honeyed fruit — something only the nobles had — a round ball of goat's cheese as

201

big as a cabbage, two loaves of the finest quality white bread, beans, vegetables and a salted hock that was so heavy they had to lift it out together. When the baskets were empty, they stared in silence at the gifts spread across the dirt floor.

'But...why?' said Mary.

Ellyn raised her eyebrows at Annie, who felt a warm glow spread from the tips of her toes to the top of her head. It seemed Joan hadn't forgotten her, after all.

CHAPTER 31

Humming to herself, Joan licked the end of her silk thread and lined it up to the eye of her bone needle. She didn't mind this sewing because every stitch was a stitch closer to the day when she would hold her child in her arms.

It was the end of October and another month closer to the birth. The dark months would soon be here. Joan shivered and pulled the furs more closely around her. She was excited about the birth, even though she'd heard tales of the pain and knew that many a woman died in the process. Still, she was certain that Ellyn would see her through.

Sir John burst into the main hall, making her lose her thread. His cheeks and nose were ruddy from the cold and his eyes were shining. 'I've been on the high road and met a traveller on his way to Oakwolde. He'd passed a drover three days away, heading this way with a large flock of sheep.' He flopped into his chair and tugged off his muddy boots. 'I'll have to speak to the shepherds in the morning.' He stretched his feet luxuriously towards the flames and wriggled his toes. 'I must have a word with Carac. We'll put the new sheep in the meadows on the other side of the village. Then, once they're settled, we can introduce those Blackface rams. By this time next year, we'll be making quality cloth.'

Joan thought about her red dye and wondered if Carac had put any men to planting her madder roots but bit her tongue. She had the baby to think of now. In a few months, she would be a mother and Eleanor would be here. She couldn't wait!

'And how are you?' Sir John said. 'Doing as the midwife tells you, I hope.'

'I'm fine,' Joan laughed. 'I'm not ill, you know, and the baby isn't due until February. Look.' She held up her stitching proudly. 'I'm actually sitting and making clothes for our child!'

'I am impressed and—' he leaned forward and gave her a gentle kiss on her cheek— 'I approve.'

They shared an amiable silence, sitting together with their wine and watching the flames flickering up the chimney. This was how Joan had always imagined married life: the pair of them sitting together by the fire, sharing their news and plans. She loved him when he was like this; his face alive with excitement and his eyes soft and warm with his care for her. Then there was the other side that she didn't love. The side when he was cold and stone-hearted like when Will had died.

She'd tried her best to help Annie, but Sir John was deaf to her pleas and, despite Joan going to Ellyn's and warning them, he had still managed to take everything Will owned. When Joan had heard, she'd been so furious that she'd stormed into the kitchen and told the maids to make up four thick straw mattresses. She'd also told Cook to put a couple of large baskets of food together, including the large salted hock, which she knew Cook was keeping for Christmas. Overhearing

Cook and the maids twittering about it, she rounded on them furiously, saying she had released Annie from her duties to look after Peter and how dare they question her! She smiled as she remembered their frightened faces.

She was glad she'd done it. She'd outwitted Sir John, which was nice. Besides, here she was with fine clothes and plenty of food, sitting in the warmth with nothing but her stitching to worry about, whereas Annie had none of those and a lot to worry about.

Joan looked down at her pleasingly round shape. Annie would be showing a lot more as well. She was glad she'd seen her, and it would be nice to see her again, but she couldn't. The walk that day had nearly killed her.

'The builders will be here tomorrow,' Sir John said.

'Everything is happening!'

'It certainly is. They'll set up a camp on the side fields. It'll be noisy and chaotic for a time, but I'll make sure that you're not disturbed more than necessary.'

'Stop fussing. I can cope. And if it all gets too much, I shall go for a gentle walk.'

'Providing it is gentle,' Sir John insisted. 'You're looking after my son, and I know you.'

Joan held out her hand to him and he took it. 'We're so lucky, John, and I am so happy.'

'I know. And so am I.'

'…and the new bedchamber will be up there—Carac, just in time! I was explaining to Joan about the new house.'

'Good morrow,' Carac said. 'I was delayed on my way over. There's more fencing blown over and broken by the winds. I've men repairing it before any of the stock gets out, but we do need to get to work on more coppicing. We're running low on hazel poles. I see the builders have arrived.'

'Yes, first thing this morning,' Sir John replied. 'They're unloading and setting up camp in the fields. I'm just waiting for Godwyn, to talk through the work.'

'Lady Joan. I trust you are keeping well?' Carac dismounted and handed his horse to the new head stableman, Mark.

'Joan is in the best of health, aren't you?'

'Yes, I am,' Joan answered with a smile. 'Although the way John fusses over me, you wouldn't think so!'

'Godwyn, at last!' Sir John beckoned to the man. 'Come and meet Lady Joan!'

'Lady Joan.' Godwyn lowered his hood and bowed respectfully.

Joan hid a smile at his peculiar appearance. Standing no higher than Sir John's shoulder he was a little goblin of a man with his bowed legs and sticking-out ears. His balding head was shaped like a goose egg, and he had a grey beard that reached to his waist in a tangle of unkempt hair.

'Now, I have something to show you. Joan, you will love this. Come with me.' Sir John strode ahead, Godwyn hurrying to keep up.

'Honestly, John's a changed man,' Joan said, walking behind with Carac. 'Ever since I told him about the baby, he's been so attentive. And he's that excited over this rebuilding.'

'Like a little boy with a new toy,' Carac said knowingly.

'Yes, that's it exactly.'

'Come on, you two! Now, stand there and imagine

this. Along here is an outside wall.' Sir John swept his arm from left to right. 'And here—' he stopped dramatically— 'is where the door will be.'

Carac frowned. 'What door?'

'The door to our new, outside kitchen!' Sir John announced triumphantly. 'What do you think of that?'

Carac sighed and shook his head.

'An outside kitchen!' Joan echoed. 'John, we're not living in a castle.'

'Not yet, but if Oakwolde Castle can have an outside kitchen, why can't we?' Sir John grabbed her hand enthusiastically. 'Look,' he said, leading her across the grass. 'The chimney and a large hearth will be here, and over there—' he turned and pointed— 'Cook can keep her pots and stores and things.'

Joan saw Carac's eyes widen and a look of alarm set on his face. She felt a bit alarmed herself. It all sounded very grand and, no doubt, very expensive.

'Can it be done?' Carac asked.

Godwyn stroked his beard thoughtfully. 'It can, but it will take time, and it won't come cheap. Chimneys are tricky things. You're talking about a completely new building. We'll need more stone and timbers and—'

'It sounds rather expensive, John. Do we really need all this?' Joan said, but Sir John wasn't listening.

'Yes, yes, I know all that. But can you do it?'

Godwyn sucked his teeth and ruffled his beard. 'Yes, but—'

'Good! Then I'll leave it to you and Carac to sort out. Just imagine, Joan: no noise and dirt, servants sleeping in the kitchen at night and not in the hall, and during the day, you'll be able to sit privately without them coming and going. And when we're entertaining, and we shall be entertaining, the servants will come in a line, carrying platters of food from outside, just like they do in the castles!'

Put like that, Joan thought it did sound rather nice. Imagine, the whole hall to herself with no chattering maids and no kitchen smells and holding banquets. That would mean new kirtles and surcoats for her and no doubt a new cote-hardie or two for him.

She looked at Carac, who was still frowning.

'It's exciting, isn't it?' she said. 'John's so full of ideas!'

Carac raised an eyebrow and pursed his lips. 'He certainly is. But I'm not sure how he's going to pay for it.'

CHAPTER 32

Joan put her hand on her bump and waited. There was no mistaking it; it must be the baby. It was the month before Christmas, and her time would soon be here. She felt clumsy, tetchy and, if she were honest, bored. The enforced rest that Ellyn had said was so important was irritating. There was only so much sitting and sewing she could do. She loved her new bedchamber, but she could hear the comings and goings in the hall below and now felt cut-off and lonely.

Agnes had laid fresh floor rushes, and the smell of thyme, meadowsweet, and timothy drifted around the room. Ellyn would approve when she arrived. Where was she? The sun was already low in the sky.

By the time Ellyn bustled through the door, the sun was down and Agnes had lit the candles.

'I've been waiting. Why are you so late?' Joan sat up, adjusting the furs covering her bed.

Ellyn dipped a curtsey. 'I'm sorry, my lady. I was making the lavender lotion you asked for, and I had to wait for it to thicken.'

'Well, at least you've got it. Come and rub some in, as mother advised.'

'This might be a little cold, my lady.' Ellyn put a small

amount of the lilac coloured cream into the palm of her hands and began working it in over her shoulders.

She lay back against the cushions and closed her eyes. 'It's very soothing, just as mother said it would be.'

'I must thank you again for your gifts, my lady.'

'It's the least I can do. Did you get the fur covers I sent over a few days ago?'

'We did and we're that grateful, my lady, please don't think we're not, but folks are talking. They get jealous, and it makes things hard for us. Maybe we've had enough gifts…'

Joan felt a little hurt. 'If that's what you want.'

'Thank you, my lady.'

Joan could almost feel the relief through Ellyn's hands. She still didn't understand some ways of the peasants. You'd think other folks would be pleased for them. Lazily, she held out an arm. The smell of the lavender was wonderfully relaxing.

'Annie is well, my lady,' Ellyn said. 'And my sister's baby is due about a month before yours. She lives upcountry, north of here and too far for me to attend her.'

What was the woman talking about? Joan let the words float over her.

'This isn't her first. She's already had four, but two died. The last one — a little girl — is sickly and demands a lot of my sister's time. I feel so sorry for her. She and Matthew have so little; the last thing they need is another mouth to feed. I know I'm a cloth-head, but I've offered to take the baby in.' Ellyn's hands abstractly circled their way across her stomach. 'Annie's going to look after the child.' Her hands stopped, and she looked hard into Joan's eyes.

Now Joan understood. 'Put that lotion down and sit

here. I want to hear all about it.' She patted the space next to her.

Ellyn held the lotion in her hands and looked at the space on the mattress. 'I couldn't, my lady.'

'Ellyn, as your lady, I am telling you to sit down here and talk to me.' Joan giggled. 'Do you know, I said the same thing to Annie once. Now, please. I don't have anyone to talk to, and I'm longing to hear how Annie's getting on. I know! Pour us some wine.'

'Wine's not for likes of me, if you don't mind, my lady. I'll just have some of my clover tonic.' Ellyn reached for her basket and then perched nervously on the edge of the mattress, sipping her drink.

'Tell me, how is Annie?' Joan asked. 'She was so sad when I came over that day.'

'Well, she's as big as a haystack and the bump's that high, I'm thinking it's a boy.'

'Can you tell? What about me? Is my bump high? Sir John wants a boy, of course. In fact, he's already declared that it is.' Joan frowned and studied her bump. It didn't look high or low to her, it just was.

'Definitely a boy, my lady.' Ellyn was relaxing a little. Maybe it was the tonic. 'And you're right, Annie is sad. She tries to hide it, but I see it in her eyes, if you know what I mean. She's had a hard time of it, and she's blaming herself for everything. I've told her so, but she won't listen.'

'I wish I could be with her. I'd soon cheer her up. She told me about the baby at haymaking. I wasn't very kind and feel awful about that. You know, it's not always easy being the lady and having to do the right thing. I do miss her.'

'She thinks the world of you,' Ellyn said. 'But I always

211

knew no good would come of it. We all have our place, and it's no good mixing things up. Anyways, the baby seems fine and happen she'll perk up once it's born.'

'I'm sure she will. I know it's strange, but Annie and I will always be friends. I'm pleased she's with you and I know she'll be a wonderful mother...to your sister's child.'

Their eyes met in unspoken understanding.

'Yes, my lady. Happen she will.'

CHAPTER 33

The cottage was quiet. Ellyn and the boys were out, and Peter was back to work. Annie drew her knees close and hugged them. The floor could do with a sweep, and the stick box was empty, but she couldn't be bothered. Her eyes itched from lying awake night after night praying for God to get rid of the baby. But He hadn't.

The lump was growing, a constant reminder of her shame. Every day, the lump grew bigger and the guilt of her Pa's death and knowing what she'd done grew with it. It wasn't fair. She was so miserable when everyone else was so happy. Joan had her baby and the new house to look forward to, and Annie was pleased to see Peter more like his old self.

What she couldn't stand was seeing Mary's smug face and having to listen to her constant whittling on about Geoffrey this and Geoffrey that. She shouldn't be jealous, but she couldn't help it. She'd let Pa down there as well. It should be her and Geoffrey getting married, not Mary. Pa would have been so proud.

She looked down at her swollen belly. Damn Aldred! She'd never get wed, and that's what maids did. She couldn't bear the thought of a man's hands mauling and possessing her. Whilst Mary enjoyed a comfortable life in the mill with Geoffrey, she would be stuck living on Ellyn's charity looking after her two boys as well as her own. A child that would remind her of him every time that she saw it. She'd never be free.

Annie wiped the salty tears from her mouth. It didn't matter what Joan said. She'd tried to cope, but she wasn't strong enough. So many feelings pushed down on her that she was collapsing under their weight. Everything was dragging her down a black tunnel of guilt, shame and misery, and there was no way out.

Ellyn said she had 'The Devil's black mood' and being shut away alone in the cottage didn't help. Things will look better once the baby's born, Ellyn said, although Annie didn't see how. If only Joan had stood by her, she might have managed. The presents were all very well, but it was understanding and support that she needed. Annie missed her so much. Unlike Joan, she didn't want her child but, for some reason, it was God's will. Now, she thought bitterly, she was told to trust in Him and make the best of it. She wasn't sure she believed in Him anymore.

Drying her eyes, Annie got up and went to the shelves. Slowly, she reached up and lifted down a jar. This would be another dreadful sin. God would send her to purgatory. At least she might see her Pa again. Either way, she didn't know or care anymore.

Holding the jar tightly in her hands, she carefully took it to the table. Then she tipped the berries from the jar into a large jug. She put a pot of water over the hearth to heat and waited. She'd practised this in her mind for weeks. When the water was boiling, she poured it carefully over the dried berries, filling the jug nearly to the top. Taking a thick stick, she began pounding the berries to a pulp.

The creak of the door made her start. Ellyn stepped across the threshold and dropped her basket to the floor with a satisfying thud. She blew out her cheeks and unwrapped her shawl, giving it a shake before folding and putting it on the shelf.

'What a morning! Old May-from-over-the-hill was that poorly with the throat sickness. Coughin' and spluttering over everything. I gave her the last of my angelica—Annie, what are you doing?'

Annie clung to the jug, her hands gripping the comforting smooth curves. Why did Ellyn have to come back now? She couldn't even get this right. Her face crumpled, and stinging tears pressed behind her eyes. A tear escaped down her cheek, then another. She gulped; she couldn't hold them back if she wanted to. Standing in the middle of the floor, her shoulders shaking, tears rolling down her cheeks, still clutching her jug, Annie cried for her Pa and she cried for Peter but mostly, she cried for herself.

Ellyn prised her hands from the jug and put her motherly arms around her. 'Come here, child.'

Annie laid her head against her and closed her eyes. Ellyn stayed with her until she could cry no more, then she wiped Annie's face with her apron and smoothed back her hair. 'Now lass, supposin' you tell ol' Ellyn.'

Protected in Ellyn's arms, the scent of her sweet herby breath and her gentle voice made Annie feel safe like a little girl with her Ma. Ellyn was so kind and she was so ungrateful and didn't deserve her. 'I'm sorry. I shouldn't have done it, but I just wanted it to end. I thought if I took enough of the belladonna berries it would be over.'

Ellyn picked up the jug, sniffed the contents, and then dipped her finger inside and tasted the mixture. 'Lass, I knew you had the Devil's mood on you, and I blame myself for this. My Ma was one of the best healers and do you know what she told me? Look to the person before you look at what ails them. I'm sorry, lass, may God forgive me, I didn't do that. I was too busy with Peter and Lady Joan. But I'm here now. Sit on the bench, I've got just the thing for us.'

Ellyn handed her a cup and sat next to her. 'Clover tonic, I swears by it. Drink up, you'll feel better.'

'I don't want this child.' Annie slapped her belly. 'I don't want any of it and everything's my fault.' She stared into her untouched drink. 'I'm fifteen birth dates and my whole life's ruined. What have I got to look forward to? All my life folks have said I'm a cloth-head. There goes silly little Annie with her head full of clouds. Cook always told me I was too stupid to do anything but scrub pans and fill pails. Even Peter called me a cloth-head with wool between my ears. For the first time, I thought I'd worked it out. I knew what to do and how to do it. But all those people were right, because I couldn't even do that, could I?'

'Now you listen to me. What you did was a wicked thing. It was against God's will. It's not for you to choose your time to die, let alone that of your unborn child. Only He can do that. You've a lot of praying to do if you're to have His forgiveness.

'What happened to you was an evil thing, but self-pity and envy, my girl, will eat you up. I know it's hard, and right now everything looks black, but we've agreed that the child will be brought up as my sister's. No one will know. You'll have no shame. Even though this baby came about in a bad way, when you hold him for the first time and look into his eyes, deep, God-given love will flood through you. Trust me. Things'll work out and it won't be so bad. Haven't you got ol' Ellyn here to take care of you?'

'I suppose.' Annie switched her stare to the stitching on her apron.

'Look at me, I'm tellin' you. Now, what you need is something else to think about. If you're so keen on crushing berries, you can help me. I'll teach you. Now, come on lass, wipe your eyes and drink that tonic.'

Annie didn't feel like learning anything right now, let alone herbs, but she didn't have the strength to fight, and Ellyn was trying to help. So she sniffed, wiped her eyes with the hem of her apron as she was told, and smiled sheepishly.

'Feeling better? Good. Then we'll say no more about it. Just one thing: where did you get those berries?'

'From the pot on the end of the shelf. Why?'

'Oh, Annie, what am I going to do with you?' Ellyn chuckled. 'If you thought those berries were belladonna, then I've got my work cut out. Why would I have belladonna? I want to heal folks, not kill 'em! They're blackthorn berries. I use them when folks get blocked up. They make you go.'

CHAPTER 34

Bunches of holly and ivy tied with nettle twine hung from the roof, their shadows dancing across the cottage in the light of the tapers. Annie arched her back and shifted her weight from foot to foot as she turned the spit.

Where were Ellyn and the others? The smell of roasting goose covered with butter and herbs filled the little room making her stomach rumble. It was the biggest goose she'd ever seen. As a treat, Ellyn bought it from the church with the extra pennies from Lady Joan's confinement.

She wiped the sweat from her brow with her sleeve and shook out her arms. They felt as though they were about to drop off. She eyed her corner longingly, but Ellyn said the goose had to be turned or it would burn. Grabbing the handle, Annie continued at her task. At last, she heard stamping feet and voices outside. The others were back from Christmas Mass.

'Outside, you two!' Ellyn shooed her two boys back out and, taking off her shawl, scurried over to inspect the goose. The skin was turning a nice golden brown, and the fire hissed as drops of fat hit the hot embers. She nodded in approval.

'Shall I put a pot on for the beans and carrots?' Mary asked, warming her hands.

'Yes; and Peter, can you take over from Annie?'

When Ellyn pronounced the goose cooked, and their mouths were watering at the thought, Peter lined up stools to either side of the trestle. Annie laid out the spoons and poured some cider into an ale cup at each place. They took their places and watched in awe as Ellyn took the goose from its spit, put it on her largest platter and carried it to the table.

They'd had no meat for a month and Annie had forgotten how it tasted. She couldn't take her eyes off it, even when Peter said the prayers. As he pierced the crisp skin with the tip of his knife, a rich, tantalising smell wafted over the table, and clear juices dribbled down the sides of the goose and on to the trestle. She remembered his tale from the gaol and caught his eye. He winked at her, grinning from ear to ear. One by one, they cut their slice.

Annie made herself chew slowly, letting the herby flavour linger in her mouth and tingle her tongue. She hadn't tasted anything so good for months. In rapt silence, they savoured this special treat, and no one spoke until they'd picked the bird clean.

Peter patted his stomach and let out a long contented sigh. 'Well, Ellyn, I must say ye've done us proud. That goose was sent from heaven, and the beans were the best I've tasted. Who'd have thought a few months ago, we'd be sittin' here with so much to be thankful for?'

'I know,' said Mary. 'You're back to work and finish your apprenticeship next year. Ma has extra work from Lady Joan and…this morning after Mass, Geoffrey, and I agreed to marry in the spring.' Her face glowed as she clasped her hands together. 'Isn't it wonderful? I thought he'd never ask. To think; this time next year I shall be the miller's wife!'

Annie smothered a pang of jealousy. Father Peter said that you reaped what you deserved in life. Well, that was true. And Mary — good, sensible Mary — deserved to be happy. She forced a smile onto her face.

'I'm so pleased, and it's not before time. And I've some good news of me own,' said Ellyn, resting her eyes on her. 'Annie will be helping me with my work. I am going to teach her to be a healer.'

'That's a lovely idea! You'll be really good at that! You must be so excited!' Mary exclaimed, sounding more excited than Annie felt.

'Yes, I am.' How Annie wished it were true. Apart from the goose she'd just eaten, she couldn't remember the last time she felt excited about anything. She'd tried telling Ellyn she wasn't clever enough to learn, but Ellyn wasn't having it. She'd simply huffed, crossed her arms across her chest, pushing up her ample bosom, and told her she was being a cloth-head. Of course, she could learn, wasn't ol' Ellyn the best healer in the area? It seemed to Annie that she didn't have much choice about anything these days.

'Well, I've got another surprise,' said Mary, grinning and springing to her feet.

She came back to the table, carefully carrying a large cloth-covered bowl. She paused and glanced around at their expectant faces. 'Frumenty pudding!' She removed the cloth with a flourish. Annie's nose tingled with the smell of the spicy porridge.

'What a treat!' said Ellyn.

'A present from Cook and Sir John, although I don't

think Sir John knows about it!'

Joan cast an approving eye around the hall. The beams were festooned with holly and ivy to ward off evil spirits, the green foliage changing shades in the flickering light from the torches.

The two rows of trestles were straight, and the pewter jugs that were filled with bunches of herbs, elder and dried flowers were sending up wafts of musky scent. Thick beeswax candles on pewter dishes flickered in between, throwing pools of pale yellow light across the boards and casting shadows on the faces of the guests already seated. The buzz of conversation competed with the soft lilt from a trio of minstrels in a corner, playing on lute, harp and pan flute.

Joan nodded. It was her first Christmas at the manor, and Sir John had deemed it her responsibility to make the day a success. The thought had terrified her, especially when he said important guests were coming. Annie would know what to do, but Joan couldn't ask her, so she'd left most of it to Cook, and what a good job she'd made of it! She must remember to thank her.

Joan loved Christmas and had deliberately kept the high table to a select five: Father Peter, Sir John, herself, Carac and his son Simon. She was going to enjoy this day and had no intention of having her meal spoiled by having to entertain people she hardly knew or cared about. That was why she'd put Carac next to her; he was always good company.

She loosened her belt a little. She was wearing the blue kirtle that Agnes had altered, but she was growing bigger every day, and even this felt tight. She fingered the new sapphire necklace Sir John had bought and insisted she wore. Many of the guests will be seeing you for the first time, he'd said. And it's a good opportunity to make our mark.

It made her feel like an object in a travelling show and did nothing to quell her mixed feeling of nerves and excitement. She hoped the feast didn't last too long, for she was close to her due date and sitting for too long gave her backache. And, pray God, she wouldn't have to excuse herself too often; these days it seemed like she always needed a pee. She mustn't drink too much. She bit her lip. She didn't want to let Sir John down.

Cook was hovering by the door leading to the new outside kitchen and nodded to her. It was their signal to say she was ready to serve. Joan leaned forward and caught Father Peter's eye to begin the blessing. As the priest got to his feet, the minstrels stopped and the conversation died as his rich voice echoed off the walls.

As soon as he resumed his seat, Cook led a line of boys bearing large pewter and wooden platters of hot food to the top table. She proudly placed her main dish of a roasted boar's head before Sir John, quickly following it with platters of venison, beef and partridge. The boys scurried to and fro with bowls of beans and steaming hot carrots seasoned with herbs and spices. When all the dishes were tantalisingly spread before them, Father Peter made them wait again as he lifted his voice and gave thanks to the Lord, making Joan wonder how many times He needed thanking and that if they didn't start soon, Cook's efforts would be in vain and she'd never hear the last of it. Finally, Father Peter resumed his seat and they were able to start.

The food was sensational. The wine flowed, guests chatted and laughed, and seeing their delighted faces picked out in the candlelight, Joan gave herself a pat on the back. halfway through the meal, the doors burst open and four brightly dressed troubadours tumbled their way down the hall, their bells jingling from their caps, amid cheers and applause from the guests.

She stole a glance towards Sir John, who was joining in, and breathed a sigh of relief. The celebration was going well and thank God, for if it hadn't, he'd blame her and go into one of his moods.

As the entertainment continued, the boys brought the frumenty pudding to everyone's delight. The feast had been a success, and it was nearly over. Slipping off her slippers under the table, Joan leaned back and relaxed for the first time in days.

Now and then, she caught snippets of Sir John and Carac congratulating themselves on the successful start of their new ventures. It seemed the timbers for the waterwheel were almost ready, the new leat was dug, the coppicing had started well and the builders had done a good job. She hoped Carac wasn't going to say anything about the cost and spoil the day.

'Let us be thankful and look forward to a bright future,' said Carac, finishing his wine. 'Now, I must take my leave. I've got an early start tomorrow. I'm giving out the bread in Holdesworthe at midday. My boy, Simon, is coming with me.'

Sir John lowered his voice. 'I dread St Stephens Day. I hate having to thank my workers and give them wheat bread. They're my workers. They owe their living to me. Why should I thank them?'

'But John, the peasants have so little and eat only the

hard rye bread for most of the year. Your gift is something they look forward to, and it shows you care,' Joan said.

'Have you any idea how much it costs me?'

Sir John would never change. She exchanged a wry smile with Carac. He knew exactly how much it cost. He leaned his head towards her. 'I wish John was as aware of costs in other areas as he is with this. The way things are going, we may yet need your red cloth.' He turned back to Sir John. 'It's traditional, and it's only once a year. Just put on a brave face. Now I really must make haste. Simon, are you ready?' Carac bowed and thanked Joan for a delightful afternoon.

'We should take our leave too. There's something I want to show you. You'll need your over-coat and hood; we're going outside.' Sir John wiped the corners of his mouth.

'You intrigue me. You're not going to show me more ideas for building, are you?' The dust had only just settled from last time, and the yard was still cluttered with rubbish, never mind what Carac would say.

Sir John laughed. 'No, nothing like that!'

Turning up the collar of his greatcoat, he led the way across the yard, his lantern swinging and making shadows on the cobbles. When he reached the end of the stables, he stopped.

'What do you make of her?' He held the lantern high, throwing a golden triangle of light into the darkness.

Two large dark eyes caught in the light and stared at them. The filly pricked her ears and took a cautious step from the safety of her mother. She was completely black, except for one small white marking in the middle of her forehead.

'Remind you of another horse?' he asked.

'She reminds me of your horse, Baron,' Joan answered.

'Just like him, isn't she? And she is all yours. My present to you, for my son.'

He never ceased to surprise her. 'I don't know what to say. She's beautiful! Thank you. You do spoil me.' Joan reached up and kissed his cheek.

He put an arm around her waist. 'You deserve to be spoiled. What will you call her?'

'She wears the Christmas star, so that's what I shall call her: Star. And one day, we'll race you and Baron along the bottom field. And we'll beat you!'

They leaned over the door watching Star, both content and confident of what the future held in store.

CHAPTER 35

The New Year came in with a vengeance, with yellow skies and north winds blowing snow and icy temperatures before them. The high moors turned white, and the land shivered under a thick blanket of snow. Black skeletons of trees bent their backs to the winds, stretching their twiggy limbs against the blizzards roaring across the land. Peasants frantically dug their way out of their cottages, but as fast as they shovelled, the snow fell in behind them. All work on the coppicing and the new waterwheel stopped as Sir John put the men to finding and digging out sheep in a desperate effort to save as many as possible.

Joan snuggled down amongst her furs. For once, she was pleased to be inside. A large willow basket pushed its way through the door followed by Ellyn.

'The devil's in the skies today, my lady,' she said, shaking her shawl and sending flurries of snow over the rushes. Flicking more white flakes off her skirts, she took off her veil and ran a hand through her damp wiry curls.

'I'm so pleased to see you,' Joan said. 'I wasn't sure you'd make it. How is it out there?'

'The tracks are treacherous with ice, my lady, and the wind's still raging like the devil himself. The snow's stopping, but mark my words, there's more to come. I fear it will lay for many a week yet,' Ellyn said, blowing on her freezing fingers. 'And how are you, my lady? Still drinking the vinegar and sugar, I hope?'

'I am, but it tastes like the worst sour wine.'

'You'll be pleased you did, my lady; it eases the birthing. And next visit, I'll bring some rose oil to rub into your sides. Some use it for the birthing, but I say that a little rubbed in now helps things along, and I've birthed most of the folks in these parts.'

'I suppose you have, so whatever you say.' She was lucky to have someone as experienced as Ellyn taking care of her. Birthing was a dangerous time for a woman, and many died. Joan shifted her position and allowed Ellyn to fuss the cushions behind her. 'I get bored sitting here. Agnes sometimes sits with me, but she can't be here all the time. My back aches, and I find it difficult to get comfortable. I'm so enormous, I'm sure there's a foal in there and not a baby!'

'Big is a good sign, my lady. It won't be long now.' Ellyn picked through the contents of her basket until she found the pot of lavender lotion. She took off the cloth top and dipped her fingers into the creamy mixture, working a small amount between her hands before massaging Joan's arms.

Joan laid back and relaxed, enjoying the company and the feel of Ellyn's practised hands. 'You're very quiet today. Is everything alright?'

Ellyn hesitated. 'Well, my sister's baby arrived four days ago, my lady.'

'Annie's had her baby? Why didn't you say? Is it a boy or a girl?' Now alert, Joan struggled to sit up. 'Sit down and tell me all about it.'

Ellyn took her seat on the mattress. 'He's a bonny boy, my lady, with a mass of thick dark hair the likes of which I've never seen. And he's a good voice when he wants. Annie, poor lass, had a difficult time carrying him, but to make up for it, he popped out so quick I nearly missed it!'

'I hope my baby comes like that. What's she called him?'

'That's what's troubling me: he hasn't got a name. Annie's not interested and refuses to give him one. I thought she'd perk up once she had him in her arms, but she hasn't.' Ellyn slowly put the lotion to one side. 'Truth is, my lady, she's maudlin. She weeps all day, doesn't eat, and refuses to even look at the little lad. It's as much as I can do to get her to put him to her breast. 'Tisn't natural, and I'm that worried.'

'Poor Annie. Is there anything I can do?'

'Not really, my lady, you being confined and so close to your time and all. Lord knows, I've tried talking to her, but she won't listen to me.'

'What about Mary?'

'Mary's head's in the clouds. Her mind's full of Geoffrey and her wedding in the spring. Truth to tell, she looks after the lad more than Annie.' Ellyn chuckled. 'I think she's practising.'

'I didn't know about Mary and Geoffrey. Being confined in here most of the time, I don't get to hear anything these days. I often think of Annie, you know, and I do miss her. She means a lot to me. I'd love to see her and the baby, but it wouldn't do, would it? I wish I could help.'

'You helped with your gifts. But you're the Lady of the Manor, and Annie was your kitchen maid. It's the way things are. The way they should be.'

'I know but...poor Annie.'

'Don't you go worrying, you've got your own baby to think of! Anyways, happen she'll come round in God's good time.'

Maybe Annie would, but whether she did or not, she needed help now. Joan bit her lip and frowned. She'd turned her back on Annie once before and lived to regret it. She wouldn't make that mistake again.

CHAPTER 36

Annie sat alone in her corner with her baby at her breast. She looked down. His face was chubby with rosy pink cheeks. His deep brown eyes stared back from underneath a thick dark mop of hair, not blinking. Was he accusing her of not wanting him? Did he know? She stroked his face with the tip of her finger and traced around the edges of his perfectly formed ears, marvelling at the softness of his skin. She drank in his milky innocence and held him a little closer. Gently, she lowered her head and brushed a kiss on his forehead. She didn't want to love him but, despite her best efforts, he had won. Her son.

His sucking weakened as he fell into a contented sleep. She didn't want to disturb him, and so they slept as one.

A loud and desperate banging on the door jolted Annie awake. The baby woke too and started yelling. The banging came again, louder and more insistent.

'Prithee, I'm coming! Shh, little one. I'll be back soon.' Annie laid her furious son very carefully on his pile of rags and hurried to the door. 'Lady Joan!'

Joan's face was twisted and she held her arms tightly across her belly.

'Whatever are you doing here?' Annie asked. 'Come in, come in out of the cold.'

'Annie, help me.' Joan doubled over and gripped her arm. 'I know I shouldn't have come, but Ellyn said you needed a friend, and I had to. The snow is deeper than I thought, and the tracks are so slippery. I got to the top of the hill and was almost here when I lost my footing and fell. Since then, I'm having these awful pains. Do you think I've hurt the baby?'

Annie didn't know what to think. 'Sit down on the bench and I'll get you some tonic. I know it's up here somewhere.' She hunted along the shelf. 'It's lovely to see you, my lady, but you shouldn't have come. Not in this weather and so close to your time. Here it is, have some of this.'

'After what Ellyn said, I was so worried about you, and I felt so guilty.' Joan gripped her arm as she handed her a cup. 'It's coming again.' She held her breath and dug her nails hard into her own flesh.

Annie knew these pains. It was the baby coming, she was sure of it. Her own child was still screaming and, torn between the two, she pulled away and picked him up. 'Shush, shush.' She rocked him in her arms. 'I think your baby's come early. It could come quickly or it could take a long time; I don't know. Oh, why isn't Ellyn here? She'd know what to do. You'll have to stay until she gets back.'

'I can't do that! John would kill me if he knew I'd come here; I'm not even supposed to leave my room. I can't have his baby here. I must get back. You'll have to help me.'

'We'll never make it.'

Joan looked fiercely into her eyes. 'We've got to make it.'

Annie had her doubts, but when Joan was determined there was no arguing with her, and Joan was still the lady and Annie the peasant. If they were careful, they might make it to the manor. 'I'll get my things, but we must make haste.'

She laid her son on a woollen blanket and tied two corners of it around her back and neck, making a carrying sling. Once satisfied her precious baby was secure, Annie grabbed her shawl, put an arm around Joan's waist and closed the door.

She'd hardly taken a step when the brutally cold air hit her, and the freezing wind whistled around her head, making her eyes water. Glancing back to the safety of the cottage, she wasn't sure they were doing the right thing. Suppose they didn't make it, and Joan had her baby somewhere out there? In this weather, a newborn would surely die. What would Sir John say about that? She held on to Joan and, as quickly as she could, set off for the warmth and safety of Court Barton.

Every time her feet slipped, Annie cursed and hugged her son protectively to her, fearful lest she fall and crush him. As they struggled forward, the cold continued to bite, turning her hands blue until she lost all feeling in them. Joan's steps slowed and her feet began to drag. Annie wasn't strong enough to support her the whole way. This was madness! She should have refused.

The snow was falling thick and fast now, the wind blowing directly into their faces. She could hardly see two steps in front of her, and the snow lay knee-deep in places, so that Annie couldn't tell where the path ended and the moor began.

Bowing her head, she kept going, half-closing her eyes against the weather, straining to see the way. They passed a large tree that shouldn't have been there, and, with a sinking heart, she knew she'd gone wrong.

'I can't walk another step.' Joan's hold almost pulled her to her knees.

'We have to. Come on.' Lady or not, pains or not, they had to keep going. The longer the snow continued to fall, the less chance Annie had of finding her bearings.

With every breath, the cold bit the back of her throat. Her feet were as wet and frozen as the land around, and she cursed her boots with their holes in the soles. She still wasn't sure where they were, and they were making slow progress. It didn't help that Joan kept stopping. The snow was falling so thickly that Annie could hardly see a hand in front of her face, and Joan was so exhausted that she could hardly lift her feet. If only they could find somewhere to rest and wait for the snow to stop! Annie would have to find it soon, or they'd be stranded in a complete white-out, with no idea where the land ended and the sky began. And if that happened, they'd be walking in circles all night, and in this cold, they'd probably freeze to death.

Annie had never been in a white-out, but she'd heard many a gruesome tale of shepherds who had been found frozen dead behind a rock, or who — despite knowing the land — still stepped off the edge of a tor and fell to their deaths. She shuddered. They had to find shelter and soon, but all she could see was the relentless curtain of snow ahead of her. There was no sign of the path, so they must be heading across the top of the hill in the wrong direction. If she was right, there might be somewhere to rest up. She wasn't certain, but it was worth a try.

Hitching Joan's arm around her shoulder and clutching her child with the other, she bent her head into the blizzard.

'We must keep moving!' she shouted into the wind.

'I can't, I just can't.'

'You can. You've got to.' Annie winced as Joan doubled over and leaned all her weight on her. Her steps slowed, and once or twice she stumbled as her burden grew heavier and heavier, until she didn't know how long she could keep going. It had to be around here somewhere.

Dear God, help us. Her legs and aching back screamed at her to stop, but she daren't. It had to be here, it just had to.

She trudged on, one heavy step after another. It would be dark soon, and the air was already colder.

They weren't going to make it. Her grasp on Joan was slipping, she was exhausted and she had to stop. Annie wiped the flakes from her eyes. When she opened them, she thought she could see a dark shape just ahead. Dear God, let it be. Just a few more steps — she gripped Joan's waist.

She could have cried. All that remained of the shepherd's hut was half of the back wall and ruins of the front. It offered no shelter. Deflated, frightened and so tired she could barely stand, Annie wanted to lie down and give up, just like the shepherds.

Her baby shifted his position in front of her and opened his eyes. She smiled and chided herself. She was his mother. He needed her. Joan and her unborn child needed her. She couldn't give up now.

'Sorry, but we've just got to push on.'

'Can't you see how I am? I can't go on!' Joan screamed at her, clutching her shoulder viciously before sinking to the ground.

'Well, the baby's coming and you can't have him here!' Annie yelled back. She couldn't waste time arguing. The snow was still falling and the sun was almost down. It would soon be dark. 'Dear God, help us!' She looked to the heavens and, putting her arm around Joan's waist, hauled her to her feet, praying to a God she'd thought she no longer believed in.

Maybe He did help, for somehow they reached the bottom of the hill and, as soon as Annie saw the old stone cross marking the way for monks travelling across the Forest of Dartmoor, from Buckfast Abbey to Oakwolde, she knew where they were. Just knowing gave her hope.

'Not far now. When we get there, we can't be seen. Will the stable lads be there?'

'Probably, but they sleep in the stables, and all the servants sleep in the kitchen now. The place should be empty. Can we make haste?' Joan was bent over, clutching her arm and panting heavily.

'What about Sir John? Will he be there?'

'He won't be back until morning. Please, the pains are getting worse and my legs won't hold me much longer!'

Neither would Annie's, and the track to the yard seemed to go on forever, but at last Court Barton stood just a little way ahead, and she had never been so pleased to see it.

Joan was right; the yard was quiet. With renewed strength, Annie hurried across the slippery cobbles and, with huge relief, to the main doors. As Joan had said, the hall was deserted.

'Nearly there. Just the stairs to go.'

Joan groaned and clung on. Taking one step at a time, Annie hauled her to the top and into the new bedchamber, where Joan collapsed onto the mattress bed.

Never had Annie felt so spent and, as Joan lay back on her bed too tired to move, she slumped gratefully on to the floor. They had made it, and she could have slept for a week. But there was still the matter of Joan's unborn child to deal with.

Her own son was still warm and safely sleeping in his sling. What a story she'd have to tell him when he grew up! Annie looked around for somewhere to lay him. In the corner of the room stood a new cradle, ready and waiting. Gently pulling back the embroidered covers, she lay him down, tucked him in and tenderly kissed his forehead. Please God, he seemed none the worse for the experience. But she couldn't linger over him, for Joan cried out as another wave of pain began.

'God's teeth, I'm such a cloth-head. I should have brought some of Ellyn's herbal poultices with me, but we can pray to Saint Margaret to ease your pains.'

Joan's labour continued relentlessly. When she sweated with fever, Annie cooled her brow with dampened rags. When the pains came with increasing ferocity, she held her hand and winced as Joan's fingers dug hard into her skin.

'Please God, don't let her die, please let it be over quickly. Please don't let her die.' She repeated her prayer over and over as the fever continued to burn and Joan screamed with every pain.

But the baby wasn't coming. Something — or maybe it was St Margaret herself — was telling Annie that things were not right, but she didn't know what to do except comfort Joan as best as she could and pray as she had never prayed before.

As light broke through the shutters, she could see the baby's head.

Thank you, God and St Margaret. 'I think the baby's nearly here.'

'I can't do anymore. I'm too tired,' Joan whispered.

'Yes, you can. Come on.'

Joan let out a scream and fell back, too tired to even open her eyes. The baby was bloody, blue, and silent. At a glance, Annie could see that the cord was wrapped around its neck.

'Oh for the love of—St Margaret and God help me! What do I do?' Frantically, she tore at the cord, but it was tight and slippery and she couldn't get a hold.

'My baby. I want my baby,' Joan murmured, then sank into oblivion.

'Is everything alright?' A voice from the stairs.

Annie jumped and stared at the closed door. Cook! She must have heard Joan's screams. Dear Lord, she mustn't come in!

'Yes, everything's well. The baby's nearly here—' She tried to keep her voice steady.

'Annie, is that you? Do you need my help?'

Just go! The last thing she needed was Cook interfering and seeing Annie's own child. 'No, thank you, Cook. Ellyn's on her way,' she lied.

'If you're sure. Come and get me if you need me, won't you?'

Annie didn't answer and heard Cook's slow, hesitant steps descend the stairs. Let her think what she liked.

She cast an eye to Joan, who was either asleep or out cold, and then to the cradle. The covers were gently rising and falling. Thank God.

Her fingers still trembling, Annie took her knife from her belt, gripped hold of the cord and started to cut. It was tougher than she thought, and she was terrified she would cut into the neck. Blood oozed over her hands and soaked into her clothes, but she kept sawing. Finally, she cut through but still couldn't free it. Her fingers refused to work, and, with tears of frustration, she tugged and wrestled.

Please, God, please. Sweat soaked her back and hot tears blinded her. Her fingers shook so hard she couldn't get a grip. Forcing them tight, she frantically tore at it until, God be praised, the cord broke free.

Annie stared at the perfectly formed child, looking for the first rise of his chest, waiting to see the colour to flood into his cheeks and to hear the sound of his first cry.

Nothing.

Come on.

There was no rise, no flood of colour and no first cry.

Come on!

Nothing.

Sobbing desperately, Annie grabbed the child and held him close, rocking him to and fro, hoping that the warmth of her body would give him life.

Breathe!

Nothing. She rubbed his chest. Still nothing.

Dear God!

Frantic and sobbing, she rubbed his back. Nothing.

Come on.

She slapped his back a few times. Nothing.

'Breathe, please breathe. Dear Lord, help me.'

Still nothing.

Annie stared into his lifeless face and realized at last that it was too late.

She picked up the dead child and lay him close to Joan, then covered her face with her hands and sobbed.

Could she have done more? If she had known what to do, would the child have lived? She'd done her best, but the poor child never drew a breath.

Joan, with her eyes still closed, instinctively reached for her baby. Her fingers touched the skin and recoiled. Her eyes opened wide and stared at Annie.

'Why?' was all she said before falling back into oblivion.

Annie didn't know why and had no words. In a daze, she found a cover and wrapped the poor dead baby. She lifted her own child out of the cradle and gently laid the dead baby in his rightful place. Holding her son close and taking guilty comfort in his life, she sat and watched her friend, now in a deep sleep.

She didn't know how long she had been sitting there when she heard heavy steps coming up the stairs.

'What are you doing h —' Sir John started. He glanced from her to the baby in her arms. Quickly, his eyes darted to Joan in an exhausted sleep and back again.

'My son?' he said. 'My son! Give him to me!' He held out his hands.

'But, my lord —'

'Did you hear what I said, girl? I want my son. Give him to me,' he ordered.

What could she do? In total awe, Annie obeyed and watched with disbelieving eyes as Sir John held her child close and studied his face. Her son's beautiful brown eyes stared at him. Spellbound, she looked on as her lord stroked her son's hand with a finger. She saw him smile as her baby instinctively grasped it tightly.

'You're a strong one,' he said proudly. 'A true Chiddleigh. My son.'

She took a hesitant step forwards. 'My lord, please, you don't under—'

She shrank under his fierce stare. 'I don't know why you're here, but go and fetch Ellyn. Tell her to come immediately.'

Annie couldn't move. She was stunned. This was all wrong. She didn't dare argue with Sir John, but her baby—yet how could she speak the truth when no one knew that she had a baby? And if she did...

'What are you waiting for?' Sir John demanded, his voice rising. 'I said you can go!'

When her lord ordered, she obeyed. Emotionally drained, exhausted, confused and shocked, Annie bent down, picked up the dead child and covered him with her shawl. Holding the bundle close to her, she walked as if in a dream to the door. As she turned to close it behind her, Sir John was holding her son close to him.

'Richard, my son,' she heard him marvel. 'One day, you will be Lord of Chiddleigh and Ashetyne.' He gently stroked the baby's hair. 'I shall teach you to ride, we will travel our estate together, and we shall go hunting. Who knows? You might even become a high sheriff, like your grandfather, and stand close to the king. Oh yes, little Richard, you and I shall build such an estate together. You will be the noblest of all the lords in Devonshire.' He laid the child next to Joan.

Slowly, Annie walked down the stairs and outside. As she reached the path to the stables, she heard Sir John run into the yard behind her. 'I have a son!' he yelled. 'A strong healthy boy!'

People came running.

'Send word to the village for the bells to ring and let us all give thanks to God,' he declared. Then, beside himself, he ran back to the house.

Annie slumped against the wall in almost the exact place where Aldred had dragged her away and into the woods nine months before. She was numb. How had she let it happen? She lifted her eyes to the sky.

Was this God's retribution for her sins? And she had sinned; she had never wanted the child. Hadn't she tried to kill them both? Was this His punishment to her? To let her love her child for just that one short moment and then snatch him away from her?

She dried her face with her sleeve. Did he even know me? What can I give him? A life of poverty and hardship. Now he will live in comfort and be a lord one day. After all, he is a Chiddleigh.

Hoping for answers, she returned her gaze to heaven, and as she did so, she heard the church bells ringing out across the land for her son. And she wept the silent tears that only a mother can weep for a lost child.

CHAPTER 37

Joan opened her eyes just a little and let her arms flop beside her. God, she had never felt so exhausted. She wished whoever it was would stop ringing those damn bells, because the noise was thumping round in her head.

What had happened? She closed her eyes again.

Last night, she and Annie had struggled through the snow, and she'd been so tired she could barely lift her feet. The snow had swirled all around them as the wind howled its rage, and she'd leaned on Annie. And the pain! Dear God, she would never forget that pain! And Annie, dear Annie, had got her home.

Joan opened her eyes and looked around her bedchamber.

'Annie? Are you there?' Her voice was hardly a whisper.

They'd come up here and...and — Joan squeezed her eyes shut, forcing herself to remember. Annie holding her hand, her distressed face, so close to her own. Annie had been frightened. Her own dread as she'd braced herself for the surge of pain building inside her. Again and again, it seemed to go on forever. She'd done a lot of screaming, she knew that. Then relief when the pains stopped and — and what?

Silence. And Annie screaming. Joan's mind hazed over. She didn't remember much after that until she'd reached for her child, and her fingers had touched —

Her eyes flew open. Dear God, the child had been cold!

She stretched out her fingers again, but the child was warm.

Had she dreamed it? She hardly dared believe but those were definitely warm cheeks. Joan turned her head and dared to look. She couldn't see much because he was wrapped in a woollen cover, which rose with each breath.

She crossed herself. Pray God, a miracle! She didn't understand it, but it didn't matter. She had to see him and hold him. She loosened the cover, and stopped.

This wasn't her child. She knew that mop of black hair. This was Annie's child. God, this was a cruel trick to play. Why was Annie's child here, and where was her child? Dear God, what had happened and where was Annie? She flopped back, eyes watering, her mind confused and too tired to think. She wanted her child.

She could hear the tread of boots on the stairs. Please let it be Annie, she couldn't face anyone else right now.

She knew by the way the latch lifted and the door opened in one rough sweep that it was Sir John. Joan bit her lip and turned her head away. He'd been so excited, and she'd let him down. If he gave her one of his cold stares, she knew she'd fall apart.

In two strides, he was by her side.

'My clever little lady!' he said, sitting beside her and stroking her hair from her forehead. 'I have a son, a healthy boy. I sent that maid, Annie, to fetch Ellyn. She shouldn't be long. The child's perfect. Look at his tiny hands and see how strongly he grips my finger!'

What was he going on about? She turned back. It was

243

true, he was a beautiful child, but he wasn't hers.

'Hold him, hold our son,' he said, lifting the child and laying him in her arms.

Her baby — no, Annie's baby — looked directly into her eyes with such innocence that her heart broke. He had long dark eyelashes and pink cheeks. He was beautiful, and she ached for him. But he wasn't hers.

Yet Sir John believed it so. Had Annie given her this gift? She'd never wanted him and God had taken Joan's own child. Annie must have seen that this way, they would both be happy. What other explanation was there?

Oh, Annie. Joan's eyes welled. She'd never seen Sir John so happy. How could she tell him the truth? And if she did, what about Annie? She held out her finger to the baby's tiny fist, and he gripped it tightly.

But what of her own child? Joan stretched her mind but couldn't even remember what he looked like. She wasn't sure if she'd ever seen him.

Glancing down, she stroked his downy cheek. It was so soft. Every instinct screamed that this was wrong, but she could pretend, just for a little while. Maybe God meant her to have this child, or why would he have taken hers? Maybe Annie was right. It would be for the best, for all three of them. She looked at him again.

'I would like to feed him myself,' she said. 'As the Virgin Mother did, and as the priest advises us.'

The baby would never know.

CHAPTER 38

Annie didn't go to fetch Ellyn as Sir John had ordered. Instead, she found herself at the log where she and Joan had spent so many happy times. It wasn't a deliberate decision, but it seemed the right place to be.

She sat for a long time just staring into the distance, totally numbed by all that had happened. The whole thing was so unreal. Had she really given her precious boy to Sir John? Her son, the one she hadn't wanted but had loved from the depths of her soul.

She still couldn't believe it, but she was shocked and too bone-tired to think straight at the time, and so much had happened. Joan turning up at the cottage like that; their struggle through the snow to get back to Court Barton; Joan's screams, her screams, and dear God — she crossed herself — Joan's poor dead baby boy.

Annie glanced down at the sad bundle at her feet and let the tears flow. She was no priest, but she had to do something for him. She started clearing away the snow and the leaves from under a small hazel tree. Then, more urgently, she pawed the surface with her bare hands. Her tears were blinding her, but she kept digging frantically until her hands were cold and raw.

Reverently, she picked up the pitiful lifeless bundle, kissed his forehead and gently laid him in his grave. She covered him with the soil and patted it into a mound. Breaking two sticks from the little tree, she used some bramble to tie a crude cross. She placed it at the head of the grave and looked up to the sky.

'Dear God, take this innocent soul into thy care. And forgive me.' She crossed herself and hoped He was listening.

As she turned to leave, the bells were still ringing across the valley in celebration of his birth.

Annie never knew how she got back to the hut. Her clothes were covered in dirt and there were bloodstains down her front and on her sleeves. She had never felt so wretched before, not even when her Pa had died. Wearily, she lifted the latch and caught the shock on Ellyn's face. Falling into her arms, she let Ellyn's motherly hands stroke her hair.

'Shh, shh,' Ellyn whispered.

Annie wanted to stay in the safety of those arms forever, but Ellyn would want answers. That was the price for her kindness. There was always a price for everything.

Ellyn looked straight into her eyes. 'Annie, where's the baby? What have you done with him?'

'Not now, Ellyn. I can't. It's all too much. Maybe later.'

The colour drained from Ellyn's face, and her eyes widened as she crossed herself.

'Dear God,' she said. 'You've killed him!'

PART II

CHAPTER 39

Annie straightened the little wooden cross beneath the hazel tree. The top had been gnawed by something, maybe a rabbit, but it still marked the spot. How could Ellyn think she'd do such a wicked thing as murder?

I'd never hurt him, she'd assured her. He's alright. I promise you, you must believe me.

Ellyn had started praying under her breath but kept holding her. They'd stayed like that for a long time. Did Ellyn believe her? Annie didn't know, but the healer hadn't mentioned it again.

She wiped her eyes with the sleeve of her dress. The cross was still leaning to one side. She bent down and straightened it.

Ellyn had given her one of her sleeping tonics, the one made with nettles and egg white, and made her lie down. Annie had curled into a tight ball with her back to the room, staring at the wall, but hadn't slept. She'd spent the time reliving every unbelievable moment, from when she had opened the door to Lady Joan to the sound of the bells.

At some time, she must have slept, because when she opened her eyes the cottage was almost in darkness, the fire just a glow of ash and last embers, and the tallow burned to a feeble flicker.

She didn't move. Mary and Peter came home and she heard Ellyn's low whispers, saying they had to be kind and not to ask questions or say anything to anyone. She knew they wouldn't. It was the unwritten 'protection of silence' when some things are best not said, even amongst kin. Their lowly lives were held in the hands of their Lord who judged and ruled over them. To survive, they had to break the rules and their only defence was keeping their actions a secret. After all, anyone desperate enough could be bribed to speak out, and no one would blame them.

The buzzards were circling high above the tors. Annie had seen them dozens of times and still loved to watch them.

The thing that struck her most about the following days was the sudden quiet in the cottage. God knows, Richard hadn't been with her for long, but how quickly he'd become part of her. There were no more contented gurgles as he lay on his rags, no more screams in the night to be fed. She still woke to the sound of his yells in her ears, and when she did, she ached with a deep primaeval pain that twisted deep inside and tore its way out. She wished she'd loved him sooner.

Sometimes, she caught Ellyn casting glances at her as if trying to make up her mind. Other days, when she was alone, Annie wrapped her arms tightly around herself and tried to squeeze out her unbearable loss. It would have been easier if he had died and she could have shared her grief honestly, but she hated herself for such a wicked thought. She had let Sir John take her sweet baby boy from her, and now she had to live with that.

At night, she lay awake. She wanted to put it right, but she couldn't. She feared to think what Sir John would do to her and Joan if he found out the truth.

No one must know. No one.

Annie stood up from her log and stretched her legs. She'd been sitting a long time and hadn't noticed the cold. She rubbed her arms and took a last look at the little cross.

'I'll come again soon,' she said and headed for home.

CHAPTER 40

Mary was coming home from the dairy with alarming tales of the baby screaming all day and Lady Joan crying. All the maids were talking, she said.

Annie didn't know what to do. It ripped her apart to think of his wails calling to her, thinking she'd deserted him. She was his mother, and he needed her.

She tossed and turned all night, and the next morning, she set out for Court Barton. It was a bright day, and the frosty ground sparkled and crunched under her steps. Shivering, she pulled her shawl close. She didn't really mind the cold, though, because soon she would be holding her son again. She still had milk and longed to feel his satisfying tugs on her breast again. All he needed was his mother's goodness, and she would give it to him.

She stopped in her tracks. She would have to give him back. Her empty days would begin again. Better if she turned back. Going forward would only make it worse.

She didn't turn back.

She knocked on the hall door and waited. Where were the maids? She crossed her arms, stamped her feet and knocked louder.

No one came. She wanted to see her boy. The handle

refused to turn. God's bones! Annie gritted her teeth, her fingers fumbling on the ring.

The door opened, and Agnes stood on the threshold.

'Annie, what are you doing here? Mary said you were helping Ellyn now.' Agnes looked her up and down.

'I am. I've got some lotion for Lady Joan.' That was her excuse for any nosy maid, and Agnes was nosier than most. Annie rummaged in her basket and held up the jar.

Agnes held out her hand. 'I'm Lady Joan's maid. I'll give it to her.'

Annie thought quickly. 'No. Ellyn said I was to give it to her myself.'

'Can't see why, but you better come in then.'

The hall was empty and silent. Where were the screams and crying Mary talked about? Glancing up the stairs, her stomach turned. Dear God, no. He wouldn't, not to her boy as well. Annie ran up the stairs and not waiting to knock, threw open the door to the bedchamber.

Joan was on her mattress, snuggled with furs up to her chin. Her face was pale but her hair was braided in neat coils behind her ears. Their eyes met. Joan bit her lip and flicked a glance to the window.

Annie dropped her basket, for, sitting on a low seat in front of the window, was a broad horse of a woman. Her grey hair was scraped back under a crisp white veil. Deep lines etched her forehead, and her mouth was set in a tight thin line as though she had never smiled in her life. The woman sat there rigidly and said nothing but regarded her with stern grey eyes. Annie stared back as she saw her boy nestled in the woman's arms and suckling contentedly at her breast.

How dare she? Who was this woman pretending to

be her? Annie wanted to run over and snatch him away from her. Her feelings must have shown on her face, because Joan cut in hurriedly.

'This is Martha, Richard's wet nurse. I...I had difficulty feeding him. Martha, has he finished? I should like to sit with Annie privately.'

Annie glared from one to the other. Richard was her son and not theirs to be passed around like a package.

'He's finished, my lady. I'll lay him in his cradle.' Martha's voice was as chilling as the woman herself. Just before she closed the door behind her, she turned. 'I suggest you leave him now. He needs to sleep. I'll be back later to see to him.'

Before the door had barely closed, Annie rounded on Joan. 'Why? You could have sent for me. She's horrible; I don't know how you can let her near him!'

Joan fiddled with her furs. She had dark circles under her eyes, and her cheeks looked sallow. She patted the space next to her. 'Sit down, Annie. I couldn't send for you, could I? You're not supposed to have had a baby. I know Martha's horrid, but she was the only wet nurse John could find. As it is, she's come from Holdesworthe and is having to stay here.' Her voice was quiet, almost apologetic.

Annie felt awful. She loved Joan and, although it hurt, she could just about live with seeing her take her place as mother, but not that cold-looking woman.

'I don't know why, but I struggled with Richard. From the first time I put him to my breast, he screwed up his face and yelled. He rejected me, Annie. He refused to even try to suckle. Again and again I tried, but he didn't want me. Do you think he knows?' Her usually bright eyes were sad and fearful.

Annie didn't know, but some said that babies knew their mother's smell.

'John hates me. You should have seen the way he looked at me, as though I wasn't fit to be a mother. I feel like a failure.'

Poor Joan. After all, she'd lost her son too. Annie put her arms around her. 'I'm sure Sir John doesn't hate you. He's just worried, that's all. I'm so sorry, I had no idea. Mary said the baby was constantly screaming, that's why I came.'

'Poor little thing was hungry, and I couldn't help him!' Joan sobbed. 'Mary was right, and his hungry screams tore me apart. Everyone blamed me. I could see it in Agnes's eyes when she came to tend me, and again when the maid brought up my food. John never said a word, except once to ask what was wrong with me? But Annie, the look of loathing in his eyes was unbearable, as though I was doing it on purpose. He made me feel so guilty when all I wanted was some understanding.'

'It isn't your fault, and I'm sure he cares.' Secretly, Annie didn't see why Joan was bothered what Sir John felt, not when everyone else thought him a cold, hard man.

Joan sniffed. 'Next thing I know, Martha walks through the door. I didn't even know she was coming. John was right to get a wet nurse, Richard had to feed, but why didn't he tell me?'

Because he's a nasty man with no feelings for anyone but himself, was what Annie wanted to say but didn't. Joan was upset. It was the last thing she wanted to hear. Annie wasn't sure she could do anything to comfort her, except hold her and let her cry if it helped.

'When she arrived, Martha gave me a tight smile, walked straight over to the cradle, ignored Richard's screaming, picked him up, went over to that chair and put him to her breast. Do you know, he looked into her face and sucked without a murmur? I could have cried.'

So could she, when she saw her boy with Martha.

'How do you think I felt when you'd given me your child and I couldn't even feed him —'

'Given him? I didn't give him to you! How could you think such a thing? Sir John took him from me.'

Joan went even paler. 'No. No, not even John would stoop that low.'

'Joan, believe me, I did everything I could but afterwards, you know…when you fell back exhausted, I wrapped your baby in a silk cover and laid him in the cradle. He looked so peaceful.' She stared into the cradle. 'I didn't want you to wake up to an empty room, so I waited, holding Richard while you slept. But when Sir John came in and saw me, he thought Richard was his and demanded I give him his son. What could I do? I couldn't tell him that Richard was mine, could I? He's a fearsome lord, and I was still dazed and shocked about everything. So I did what he asked and gave him my son.' It pained her to say it. She still found it hard to believe.

They looked at each other in silence.

'And what happened to my boy?' Joan asked.

'I couldn't leave him for Sir John to find, so I took him with me and buried him. Properly, with prayers and a cross and that.' It didn't sound like much now. Annie sniffed and shook her head in despair.

'Dear God.' Joan's voice was very soft. 'What have we done?'

Joan was like a sister to Annie, and she wished she had the answer, but there was nothing she could say or do to help. Holding each other, they sat, crying into each other's shoulders.

'I want him back,' Annie said in a voice barely above a whisper. 'Please, Joan. I just want him back.'

Joan bit her lip. 'But how? What would we say? That we knew you were with child all the time? That we kept it a secret from everyone? What would I tell John? And what about Richard? I'm sorry Annie, we can't, it's too late.'

Joan was right, but to hear the words spoken somehow made it so final. 'I know, you're right. Even if I could have him back, I'm only a peasant and he would be one too. With you, he'll never go hungry, he'll live in this beautiful house and he'll be the Lord of the Manor one day, giving the orders instead of bowing to others.' The difference between them had never mattered as much as it did now. Annie would gladly sacrifice everything for her son but Joan was right. It was too late and she would just have to cope with her guilt and grief somehow.

'It doesn't seem fair, does it?' Joan said. 'But you must still see him. You can say you're running an errand for Ellyn. It could only be once a week; any more and it might look odd. And—' she bit her lip— 'later, when the madder roots are ready, you could help me with my new idea. I want to make a scarlet red dye. You know herbs and things, you'd be just the right person, and it would be an excuse for you to come here. You'll still see him, so it won't be so bad.'

That was easy for Joan to say. Annie was busy enough without playing with dyes, but if it meant seeing more of her boy, then she would do it. It was all the hope she had.

CHAPTER 41

Ellyn took Annie under her wing like a mother hen and taught her about herbs and healing. It was just what Annie needed: someone to fuss over her and make decisions for her so she didn't have to think, just do as she was told. And she liked Ellyn; she was so easy going. Her two boys, Mark and Luke, were a bit of a handful, but Ellyn had a way of making Annie feel like part of the family. She needed that.

Ellyn loved her herbs, and Annie was amazed by how much she knew. They went for walks, and Ellyn named different plants by the feel and shape of their leaves and by their smell. Annie learned that foxglove flowers and leaves were poisonous, although their seeds helped to heal wounds if ground into a powder and taken in tiny amounts.

'But don't you go tellin' folks it's foxglove, or they won't take it,' Ellyn said one morning when they were out.

Annie wrapped her woollen shawl tighter around her. Her fingers were blue with cold and her ears throbbed. How she wished she had fur-lined gloves and a hat like Joan. If Ellyn showed her one more herb, her mind would explode, but Ellyn was determined to take her on a walk and show her what few plants were around in the winter.

'Now you know the ivy.' Ellyn stopped by a hedge. 'See these black berries? They're poisonous and only fit for birds. And the yew, like the big tree by the church, don't you be fooled by the pretty red berries! They're poisonous too.'

Good Lord, she wasn't going to walk down to the church, was she? 'I know the yew tree,' Annie said, rubbing her arms and trying to stop her teeth from chattering.

'Are you cold? 'Tis getting late. Pick up sticks on the way back, and we'll get the embers going when we get home.'

What a lovely thought. Usually, Annie enjoyed Ellyn's walks, but tomorrow was her first visit to see her boy, and that was all she could think about. Her stomach had been twisting itself in knots for days. She even had no taste for Ellyn's best bread, which she usually couldn't get enough of.

That night, she took a spoonful of the poppy tincture that Ellyn said would send her to sleep. It didn't work, and she lay awake pretending that her boy was with her. She talked to him under her breath and saw him look at her with his huge brown eyes; she heard his gurgles and shared his smiles.

She must have slept at some point because, when she woke, the sun was squeezing narrow strips of light between the gaps in the walls. At last, she was going to see her son! Annie felt like a little girl again and dressed quickly, putting on her best kirtle and apron, the one with the herringbone stitching. It was silly — her boy was only a baby — but today was a special day, and she was going to make the most of it.

Joan had told her not to come until after the midday bell, when Martha would be gone for the afternoon.

Ellyn was out visiting so Annie had the whole morning to fill. Perhaps she shouldn't have put on her best clothes so early. She'd wear one of Ellyn's large over-tunics to keep them clean.

She fed the fowl, fetched the water and swept the floor. Anything to keep busy. It seemed as though the morning would never end, and she kept checking the sun in case she missed the bell.

As she stuck her shovel in the last row of the vegetable patch, she heard the solemn toll of the church bell ringing across the valley. She threw down her shovel, pulled Ellyn's tunic off over her head, leaving it on the ground where it fell, and rushed inside. Grabbing her basket with the tincture of poppy seeds carefully placed in the bottom, Annie took her shawl and let the door slam shut behind her.

She was walking briskly, but the path seemed to go on forever. She ripped off her veil and started to run, her basket banging against her knees. She reached the top of the hill, her heart pounding in her throat, and looked down on the manor house. Her boy was in there. Picking up her skirts, she scurried down the hillside as fast as she could and ran across the yard, ignoring the surprised look on the maids' faces.

God was with her, for she saw no sign of Sir John. She couldn't face him so soon, and if he saw her, she wouldn't have an excuse to stay after leaving the tincture for Joan. Standing before the hall doors, Annie checked her appearance and straightened her skirt. It was silly, he was a baby and wouldn't know any different, but still...

With her stomach dancing, she knocked but was too impatient to wait for a reply, so she turned the heavy iron ring and went in.

The hall was empty. She'd left her muddy shoes by the door, the slab stones cold under her feet as she hurried to the stairs leading to Joan's bedchamber. Her heart racing, she ran up the stairs, opened the door, went straight to his cradle and peered in. Her precious boy was sleeping and looked even more beautiful than she remembered. Gently, she stroked his cheek with the back of her hand, his milky cream skin so smooth to her touch. She marvelled again at his long dark eyelashes and his thick mop of black hair.

Her eyes filled, and she wiped them quickly with the back of her sleeve, and then looked at Joan and beamed proudly. 'Isn't he beautiful? Can I pick him up?'

'Of course. Martha's fed him, so hopefully he won't wake up and start screaming and yelling.'

Annie reached into the cradle and lifted him to her. Cradling his head in one hand, she snuggled him close. She had waited a whole week for this, and it was worth every agonising moment. She took in every part of him from his face to his perfectly formed fingers and tiny nails. Gently, she stroked his hair and smiled at his neat little ears. 'Thank you for keeping his swaddling off. It wouldn't be the same if he was bound and all I could see was his head.'

'I had a fight with Martha about that, I can tell you. She went into a huff saying that his arms and legs would grow crooked if he wasn't tightly bound. I suppose she's right, but I insisted she kept them off for just a short while. How are you, Annie? I've been thinking about you.'

Annie was touched by Joan's concern. 'I'm better now I'm here, but the days have dragged by. Ellyn keeps me busy. I'm learning to be a healer,' she added proudly.

'I wish I was busy instead of being stuck in here. I get so cross with John. He insists I stay inside. I can't imagine what he thinks will happen to me if I go out. But you know me; I sneak out when he's away.' Joan giggled. 'And anyway, on Sunday, I'm going for my churching when the priest will welcome me back after the birth of my son and allow me to take the sacraments again. John can't stop that.'

Annie ought to go to church again. She'd missed so many Masses, and her confessions would take forever. Only small things, though; she'd never speak of this latest sin, not even to Father Peter. She hoped God would forgive her. 'What about Richard? You won't leave him on his own, will you?'

'Of course not! He's got Martha.'

'No need to look so indignant. I know you. You can be so determined sometimes that nothing will stop you. I couldn't leave him.' Annie smiled fondly at him. 'I wouldn't want to miss a moment—Oh, quick, he's smiling! Can you see?'

'He's probably got wind,' Joan said with a touch of boredom.

'How can you say such a thing? If I was you, I'd have him with me all the time and…' Annie's voice trailed off.

It wasn't fair that Joan was the one who was with Richard every day and not her. She saw the pity in Joan's eyes as she sat close and put her arm around her shoulder. 'I know you would, but you're here now so don't dwell on it and enjoy him. He looks very content with you.'

He was content and so was she, but she'd have to hand him back. Annie pushed the thought away. She already felt so guilty, and when he stared into her eyes, she thought she would break. No matter how many times she visited, that feeling would always be there. But that was her penance from God.

CHAPTER 42

Joan paced the hall floor with quick, agitated steps. This was the last thing she needed. 'Why now? It's spring, and everyone is so busy ploughing and planting.'

Sir John sat in his chair, his legs crossed with an air of quiet assurance that came with his title. 'To celebrate the birth of my son, that's why. It's the perfect reason to hold a banquet. The tracks are clear, and the house has been finished. Finished at great expense, as Carac keeps reminding me, but it now befits my status. It's time to make myself known to the right people, such as Lord Tamworth and his lady. She's well known in high circles, so she's one for you to make an impression with. I'm also inviting Lord de Mareux and Lord Carneworthe, amongst others, and Roger Coute. Regrettably, he's not titled, but he is necessary. His manor adjoins mine, and I've an eye on his fields by the river. It wouldn't do to slight him. And, of course, the Earl of Devonshire and the countess. Out of all of them, she's the one you must make your friend. If I leave it much later, we'll be celebrating Richard's first birthday.'

The thought of having to entertain such women with their idle gossip did nothing for Joan's temper.

'Richard's only two months old. There's plenty of time. It's the end of the season, stocks of food are low and nothing's growing yet. What's Cook supposed to produce for this fancy banquet of yours?'

He put down his goblet with just enough noise to show his annoyance. 'I don't know! She's a cook, isn't she? Well, tell her to cook! But it's got to be good. I leave that to you, but we have to impress. And you'll need a new kirtle and jewellery.'

'I can't have a new kirtle made in two weeks! Why can't you wait until the beginning of June, before the haymaking? That'll give me and the servants more time to prepare, and we might just have something fresh from the kitchen gardens by then.'

'I can't wait that long. I want to show off my son, and I've already sent the messengers. So, no; the banquet will be in a couple of weeks.'

Joan crossed her arms and paced furiously up and down, her slippers slapping the flagstones. He didn't care what she thought. The way he ordered her, she might as well be one of the maids. And what had happened to the soft voice and tenderness he'd shown her when she was with child? That had slipped over the weeks. Never once had he called her Joannie or asked after her; all he thought of now was his son and his status. It was as though she had fulfilled her task and didn't matter anymore. And if the banquet was a failure, it would be her and Cook's fault and nothing to do with him.

God's teeth, he really was the most infuriating and selfish man!

'Good, you're home,' Carac said as he opened the door and saw the pair of them. 'God's speed —' he glanced from Joan's agitated face to Sir John's determined one. 'I don't wish to intrude.'

'God's speed,' Joan answered, 'and you're not intruding. It's good to see you. John wants to hold a banquet two weeks from now. I've been trying to explain how impossible it is, but he refuses to listen. Maybe you can dissuade him.'

Carac raised his eyebrows. 'Two weeks does seem a little hasty. It doesn't allow much time to prepare.'

'You see?' Joan said. 'Carac agrees with me.'

'Why is a banquet necessary? With the building and other expenses, which I have here to discuss with you, John —' Carac patted his leather bag — 'I should have thought —'

Sir John rose, his face burning, his eyes steely grey. 'If you say one more word about the muxy expenses to me, I shall build another hall just to vex you! I am the lord here and I will have this banquet! So, my lady, you will need to tend to it, and Carac, I'll speak with you later!' He strode towards the door, forcing Carac to step aside, and then turned, his face dark as storm clouds over the moor. 'Did I mention that I want everywhere and everything thoroughly cleaned? Get the maids on it.'

The door slammed behind him, the echoes bouncing off the walls, and Carac held out his hands in a helpless gesture.

'So that's that.' Joan sighed and dropped into a seat. 'He won't change his mind. I shall have to do the best I can, but he makes me so angry. When he gets an idea into his head, nothing will move him. Sit down and have some wine. I'm sorry you've had a wasted journey.'

'Indeed. I trust I haven't made things worse, but I do need to speak to John about the figures.' Carac sat down opposite Joan and carefully placed his leather bag on the floor beside him.

Why couldn't Sir John be as calm and reasonable as Carac? It would make her life a lot easier. 'Are things that bad?' Joan asked.

'No need to sell your jewellery yet.' Carac smiled dryly. 'But John does need to curb his spending this year. He can't afford to hold banquets.'

'That won't stop him. He even wants me to have a new kirtle and jewellery. There's nothing wrong with the ones I have. Some of them I've only worn once, and the guests haven't seen them, so they won't know the difference. I doubt if John would either.' She smiled mischievously. 'That'll save a few pennies.'

'I'm glad you understand. And the jewellery?'

'I can't stop him buying something, but I'll tell him my emeralds or whatever are just perfect. He might listen. He's invited the Earl of Devonshire, no less —'

'The earl?' Carac put his two hands together as though in prayer, lightly resting his chin on his fingertips.

'You do that when you're thinking or worried. Is there something I should know?'

'I'm not worried exactly, but the earl is a wily fellow and totally unscrupulous. John would be wise to be on his guard. Leave it with me, I'll mention it to him.'

'And the countess? I have my orders to make friends with her. Should I be on my guard too?'

'I have been introduced on one occasion, and I confess that once was enough. She does have a reputation for being the most vicious gossip and is by far the most tedious woman I have ever met.' He shook his head. 'I wish you luck.'

'Then I'll make sure you're sitting the other side of her, so you can come to my rescue.'

'God forbid! I'm quite sure you are capable of handling the countess on your own. No, I should be better placed closer to the earl.'

'Pity, but as you wish. I shall seat the earl between you and John. That way you can hear what they're saying. More wine?'

'A little, then I must be on one my way. The men are harrowing two newly ploughed fields ready for sowing, some of the harrows need new nails or the soil won't break down, and I want to see how things are progressing.'

Joan smiled. She liked talking to Carac; he had a certain reassuring way about him. 'Do you know, I sometimes think I'm not a very good lady. I'd much rather be with my horses or preparing the dying shed than entertaining boring old countesses.'

'It would be time better spent, for we may need your red dye to help balance the figures.' Carac wasn't joking; the serious tone of his voice told her that.

'I fear it will take a little time, but I am determined to try. I've found an empty shed to work in and a few tun barrels to get me started, and I've ordered some lime from the kilns at Okewolde. Lime's not expensive.' Joan smiled at him. 'I'll need some tenter poles and trestles made.'

'Some things are worth a little investment, for if you succeed, the rewards will be high. I'm impressed you know so much about the process.'

Why couldn't Sir John take her seriously like this? 'I got most of it from Annie who asked the womenfolk. She's going to help me.'

'That's a good idea. I'll ask the reeve to have a word with you about setting up. Let me know if you need anything else.'

'Thank you, your support means a lot. John's still not interested.'

Carac smiled knowingly. 'He will be as soon as he sees the money rolling in. Now, I must go. As always, it has been nice to share some wine. I'll see you at the banquet with the Earl and Countess of Devonshire.' He raised his eyebrows, and she knew exactly what he meant.

CHAPTER 43

Annie burst into the hall and, with a quick nod to Joan, rushed across to the cradle.

'It's so good to see your happy face after only having sour-face Martha to speak to,' Joan said. 'I can't tell you what it means to me, especially after the week I've had. Just after your last visit, John declared that he wants a banquet at the end of next week for the right people, as he calls them. I've two weeks to get it ready, and he expects everything to be perfect. Honestly, the maids are working every hour sweeping the floor, cleaning the pewter and waxing the trestles, and Cook is unbearable.' She straightened her furs irritably.

'I bet she is, but it's a strange time to hold a banquet, isn't it? I mean, there's little food in the stores after winter.' Annie lifted Richard from the oak cradle, closed her eyes and kissed his cheek.

'You try telling John that.' Joan sighed. 'Anyway, I'm doing what I can, and I deserve this time with you.'

Annie flung her veil to the floor and settled by the hearth with Richard. 'It's just like old times, isn't it? Us both escaping and meeting in secret. I've brought some primrose lotion; I thought I might as well bring something you can use.' She offered her little finger and cooed when Richard grasped it tightly.

'How come he's always so quiet and peaceful with you and not with me? What do you do, that I don't?'

Annie shrugged. 'I don't do anything. You're just being silly. Here, you hold him. See? Offer him your little finger, he's surprisingly strong.'

Richard took Joan's finger, then slowly his cheeks puckered and his chest swelled. She knew what was coming. He creased his face to an ugly red, opened his mouth and yelled with all his might.

'He always does that.' Joan handed him back. 'Anyway, it's your time with him, you make the most of it.'

'Hush, hush, little one, it's alright. I'm here now.' Annie gently kissed his forehead and rocked him.

Immediately, the wretched baby was quiet. Why did he only scream with her? Joan wondered. Was she really so useless? She wouldn't pick him up in front of Annie again.

'Babies are fickle, that's all. He'll soon settle to you, I'm sure,' said Annie. 'Anyway, when are you allowed out? You must be going mad in here on your own.'

'I am, believe me. I sometimes wonder if John thinks about my feelings at all.' Joan sighed. 'On the one hand, he expects me to rush around getting his damned banquet ready, and yet he still doesn't want me to go out and about. Mind you, I still sneak out when I can, and when I can't, I pace up and down calling him all sorts of names under my breath.

'Sometimes, I stare out of the window watching the dairy maids coming and going across the yard. There are days when I wish I was one of them instead of being cooped up in here. Do you know, I've counted every knot and nobble on these beams? Still, the physician's coming on Friday, and I'm hoping he'll say I can go out. Between you and me, I don't care what he says, because I shall tell John I can go out anyway. And the first thing I shall do is see the horses and then take a look at the madder plants and I can't wait.'

Annie giggled. 'Fighting talk, that's more like you — Oh look, he just smiled at me.' Her face glowed with delight.

Of course he did. He'd probably saved it deliberately for her. Joan smiled weakly with feigned joy. 'That's wonderful. I've been thinking about the dyeing. There's so much to do to get things ready for harvesting the roots at autumn time. We'll use one of the old hand carts by the stables, and I've got some large barrels put by. I've ordered some lime, although I've no idea how much we'll need, and Carac's getting the men to make some tenter poles to stretch the cloth. I suppose we'll need iron to deepen the colour, but I'm not sure about the rest of it. Do you know?'

Annie shook her head. 'Not much. I'll ask Ellyn again. It sounds like a lot of work, but I'll get here as much as I can. I will see Richard, won't I?'

'I'll bring him over to the dyeing shed especially. It'll be fun! I can't wait to get started.'

Annie stayed until they could hear Martha's steps coming across the yard. Quickly gathering her things, she laid Richard back in his cradle, tucked him in and, with a reluctant last look over her shoulder, passed Martha in the doorway.

Annie was smiling again now, and her face had that healthy pink colour. She was obviously happy with Ellyn and she was seeing Richard.

Joan felt the loneliness fold around her like a cloak.

Not caring what Martha might think, she burst into tears. Richard never smiled for her.

CHAPTER 44

'No, no, no! The benches have to line up to the trestles; I can't have my guests banging their knees against the legs! Straighten them up, you cloth-headed peasants!' Sir John turned sharply to a young maid trying to scurry past unnoticed. 'And you, girl; wax the tops! They're filthy!'

Joan sighed. Sir John had been driving her mad all week, and now the day of the banquet was here, he was causing chaos in his anxiety to have everything perfect.

'It's alright, Tilda. Go back to Cook. John, the trestle tops have been waxed three times already. If they're waxed any more, the platters will slide off.' She put her hand on the small of his back and steered him to the stairs. 'Why don't you go and get ready and leave this to me? The guests are due at the third quarter. We've only to put out the hand cloths, and we're finished.'

She'd almost got him to the foot of the stairs before he stopped. 'You have greenery for the tables?'

'There's only enough greenery for the high table, and that's from the herb garden because as I told you, it's the wrong time of year for flowers.'

His foot was on the first step. 'And the candles are beeswax —'

'Yes, from the monks at Tavistoke. The ones in the wall sconces and on the tables are beeswax, I promise. Now leave it to me and go and get changed!'

She waited until she heard the bedchamber door safely close, let out a long sigh of relief and pushed back her hair. She and the servants had worked day and night to get everything ready. The stable lads had even raked and weeded the yard and shut in the fowls as Sir John had wanted, although why he'd insisted on that, Joan couldn't imagine. Everyone was worn out, and she would be pleased when the banquet was over.

Putting her hands on her hips, she glanced around the hall. Had she forgotten anything? If she had, she'd never hear the last of it.

The silver goblets on the high table gleamed and, although not extravagant, the three small arrangements of herbs added a pleasing touch. A water bowl filled with sage water for hand-washing was at each place. Joan continued to inspect the tables, ticking items off with her fingers. A pewter platter, spoon and a goblet for each guest; candlesticks with a yellow beeswax candle neatly lined down the centre of the trestles; iron sconces on the walls free from cobwebs and holding new torches ready to light. She watched a maid place the last hand cloth and nodded in satisfaction. It looked good. Now she should call Agnes and get scented and dressed before the first guests arrived.

Agnes fastened the green emerald necklace around Joan's neck. It had a thick gold chain and weighed heavy against her skin. The five large drop stones, which were supposed to sit enchantingly beneath her throat, bunched together like a pile of rocks. It didn't feel right, but it was what Sir John wanted her to wear.

Agnes had also altered the neckline of an old kirtle, but Joan hadn't had time to try it on. Too late, she now realised that it exposed more of her bosom than she felt comfortable with. Agnes had done a good job with narrowing the wide sleeves, and with the side seams and added little bit of embroidery here and there, it looked like new. Joan smoothed the fine silk close to her shape. It was nice to have her figure back and wear something special again.

'The new gown suits you, Joan,' Sir John said, 'and the emeralds go well with it.'

Joan smiled to herself. Sir John didn't know one kirtle from another.

'What do you think?' he asked, straightening his attire and standing before her.

Joan thought that he'd overdone the sage lotion, but he looked handsome laced in his royal blue cote-hardie tied in at the waist and hanging full to his knees. Red and green jewels glistened on his belt, and she noticed a new gold brooch on his shoulder. She glanced down and choked back an urge to giggle. 'What have you got on your feet?'

'What do you mean? According to my bootmaker, these are the latest fashion in London.' Sir John held out a foot, turning it approvingly from side to side. The blue cloth shoes were nearly a foot long and came to a sharp point at the toes, which curled up at the end like a snail's shell.

'You'll fall flat on your face in those.'

'No, I won't. Look.' He stepped slowly across the bedchamber, putting his heel down first, the ends of the shoes slapping onto the floor with each step.

Joan stifled a laugh behind her hand. 'Don't try

dancing in them, for God's sake.'

'You can laugh, but I need to be with the fashion. Such things matter to the high nobles, and you won't be laughing when I'm friends with them and they invite us to their castles.'

No, she wouldn't.

Frederick de Gravesmire, the Earl of Devonshire, sat at the high table to Sir John's left. Curious to see the wealthiest man in the shire, Joan leaned forward. The slight lift of his chin emphasised his arrogance, and one corner of his mouth was raised just enough to show his superiority as he appraised those around him with narrow green eyes. Every item of his clothing was immaculate, from the fur-lined red over-tunic to the white linen underneath. His ginger hair and beard were both perfectly trimmed. His jewelled shoulder brooch and rings sparkled in the candlelight as he clasped his hands confidently above his richly embellished belt.

He was every inch a man of power and influence, and he clearly knew it. Hardly the sort of man she warmed to. As promised, Joan had placed Carac next to the earl, and she sat to Sir John's right with the countess next to her. The countess's large frame overflowed the sides of her chair. Discretely, Joan shifted her chair toward John. Carac leaned forward, acknowledging her and the countess with a polite nod. Joan caught his raised eyebrow and they exchanged a thin smile.

'Lord Courtesy —' said Sir John.

'Call me Frederick.' The earl waved his hand nonchalantly. 'All my friends do.'

Sir John puffed out his chest. 'Frederick —'

Good God, she hoped Sir John wasn't going to be too ingratiating. Putting on her broadest smile, Joan turned to the countess. The overpowering smell of cloves from the woman's hair almost choked her, but she smothered it with a polite cough and a smile.

'Lady de Gravesmire. Or do you prefer Lady Courtesy?'

'Lady Courtesy is appropriate, Lady Joan.'

That put her in her place, but she held her smile. 'Lady Courtesy, I hope you had a good journey.'

'Tedious, long and cold. It is chilly in here. I do hope it'll warm up as the evening progresses.' The countess shivered dramatically and wrapped her furs around her.

Joan bit her tongue and, playing the perfect hostess, called for a boy to lay more logs on the hearth whilst keeping the smile on her face. It was going to be a long evening.

Sir John offered the earl some wine. The man regarded its contents before taking a cautious sip.

'A little sharp perhaps? The best wines come from Burgundy, if you can afford them. Remind me to give you the name of my merchant.'

'Very gracious of you, Frederick. I admit I've not been satisfied with my supplier of late. The wine is, as you say, a little sharp,' said Sir John.

Joan nearly choked on her wine. Sir John had said only yesterday that the wine was the best he'd tasted for months! Sharp or not, it didn't stop the earl from holding out his goblet for more.

'Lady Joan, did you hear what I said?'

Joan shook herself and turned back into the countess. 'I'm sorry, I —'

The woman tutted and leaned close, making Joan

277

flinch away from the stench of cloves. 'I was warning you to be careful of the Lady Tamworth. She's a dreadful gossip. Of course, she's not from the highest family. I was saying only last week to the Countess of Dorchester, there's—' she lowered her voice— 'madness in the bloodline.' She sat back, folded her arms beneath her voluptuous bosom and nodded knowingly, and then leaned in again. 'But, of course, if one marries beneath one...'

The monotonous voice droned on. God's teeth, she had a whole evening of this to endure. Thankfully, the maids had just entered and were waiting for her signal to bring in the food. A welcome respite and, letting the countess's words drift over her, Joan turned to Sir John.

'The food's ready. Shouldn't you give a toast to Richard?'

Sir John stood up and cleared his throat. 'To my son, Richard, the next Lord de Chiddleigh. May he live a long and prosperous life!' He raised his goblet with a flourish.

Everyone stood and raised their goblets. 'To Richard!' they replied.

Raising hers, Joan wondered what they would say if they knew the truth. She nodded to the maids. The show could begin.

'Boar's head and goose, Lady Courtesy. Cook does marvellous things with goose. Wait until you taste it,' Joan said with exaggerated enthusiasm.

Boar's head, the traditional Christmas dish, wasn't exactly top banquet fare, but at such short notice, Cook hadn't been able to get any swan or peacock. Goose was such common meat, but it was the best Cook could do and it was beautifully presented with sprigs of sage and roasted apples. Rather too many apples, but then, they still had plenty of those.

The countess sniffed and her mouth turned down in disappointment. Joan thought that the woman would react the same no matter what was put in front of her.

The boys brought in the dishes piled with beans and carrots but cleverly disguised with sauces and different herbs and spices. Now it was on the table, it all looked rather plain. Well, too bad; it was the best she and Cook could do.

'Boar's head, John? Late for Christmas, are we?' The Earl's hearty laugh ricocheted along the table. Sir John joined in, but not before he shot a scowl in her direction.

What did he expect? She wasn't a sorceress, able to magic something out of thin air.

'I suppose it's fair enough for such a small occasion, but I always insist on peacock for my banquets. Get your good lady to have a word with the countess.'

'I believe she tried to get peacock, but the merchant—'

'Merchant trouble again? You really should sort that out. Don't let them hoodwink you. You must be firm.' He laid a hand on Sir John's arm. 'I insist on only the best, and no supplier of mine would dare to send me anything else. When we received your invitation, the countess remarked that it's a strange time to be holding a banquet. Nothing left in the stores, apparently. I'm surprised Lady Joan didn't tell you.'

Sir John looked crestfallen.

Carac had told Joan that the Earl was wily. She couldn't make up her mind if the Earl was deliberately playing with Sir John, or whether he was simply very rude. Either way, she wanted to knock his superior head off his shoulders. But she smiled sweetly and nodded graciously. At least the countess had stopped talking and was eating well. Joan herself didn't have much of an appetite. If only Sir John had waited for this banquet, they could have done so much better.

As soon as the guests had finished and the dishes were cleared, the countess resumed her monologue. Joan switched off. She couldn't care less who was wearing what and when and whether Lady So-and-So's third daughter would ever get married. Carac was talking to the earl, now that would be much more entertaining. She strained her ears.

'...and the new waterwheel is fifteen feet wide —' he was saying. 'We are digging the leats now, so we should be ready for the new fleece this year, and we've new, larger looms to take the extra wool.'

'You'll need a lot of sheep to feed that,' the earl commented dryly.

'I bought in another two hundred last year and a few blackface rams from the northern shires,' said Sir John proudly.

'Two hundred? Is that all? You'll need more than that.' The earl's eyes narrowed as he sipped his wine. 'Tell you what: I like to support up and coming young knights like yourself, and when you run as many sheep as I do, there's always a few to spare. I'll have the drovers bring them over to you. At a fair price, of course. Wouldn't want to fleece you!' He laughed loudly at his own joke.

The wily old devil, Joan thought and matched the raised eyebrow on Carac's face.

'Thank you, Frederick. Most kind,' said Sir John meekly.

'It is indeed most gracious, but are we ready for more sheep, my lord?' Carac said.

'Of course we are, and I'm never one to pass by a

good opportunity.' Sir John nodded conspiratorially to the earl. 'I'm always telling Carac that he worries too much.'

Carac's mouth tightened, his eyes boring into Sir John, who avoided them determinedly.

Joan caught Carac's eye, and he raised his eyebrows in a helpless expression. No doubt he was already calculating the implications and costs.

The evening dragged on, as did the countess. Would the woman never run out of social drivel? Joan wondered.

The candles burned low, and she prayed the guests would leave before they needed replacing, for, with Carac's cautionary words in her ears, she didn't have enough.

At last, the Earl wiped his hands and turned to the countess.

'Are you sure you wish to take your leave?' Joan asked as she forced her mouth to turn down in disappointment.

They did. With feigned reluctance, she called for the maid to show them to their bedchamber.

In her own bedchamber, she waited for the sound of Sir John's steps on the stairs. If he started complaining, she was ready.

As soon as he came in, she tried to gauge his mood by the look on his face, but his jaw was surprisingly relaxed, and his eyes didn't look hard or steely. He sat on a stool, took off his new shoes, threw them in the corner and rubbed his feet.

'Muxy things! I could hardly walk in them and they pinched my toes all night. Get that maid of yours to bring in a bowl of warm herbal water for these feet.'

'John, I'm so sorry about the evening—'

'What for? I thought it all went rather well in the end.'

281

'But the food...I heard a lot of what the earl was saying. He was so demeaning to you, and the way he foisted those sheep on you! I'm not sure I like him or his wife.'

'Really? I thought Frederick was charming and very understanding of the boar's head. And he's quite right; I should look to my suppliers. But I must have made the right impression or he wouldn't have sold me those sheep.'

Joan's heart sank. Sir John was completely taken in with his new high connection, but she had a feeling that it might not be a good thing.

CHAPTER 45

The trees were tinged with yellow, and the horses were getting their winter coats. Joan returned the brush to the shelf and looked at the dirt on her hands. Merek could have groomed Star, but she enjoyed doing it and it gave her a break.

She washed her hands in the trough. She rarely saw Sir John these days. He was always out. She missed him, but she doubted he missed her. If he did, he never showed it.

Did she love him? Had she ever loved him, or had she just been smitten with his good looks and title? She wasn't sure anymore.

Did he even care for her? He'd behaved wonderfully to her before Richard was born, but now he was different. Maybe it hadn't been her but his unborn child he'd cared about.

It was certainly Richard he cared about now. But surely he didn't still hate her for not being able to feed the child? Lord knows, she'd tried.

Richard was six months old now and starting to crawl. Sir John doted on his boy, getting down on his hands and knees and making bear growls as he crawled after him around the hall. Once, Joan had hitched up her skirts and tried joining in, but they hadn't wanted her. It was a game for just the two of them.

Martha had returned home early. Family matters, she'd said, but Joan wasn't convinced. She'd probably received a better offer from elsewhere. Still, she wasn't sorry to see her go. At first, she'd worried that Richard wouldn't get the natural milk he needed. Joan would have expected any wet nurse to feed her child for at least another year.

Annie, surprisingly, wasn't concerned. As she said, peasant women didn't have the time or the nourishment to keep their children to the breast for so long. Richard was given sheep or goat's milk to drink from a horn and fed what Cook called mush, a disgusting grey gruel made from bread and sheep's milk. When he yelled, Agnes gave him a rag soaked in milk to suck, which usually quietened him. He seemed to like her, and Agnes had slipped into the role of his nurse. Richard was cared for and content.

So why was Sir John back to being so cold towards her?

The sound of wheels on the track distracted her thoughts as she watched a wagon turn into the yard. She wasn't expecting anyone.

'J-Jay! Jay!'

There was only one person who called her that. Joan's heart leapt with joy.

Eleanor jumped off the wagon before the wheels had barely stopped turning and ran across the yard, one hand holding the veil on her head, the other waving like fury. Her round face glowed pink as Joan hugged her.

'Eleanor! What a wonderful surprise! I never got a message. It's lovely to see you after—how many years? Stand back, let me look at you.'

Eleanor posed, holding out her arms and grinning. She hadn't changed that much. A little more round perhaps — she'd always been what Joan's father had called well-covered — and her face was still round and rosy as an apple.

'Dear Eleanor! After all this time, I can't believe you're here. Merek! Get a couple of the boys to take Eleanor's bags to the upstairs chamber. Come on, I'll get Cook to find you something to eat. You must be starving after your journey. I'm thrilled you're here and can't wait to hear all your news. Have you seen Mama and Papa?' Eleanor was just what Joan needed to put a stop to her maudlin thoughts, and, linking arms, she steered her towards the hall.

Two boys scurried from the stables, bowing as they rushed past to unload the wagon.

'You are the Lady of the M-manor, aren't you?'

Eleanor hadn't grown out of her stammer then. 'Yes, I suppose I am.'

'I c-couldn't write. I'm not very good with letters.'

'You're here now and that's what matters. You've got the upstairs bedchamber. John says it's for important guests, but don't mind him, they'll have to go somewhere else.' Joan giggled, opening the doors.

'What a room!' Eleanor turned a circle, her eyes wide as she gazed around the hall.

Joan looked around with her and felt ridiculously proud.

'And you've got stairs!' Eleanor added.

'Those are to my bedchamber and those—' Joan pointed— 'go to yours.'

'C-can I, Jay?' Eleanor rushed over and ran up to the top of the stairs and back down again, her face beaming.

Her cousin was behaving like a child. It made her feel old, but then she was a married lady with a son.

Eleanor flopped back in her chair, sighed contentedly, licked her fingers, and slapped her tummy. She had eaten every one of Cook's oatie cakes with enthusiasm. It was just as well Joan hadn't wanted any.

Agnes came into the hall, holding Richard in her arms. 'He's eaten well, my lady, and is sleeping. I thought —'

Eleanor leapt to her feet and rushed over. 'Let m-me see! Oh, he's lovely. C-can I hold him?'

'Sit down, and Agnes will pass him to you.'

Eleanor wriggled in her seat and held out her waiting arms. Her faced creased in a broad smile as she snuggled the baby close, cooing and kissing.

Richard didn't even murmur, unlike when Joan tried. 'Tell me about your trip,' she said quickly, pushing away the tiny pang of jealousy.

'Well, it t-took ages and …'

Eleanor chattered away, barely pausing for breath, and soon got on to old memories of her visits to Joan. 'Do you remember that t-time when we were riding around the fields and you jumped that enormous hedge and fell off on the other side?'

'I do! I hurt my foot and couldn't walk properly for days. We couldn't have been more than eight or nine birth dates —'

'And your P-Papa was furious because he'd t-told you to go quietly and said we c-couldn't ride for a week? We still did though, didn't we?'

They both fell into a fit of giggles. 'Yes, we did!'

Annie bustled in, a large welcoming smile ready for

her boy. Seeing Eleanor with Richard, she stopped. Her face dropped and she looked to Joan, who bit her lip. In the excitement of Eleanor's arrival, she'd completely forgotten about Annie's visit.

'Annie! I was just saying to Eleanor that you were coming.'

'J-Jay, we were t-talk—'

'Come over and meet my cousin, Eleanor. I told you ages ago that she was coming to be my companion, and she's finally here!' Joan blustered on. 'I had no idea she was coming today! Isn't it exciting?'

Annie bobbed politely to Eleanor, her eyes never leaving Richard and looking a little lost. Joan felt dreadful. What must Annie think?

'Eleanor, this is Annie. She's been helping me with Richard. Why don't you let her sit and hold him for a while? I'm sure your arms must be aching by now.'

Annie settled herself with Richard on her lap, and Eleanor pulled up a stool and continued chatting. Thank goodness the girl never stopped talking. It gave Joan time to compose herself again.

Eleanor prattled on about their childhoods, about their time together playing ring toss and other games, but Joan wasn't really listening. She was watching Annie, who kept her attention on her son and was very quiet. How was she going to explain their friendship to Eleanor?

'J-Jay, do you remember that M-May Day, when your M-Mama invited all the local farmers to celebrate? We danced around the m-maypole, but I went the wrong way and my ribbon got t-tangled. Everyone got cross with me, so we went and picked M-May blossom instead. And I'll never forget your

M-Mama taking us into Dorchester to get cloth for new kirtles. I chose a beautiful green, and you argued because you wanted the yellow but there wasn't enough silk.' She turned towards Annie and frowned. 'Why are you wearing a loose kirtle, like a p-peasant?'

Joan wanted to climb into a hole and disappear. 'Annie's a heal—'

'I don't wear fashionable clothes. I'm learning to be a healer.' Annie lifted her chin as if to say I'm as good as you.

'How strange. I thought only p-peasants did that.'

A little bit of something died inside Joan. 'Eleanor, why don't you go over the stables and look at the horses? Merek will show you.'

'Oh, c-can I? And c-can we go riding t-tomorrow? You could come with us.' She looked at Annie. 'It'll be fun.'

Joan bit her lip. The quicker she could get Eleanor out of the room, the better.

'I can't,' Annie answered. 'I'm helping Ellyn pick marigolds. We've a good crop this year.'

'Why would you want to do that?' Eleanor wrinkled her nose.

'Because we eat them and use them for healing. Ellyn's teaching me tomorrow.'

Good old Annie, Joan thought. She could look after herself.

'You are strange,' Eleanor said, practically skipping out the door.

Joan shook her head and moved over. 'I am so sorry. I love Eleanor to bits, but she doesn't think before she speaks, never did.' It sounded lame, but it was the best she could do.

Annie smiled weakly. 'It's alright. It sounds like you had good times when you were girls.'

'Yes, we did. But tell me about the marigolds. Am I going to be getting some lovely scented lotion soon?'

'I do understand, you know. Eleanor's your cousin, and you haven't seen her for a long time. But tell me—' Annie bent her head close— 'how old is she? I think she's the strange one, behaving like a child.'

'I'm glad you said that. I was thinking the same thing. She's only a birth date younger than me but hasn't changed since I last saw her. Maybe she's just excited at being here.'

Annie puckered her brow. 'Maybe. Richard's waking. He's quite a weight now, and my legs are numb. I'll let him crawl on the floor.'

'The madder plants for my dye are doing well and need pulling. Carac will get the men to do that, and the shed is set up so we can begin soon. I've a rough idea how to dye cloth but not how to get the colour I want.'

'What does Sir John say about it?'

'Not much. He thinks I'm wasting my time and that I'd be better employed sewing or something equally boring. That's all the more reason to prove him wrong.'

'Good for you. Let me know and I'll help.'

'I will. I'm looking forward to it. Working together will be fun.'

'You'll bring Richard to the dyeing sheds, as you promised?'

'Of course. I said so, didn't I?'

Annie didn't seem that keen, Joan thought. No matter. With her help, the task didn't seem so impossible now.

She glanced at the door. She should be with Eleanor, but it didn't seem fair to desert Annie.

'If you want to go to the stables with Eleanor, I don't mind,' Annie said. 'I'll be more than happy here with Richard.'

'Are you sure you don't mind? She's only just arrived; I can't abandon her so soon.'

'Of course I don't mind. If anyone comes, I'll just say you popped out for a moment and I've got some more lotion for you, just in case. You go.'

Annie certainly didn't look as though she minded. She probably liked the idea of having Richard to herself. 'Annie, you're the best friend. And next week, we'll take Richard to the orchards and have a picnic. I'll get Cook to do your favourite oatie cakes, but you'll have to be quick; Eleanor likes them too!'

With a pang of conscience, Joan made for the doors. She ought to say something, give Annie some reassurance that Eleanor's arrival wouldn't change anything but, glancing back, she saw that Annie was already trying to distract Richard away from the hearth. He was fascinated by it, and he was also at the stage where everything he found went straight into his mouth, including the ash.

Joan was sure she was overreacting. Eleanor would soon settle in, and there was no reason why the three of them shouldn't be friends. After all, everyone liked Eleanor.

CHAPTER 46

Annie checked her basket and smiled as she saw the rag ball inside. It was her boy's second birth date and she had been looking forward to it for weeks. Three days ago, Ellyn had come home in a flurry, saying that Joan had given birth to another fine boy. This one had been an easy birth, so there was the new baby to meet as well. What an afternoon it was going to be!

Lifting her skirts and humming to herself, Annie stepped across boulders by the mill. Richard was already a strong healthy child and had started walking by his first birth date.

Her chest swelled with pride. She'd so wanted to see his first steps, but she'd missed them. But then, she'd missed a lot of things.

Her visits were still the best part of her week, but now Eleanor was always there with her high babyish giggle that set Annie's teeth on edge. And her constant chatter! It was all Joan and I did this and Joan and I did that.

It was the same when she and Joan were in the dyeing shed. It had been fun in the beginning, but then Eleanor had started coming and fussing over Richard, which irked Annie. She'd never said anything to Joan, but she hated going to that shed. Her back ached from grinding the roots, her hands were stained red for weeks, and Ellyn complained that she smelt of piss. She'd only agreed to help in the first place because Joan had promised to bring Richard. Last season, she hadn't always done that either, saying he and Eleanor got under her feet in the shed and were better out of the way.

Annie didn't like Eleanor much. She talked about her boy as though he were hers, and Annie had to admit that she was jealous of the girl's friendship with Joan. Eleanor couldn't help herself, and Annie knew that she should feel sorry for her being like she was, but just having her around made her feel like an outsider.

Reaching the other side of the river, she shook her skirts, which were only a little wet around the hem. Checking the rag ball was still safely in her basket, she walked on.

Her boy seemed happy, and she should be grateful for that, but from what she could see, Eleanor had more time for him than Joan did. And Sir John spoiled him. According to Joan, Richard only had to pucker his face and Sir John would give him want he wanted. He didn't like to hear him scream, she said.

But children needed some discipline, and Annie worried that her boy wasn't getting it. She'd even tried to say as much, but Joan had refused to listen. She'd talk to her about it again, but not today. Today was special.

Annie pulled her veil over her ears as she passed the monks' cross. It was a fine day, but there was a sharp nip in the air, and the frost still lay crisp and white on the ground.

She was nearly there, and as always, her heart began to race. She reached into her basket and smiled at the rag ball in her hand. She'd had one when she was little. It had been Peter's and was very worn by the time she'd got it, but she'd still loved it. She hoped Richard would like his. It had taken her many evenings to make. She hadn't had enough scraps to finish it in the end, so she'd ripped some strips off the bottom of her skirt and told Ellyn she'd caught it on a briar.

Annie's heart thumped and her stomach turned over as she entered the hall, clutching her son's present in her hand. She couldn't wait to give it to him and see his eyes light up!

The room was empty. Disappointed, she climbed the stairs to Joan's bedchamber.

Richard was sitting on the floor and, to her dismay, Sir John sat beside Joan on the mattress with his back to the door. He turned sharply and bore through her with his cold eyes.

'How dare you come in here?' he shouted. 'Get out!'

Joan looked past him as Annie shrank back, edging her way out the door.

'No, don't go, Annie. I want you to stay.'

Annie hesitated between Joan's welcoming face and Sir John's decidedly unfriendly one. Not knowing what to do, she stayed where she was, hovering in the doorway.

'John, Annie is here to check on Thomas and myself,' Joan told Sir John firmly. 'Come in, Annie, and take a look at this.'

Sir John's piercing glare kept her frozen her to the spot. He was such a cold man. Annie dropped the rag ball into her pocket but dared not move.

At last, Sir John sighed audibly and turned his back on her.

'Richard, this is your new brother, Thomas. Give him

a kiss,' he said, lifting his son and holding him close to the baby.

Richard lifted his arm and slapped it down on baby Thomas's head.

'Richard! No!' Annie couldn't stop the words.

'Take him away; he's upsetting Thomas,' Joan said, clutching Thomas protectively to her.

'Very well. I've important matters to see to. I'll leave you with your...healer.' Sir John put Richard back on the floor and took hold of his hand.

As Richard toddled towards her, the malicious smile on his face made Annie's skin crawl. She'd seen the same expression on Aldred's face. Sir John glared at her as he brushed past, forcing her back against the door. Staring at the floor, she bobbed a curtsey.

'Don't mind John, Annie; he has his moods. Come and see baby Thomas.'

Easy for Joan to say, but she did mind Sir John. He frightened her, both as a man and as her lord. She didn't know how Joan put up with him.

Joan was surrounded by furs on the bed and looking very smug. Her son was suckling. She couldn't have seen the look on Richard's face as he left. Should she tell her? Annie wondered.

No, she was just being silly, Richard was just a little boy. It didn't mean anything.

'Isn't Thomas just the most gorgeous baby you've ever seen?' cooed Joan.

'Richard shouldn't have hit him. Why didn't you say something?'

'Like what? Children do that sort of thing. He'll get used to Thomas.'

Annie disagreed. Her boy needed to know if he did wrong, but she let it go, not wanting to spoil the moment.

Joan was glowing, her eyes tender as she gazed down at her son. She'd never looked like that for Annie's boy. And Thomas seemed rather plain and sickly and not nearly as lovely as her Richard. He was the image of Sir John with the same long face and straight nose but he didn't have the fine mop of hair her Richard had, nor the same rosy round cheeks.

'He's beautiful and he's feeding,' Annie said, sitting next to Joan.

'He's no trouble at all. He feeds, he sleeps. He does cry of course, but little whimpering cries. Not like Richard, who screamed the house down.'

'He sounds perfect,' Annie said, biting her tongue hard.

'He is. I'd let you hold him, but he's just finished and likes to fall asleep on me. I love that.'

Annie had been looking forward to holding the new baby. She'd never seen Joan so smitten, her face glowing with pride like that. For the tiniest moment, she felt jealous.

'And just look at this! John's present to me as a thank you for Thomas. Wasn't it kind of him? He's not always heartless.'

Annie didn't think Sir John knew what the word kind meant, but she didn't say so.

Joan handed her a shiny object about the length of two hands. It looked like one of Cook's large flat spoons she used to stir the frumenty pudding with at Christmas. It was heavy and shone like gold. The round part was beautifully decorated with engraved swirls and coloured stones. Annie didn't know what they were, but she was sure they were expensive. Lightly, she ran her fingers over them. 'What do you need a fancy spoon for?'

Joan giggled. 'It's not a spoon, cloth-head! Turn it over.'

'Oh!' Annie jumped back and dropped the—the thing onto the bed as if it had burned her hand.

Joan burst out laughing. 'That's just what I did! Look again, it won't hurt you.'

Annie didn't trust it but, curious, she picked it up, holding it at arm's length. Slowly, she tilted her head to the right and then to the left. She touched her cheek and frowned. Quickly, she put the thing facedown away from her. 'What is this magic?'

'It's not magic, there's no need to be afraid. It's called a looking glass. It's the very latest thing. It must have cost John a fortune.'

Annie shifted a little away. 'It's magic, it must be. I was in there. I saw it with my own eyes,' she said pulling her shawl together.

'Oh, Annie, it won't hurt you and once you get used to it, it's wonderful. I had no idea I had so many freckles.' Joan picked it up and peered closely.

'I want no part of it. A puddle's good enough for me.' Annie felt the rag ball in her pocket. Joan hadn't even mentioned her boy's birth date. 'Where's Richard gone?'

'John's probably taken him over to the stables. Do you know Richard says horsey now?'

She didn't. That was another thing she'd missed.

'John had him sitting on Baron the other day.'

'Isn't that dangerous? He's such a big horse.'

Joan laughed. 'Not on his own, silly! John sat with him and held him. It's how I learned to ride with Papa. Thomas will one day too, won't you little one?' She bent and kissed the top of his head.

How was Annie to know? She'd never sat on a horse. 'Richard loved it and kept screaming to go faster. I watched it from that window. John's bought him a pony for his birth date. If you look out, they'll be in the field soon. And you should see all the other things he's got. John had a joupon made for him, it's so tiny. And Eleanor made him a kerchief of the finest silk. She stitched an 'R' in the corner; she's very clever with a needle. And Carac, dear Carac, gave Richard his first set of quills, although I don't think he'll be using them just yet. Take a look.'

Reluctantly, Annie went to the pile on the floor and held up a smart deep blue jupon. How silly! It was far too old for a child his age. Richard would be much better off wearing a sensible tunic and hose. She laid it down again. There were wooden blocks, a push-along wheel on a handle, a beautiful metal toy horse — black like Baron, of course — and other things, but she'd seen enough. 'Is it a good idea to give him so much? You don't want to spoil him.' She hadn't meant to say anything, not on today of all days, but the words just came out.

Joan stiffened. 'We're not spoiling him, and I wish you wouldn't keep saying that. Last time you were here, you told Eleanor off for giving Richard a honey cake and said she was spoiling him. If John wants to give his son nice things, why shouldn't he?'

'I didn't tell her off. I only said that she shouldn't let him have his own way just because he screamed. And you'd already said he couldn't have another one.'

'Yes, well, Eleanor was very upset.'

'I didn't mean to upset her—'

'Anyway, I should have thought you'd be pleased that Richard has so many nice things.'

There it was again, the difference between them. An argument was the last thing Annie wanted, but Joan always had to have the last word these days, and it was beginning to get annoying. She might as well have said things you can't give him because that was clearly what she'd meant.

Annie looked again at the pile of presents. This was what noble children enjoyed. Joan was right; wasn't it what she wanted for him? She fingered the rag ball in her pocket. It felt out of place now, a little like her. Today was supposed to be such a special day, and now it was ruined.

'I was only trying to help,' she said quietly.

Joan was too busy gazing at Thomas and stroking his head to answer, which was answer enough: Annie wasn't needed.

'I'll be going now.' She headed for the door.

'Don't you want to see the pony?'

Annie shook her head. 'Another time, I've seen enough.' She'd give the rag ball to Isobel's little girl; she'd love it.

CHAPTER 47

July 1336

Joan stood by the window, her arms folded tightly across her chest, and bit her lip. It was the first day she'd had to herself for weeks and, instead of being outside doing what she wanted, she was stuck indoors again, and it was such a beautiful summer's day. She wished she'd been out and not got Annie's message, because now she was obliged to wait.

Richard was five years old, and Joan wondered how much longer Annie's visits could continue. Richard was out with Sir John most days, anyway.

In the beginning, when Richard was a baby, she'd looked forward to Annie coming. She'd even started bonding with Richard and thought of him as hers. It was a happy time, playing clap games and hide the ball, and, when he'd sat up at around five months, they took him outside for the first time. How they'd laughed when his face lit up, his brown eyes wide with wonder when he saw his first butterflies. Annie had insisted they put cushions all round him in case he toppled over. She was always too protective.

Then Thomas had been born and everything had changed. Joan had felt an immediate bond with him and realised what she'd missed. Agnes and Eleanor were only too pleased to take care of Richard, and she was glad as it gave her more time with Thomas. It was strange, but it was at about that time that Annie stopped coming every week. Joan often wondered if she had upset her in some way, but as Annie told her, she was a busy healer, and Ellyn wasn't getting any younger.

The door flew open and Annie's feet clipped across the stone floor. By the look of her flushed cheeks, she'd been hurrying.

'You got my message? Sorry I'm late, but by the time we finished gathering the hay last night, the moon was high and I was that tired, I slept late this morning. Then I had to run errands for Ellyn, but I'm here now. How's my boy?'

'He's not here.' And he's not your boy, Joan thought.

Annie sighed. 'Not again. I made such an effort to get here. I've not seen him in ages. I suppose he's out with Sir John again.'

'No; for once John couldn't take him. Anyway, we can't run the estate around you. I never know when you're coming these days. He's actually with Eleanor, Thomas and Maria in the orchards.'

Annie looked taken aback. God's teeth, Joan thought, she'd better not start on any more of her helpful suggestions for Richard, or she really would lose her temper.

'Come on, let's not waste any more of the afternoon.' Her quick steps echoed across the hall, her skirts swishing furiously as she strode ahead to the orchards.

'The apples are coming nicely,' said Annie, trying to keep up.

'Yes, they are.' Joan was in no mood for idle chatter. Ahead, she could hear Thomas's high voice and Eleanor's girlish laughter. She smiled; that sound always cheered

300

her up. Eleanor was sitting on the grass with Thomas, now three, and his one-year-old sister, Maria, teaching them to make daisy chains.

Thomas lifted his proudly. 'For you, Mama!'

Joan held it up as though it was made of diamonds and pretended to put it around her neck, although it was far too short. Thomas's face crumpled, but Eleanor said not to worry; only a few more daisies and it could be a bracelet. Joan hugged him and said she loved it anyway.

Richard was sitting apart as he always did. She'd given up trying to include him. He'd only say something in that belligerent way of his. Annie would sit with him; he'd prefer that anyway.

Thomas finished the daisy bracelet and, grinning with delight, gave it to her. Joan slipped it on her wrist. 'It's the nicest bracelet I've ever had. Come here,' she said and gave him a warm kiss on his cheek.

'Let's p-play bears!' Eleanor jumped up, screwed her face tight, and put both her arms out, making bear noises. Thomas squealed with delight and ran away. Eleanor went after him. Joan spread her arms and growled, chasing them in and out of the trees.

'I'm a bear too! Chase me, Mama!' Richard spread his arms wide and roared at the top of his voice. He ran around them, his arms brushing the top of Thomas's head until the younger boy started to cry.

'Don't be silly, Richard,' Joan said. 'You'll hurt Thomas.'

'I'm a bear!' Richard roared, running in smaller circles, swooping in and out.

Eleanor stopped being a bear, and Joan stood behind Thomas, holding him. Richard slowed down and stopped in front of her, panting. Wide-eyed and red-faced, he looked first at Joan and then at Thomas. His face clouded over, he clenched his fists, and then, turning on his heels, he raced out of the orchard.

'Richard!' Annie started to run after him, but he was out of the gate and down the track before she was halfway across the field.

'You're not going to let him go, are you?' Annie's eyes challenged Joan.

'He's just sulking. What am I supposed to do? He always plays too rough, and it always ends in tears,' Joan said, kissing Thomas on his brow.

'He only wanted to play bears with his Mama, like Thomas was, but he said you'd be cross. I told him you wouldn't, and now I feel awful. You should have let him join in. That was all he wanted.'

Maybe it was, but Joan was sick of Annie's helpful suggestions, constantly telling her what to do and how she should do it. 'I think I know better than you what Richard wanted—'

'Do you? I don't think so. You give all your attention to Thomas, and Richard feels left out. He's just a little boy who wants his mama to notice him. That's all.' Annie's cheeks were flushed and her eyes blazed.

Joan pressed her hands together and bit her lip. 'Are you accusing me of ignoring Richard?'

'You should spend more time with him. Do you ever give him a kiss or a cuddle, like you do Thomas?'

How dare Annie stand there looking so smug and criticise her? Joan thought savagely. She should try being a mother! 'What do you mean? Of course I do!'

'I've never seen you.'

'Well, I do. You're just never here.' Did she? Richard never struck her as the cuddling type.

'Richard just wants your attention. Maybe you should try it.'

Annie made it sound so easy. 'You've no idea how difficult Richard can be, and I refuse to discuss it further.'

Annie held her ground, her eyes still blazing. Eleanor and the children had gone quiet. Joan glared back long and hard, determined that she would not be the first one to give way.

At last, Annie dropped her eyes and shook her head. 'I'm sorry if I've upset you. I was only trying to help. But please Joan, give him a hug now and again. He's such a little boy.' Her shawl trailed behind her as she walked away.

Damn it. Now Joan felt angry and guilty, not only because she'd upset Annie, but because, deep down, she knew she was right.

CHAPTER 48

April 1338

Annie had promised to call in at the forge. It had been a proud day a few years ago when John Forge had said that Peter and his new wife, Janet, could make a home there. Now they had a son, William, and Peter was all but running the place. Janet was the twitchy sort and reminded Annie of a nervous sparrow with her thin frame and straight brown hair.

John Forge's cough wasn't getting any better, and many a day he struggled to breathe. What more could she do? She had tried syrup of angelica and then horehound drink, but he refused to take any more of that because he said it reminded him of the swill channels in Okewolde's streets. So she had given him some mint ointment to rub into his chest, but that didn't seem to help either.

Annie checked her basket. Hopefully, this new angelica and rosehip mixture would work.

Reaching the edge of the village, she crossed the grass track and spotted a small wiry woman dressed in green just ahead of her. 'Cecily!'

'Annie! Busy as always?'

'Yes. How do you fare?'

'Mustn't grumble, though I'm pleased to see a bit of

sunshine. It's been a hard winter. Let's pray we have an early warm spring,' she said, as the two women ambled past the cottages together.

'Are you using the barley poultice on your leg?' Annie asked.

'I am, and the bad humour is still coming out.'

'Good, that's what you want. Let me know if you need any more.'

'I will, and I'm that grateful, but I can't pay you —'

'I understand,' Annie interrupted. 'Wait until later, when things are easier.'

It was always the same at this time of year. The few things folks could store for the dark months were used. Food was meagre, there was nothing to take to the market and there would be nothing growing for weeks.

'Is that Master Richard coming this way?' Cecily said suddenly. 'I'm turnin' down here. I've no likin' to dip a curtsey to that one. God speed, Annie.'

Annie's heart gave a small lurch. She remained where she was, watching her short stocky boy of seven summers with his thick mop of dark hair bobbing up and down on his head and shoulders. He didn't so much walk as swagger through the village towards her.

William was outside the forge, squatting at the edge of the lane and playing quietly with knucklebones. Richard saw him, reached for the leather catapult on his belt, smiled wickedly, and picked up a stone. Pulling back the leather string, he took aim and let the stone fly.

Oh, Richard.

'Ow!' William gripped his arm and, as he looked up, another stone hit him hard on his shoulder. He burst into tears.

Richard was just a few feet away, his legs rigid and slightly apart.

'Crying, peasant boy?' he taunted.

William looked up. 'You did that on purpose!' he said between sobs, rubbing his arm and shoulder.

Richard leered down, tossing a stone in the air from hand to hand. There it was. That same look that Aldred had once given her. But dear God, not on her boy! Would she never be free?

Peter hurried out of the forge as a rider on a black horse trotted across the ford.

'That's my father! Now you're for it.' Richard waved his arm high over his head. 'Papa, quick!'

Sir John pushed Baron into a canter, pulling him up short in a spray of dirt. 'What's going on?'

'I was just walking to the forge to collect my pony when that peasant boy threw a stone at me!' Richard pointed his finger at William. 'Look! It got me on the arm. I can hardly bend it.'

William hid behind his Pa.

Sir John dismounted. 'Let me see.'

Richard yelled dramatically as he rolled up his sleeve and held out his arm for inspection. 'It hurts,' he whined, screwing up his face.

'You! Are you the boy's father?' Sir John demanded, turning his attention to Peter.

Peter removed his cap. 'Yes, Sire.'

'Then you would do well to teach him some manners. Keep him indoors where he can't be a menace to his betters.'

Peter twisted the cap tightly in his hands as the colour rose up his neck, a sure sign he was about to lose his temper. Annie held her breath. It would only make things worse if he did. To her relief, he bowed his head. 'Yes, Sire.'

306

'Fetch Master Richard's pony. I assume you've shod him? And don't expect any payment. Let it be a lesson for you to keep better control over your son.'

'Yes, Sire.'

Peter's face was grim as he led the bay pony from the forge and stood him square for Richard to mount.

'Give me a leg up then!'

Annie could see her brother gritting his teeth, but he put his two hands together, taking Richard's weight as the boy used him as a step to mount his pony.

Sir John fixed his cold eyes on Peter. 'You'd do well to remember what I said, blacksmith.'

Annie watched them go. Hadn't she said years ago that Sir John was spoiling him? But Joan wouldn't listen, and now look at her poor boy. After just a few yards, Richard turned in his saddle and grinned triumphantly, then turned back as he and Sir John galloped up the hill. She pursed her lips and watched until they were out of sight. Something had to be done about that young man, but right now, William needed her attention.

Annie stepped into the warm glow of the forge. Peter was the colour of the red embers as he paced the dirt floor, his fists clenching and unclenching.

'I saw everything. Master Richard deliberately flew two stones at him,' Annie said. 'How are you, William? Roll up your sleeve and show Auntie Annie your arm.'

'I knew it! I swear, one day I'll swing for that man. And as for that arrogant little —'

'Peter, calm down. I know how you feel, but it's not worth getting yourself worked up,' said Janet, as she went to put an arm around him.

'That muxy boy—' Peter shrugged off her arm, picked

307

up a hammer and brought it down hard onto the anvil with a resounding clang.

'William was just playing by the door,' said Annie crossly. 'Sorry, William, but does this hurt?' She pressed his shoulder.

'A little,' he said, watching his Pa and wiping his nose with his other sleeve.

'And then, Master Richard stood over him gloating while he watched William cry.' Annie rolled down William's sleeve. 'There's nothing broken, but your arm will turn blue and yellow and be a bit sore for a few days.'

'It hurts, Auntie Annie,' William sniffed. 'Why did that nasty boy throw stones at me and call me a peasant?'

The three adults looked at each other.

'Because he is a nasty little bully who thinks he's better than all of us, just because Sir John is his father—'

'Peter, don't!' Janet protested. 'You shouldn't say such things.'

'What things?'

John Forge leaned against the door frame. The past seven years had not been kind. His face was pale, his skin taut across his sallow cheeks, and his once strong hands that could hold any horse's hoof were now distorted with knobbly growths on the fingers.

'I was just saying that Peter shouldn't talk about Sir John like that in front of William,' Janet said. 'The boy's too young to understand.'

Peter stopped his pacing and began fiercely pumping the bellows, sending thick plumes of grey smoke billowing up the chimney and into the room. 'If Master Richard was my son, he would feel the back end of my belt. That's what he needs. But Sir John's precious son can do no wrong. God's bones, it gets my blood up.'

What they said was true, but it still hurt Annie when people talked of her Richard in that way. Every time, she had to force herself not to leap to his defence, as any mother would.

But she wasn't any mother, and she had to be careful.

'You can't blame Richard—' she began.

'It won't do, lad,' John wheezed. 'Your hatred of Sir John is eating you up. Let...it...go.' He struggled to get his words out as the cough forced its way up from the depths of his chest. 'And by the Lord's balls, stop working those bellows or you'll be sending me to my maker!'

'He's right, Peter,' Annie said. 'I don't like Sir John any more than you do, but it's not Richard's fault. He's only a child. Now William, come and sit on my knee and give me a cuddle.' She patted her lap and began rummaging in her basket. 'I've brought you some of this new mixture,' she added, holding out a jar to John. 'It tastes quite nice, and I'm hoping it'll work.'

John took out the reed stopper and sniffed the contents. 'Smells alright. Thanks, lass, I'll give it a try. You're a right little angel and no mistake.'

'Big Papa John!' William wriggled off her lap. 'See my arm!' he said, pulling up his sleeve. 'Is it yellow and blue yet?'

CHAPTER 49

Annie left the forge but, instead of heading home, she carried on along the path towards Court Barton. The clouds hung low and heavy over the moors and were darkening. It would rain soon. She lengthened her strides. If she was lucky, she would be home before the heavens opened.

Pausing at the top of the hill, she looked down at the manor house. A few maids scuttled to and fro between the kitchens and the dairy. She made her way down the hill and entered the cobbled yard. Joan came out of the stables, brushing horse hairs from her skirts.

Annie took a deep breath. 'I was in the village earlier and had to see you. Are you alone?'

'Annie! Yes, I am, for once. Have you brought it?'

'Brought what?'

Joan sighed audibly. 'The clove paste for Maria's toothache. Surely you haven't forgotten.'

Annie knew nothing about that. Ellyn must have forgotten to mention it. She seemed to be forgetting a lot of things lately. Pretending to look, Annie rummaged in her basket. 'I'm sorry; I'll bring it straight down.'

'Do; the poor child's in agony. Richard's with John, and I am rather busy.'

Joan was almost dismissing her, and after everything they had been through, Annie wasn't going to be dismissed. She didn't know how Joan was going to take this, though, and wiped her hands on the back of her skirt a little nervously.

'I saw Richard in the village earlier. I'm sorry to say he deliberately used his catapult at a little boy, William. And when Sir John turned up, Richard lied and said his arm hurt and that the boy had thrown stones at him. Sir John believed him, of course, and Peter took the wrath of his tongue and lost payment for his work.' Joan was eyeing her frostily now, but for Richard's sake, she had to say what she came to say. 'It's not the first time Richard's done this sort of thing. I thought you should know. I hate to say this, but he's turning into an arrogant bully. It hurts me to see him like that, and folks are talking. The boy needs discipline.' Annie felt better for saying it, but Joan had stiffened and was biting her lip, a sure sign that she was either thinking or agitated.

'Sir John and I will be the ones to decide that—'

'When?' Annie interrupted. Joan wasn't going to play the lady with her, not when her boy was at stake. 'If you don't do something soon, who knows what he'll do next? Sir John spoils him and won't have a word said against him, as you well know, and as you've told me more than once, Richard won't listen to you.'

Joan winced, then her eyes flared. 'How dare you! Richard is difficult, but I do my best, despite your constant interference over the years—'

'I wasn't interfering, I was trying to help. I could see you were struggling with him. You said as much yourself.'

'I wasn't struggling that much, and I don't just have

311

Richard; I have Thomas and Maria to think of as well!' Joan's hands were on her hips, her shoulders raised and her eyes still blazing. Annie had never seen her so angry.

Well, she was angry too. They were ruining her precious boy.

'Oh yes, your perfect Thomas! The first day I saw you with him, I knew my boy was forgotten. You just handed him over to Eleanor; don't think I didn't notice. As soon as Eleanor arrived, I was pushed out. You and her talking about things I didn't understand, because you're both from the same families, and I'm just a peasant. Do you know how left out I felt? After all the years and everything we've been through, do you have any idea how much that hurt? I can't believe how thoughtless you were, but then you always were selfish and full of yourself!' Annie didn't know where the words came from, but they must have been brewing for a long time.

'You keep Eleanor out of this! She's good and kind and hasn't a nasty thought in her head. And I never pushed you out. You just stopped coming so often. You never said why —'

'Well, now you know why. And you only ever had eyes for Thomas. Poor Richard was always left out. He desperately wanted your attention, but you couldn't see that. It was always Thomas, Thomas, Thomas, and it still is!'

'That's not true! I love Richard as though he were my own.'

'That's it, isn't it? Thomas is yours and Richard isn't. What about that time in the orchard when you were playing bears with Thomas? Or when Richard found the stag beetle and was so thrilled he wanted to show you. What did you do? You shrieked, said it was a nasty, dirty thing and told him to go away. I'll never forget the disappointment on his face.'

'Well, it was nasty. Anyway, we had loads of lovely picnics by the river.'

'He just wanted you to notice. And when you didn't, he had to make you notice. It's no wonder he started bullying Thomas. He was jealous of him. But you never saw it.'

Joan was facing her, her eyes wide and every muscle tight in her face. 'You were jealous too, though, weren't you? Jealous that I had another friend, jealous that Eleanor was with Richard and you weren't. God's blood, Annie, I never thought you were like that. Anyway, Richard is out riding with John most days now, so none of us see much of him.'

She had been a little jealous, that was true, but it was more that she felt betrayed by her lowly status. Joan would never understand that. 'Oh, yes; Sir John got him on a horse before the boy could hardly walk, but then that's what nobles do, isn't it? They sit on their high horses looking down on the rest of us. Well, I don't want my boy to be like that—'

'He isn't your boy any longer, and it isn't for you to say how you want him! Sir John is his father, and I am his mother! You need to accept that.' Joan's eyes burned into her. She was being every part the Lady of the Manor. Even her voice had that superior direct tone, although her face was red and her lips pressed hard together.

Annie glared back. How could Joan be so cruel? The lady had put the peasant in her place, and it felt as

313

though she'd punched her in the stomach. Suddenly, she'd run out of words. She wished she'd never come, but all those hurtful things they had just said to each other would probably have been said sometime.

The difference between them had finally won. Unable to look at her old friend any longer, she dropped her eyes to the ground.

'Annie, I'm sorry,' Joan said in a quieter tone. 'I shouldn't have said that. I never realised how you felt, and I should have. Believe me, I don't want to upset you. We're friends, you know that. But you must see that now Richard is older, things have to change. The boy can't have two mothers, can he?' Joan dropped her hands, and her eyes were as soft as they usually were.

'I only came here to help. I never meant for us…' Annie swallowed and fought back her tears. Despite her words, Joan didn't need her. 'I think Ellyn should come in future, and I don't think I can help with the cloth dyeing anymore. I'm sorry.' She picked up her basket and turned to go.

'Annie, come back! Annie!'

Annie kept walking, not even turning around. Joan was right. Her boy was growing up and, as hard as it was, it was time to let go and watch from afar.

CHAPTER 50

Eleanor watched her steps on the flagstones, her arms swinging listlessly, pacing to the end of the hall she turned. 'Oo, twaye, thray.' Another step and she hesitated.

'J-Jay? What comes after thray?'

Joan put down her stitching for the third time. 'Four, Eleanor. Four, five, six, but do stop pacing up and down and find something to do! Why not play with Maria and her poppet doll or something?'

'I'm bored, J-Jay. Even Annie hasn't been to see us for t-two weeks,' Eleanor said, counting her way over to the window. The shutters were drawn back and she gazed out, leaning on her elbows, her chin resting in her hands. 'I miss seeing Annie. Why hasn't she been?'

Annie hadn't come to see them since they'd quarrelled, and Joan wished that she would. There was so much she wanted to say. Sorry, mainly. Not about Richard — on that score, she was right — but she could have been kinder.

'It's such a lovely day, why c-can't we go outside? You'd like that, wouldn't you, Maria? Oh, say we c-can, Jay.' Eleanor's apple-round face lit up and, rushing over, she threw her arms around her. 'Please?'

Joan sighed. She loved her cousin, but in Eleanor, she had a nine-year-old child on her hands, not an equal. Aunt Philippa must have praised God when she received her mama's plea for help. It solved her problem of what to do with her unmarriageable daughter, she thought sardonically.

Eleanor was such a loving and innocent girl, always happy and willing to please and a joy to be with. It was just that, somehow, she'd never grown up. Thomas and Maria, now five and three, adored her. Just as well, since the four of them spent so much time together.

She seldom saw Richard now, who was always with Sir John. It was easier that way. Her other children were compliant and a delight, but Richard was truculent and deliberately disruptive. He teased Eleanor mercilessly, took a delight in making his little sister cry and intimidated Thomas. The children were scared of him, and she had to admit that she'd never understood him, but then, he wasn't truly hers. Was Annie right? Did he just want her attention? She must try to include him more.

'Alright, Eleanor. Get the children ready and we'll go to the new fish ponds. They should be finished by now.'

Stepping outside and feeling the warmth of the sun put a smile on her face. The dark months were behind them at last and spring was on its way. Eleanor was right: it was a lovely day, and it would do her good to blow away a few cobwebs from her mind, and the children could gather some herbs for Cook on the way back. If they took the path through the orchards, they might find some early primroses. Joan loved primrose petals coated in honey.

Eleanor and Marie skipped ahead and turned into the meadow. Joan liked to let them go ahead; it gave her just a few moments with Thomas all to herself. She was about to follow when she saw Sir John and Richard riding along the track towards her.

'John, you've arrived just in time! I'm taking the children out. Why don't you and Richard come with us?'

'Papa, you said that when we got back, I could practice my archery, as knights do,' Richard piped up.

'Yes, yes I did…'

'You can do that afterwards,' Joan said. 'You'd like to see the new fish ponds with us, wouldn't you, Richard?'

'Why should I want to see some silly fish ponds? Knights don't fish. I want to do archery.'

Sir John wouldn't want to disappoint Richard, but Joan hoped that he would come. They rarely did anything together now, and Thomas needed a father figure.

'I did say —' Sir John began.

'You promised!' Richard pouted, tightly crossing his arms.

'Yes, I did. But your mother's right. We can do that later —'

'You told me that you should never break a promise,' Richard persisted.

Sir John shrugged with an inevitable smile. Joan couldn't believe it. He was going to give in again.

'He's right. I did promise.'

'Can't you at least take Thomas with you? He'd like that, wouldn't you, Thomas?'

Thomas sidled behind her skirts and kept his head down, not answering.

'He can't keep up,' Sir John said. 'Maybe when he's older. You do understand, don't you?'

Joan bit her bottom lip. 'Oh, yes, I understand perfectly. And, by the way, Carac was over earlier looking for you.' She gathered her skirts in one hand and swept past him.

She heard Richard's voice behind her and, glancing back, saw Sir John lay a hand on the boy's shoulder as they rode away together in the opposite direction, everything else already forgotten.

Joan walked quickly, her strides getting longer and faster as her boots furiously hit the ground. Annie was right, she knew that now. She just hadn't been able to admit it at the time. Richard was getting far too much of his own way. It would do him good for his father to say no once in a while. She'd tried to tell him that, but Sir John had said she was being too hard on the boy. What more could she do?

'Mama, slow down.' Thomas tugged at her hand.

Smiling, Joan crouched down and stroked back his hair. He was a frail little boy with his elfin face and fair hair flopping into his eyes. He wasn't as strong as the others and sometimes had problems breathing. Ellyn and Annie had tried everything but nothing worked, so Joan had sent for the physician from Exeter. He couldn't help either. He'd just sold her some expensive angelica tincture and said that Thomas would grow out of it. She hoped he was right.

'Sorry. This way, girls. Let's see how many fish we can count.'

Eleanor cautiously stood on the edge of the pond. 'Where's the water?'

One by one, they all peered in. Instead of sparkling clear water full of large carp fish for the kitchen, there was nothing but a very large, muddy pit.

'I don't know,' Joan said. 'Let's go to the other pond.

Maybe that's got water in it.'

There was nothing there either. No hole, no mounds of dug out soil; nothing but grass.

'I want to see the fish,' Maria said sadly.

'So do I, Maria. So do I,' Joan answered. 'Eleanor, take Thomas and Maria over to those trees and wait for me. I'm going to find out what's going on.'

First Sir John, and now this. It was turning into a very trying morning. With a frown, she walked briskly toward the straggle of makeshift hovels in the next field, her skirts swishing through the grass. By the time she got there, she had blamed her husband for everything, cursed her quick tongue, cursed Annie's stubbornness and was in no mood to argue.

'Who's in charge here?' she demanded, placing her hands firmly on her hips.

A thin, wiry man came forward and took the piece of grass he was chewing out of his mouth. 'I am, my lady.'

'Why are you all sitting here and not working? Sir John doesn't pay you to sit around. The ponds should be finished by now. You haven't even started on the second one.'

'But that's just it, my lady. We're waiting for Sir John to tell us where to dig and what size. He said two weeks ago that he'd be back and show us, but we're still waiting.'

Oh, that man! 'That's no excuse. You've sat here for two weeks getting paid, when you could have asked me. Get your shovels. You've time to make up.'

The Lady of the Manor had spoken.

Joan wasn't sure what size the ponds should be, but she remembered seeing some at one of the estates that she and Sir John had visited. Someone had to get things organised, and it wasn't going to be Sir John.

She lifted her chin and confidently paced out the area she thought was about right, and then stood back with her arms crossed and a haughty look on her face as she watched the men pick up their shovels and start to dig.

'Ah, I see work has started on the ponds at last,' said Carac, striding toward her from the direction of the orchards.

'Hail, I trust you are fair? And yes, the work has started, but only because I brought the children over to see the fish in the new ponds that aren't here and then set the men to work myself.' She drew Carac out of the men's hearing. 'I'm furious with John. Apparently, he said he'd tell the men what he wanted but never did. Now I've got to go back and tell Cook that her supply of fresh carp will be another God knows how many weeks, and she won't be happy. And if Cook's not happy, the entire household knows it. And it's not the first time; John promised to arrange for the saddler to come and repair the harnesses ready for the oxen and harrowing this month, but the harnesses were still sitting on the racks three weeks later. It was only by chance Mark bumped into the saddler in town and learned that he knew nothing about it. The weather and ground are perfect to start work, but now we've only one set of harness while we wait for the others to be repaired.'

Carac frowned and kept watching the ground as he walked. 'I did wonder why only one ox was working. I shall have to set the men to drag the harrows themselves. They won't like it, but we can't wait or we'll never get the wheat sown in time. By your words, I understand that John is not here?'

'Don't be silly; you must have noticed that he's never here these days. He's either away connecting with the right people, as he puts it — in other words, wining and dining — or enjoying himself at some hunting party or other with his new high noble friends. And when he is at home, he's out teaching Richard about the estate, or so he says. They're practising archery at the moment. Meanwhile, I'm left to cope, not knowing what he has or hasn't done.'

They'd reached the tree where Eleanor and the children were making chains with early buttercups. 'Come on, let's go home,' Joan said wearily.

'I'll accompany you if I may. Tell me, is John seeing anything of the Earl of Devonshire on these trips of his?'

'Sometimes, I think he is. And as you know, John's dragged me to I can't recall how many banquets to be seen, and 'maintain my presence with the ladies." Joan put a hand over her mouth to cover an exaggerated yawn. 'I can think of nothing worse, and I have a horrible feeling he's brewing up to hold another banquet here with plans to invite the earl.'

'Is he, indeed? He must feel confident in his position with the earl, particularly after the last time he was here. I seem to remember the earl was more than a little disparaging on that occasion.' Carac held open the wicket gate and waited for Joan to pass through before closing it behind them.

'He certainly was, but in John's eyes, the man can do no wrong. When I do see John, it's either Frederick this or Richard that. He never asks after me or the children. I don't think we feature in his world at all.' She bit her tongue. 'Sorry, I'm having a bad morning and I shouldn't go on like this. It's just that I get so frustrated with him! Were John's parents sociable people?'

Carac raised his eyebrows and laughed. 'Good Lord, no! Old Sir James was a High Sheriff and often away for months on the court circuit. He didn't have much time to hold banquets. Hilde—well, she became a...a solitary sort of person. But, tell me, how you are progressing with the scarlet red dye? Last time we met, you were about to try a different mix with madder and—what was it again?'

Was it her imagination, or had Carac just switched the subject rather deftly?

'Murrey berries from the mulberry bush and iron, but I'm afraid the result was too dark. I was so disappointed. We've made some nice red dyes but not the elusive scarlet, and that's the one everyone wants.'

'And the one that fetches the highest price.'

'Yes. I'm determined to find the right mix.'

'And I'm sure you will. Annie must be a help to you.'

'Sadly, she's not helping me at the moment.' And how Joan wished she was. Annie was so knowledgeable about berries and plants. She would know what to try next.

They had arrived back in the yard. 'It was nice seeing you, Joan, but I must make haste. Do tell John that I need to talk to him. The reports and figures are up to date, and it would be nice if he looked at them once in a while.'

'I will.' It seemed she wasn't the only one who was frustrated with Sir John.

CHAPTER 51

Sir John threw himself into Carac's best chair beside the hearth, slumping back with his legs stretched out before him. Richard sat opposite, mimicking his father.

Carac surveyed his spotlessly clean flagstones and tutted. Richard had stamped his filthy boots right across, leaving clear prints to where he was now slouching in his chair. The boy even managed to drop more dirt by the hearth.

Carac had no idea why Sir John had to bring Richard on every visit, but regrettably it was the way of things now. He would never say so, but he didn't like the boy. Richard strutted in his father's shadow, as though he was already the lord, and his arrogance wasn't becoming in one so young. It was enough to test the patience of a saint.

'A hard ride?' he asked.

Sir John chuckled. 'We didn't spare the horses, did we, son?'

Richard bounced in his seat, rubbing his hands together. 'No! And I was holding him back; I could have gone faster if I'd wanted! And—'

Carac had no intention of including Richard in his conversation and cut him off. 'Why the haste?'

'All in good time, Carac, all in good time,' Sir John answered. 'Now, your best wine! We have something to celebrate.'

Carac raised an eyebrow. He didn't like surprises; they unsettled him. He much preferred to keep his feet on the ground and know where he was. With a little reluctance, he went to his store outside. Selecting a barrel that wasn't quite his best, he took a flagon, checked it was clean and filled it.

Sir John took a long draught of the deep red wine, put down his goblet with a flourish and sat forward, his eyes shining with excitement. Carac had seen him like this many times and not always for the better. He took his seat with a sinking heart and waited.

'I have been granted three Knights Fees from the Earl of Devonshire,' Sir John announced. 'Even one would have given me enough land to support myself, a bailiff and servants, but three! He was most generous. That means my estate now stretches an extra ten miles north from Holdesworthe and a further twenty miles south, bordering the Forest of Dartmoor down to the village of Dunsford. Drink up; I think we'll need another flagon before the morning is out.' He relaxed back with proud satisfaction.

Carac was speechless. He'd had no idea Sir John was on such intimate terms with the earl, but he should have had. He made it his business to know everything about Sir John and the estate. How else could he keep an eye on him and run things? But this had slipped him by, and he was annoyed with himself.

'Well, have you nothing to say?' Sir John demanded. 'I thought you'd be overjoyed. Just think of all those extra acres and good rolling pasture. We can expand our sheep flocks more quickly, make more cloth and branch into other things. I've already got a few ideas.'

Carac didn't doubt that for a moment, but he would be the one who'd have to keep Sir John in check and curb his impulses all the time, especially since the coffers weren't exactly overflowing. He'd always assumed that Sir John would settle down and mature as he got older. When that hadn't happen, Carac had hoped that a wife's influence might have made a difference. But that obviously wasn't to be either.

He chose his answer very carefully. 'The acquirement of any land is an asset, although I should have preferred it to come from a different source. I would strongly advise caution.'

'What do you mean?' Sir John sat up, eyeing him over his wine.

'The Earl of Devonshire is a very powerful man. He is known to be ruthless and...what shall we say? A little clever in some of his dealings?' That was being kind, Carac thought. Devious was nearer the mark.

'Are you saying that I shouldn't trust the very man who has shown such faith in me?'

He had spoiled Sir John's good news and, as expected, the man was going to argue. Carac had seen it all before, and he was getting too old for it. 'I didn't exactly say that—'

'Then what are you saying, exactly?'

'I'm saying that you should be aware, that is all.' Carac took a breath and a sip to curb his growing irritation.

'After all the years I've spent cultivating his friendship, am I to refuse his patronage? Is that what you want? God's teeth, Carac, the man's an Earl! This is the opportunity I've been waiting for.' Sir John poured himself some more wine, gulped most of it down in one go and put his goblet down hard on the table.

'I'm simply saying that we should be vigilant,' Carac insisted. 'The cloth trade was down last year. We've had two years of wet summers and brutally harsh winters. We lost a good quarter of our lambs last winter because of the weather and not having enough feed. Suppose we have another bad year? The money reserves won't last forever —'

'You're always going on about money. You're too cautious, that's your trouble. The estate has gone from strength to strength over the past seven years. Yes, we've had a couple of poor years, but we must still be in profit.' Sir John's voice rose on the last words and he stared at Carac, a clear challenge in his eyes.

Carac gripped the arms of his chair. Somebody had to watch the coffers. It was true the estate had done well, but they still needed to build reserves. He had put in a lot of effort behind the scenes into doing just that. He wouldn't have Sir John rushing in with some ill-thought-out scheme and spending it all. Things should be planned and conducted in an orderly manner.

'John, listen to me. We're still making money, yes, but not as much as before. We've produced less cloth over the last two years, and the quality of the wool hasn't been too good either, you know that. You've spent a lot of money on entertaining, building, buying stock and hiring more and more men. We do need to proceed diligently. The records speak for themselves, if you'd care to take a look.' Carac rose to fetch his parchments from where they were neatly piled on his table.

Sir John's cheeks were flushed and his voice bounced

around the room. 'No, I wouldn't care to take a look! All the plans we put into action seven years ago have paid off, and the estate has prospered. The Earl of Devonshire granted the Knights Fees because of it. Bringing in those Blackface rams was one of the best ideas I've had. Ashetyne has become well known for its cloth and good quality wool. The coppiced woods are a success, and hiring men is more flexible than relying on estate peasants. I don't understand your attitude, Carac.'

He'd never persuade Sir John to look at the records while he was in this mood. Reluctantly and with a sigh, Carac returned the parchments to their allotted place and put his two hands together, as if in prayer, and slowly began pacing the length of his hall. He needed to calm himself and think, and he thought better if he paced.

He proceeded slowly and turned at the far end of the hall. Sir John was fidgeting and drumming his fingers on his knee.

'You're right. For the first few years, the estate did do well, but we don't control the markets. Last year, the Flemish merchants wanted a better quality cloth than ours. Joan is making good headway with the red dyes and has a few of the women working on it now. If we put more effort into that, we really could increase the value of our cloth. That's where the exports are, and red cloth fetches the highest prices.'

Sir John stopped his drumming. 'If it keeps her amused, let her play. Personally, I don't see how she thinks she will succeed where others have failed.' He waved his hand dismissively.

Carac hated it when he did that. He sighed and

returned to his seat. The man was impossible. 'You underestimate your wife.'

'I don't think so. Anyway, the reason the cloth wasn't as good last year was because of the weather. It wasn't our fault.' Sir John's voice had a hard edge, his jaw was set firm and he sat rigidly upright, rapidly swirling the wine in his goblet.

'Quite right, Papa.'

Carac silenced Richard with one piercing look. 'Exactly my point. We can't control the seasons which is why we should be careful. We need to plan. Keep reserves. We can't just assume that every year will be a good one —'

'I know that!' Sir John interrupted. 'I'm not a numbskull!'

Carac wasn't entirely sure about that sometimes. Fighting to keep his voice level, he continued. 'These lands from the Earl of Devonshire could be an asset, but we shouldn't rush into things. I suppose you'll be visiting them?'

'Of course —'

'Because I can't run things here and take that on as well, even with Simon helping me,' Carac said firmly.

Sir John glanced around. 'Yes, where is Simon?'

'Who's Simon?' Richard interrupted again.

'Simon is my son.' The boy was getting on Carac's nerves. Sir John should teach his son to keep quiet in matters that didn't concern him. 'He's with the woodsmen. And that's another thing: we reduced our felling of mature trees and now we're losing out on orders for large timbers. There's more demand for house and shipbuilding again —'

'King Edward's wars with France, I suppose?'

'Indeed, and those orders are now more valuable

than coppicing.'

'Are you now saying that we were wrong about the coppicing?' Sir John demanded.

Carac sighed. Sir John really couldn't take even the tiniest criticism without getting defensive. 'Not entirely, no, but I do believe we should begin felling again —'

'I don't agree.'

'I'm telling you, we're missing out on a lucrative trade and we can't afford to. Let me set out some areas. I've got a few contacts, we can easily get back into it.' In fact, Carac had already made a start, but he thought it wise not to say so. Sometimes it was easier if Sir John didn't know everything.

'No. I intend to focus on my new lands.'

Damn the Earl of Devonshire. 'Will there be a bailiff for these new lands? Only there won't always be Simon and me. I'm not getting any younger, and one day he'll be on his own. It'll be too much for one man. That will mean you'll have to pay for someone else. Have you thought of that?'

'Don't worry. There's a bailiff, and I shall be meeting him when I visit. But before I do, I shall hold a large banquet to celebrate my new Knights Fees and invite the Earl of Devonshire.'

Joan was right. Carac shook his head. The man was exasperating. Was there nothing he could say to make him understand? 'Do you need to hold an expensive banquet?'

'God's teeth, Carac, will you stop thinking about money?' Sir John slammed his fist down on the table. 'Of course I need to hold a banquet! I have to honour the Earl's trust in me. Despite what you think of him, I happen to like the man. Through him, I am making

329

myself known to all the right people. People who matter. I always said I would make this the best estate in Devonshire, and I will, with or without you.' Sir John's eyes were cold and hard as he glared at him.

Carac could feel the heat rising up the back of his neck as he clenched his teeth. He rarely lost his temper, and he would not do so now. Consciously, he relaxed his jaw, took a long deep breath and ran his hand over the back of his neck.

'I am sorry you feel like that, John. I have no wish to fall out with you over this, but I would be failing in my duty if I wasn't honest with you.' He pursed his lips tightly, not wanting a row. He picked up Sir John's gauntlets and held them out to him. 'I think we both need time to reflect, but I beg you, don't do anything rash.'

Sir John stared at the gauntlets and back at Carac, astonishment written all over his face, then drained his wine.

'Come on, Richard,' he said, snatching the gauntlets and striding out of the hall.

Carac cursed himself. He should have handled it better. Sir John wouldn't reflect on anything; it just wasn't in his nature.

CHAPTER 52

Agnes brushed Joan's thick chestnut hair. Falling to her waist, it hung in thick luxurious waves. It was her best feature, and Joan would have liked to wear it that way, but it wouldn't be seemly on such an important occasion. She tried not to fidget while Agnes plaited two braids and coiled one over each ear, then curled the rest on top, leaving just a few strands to cascade down her back. Carefully, Agnes entwined spring flowers through her creation, stood back, smiled, and nodded.

Joan picked up the looking glass and turned her head this way and that. It was a marvellous thing, and whilst not as clear as looking in a still pond, she still loved it. It was a generous gift. Sir John had almost bounced into the bedchamber with a huge grin on his face, hiding it behind his back. Baby Thomas had been suckling at the time. She could feel the rhythm on her breast now: one, two, three, four, pause; one, two, three, four, pause.

She had fed him until her milk dried. He would have been just on his first summer by then. He hadn't been an attractive baby; he was small, pink, wrinkled and, if she were honest, rather ugly, but to her, he was the most beautiful child ever born. The moment Ellyn had put him in her arms, love had flooded through her with such force, she would have killed for him.

She'd never felt that with Richard.

Putting the glass down, Joan ran her hands over the delicate silk of her new dress. In the new fashion, it hugged her figure to a low waist with a thin cord tied loosely at her hips. She straightened the close-fitting sleeves and fingered the tiny buttons running down the front to her waist. Buttons! What a marvellous invention! No more standing while Agnes fiddled with laces at the back. She loved them.

Sir John came in, taking in her appearance with one sweeping glance from top to toe. 'The red suits you. Wear the rubies with it. This banquet is the most important I've given. There are guests here who have a lot of influence in this shire and beyond. We have to make a good impression.'

He was brusque because he was nervous. She knew that. He held out his new rich red jupon in front of him. 'Look at this. It's made from the finest cloth.'

'It's very nice,' Joan said, although she wasn't really interested. These banquets still bored her, and she would have to endure the Countess of Devonshire sitting next to her with her eternal gossip and talk of mundane topics. She doubted if the woman had anything in her head at all.

'It's such a shame Eleanor and the children can't come,' she said. 'They would so enjoy it. There's still time for them to get ready—'

'No. I'm not having that fool of a girl embarrass me at my own banquet.' Sir John picked up his new green hose.

'That's a bit harsh,' Joan protested. 'She's—'

'A girl in a woman's body. She can't even speak properly.'

Such were not suitable words for a maid's ears, as they would delight in spreading the gossip to anyone who would listen, and Joan glanced over her shoulder.

'Agnes, you can go.' As soon as she heard the maid's steps on the stairs, she lowered her voice and continued. 'It's not Eleanor's fault —'

'She's not coming and that's that. She can stay here and look after Thomas and Maria.'

Sir John never allowed them to these occasions, and Joan was always the one who had to soothe their disappointment with excuses and promises of next time. It wasn't fair. 'If you'd allow her to come for even part of it, she could sit with them. But it's just Richard again, I suppose.'

'What do mean just Richard again?' He pulled his white over-tunic over his head.

'You know what I mean. It's always just Richard. You never have any time for Thomas and Maria.' Joan fastened the jewelled necklace around her throat and looked in her glass. It wasn't right — the gold pendant would have looked much better — but she couldn't be bothered to argue.

'I could say the same about you. It's always Thomas and Maria.'

Joan slammed down the mirror. 'That's not true! I treat all my children the same!' Yet even as she said it, she wondered: did she?

'It's just as well I've taken care of Richard's interests, for he seldom enjoyed the attention of his mother, and I know how —'

'And you know how that feels? Tell me, what did happen all those years ago? Was it to do with Aldred's family? In all the years we've been married, you've never once said.'

Sir John stiffened, his jaw tightened and he turned to her with those cold eyes she was so familiar with. 'This is not the time, woman. Richard will be Lord of the Manor one day, and he needs to meet these people. Thomas does not.' He lowered his voice and leaned close. 'You do realise that some of these guests stand next to the king? That's what I want for Richard. Anyway, Thomas is nothing but a weakling, and Maria's a girl and too young.' He straightened his belt to ensure the large gold buckle was in the centre. 'Now, are you ready? We mustn't keep our guests waiting.'

'I'm ready.' And, fixing a broad smile on her face, Joan walked dutifully down the stairs to greet his guests waiting in the hall.

CHAPTER 53

As Carac had expected, he hadn't seen or heard from Sir John since his visit about the Knights Fees and had received no notice of the banquet. How could he do his job if he didn't know what was going on? It was intolerable. He had no choice but to make the first move.

Sir John had feigned surprise, saying of course Carac was invited, but Carac had seen that blustering before, and if he hadn't asked, he wasn't so sure he would have been. He had tried further conversation, but it was obvious Sir John had no intention of discussing anything with him.

So be it. He would have to keep informed in other ways.

He'd hoped to be seated next to the Earl of Devonshire, but annoyingly, Richard was between them. Well, he should be able to hear; the earl had a loud enough voice. Carac leaned forward and stole a glance. Every item of the earl's clothing was as immaculate as ever, and his ginger beard was even more severely trimmed this time. The laces on his cotehardie strained across his stomach — too much good living, no doubt — and his small green eyes darted everywhere. Clearly, the earl didn't miss much.

Glancing further along the table to Lady Joan and the countess at the far end, Carac caught her eye and nodded his respects. Poor Joan, having to listen to that woman's drivel all night. He switched his attention back to Sir John and the earl.

'Lord Courtesy—' Sir John turned to the earl.

'Frederick.'

Sir John puffed out his chest just as he had before. 'Frederick—'

Carac sighed.

'Ah, my favourite: roasted peacock.' The Earl closed his eyes dramatically as he breathed in the rich aroma of the dish placed before him.

No boar's head this time. Carac smiled to himself. He had to admit the bird looked magnificent placed on a gleaming silver dish, on a bed of roasted apples and carrots and adorned with a crest of three bright blue feathers and a luxurious tail of brilliant turquoise and green.

'Boy!' Sir John snapped his fingers. 'Wine for the earl!'

'French, I presume?'

'Of course, and only the best.'

Didn't he know it, Carac thought bitterly. Sir John had it delivered all the way from Plymouth at huge expense.

He kept watching. The earl tasted his wine, nodded in approval, and carefully dabbed the corners of his thin lips with his hand cloth.

'The Lady Joan is a credit to you, and you've done well here. But tell me, what do you intend to do with your new lands?'

'I haven't been able to see them yet, but I've some business in Exeter and will be visiting them next week.

I've been busy with—'

'Doesn't do to tarry! Make haste and talk to the bailiff. You'll find he's a good man.'

'Yes, I intend to. I thought I might...'

Curse those minstrels, they were drowning the conversation. Carac leaned forward a little and tried to concentrate.

'...And your Richard's a good lad. How old is he?' The earl eyed up the sugared fruit desserts.

'He's seven summers and can already hit the mark with an arrow at fifty paces,' Sir John boasted.

'One hundred paces,' Richard corrected him and puffed out his chest, in the manner of his father.

'Well, if you can do that, you have the makings of a real knight.' The earl bestowed a broad smile on the boy.

Richard glowed with pride and swung his legs vigorously back and forth under the table, kicking the legs. Carac hastily grabbed his wine before it could spill.

The earl paused and examined his goblet, turning it slowly in his hand. 'Tell you what: when the lad's a bit older, he must come and spend some time with me. Improve his education.' His foxy green eyes narrowed to slits as they fixed on the boy. 'We'll teach you how to be a real knight. You'd like that, wouldn't you?'

'On a horse? With armour and things?'

Now the wretched boy was bouncing in his seat, his hands on the table. Carac kept a tight hold on his goblet. It would be a shame to spill such good wine. He didn't trust the earl, but such procedures were usual in noble families. It might even do the boy some good.

'Yes, on a horse, with armour and things. I'll show you how to knock a man from his horse with a lance and how to use a mace,' the earl said.

That wasn't so good. The Chiddleighs had never been a fighting family, preferring to keep their heads out of politics and work their estates. Carac listened carefully.

'And can I go into battle?' Richard swung his arm from side to side as though he was already there.

'You're too young, Richard, and you need to learn the ways of the estate.'

Carac breathed a sigh of relief. For once, Sir John was thinking the same as him.

The earl waved his hand nonchalantly. 'Of course,' he said. 'But one day, young man, one day.'

The earl bent his head towards Sir John and lowered his voice to such an extent Carac couldn't hear. If only he could swap places with Richard, but that wasn't possible. He caught the odd word but frustratingly, couldn't make sense of it.

Sir John leaned back. 'Yes, yes, of course. Totally loyal, Frederick.'

The earl smiled. 'I knew I could rely on you.'

Carac raised his eyebrows. He didn't like the sound of that. What was that old fox up to?

CHAPTER 54

Annie twiddled her thumbs. Ellyn only had one visit to make and she should have been home by now. She couldn't just stand there, doing nothing. There was a pile of dried nettles needed sorting. She picked them up, and then shoved them irritably to one side. They could wait.

Where was Ellyn? She straightened the already straight jars on the shelf, then poked the embers in the hearth. Crossing her arms, she went outside and glanced along the path towards Will's old place but there was no sign of anyone. She turned left and walked a little way, hoping to see Ellyn's stocky form with her familiar rolling gait hurrying towards her, but no. It was no good, she couldn't put it off much longer.

Back inside, Annie returned to the nettles and furiously starting stripping their leaves into a pile for tonic and putting the stems to one side for twine. She was halfway through her task when she finally heard the sound she had been waiting for: the click of the door latch followed by the welcoming sight of Ellyn bustling in.

'Ellyn, at last! I've had word from the manor: Master Richard has a cough. Can you go?'

Ellyn blew out her cheeks. 'I would, lass, but Wini started this morning. She knows what she's about, this is her fourth and she's sure something's wrong. I'm just getting my things and I'm back out to her.' Ellyn spoke over her shoulder, grabbing jars and lotions and dropping them into her basket as she went. 'I'm sorry, but I've to make haste. You can see him, can't you?' Her words drifted after her as she threw open the door and hurried outside.

Of course she could, Annie thought. There was a time when she'd have leapt at the chance, but it was only a month since her row with Lady Joan, and she was still shaken. They'd both said dreadful things, but she had crossed the invisible line between their friendship and Joan, Lady of the Manor. Annie wished Joan had said something to her before. It might have saved the bad feeling between them.

There was nothing for it; she would have to go, and no matter how Joan behaved, she had her pride. Resigned, Annie searched along the shelf for the tincture of horehound and, draping her veil over her head and throwing a shawl around her shoulders, stepped outside to the first drops of another shower.

By the time she reached the manor, her shawl hung heavy and wet over her shoulders and water dripped from the ends of her veil. As she walked across the main hall, she shivered then cursed. It was the rain, nothing more.

Joan was sitting by the hearth with Thomas and Eleanor, who was cuddling Maria on her lap. They made a contented group. Richard sat apart from them on the floor, his legs crossed with his back turned towards his family. Nothing changed. It was nice to see that he was playing with the small wooden knight she'd given him for his fourth birth date. He thrust it forward, shouting 'Charge!' watching it fall on its side before picking it up and repeating the game.

Butterflies danced in Annie's stomach as they always did when she saw him. She couldn't resist a brief moment to watch her boy—no, not her boy; she wasn't allowed to think that anymore.

'Annie!' Eleanor beamed. 'Where have you been? We've m-missed you.'

'It's true, we have missed you, and it's good to see you. You're wet through! Put your shawl near the fire to dry and come and sit next to me.' Joan moved up to make space. 'We need to have a chat, but not now,' she whispered, nodding her head towards the others.

Joan seemed pleased to see her, but she'd made her position very clear that day and it still hurt.

'I think we've said more than enough to each other. I won't sit if you don't mind, my lady.' Annie dipped a prim curtsey and remained standing. 'How is Master Richard?'

'Still coughing.' Behind her hand, Joan whispered, 'and he's sulking because he can't go with Sir John on his visit to see the new lands. Richard, come over here, Annie's brought something to make your cough better.'

Joan was acting as though nothing had happened, but Annie thought that she couldn't have it both ways. Either she was the lady or she wasn't. She lifted her chin and remained standing.

Richard didn't move.

'Richard, come here, please,' Joan repeated.

His back still turned, Richard continued his game. 'I want a proper physician,' he demanded.

Was Joan going to let him talk to her like that? She should go over, give the boy a slap and make him do as he was told.

'I'm sorry,' Joan said. 'He's disappointed at not going with John. You go over and see if he'll take it.'

Annie crouched down next to him, her heart beating so loudly she was sure he could hear it. She loved his long eyelashes that curled over his deep brown eyes and the way his thick mop of hair waved and shone. He was beautiful and he was hers, and Joan was cruel to say otherwise.

He mustn't see her hurt, so she put on a bright smile. 'Master Richard, I'm here to help you. Look.' Trembling a little, she searched her basket and took out a small wooden spoon and an earthenware jar of cough tincture. 'This will help your cough. A small amount, two times a day and you'll feel much better.' She poured a dose into the spoon and offered it to him.

He eyed it suspiciously. 'How soon will it work?'

'Quite soon. Try some; it'll do you good.'

He frowned but took the medicine. His face creased into deep folds, his nose furrowed into wrinkles and his eyes closed as he spat it out all over her. 'That's disgusting!' he shouted, wiping his mouth with the back of his hand.

It was an excuse for Annie to put her arm around him, but he shrugged her off. 'Get away from me, you peasant! You're not a physician, you're a witch!' He looked at her as though she was a piece of dirt on his shoes, and something inside of her died right there. To him, that's all she was: a peasant.

'Richard! Apologise to Annie at once —'

'It's alright, really,' Annie said.

'What's going on? I could hear Richard from outside.' Sir John's long strides echoed across the hall.

'She's an evil witch and she's trying to poison me!' Richard pointed at Annie. 'It tasted foul, so I spat it out.'

'Annie was just giving Richard some tincture for his cough,' Joan explained. 'He's being very difficult because he can't go with you. Can you reason with him? He'll listen to you.'

Sir John stroked his beard thoughtfully. 'Richard,' he said at last. 'I'm as disappointed as you are that you can't come with me, but I've many miles to cover and need to ride hard. With that cough, you won't be able to keep up. The medicine's good for you. Won't you take some, for me?'

Annie cringed but bit her tongue. Were they frightened of the child? If only she could intervene and take a firm hand with him. That was all he needed.

'I don't want that stuff. It tastes horrible. I want to see a physician.' Richard's eyes were challenging. 'And I don't want her.' He pointed at Annie again.

'You're right, and you shall have a physician. I'll send word to Exeter. You can go.' Sir John dismissed Annie without even a glance.

'No, Annie, wait,' Joan interjected. 'I don't think you should give in to the boy, John. Annie's perfectly capable —'

His cold eyes turned to Annie, and he repeated his command, emphasising every word. 'I said that you can go.'

Angry and humiliated, Annie bobbed a curtsey and picked up her basket. Joan was flushed, her head turned slightly away. She was too embarrassed to look her in the eye. Once outside, Annie stood by the doors, put down her basket and fought back her tears.

'How could you do that? You can't let the boy dictate—' Joan's voice carried through the doors.

'The boy's right. He should have a proper physician, not some peasant healer with her potions.'

'Annie's not—'

'And as soon as you get back you'll tell me all about the lands and take me with you next time?' Annie couldn't mistake the note of triumph in the boy's voice as it rose over his mother's.

'Of course I will, son, but now I must take my leave. I'm not sure how long I shall be away. A few weeks perhaps, maybe more.'

Heavy footsteps approached the door. Flustered, Annie grabbed her basket and hurried across the yard. Her poor beautiful boy. What were they doing to him?

CHAPTER 55

Joan sat by the window, the bone needle threaded with red silk held idly in her hand, her unworked tapestry on her lap. What was happening to them? She and Sir John were distant, Annie was refusing to talk to her and Sir John was at odds with Carac. At least with Sir John gone, she had a chance to spend time with Richard on her own. It was as if Sir John were protecting the boy. From what? Her? Maybe he still thought her cold and unloving to his son.

If her feelings were so obvious to him, did Richard feel them too? That would be unbearable. Lord knew she had tried, but Richard had always been so...removed. Joan didn't understand why she found it so hard and had lived with the guilt every time she saw Annie, and even when she didn't. And Sir John's indulgence didn't help; it just made her out to be the hard unloving one in Richard's eyes. Well, she had two, maybe three weeks to put things right.

'I shall be a knight galloping into battle and charge right over the top of the hill to the old shepherd's hut. I bet you won't catch me!' Richard ran around the room, his arm outstretched holding an imaginary lance.

'Thomas is riding Mead. I'll have him on a leading rein, so there'll be no galloping.' Joan handed Thomas his boots and reached for her own.

Richard stopped, his face fell and changed to a pout.

'If you don't want to come, you can stay here with the girls,' Joan added, knowing he wouldn't.

They took the path through the woods towards the mill and stopped at the ford to let the ponies drink. Joan loved this spot. She liked to sit in the stillness and listen to the birds and watch the sunlight sparkle on the water, especially after she and Sir John had crossed words. It was one way she could regain her calm. Richard was behaving himself, and so far all was going well. Maybe she had been too hard on him.

She knew the path well. It led to the top of the hill and what she would always think of as Annie's log. She hadn't been there in years.

Halfway up, the path straightened and levelled out. With a mischievous grin over his shoulder, Richard dug both heels into his pony's sides and shot off at a gallop, leaning forward and swinging an imaginary mace.

'Charge! Take that, and that!' His voice trailed into the distance.

'Richard! Come back! I said no galloping!' Joan's words were lost in the thunder of hooves.

Star tossed her head and fidgeted, keen to follow and Mead pulled at the leading rein. Joan held on, but Thomas lost his balance, screamed, and hit the ground with a sickening thud. The leading rein slipped out of her hand, and she watched helplessly as Mead disappeared in a clattering of hooves and a cloud of dust up the path.

Thomas had landed on his back and was gasping for air. Joan threw herself out of the saddle. He was having one of his attacks.

'Sit up and lean forward. Deep slow breaths, remember?'

Thomas's face contorted as his chest heaved in the effort. Every time he had an attack, or a fit, as Sir John called it, as though Thomas were the village fool, Joan feared for his life and prayed he'd pull through.

Rubbing his back, she watched him wince with each hard-fought breath. Together, as Ellyn had told her, they counted each breath in and out until his breathing slowed to a gentle rhythm and the rattle of his rasps give way to gentle breaths.

Joan breathed out herself and sat back in relief. 'Thank you, God.'

Richard trotted nonchalantly back towards them, leading the now docile Mead with a grin on his face. Well, that was something.

'You cloth-head! You could have killed him!' Joan yelled.

'But I didn't, did I? Anyway, he'll get over it.'

Joan was beyond words. The morning spoiled, they made their way home in silence. Richard hummed to himself. He was showing her he didn't care, which he probably didn't. He was mimicking Sir John's behaviour to his peasants, and that was a worrying thought.

Richard slammed the door behind him and stormed across the hall like a raging bull.

'Where's Dart? I want to go riding!'

Slowly and deliberately, Joan continued her stitching. She

didn't look up, even though he was standing so close she could feel his breath on her cheek. 'He has been turned out to the far fields, on my orders,' she said, breaking the thread with her teeth.

'You've no right —'

She looked up at him. 'On the contrary, Richard, I have every right. I told you, your punishment would be no more riding or going out on your own for the rest of the week.' She selected a new thread.

'You're just my mother,' he spat. 'You wait till Papa gets back and I tell him what you've done.'

And when he did, she'd have a few things to say as well.

It was the beginning of a difficult few weeks. No matter what she did, Richard challenged her and was belligerent when she refused to back down. Joan tried to include him, but he simply turned his back and played with his toy knight. It was like when he was a baby and wouldn't suckle; he didn't want her. And, just like then, she screamed inside with frustration and hurt.

One day, when the children were reciting the Pater Noster, something they heard every Sunday in church, Richard stumbled over his words. Eleanor laughed, Maria giggled behind her hands and Thomas finished the prayer for him, word perfect. Richard stomped off to the corner of the hall, turned his back and refused to speak to any of them again for the rest of the day.

And things got worse as he sought his revenge. He pinched Maria until she cried and then denied ever touching her. He taunted Eleanor until she lost her temper and enraged her even more by mocking her stutter. And he bragged to Thomas about his skills in archery, riding, and sports, mimicking his brother's fits and calling him a girl and a weakling.

No matter how many times Joan stood her ground, Richard always defied her and found a way to create tension within the group. By the time the physician arrived at the start of the second week, she was almost at the end of her tether.

The physician, a round, balding little man of few words, looked into Richard's mouth. He peered down his throat and stated that no amount of tincture would help.

'The boy needs to be bled,' he declared. 'The bad humours have to come out. I'll do it in the upstairs bedchamber.'

They watched the physician climb the stairs, ceremoniously carrying a large bowl, a cloth and a knife in his hands. Richard followed with a defiant look on his face, but he didn't fool Joan. She could see the fear in his eyes as he paused and gripped the post at the foot of the stairs.

In the hall, they waited. There was a long period of silence, and then they heard deep heartfelt sobs. The children nudged each other and grinned.

Later, the physician trod heavily back down the stairs, his bowl covered with the blood-stained cloth and a bloodied knife in his hands. Richard was to stay in bed for the whole of the following day. The children's faces lit up and, secretly, so did Joan's.

Thomas and Maria were to spend the day with Cook. They would have a wonderful time getting their hands into sticky dough and licking their fingers after making honeyed fruit, giving her a peaceful day out with Eleanor. It would be a chance to unwind.

Not wishing to waste a moment, Joan and Eleanor set out early next morning and strolled to the river where the bank was shallow and they could dangle their feet into the water. Joan watched the first skylarks spiralling upwards until they were tiny black dots in the blue sky, which disappeared and left only their sweet trilling song behind, and her spirits rose with them.

When the midday sun was overhead, Eleanor insisted on unpacking the food, her pink cheeks shining with childish delight as she untied the willow twine and unfolded each neatly wrapped cloth parcel. Her smile grew as each revealed its tempting contents; hunks of bread, a block of goat's cheese, a slice or two of salted ham, apples, some of Cook's pickled beans and—yes, Cook had remembered her favourite oatie cakes.

Later, when the empty wrappings lay strewn across the grass, Eleanor leaned back on her arms and watched the clouds lazily sail across the sky.

'That was the best p-picnic ever, J-Jay,'

Joan agreed and, closing her eyes, lay next to her, basking in the peace and warmth of the sunshine. She hadn't realised how tired she was and dozed off until the sound of approaching hooves caused her to lazily open her eyes. A large chestnut horse was ambling towards them. The rider, whoever he was, was obviously in no haste. As he approached, she recognised him and waved.

'Carac! What brings you this way?'

'Lady Joan. Eleanor.' Carac removed his cap and nodded. 'I'm on my way to the high fields to see if the men can start harrowing. The wet winter has saturated the lower lands and we can't get the ploughs through. The men have started breaking the clods of soil with

350

mallets, but it's slow work,' he said, dismounting his horse.

Eleanor jumped up and shook out her skirts. 'I'll hold him. He's lovely. What's his name?'

'He's called Victor. You can let him graze over there if you like,' he said, handing her the reins.

She stroked the horse along his light brown neck. 'C-come on Victor, have some of this nice grass.'

'Sit down, Carac.' Joan patted the grass. 'It's so beautiful here.'

'Are Thomas and Maria not with you?'

'We left them behind. Causing chaos in the kitchen, I expect.' Joan shook the cider jar. 'There's a little left; would you like some?'

'No, thanks. I trust you are all well?'

Joan bit her bottom lip then drank the last of the cider. 'Carac, can I talk to you for a moment?'

'Of course.' He settled down, his elbows resting his knees. 'The scarlet dye still proving difficult?'

'Yes, and I miss Annie in the dye shed, but it's Richard I want to talk about. He's at home while John's visiting his new lands, and he's being so difficult. I've tried everything I can think of, but I feel as though I've won the battle but not the war. John has spoilt him from the day he was born. He denies him nothing, and I hate to say this but he's turned his son into a nasty, selfish little bully. Folks are talking. They don't like Richard, you know.' She didn't add that neither did she. 'John's obsessed with the boy. He can't or won't admit to what his son has become or what he might grow into. If something isn't done soon, it will be too late. Richard will be lord of all this one day, and right now, I dread to think what sort of a lord he will be. I'm not sure what more I can do. I've tried talking to John but he won't listen. And he's letting things slip. Take those carp ponds, for example; they should have been finished weeks ago. He's so full of being with Richard, improving his status and being with the people that matter, that—oh I don't know! It's like he's blind to what's happening under his nose.'

It was true, and nothing she said or did seemed to make any difference. Sir John didn't even notice her these days. She had fulfilled her duty by giving him an heir, and she suspected that was all he had ever really wanted from her. Sometimes, particularly when she spoke to him of Richard's manner, Sir John's eyes became cold and hard, like that time with the blacksmith's son and the stone. After hearing Annie's story, Joan had mentioned it to Sir John, but he refused to believe his son was anything but perfect.

He didn't listen to her anymore—no, it was more than that, he didn't care what she thought. From the beginning, he'd never been exactly warm towards her, but he had listened sometimes. Now he only had two aims in life: Richard and raising his status amongst the nobility, and she didn't feature in either.

Joan sighed. She felt better for talking, and Carac was such a good listener. She should have asked for his advice earlier.

'It is not for me to tell you or John how to raise your son. However, I can appreciate your concerns. How old is Master Richard? Six or seven?' he asked.

'He's seven summers.'

'Then have you considered sending him to school?'

'John and I haven't actually discussed it, but I always assumed Richard would go some time.' Joan tilted her head to one side. 'You might have something there.'

Dear, wise Carac; he always knew what to do. 'It will do John good too. Maybe get his mind back to things that matter. And people,' she added softly.

Carac smiled sagaciously. 'At the banquet with the Earl of Devonshire, did you happen to hear any of his conversation with John?'

'No, I had the high-and-mighty countess to entertain. A more tedious woman I have never met. Why?'

'Oh, nothing. I just wondered.'

Walking back later that afternoon, Joan thought about her conversation with Carac. It made sense. It would be good for Richard to be with other boys and away from Sir John, and a bit of school discipline wouldn't do him any harm.

Her mind wandered to Thomas. He was the image of his father with his fair hair, blue/green eyes, and slender build. He wouldn't be as tall. She prayed that he would grow out of his breathless attacks. They stopped him from doing so many things. Then again, Thomas was very clever. He was only five but remembered perfectly after hearing things only once and picked up on details. He was always asking why or how until she ran out of answers; Richard had never done that. And whereas Richard was thick-set and always full of aggressive energy, Thomas was quieter and gentle. One was so petulant, the other so affable. Richard confounded her whereas Thomas amazed her.

The rain rattled against the shutters of the main hall. Joan sat by the hearth watching the flames flickering into the cavernous mouth of the chimney. Sir John had been away for nearly three weeks. Surely it wouldn't take him all that time to see the new lands and speak to the bailiff. What else was he doing? She never knew where he was or when he would be back, and it was getting very annoying. When he did come home, she would ask after his travels but he would be non-committal. Was he hiding something?

She turned her attention to Eleanor and Maria, who were sitting on a bench near the window, their heads bent close together. Eleanor was teaching Maria to sew. That was something Eleanor could do well. She had endless patience, unlike Joan, and her stitches were so neat and tiny. She was good with Maria too and would have made a wonderful mother. What a pity it would never happen.

Thomas was arranging wooden cubes one on top of the other to make a tower. Richard was playing with his toy knight in his usual place, sitting on the floor with his legs crossed and his back to them. For once, all was quiet.

Thomas's tower crashed to the floor, clattering blocks everywhere and smashing her peace. Whether it was the furtive glance Richard shot over his shoulder or the way he quickly tucked his leg back under him, Joan was sure he had done it deliberately.

The girls bent their heads back to their stitching. Thomas picked up a cube and diligently started to rebuild his tower. Peace was restored.

Thomas placed the third cube on the top of his tower. 'You blubbed,' he said quietly, picking up another cube. 'You said you would be a knight one day. Knights don't blub.' Carefully, he balanced his cube on top of the others.

Richard held his knight in mid-air. 'I did not blub!'

'Yes, you did,' Maria piped up. 'When you were upstairs with the physician, we all heard you. Didn't we, Elly?'

Eleanor nodded. 'Yes, we did.'

Richard threw his toy across the floor and spun round to face them, his face black as thunder. 'I did not blub and I will be a knight one day. The Earl of Devonshire said so.'

'Richard, calm down,' Joan said. 'Let's all of us just forget it.'

But Thomas wasn't finished. 'We all know the truth; you're just a crybaby!' he taunted.

Richard's rage erupted like a volcano and, roaring, he threw himself on Thomas. Before Joan knew it, they were wrestling across the floor in a tangle of flailing arms and legs.

'Richard! Thomas! Stop that at once.' She leapt from her seat as Eleanor screamed and Maria wailed, her eyes wide in horror.

A stray ankle shot out of the melee. Joan grabbed it with both hands and dodging the flying limbs, pulled as hard as she could.

'Stop it, you two!' A foot lashed out, catching her on the chin. 'God's bones!' She gritted her teeth and clung on. Slowly, the ankle unravelled itself from out of the chaos, followed by the knee and the rest of the leg. Taking a fistful of red tunic, she dragged its owner clear. It was Thomas.

Straightening up, Joan blew out a long breath, sending a wisp of hair off her face. She wiped her brow with the back of her sleeve and rubbed her chin, checking her hand for blood. There was none.

'Girls, be quiet!' she yelled. 'Richard, how could you?'

'He called me a coward.' Richard's eyes challenged her as he thrust an accusing finger at Thomas.

'I don't want to hear it. Thomas, are you hurt?'

Sulking, Richard stomped back to his usual place as Joan sat Thomas on her lap and checked him over. No cuts or bumps and, thank God, he was only out of breath and not having an attack. She held him for a while, her face close to his.

'Eleanor, take Maria and Thomas outside, now. Not you, Richard. You stay here.'

She waited for them to leave. 'Come over here, Richard,' she said gently, offering her hand.

He stared at her but didn't move.

'Why? Why do you do it? Thomas wasn't doing anything to you.'

'He said I'll never be a knight, and I will. I'll show you!'

'You're much bigger than he is. You could have hurt him. You know that, don't you?'

He didn't flinch, his eyes holding hers.

'You're constantly disruptive. Do you enjoy upsetting people? I've heard tales of your manner in the village and elsewhere too. You have to learn to think of others.'

'Why should I? They're just peasants. They don't count.' His mouth twisted into a sneer.

That was what Sir John said, and he was wrong. Peasants like Annie did count. They had feelings just like them, but Joan could never make him see that. God knew, she'd tried and failed enough times.

'You deliberately knocked down Thomas's tower, didn't you?'

Richard smirked. How that smirk always riled her. It made her want to slap it off his face, but she bit her lip.

Annie said Richard needed cuddles, so she held her out hands, her voice soft, almost imploring. 'Richard, please come here. I'm trying to help you.'

He didn't move.

'I'm your Mama and I love you.'

The smirk faded, he lowered his eyes, and to her surprise, his chin began to wobble. He tightened his mouth hard to fight it.

'Come on, come here.' She opened her arms to him.

He took a hesitant step towards her and another. Maybe this was the turning point. Maybe she had reached him at last. Joan kept her arms open and smiled.

He stopped. His head shot up, his eyes piercing and tearful.

'I hate you!' he screamed. 'I hate you, I hate you, I hate you!'

CHAPTER 56

Annie may have been just a peasant to Richard, but he was still her boy. Others had refused to take the horehound medicine too. She would make a new recipe, one with a better taste, one he would like. After days of pounding, mixing and tasting, she came up with a syrup of horehound, angelica and rose, with just a little honey to sweeten. Ellyn liked it and John Forge said it was an improvement, so with high hopes, she set off to Court Barton with a jar of the new tincture for Richard. She wouldn't stay. She'd just give it to Lady Joan and leave.

Being in no hurry, she savoured the afternoon sun on her face as she ambled along, humming to herself and gently swinging her basket in rhythm with her steps. When she arrived at Court Barton, the shutters were open and she could hear Sir John's and Lady Joan's raised voices coming from inside.

Annie knocked and waited. No one came, so she knocked again. Still no one answered.

Opening the door just a crack, she peeped in. The hall was empty, so she stepped inside. The voices were coming from the upstairs bedchamber. Annie tiptoed to the bottom of the stairs and hesitated, her hand on the post. She couldn't intrude. She'd leave the tincture on the table for Lady Joan to find, but the voices were getting louder and she could hear every word.

'John, I'm telling you. The past weeks have been a devil's dream. That boy is out of control—'

Part of Annie wanted to leave, but the temptation was too great. She listened, one hand still on the post.

'From what you've said, I think it's you that has the problem,' Sir John answered. 'I don't have any trouble controlling him—'

'That's because you don't control him! You simply give into him! You've spoiled him, John. It's not me who has the problem, it's you!' Her voice was higher and louder, and Annie could imagine Joan standing with her hands on her hips and her chin lifted high.

But what Joan said was only partly true; she gave into Richard as well.

'You've always had a problem with him from the moment he was born. You can't deny it. It's a good job I did step in, because you were never a mother to him. And a boy needs his mother,' Sir John added, his voice less abrasive.

Annie winced, knowing how much Joan would be hurt by Sir John's cruel words.

The voices fell silent. Part of her wanted to rush up the stairs and tell Sir John what a cold heartless brute he was, but she daren't.

'Maybe we should think about sending Richard to school,' said Joan. 'He is seven, after all, and it would do him good to mix with other boys.'

Annie's knuckles whitened on the post. Joan wanted to send her boy away. She wouldn't. She couldn't!

Richard was too young, and how would she cope not seeing him? Annie listened harder, straining her ears.

'One day, I shall send him to school,' Sir John agreed. 'He will need to be educated to hold his place in society. But for now, I need him here to learn more about the estate, especially now I have extra land.'

'When will you send him?' Joan demanded.

'Maybe in a year or so. You know as well as I do that I've spent years building this place up and making connections with influential people. I'm now accepted in the Earl of Devonshire's circle, and I need Richard with me, to make sure he's known. One day, Richard will rub shoulders with King Edward III, no less.'

Annie heaved a long sigh of relief. For once she agreed with Sir John. It was far too early to send her boy away.

'That's all that matters to you now, isn't it, John?' Joan said, her voice rising again. 'Money, Richard, and rubbing shoulders with the King. You can't see beyond that. We never talk or ride out as we used to. You've no time for your other son, Thomas, who is desperate for your attention. And as for Maria, I don't think you know she even exists.'

'Not this again. You know my opinion of Thomas, Joan: he'll never be of any use to me. He's weak and feeble, he has one of his fits every time he sits on a horse, and he lives in some sort of a dream world—'

Joan was shouting again now. 'Don't you dare speak like that about Thomas! He's a beautiful, kind and clever boy. You don't know him, and all the time you're besotted with that spoilt son of yours, you never will. And as for the estate, you spend so much time with your precious Richard, you're neglecting things. Carac was only saying the other day—'

'Ah, now I understand where all this is coming from! You and Carac have been talking behind my back and turning the knife, I'll wager. I bet it was his idea to send Richard to school.'

'He may have mentioned it,' Joan said, 'but we weren't talking behind your back. We're concerned. No, more than that; we're worried. We've lost most of the large timber trade, and the estate is now so reliant on the extra sheep for the mill that one more bad harvest means we won't have enough grain to feed the sheep or money to pay all the hired men. No one is beyond the will of God, John. Not even you.'

'Will of God or not, I am lord here. Richard is not going to school and that's an end to it. What I do with my son and my estate is my business, and what you do with Thomas and Maria is yours. Good day!'

Annie could hear the boards creaking as he stormed across the room. She'd no wish to meet with her lord's anger again, but she'd never reach the door in time. Casting around, she saw there was nowhere to hide and flattened herself against the wall as he stamped down the stairs. Annie held her breath as he passed her, so close that she could see the veins on his neck standing out like blue rope. He marched down the hall and slammed the door behind him.

For a moment, she didn't dare move in case he came back. She should have left right at the beginning, and then she'd never have heard. She had no idea things were so strained between Sir John and Joan. Their lives were founded on a single lie, a lie that Sir John had unwittingly created by taking Richard. It was tearing them apart, and she had allowed it to happen.

CHAPTER 57

April 1340

Annie shivered and pulled her shawl around her. It was still early. Passing the communal fields, she nodded to Mark and Luke, Ellyn's boys, who were working on clearing the ditches. Walking on, she waved to Isobel's husband, Cedric, where he was working the oxen and plough through the red soil in the opposite field. Two goaders walked ahead, keeping the furrow straight and leading the oxen on long ropes. God had been kind, giving them a warm spring, and soon they would start sowing the corn.

Quickening her pace, Annie tutted at herself and then smiled. She was too busy for this, but she didn't want to miss him. It was all such nonsense, parading the boy through the village as though he were already the Lord of the Manor; not that he wouldn't enjoy it, of course. Now that she wasn't visiting the manor, she only caught a few precious glimpses of him as she made her visits to folks.

Her boy was growing up fast. It was hard to believe he was nine summers and off to school. He'd be back later in the year and by then he would have grown some more. She wondered if she'd recognise him, but that was being a cloth-head; she'd always know him.

Reaching the village, she passed the pillory. Rodin stood miserably with his neck and hands held in the wooden bars, his hair shorn like a sheep. No doubt he'd been caught by the ale tasters again for adding sugar or something worse to the ale. Last time, he'd been fined a penny. She shook her head at his folly. There would be no certificate of quality or sprig of evergreen to hang over his inn door.

Annie pushed her way through the clusters of folks lining the track just as Sir John had ordered. They huddled in groups, stamping their feet and swinging their arms, their breaths freezing the cold air in silver plumes before melting in front of them. They didn't want to be there, and it showed on their long faces. They didn't have time to waste on their lord's whim; they needed to make the most of the daylight, for there was ploughing to finish, manure to spread on the fields and lambs to be born.

Janet and William were standing by the ford with Mary, Geoffrey and their daughter, little Rose. She was a pretty thing with the same wiry curls as Mary and big blue eyes like her father. If Annie had a daughter, she'd want her to look like that.

She sometimes wondered what would have happened if Richard had been a girl. She wouldn't be standing here waiting for him to be paraded off to school, that was for sure.

'Hail, how go things at the forge and the mill?' Annie crouched down and gave Rose a hug. 'You're taller every time I see you. How old are you now?'

Rose counted out her fingers and proudly held up one hand and the thumb of the other. 'Six! Do you like my daisies?' she said, proudly holding up a wilting daisy chain.

Annie laughed, 'Yes, I do! And how are you, William?'

William shuffled his feet in the dirt and mumbled something she couldn't make out.

'The children are bored waiting,' said Mary, looking hopefully down the lane.

'They're not the only ones,' Geoffrey muttered under his breath. 'I've loaves in the bread ovens. If Sir John and his precious son don't arrive soon, they'll burn.'

'Peter not with you?' Annie asked Janet.

Janet shook her head. 'No, he stayed in the forge. He says that he's got far more important things to do than take off his cap to the likes of them, and I won't tell you what he called Richard. He said the most Sir John will get out of him is a quick poke of his head over the door as they go past. I wish they would hurry up and then we can all get on.' She rubbed her hands together and tucked them under her shawl. 'It's cold this morning.'

'I'm sure they won't be long,' Annie said. 'And Richard's not all bad —'

Geoffrey raised his eyebrows. 'Well, if you believe that, you're the only one who does. Everyone knows what a nasty little knave he is. I'm pleased he's going away. The whole estate will be a better place without him.'

'Geoffrey! You shouldn't say such things,' said Mary.

Annie sighed. She heard such words from a lot of the folks she visited. 'He's only a boy. I'm sure he'll grow out of it —'

'Are you? I'm not. There's bad blood in them Chiddleighs. Look at old Sir James's brother, Boren, and his sons. Nothing but cheats and thieves. And that Aldred got what was coming to him.' Geoffrey folded his arms and nodded, satisfied with his conviction.

'I don't think Master Richard is a thief,' said Mary.

'Not yet, but come to think of it, Richard does look a bit like Aldred. You mark my words, there's bad blood in him.' Geoffrey nodded again as if to prove his point.

Annie went cold. Just the sound of Aldred's name made her shudder. Geoffrey was right though. Sometimes, particularly when he had that menacing sneer on his face, her boy looked just like Aldred. She didn't like to admit it, but now someone else had seen it.

'You're wrong! Master Richard doesn't look a bit like Aldred. He's young and a bit head-strong, that's all.' The force in her voice surprised her and she picked up her basket, flustered now. 'I've just spotted Isobel, I need to see her.' She fled, hearing their voices behind her.

'Honestly, now see what you've done!' said Mary.

'Just speaking the truth,' Geoffrey replied. 'Anyway, I don't see why she should take on so.'

CHAPTER 58

At Court Barton, two lads heaved three trunks on to the wagon. Joan watched Richard swagger across the cobbles and climb up to sit next to the driver. He was scowling and sat dead still, as though awaiting his fate.

She stepped back a little from the window. No emotional Goodbyes, no hug for his mother. It was as she expected, but a small part of her deep inside had still hoped. Ever since that day when he'd screamed that he hated her, he'd kept his distance.

Earlier, she'd gone up to see him especially, thinking they could have a chat and part with a kind word, but he'd pushed past her and she'd lost her chance. She could have ordered him to come back, but he probably wouldn't have listened. Even if he had, she didn't want to hear his disdain or see the look of loathing on his face that she'd come to expect.

The hardest thing to cope with was not understanding why, or in truth, not being able to admit it. Hadn't she done her best to hide her guilt and treat him like the others? But she didn't feel the same towards him; she never had. The boy was getting older. Surely he didn't sense her inner feelings? She couldn't bear that.

Sometimes, she thought that Sir John was deliberately turning Richard against her, but he didn't need to. Whatever he was, Richard followed. That was all it was. Richard would come back from school in the summer and things would be better.

A lad led Baron from the stables. The horse's glossy black coat shone in the light, and his leather saddle gleamed. Sir John mounted the horse and gathered his reins. He was still as handsome as ever.

The driver flicked his whip. The horse leaned forward into his collar and the heavy solid wheels rumbled forward.

'When will you be back?' Joan called down.

'I have no idea,' Sir John answered. 'I've some business in Exeter.'

'Carac wants to see you. What shall I tell him?'

'Tell him he can wait.' Sir John turned and trotted to catch up with the disappearing wagon.

Joan watched them leave the yard, turn left on the path that led to the village, and go round the bend out of sight. It would have been nice if Sir John had said something to her; asked her how she felt about Richard leaving or even given her a clue about his feelings. He hadn't, of course, but he wasn't happy. She could tell that by the terseness of his voice, the hard set of his jaw and the way he over-enthused with Richard about how much fun he would have with the other boys, and how he would be home for the summer before he knew it.

Well, the boy was away, and now was their chance to close the gap that still divided them.

Thomas tugged her sleeve. 'Has he gone?'

'Yes,' she said softly. 'They both have.'

'Good. Now I can do archery.' Thomas grinned. 'And I shall use his bow.'

'Good idea,' she said, ruffling his hair. 'That's a very good idea.'

CHAPTER 59

'Hail! Has Sir John returned from Exeter?' Carac covered the cobbled yard in a few long strides, his face breaking into a hopeful smile.

'Hail. I'm sorry, no.' Joan leaned on the edge of the stone water trough and shook her head.

Not again! Carac thought. Sir John was more than a little irritating, but he always enjoyed spending time with Joan. He felt younger when he was with her.

'This is too much! He knows I want to speak with him. When will he be home; do you know?'

'I don't. He never tells me anything these days. He just said he had business to attend to after he'd taken Richard to school. Do you know what he meant?' Joan plunged her hands into the water, grimaced at the coldness, and began washing her hands vigorously.

'Indeed I do not. It seems he takes neither of us into his confidence.' Carac perched wearily on the edge of the trough. He sighed. It was always the same these days, and he was tired of it. Not physically tired but dispirited was a better word. Judging by the tiredness around Joan's eyes, she was feeling the same. She was a fine woman and deserved better. Carac had an overwhelming sense of wanting to say as much, but he knew it wouldn't do.

He glanced down at his clothes. Tutting to himself, he straightened his over-tunic and stroked his beard. It needed a trim. Whatever must she think? He must keep himself together.

Joan examined her hands and sat next to him, wiping them dry with the bottom of her apron, making pale streaks of red on the white linen.

'You look troubled, Carac. Can I help?'

She had lovely hands; not particularly graceful but good, honest hands. He liked that in a woman. Carac pushed the thought aside. He shouldn't speak of Sir John behind his back, it wasn't worthy of him, but he had to know what was going on. Else how could he keep the affairs in order and, more importantly, keep an eye on the coffers?

'Maybe you can,' he said at length. 'John is avoiding me. It's been two years since we quarrelled over his new lands from the earl and, since that day, he has been...how shall I say, reticent? He seldom visits and tells me little or nothing. I did take it upon myself to visit the new lands and speak with the bailiff. In fact, I have been twice. I first visited about six months after John's acquisition. The bailiff is a good man but knew little more than I. The only fact I gleaned at that time was that John was planning to farm rabbits.'

'Rabbits?' Joan echoed. 'That's the first I've heard of it. Why would he want to do that?'

So she knew even less than he did. 'I believe there is a high demand for their meat and fur amongst the wealthiest. It is the latest fashion.' Carac raised his eyebrows at the folly of such people.

'Then I'm surprised that meat hasn't appeared on our table. You said you visited twice? When did you go again?'

'Just a few months ago. I was astounded by the size of the venture. There are acres and acres of it. The entire area is enclosed by huge boundary banks about six feet high and twenty feet wide, and along the top of them he's planted hundreds of gorse bushes, presumably to keep the rabbits in and poachers out. Then there's another large area with numerous mounds of earth where I saw a lot of young rabbits running around, so I assume those are the breeding warrens. It must have cost a fortune to build.'

'If it's that's big, he must be making lots of money.'

'If he is, I don't know where it's going. Do you know what he's up to?' he said.

'I'm sorry. As I said, he says little to me. He does seem very preoccupied though. I think it's because Richard's away. He must be missing him.'

'Indeed, although I do believe sending him to school was the best thing for all of us.' He smiled sagely and felt the tiniest of jolts when she smiled back.

Joan dropped her gaze to the ground. 'I had hoped to see more of John, but if anything, I see less. I've no more of an idea than you do, I'm afraid.'

He riled at the sadness in her and fought the impulse to hold her and let her cry on his shoulder. He was being ridiculous; a man of his age! Better to return to the matters in hand. 'My real difficulty is that John won't talk to me. As a result, I cannot keep my records and accounts accurate. I have no true idea of how the estate stands financially, and I suspect that neither does he,' he said.

'That's not good.'

'Indeed, it is not. The last two years were wet, and the harvests were poor. We need corn driers. On the few

371

occasions when we have spoken, I have said as much, but he won't listen. He says he can't afford it.'

Joan frowned. 'I don't understand. Despite the disappointing years, I assumed the coffers were full. Our first batch of red cloth sold well, which helped, and I'm sure we can do even better.'

He liked her spirit. 'The sales were most encouraging. When he does return, please ensure he understands my urgency to speak with him. Best not to mention why, or I'll never see him.' Carac didn't hold out any hope and, regrettably, was beginning to lose the will to care. It was maddening!

Frustrating as it was, he could do no more for now, so he got to his feet.

'I understand,' Joan said. 'Truly I do, and I will tell him. But before you go, let me show you my new dyeing sheds. I'm rather proud of them.'

Her eyes shone with enthusiasm. Joan was no fool, Carac admired that, and she was genuine. There were no cat-and-mouse games with her, and it was heartening to see someone still passionate about something. It would be a pleasure to spend more time in her company.

Carac followed her into a long open shed behind the stables. A mixture of various smells hit his senses, not least that of urine. He winced and held his kerchief to his nose.

'It is a bit strong.' Joan laughed; such a beguiling laugh! 'They've just finished adding it to the latest batch of dye. We use it to fix the colour. You get used to it.'

Carac, whose eyes were now watering, doubted that very much.

In a line down the middle of the shed were six large open-topped tun barrels. Along the back wall, row upon row of hazel drying poles were suspended from the beams by willow twine and draped with panels of cloths in various shades of red. On one side, crude wooden trestles bowed under the weight of bowls and containers of all sizes filled with a variety of powders. Smaller pails and tubs lie scattered around the shed.

Carac was impressed. A lot had been happening since his last visit.

'Look at this,' she said proudly, reaching up to one of the poles and carefully pulling down a rectangle of cloth.

She draped it over her arms. Carac couldn't help noticing her milky white skin. 'This is the closest I've got to scarlet so far.' Carefully she laid it down and he switched his attention to the cloth. 'It takes ages to remove the stain. I believe it will hold to the cloth and not fade. It's still a little wet, but I shall know for certain when it dries.'

'It is a remarkable colour. Forgive me if I don't touch it. It wouldn't do if my fingers were to leave red stains over my parchments.'

'Carac, you do make me smile.'

He knew that many saw him as over-particular, but no matter; standards should be maintained. He tore his eyes away from her and gave an almost indiscernible nod. Inside, he was childishly pleased at her approval. 'How have you achieved such a colour?'

'The main source for red dye is the madder herb. That's well known. It's one of the difficulties because we use the roots and can only harvest them once a year. A bad year means poor roots. Then, of course, we have to replace those plants and wait for the new ones to grow big enough to use. I have areas of them growing in various stages behind the orchards.'

'If you are to proceed seriously with this red dye, I presume you will need more land to grow more plants?'

'Yes. John can't see it. He's never taken this project seriously.' Joan shrugged.

Carac shook his head. If only Sir John would take an interest in his lady and see her potential.

'Why so cross?' she asked.

'Not cross, merely frustrated.'

Joan had done well, working entirely on her own for years. When her ideas didn't work, she simply tried again with even more determination. She deserved to succeed, and if she wasn't getting any encouragement from Sir John, she'd get it from him.

'Leave it to me, I will make some labour available to you. Just tell the men what you need doing.'

'Thank you. With your support, I don't feel I'm doing all this for nothing. I am grateful, truly I am.' She put her hand on his arm.

Carac swallowed. 'I'm pleased to be of assistance. If you need anything, anything at all, I will always be here.' Awkwardly, he felt around the inside of his collar. 'Tell me, how do you use the roots once you've harvested them?'

'Come with me.' Joan led him to the first of the line of tun barrels. 'We put the roots in here and boil them in water until they turn to pulp. Then we strain the pulp through these wooden sieves.' She moved on to the next barrel. 'Then we add alum if I can get it, but I've found a moss from the moor that works equally well. It took me months to discover that and learn how much to use. In the beginning, I was adding too much and the cloth went sticky. We boil it together in limewater.' She spoke quickly, her voice full of enthusiasm.

'In this barrel, we do the exciting bit. This is where I add other ingredients to get different shades of red. Some woods, like brazilwood, are good, but again, they're difficult to get and expensive. I tried sycamore but it was a poor substitute. A black dye will give a darker red, and the berries from the mulberry tree make a purple-red. But this,' she turned around and lifted a heavy bucket on to the trestle. 'This is magic.'

She put in her hand and lifted it high, letting grains of fine red soil fall through her fingers. Her face was bright with excitement and proudly she broke into a broad grin. 'Good Devonshire red soil. The answer was here under my feet all the time. It was the women, you see. After they'd pulled the madder, their hands and aprons were stained red, not from the roots but from the soil. They were always complaining they couldn't get rid of it, and that made me think. If the red from the soil didn't wash from their hands and aprons, wouldn't it stain our cloth? I don't understand why it works, but it seems to.

'The women sieve the soil until it is really fine, and then add it to the final barrel, boil it, and strain. The scarlet I showed you comes from months of trying different amounts of soil and madder. We now have a dye for red scarlet, and that is the colour that will sell best. I'm sure of it. I have to wait to see how it dries and stands up to weather but I am hopeful, I really am.'

Her cheeks were flushed as red as her soil and there was a liveliness about her. She reminded him of the day all those years ago when, as the new and innocent Lady of the Manor, she had sat at his table for the first time and shown such interest and enthusiasm for his and Sir John's plans.

'You have done well. I congratulate you.'

'We'll need to produce more of this scarlet cloth and get the Guild seal. We shall be known for this cloth. I thought I'd call it Chiddleigh Red Scarlet, what do you think?'

He hated to disappoint her. 'A fine name, but I don't think it will be possible for you to get into the Guild.'

She frowned, 'Whyever not? It will prove our standard and give buyers confidence. Without it, we shall be at a distinct disadvantage.'

There was no nice way to say it. 'They don't allow women.' Carac shrugged apologetically.

'So what you're saying is that if Sir John had done all this, and not me, we would get the seal?'

'Indeed. Without it, you can still sell at the markets but not in the town, and you can't give it a name or display the seal of course.'

She sat down heavily. 'After all my work, it's not fair. There must be a way.'

He felt for her. After all her efforts, she deserved the reward of the seal. 'Leave it with me.'

It would do him good to dwell on a worthier cause than Sir John.

CHAPTER 60

Joan folded her arms tightly across her chest and watched Sir John leave the yard. No sooner had he come home than he was off again. God's teeth, he was exasperating! She still didn't know what business he had in Exeter; he was as reticent as ever on the subject. With Richard away, she'd hoped they would become closer again, maybe go riding over the estate together. She'd looked forward to helping him, and imagined them sitting by the hearth in the evening, discussing matters over a companionable goblet of wine as they used to.

That seemed like a lifetime ago.

She leaned against the wall of the house and despondently kicked a stray stone with the side of her shoe. It hadn't happened like that of course, and she was beginning to think it never would. He always had something more important to do, and he didn't need her help. She knew he wasn't interested in the red dye, but if she could just show him and explain, he'd understand how profitable it could be.

Joan ran her fingers through her hair and sighed. It was much too nice a day to dwell on all that. She'd promised Thomas she'd watch his archery, and Carac was coming over.

The arrow wavered just a little in the breeze, levelled, and then went straight to its target.

'Well done, Thomas! Another one in the centre.' Joan clapped.

'Almost as good as Richard,' Thomas said, beaming.

Carefully, he nocked another arrow, brought his arm up smoothly and lined the arrow against his right ear. Then he shut his left eye and, with the tip of his tongue held between his teeth, slowly pulled back his arm. The bow bent with tension; Thomas adjusted his aim and let the arrow fly.

'My best yet! Bang in the middle! Come on, let's see.' He ran towards the target.

Joan smiled proudly. It was wonderful to see him so confident and full of life.

'I can't wait to show Papa how good I am. Do you think he'll buy me a bow? Only Richard's is a bit big for me.'

'I'm sure he will, and he'll be so proud of you,' Joan said, although she doubted both statements.

'Can I go out and meet Simon and Carac now?'

'If you want to, but stay on the high road and go no further than the forked path.'

Thomas ran off, jumping over the buttercups with his arms flying out. He was a different child. Gone was her shy retiring little boy, always indoors and hiding behind her skirts. Now, he had a zest for life that she'd never known he was capable of. She hardly saw him these days; he was always out fishing, chatting with the stable lads or riding with a lot more confidence, she noted. He was a normal seven-year-old boy and flourishing.

Joan's chest swelled with pride. He hadn't had one attack since Richard had gone to school, and the girls were happier too. But in just two short weeks, Richard would be back for the summer, and that was a sobering thought.

The sun was almost in the third quarter. She ought to get back for Carac. Picking up the quill of arrows, she slung it over her shoulder and headed for home.

Carac swilled the wine in his goblet. He sat in her hall with his legs crossed, his foot moving rapidly up and down. 'So I've missed him again, and I've got to wait for the corn driers.' His voice had an unusual edge to it.

'I'm sorry, but that's what he said.' A little awkwardly, Joan adjusted her headdress.

'It's madness! We've had two wet summers and poor harvests in a row! He's keeping more sheep every year to feed the cloth mill, and this year we lost lambs because we didn't have enough to feed the ewes. Last year was the same, and the fleeces were poor as a result. God's teeth, what does John think he's up to? If we get another bad year and don't have corn driers to save the wet grain, we won't be able to feed ourselves, let alone the sheep.' He finished his wine in one angry swallow. Mouth taut, he sat stiffly in his chair with deep lines furrowed on his brow. Joan had never heard him swear before, and seeing him like this was unnerving. He was her rock, someone she relied on.

'He must know that,' she said.

Carac poured more wine, spilling a little on the table. 'I'm sure he does. Has he said anything to you?'

'Only that he can't afford them.'

'I've got a good mind to just go ahead and build them anyway. The final reckoning after last Michaelmas left us with enough to pay for one, if not two, corn driers. Something's not right, and I need to find out what.' He put his goblet firmly on the table.

'I feel terrible,' Joan said. 'I do try to talk to him, but he tells me nothing. I don't know what more I can do.'

'It's not your fault. The situation is most frustrating, and I admit that I am more than a little vexed.'

Sometimes Joan wondered if it was her fault. She and Sir John were hardly the happy couple they pretended to be. If Carac was concerned, there must be something wrong, and that made her as unsettled as he was.

'Thomas loves going with Simon and is making the most of the archery targets before Richard comes back,' she said, by way of lightening the conversation.

'Indeed. The boy is showing an intelligent interest in the estate. He reminds me of his grandfather, old Sir James. He was a good lord, one of the best. He knew every one of his workers, their troubles and hardships, and he cared. In the leanest months before spring, he gave out spare corn from his store, and many a time I saw a maid taking home a goat's cheese or leftovers from the kitchen. It was a sad day when the good Lord took him.'

Carac's frown was gone and he was sitting more easily in his seat. Joan poured him some more wine.

'What happened? I know there was a rift between Sir James and his brother, Boren, but John won't speak of it. He did say one time that he never knew his mother, but whenever I ask, he gets that cold look and refuses to say. He didn't like Aldred, did he?'

Carac pursed his lips. She could almost see his thoughts going round in his mind. He put his two hands together, just like he always did when he was thinking.

'Please tell me,' Joan pleaded. 'I feel as though there's a huge part of John I don't know. And I want to know.'

'I cannot betray his confidence, but I can explain a little. You are right. The two brothers did quarrel, and Sir James banished Boren to a remote farmstead called Combe Hide on the furthest part of the estate. It's a poor place, with just one hundred acres of mostly water meadows. He and his wife — Margaret, I think her name was — took their young son, Gilbert, and settled there. I don't think Boren ever forgave his brother. John would have been about six at the time.'

'He said he never saw his mother. He seemed very bitter about it.'

Carac studied his goblet thoughtfully, choosing his words with care. 'Hilde was never what one might call a natural mother. She—what shall I say? She found God and rarely ventured out.'

'Poor John.'

'Indeed. It was difficult for such a young boy. Sir James found the situation with Hilde intolerable, and when he moved his manorial seat to here, she remained in the old manor house in the north of the estate. The idea of a move was something we had discussed many times. The old house was too far from the high drovers' road and Oakwolde for trade. John and the servants came too, of course. John was seven by then. That's when I became his tutor and guardian alongside Sir James. When John was nine, he went to school. I continued my duties as bailiff and was guardian to John when he was home.'

'It must have been hard for him growing up,' Joan said softly. 'Did you know he once accused me of never loving Richard? He said that a boy needs a mother's love. He was referring to Richard at the time, but from what you've just said, I think he was talking about himself as well.'

'I'm sure that's not true. You are an exemplary mother—'

She leaned forward, her voice soft and quiet. 'I wish it was so. I've never admitted this to anyone, but I always found Richard difficult, and John saw it. From what you've just said, I think he didn't want Richard to suffer as he had, so he gave him the love and childhood he never had. Only he gave him too much. I see it all now. If only he'd told me, I'd have understood and things might have been different.'

She slumped back. She never intended to say anything and wasn't sure why she had. Carac was twiddling his thumbs around each other and staring at the floor. She had embarrassed him. 'What was the argument about?'

Carac held up his hand. 'I have said more than I meant to. I cannot betray Sir James's confidence. You will have to ask John. It is for him to tell as he wishes.'

Joan was disappointed, but at least now she understood her husband a little more. She wouldn't press Carac.

'I understand.' She put her hand on his arm affectionately. 'And thank you. You're a good friend.'

He coloured and flustered to find his things. Dear Carac, she had embarrassed him again.

CHAPTER 61

Joan stretched her legs and wriggled her toes in front of the fire. Even though it was May, the hall was chilly. Her conversation with Carac the day before played in her mind. She hadn't meant to say all those things, but he was such a good listener, and she had no one else to talk to.

She'd used to talk to Annie. It had been two years since their quarrel, and at the time, Joan hadn't appreciated how much she would miss her. Did Annie miss her? It would be good to see her and chat like old times.

Eleanor was playing hide the thimble with Maria, Thomas was out with Simon, and Sir John was still away. If she rode fast, Joan would just have time to get to Ellyn's cottage, see Annie and be back before the midday bell.

Yes, that was what she would do. It was time they settled old differences. Feeling excited at the prospect, she hastily stuffed her tapestry back into her work-basket. She had no heart for it, anyway.

'I have to go out this morning, Eleanor. Can you look after Maria for me? I'll be back for the midday meal.

'C-can't we come?'

'Not this time. We'll go out this afternoon. Think about what you'd like to do while I'm gone.'

'Alright, J-Jay. It's your turn t-to hide.' Eleanor gave the thimble to Maria and put her hands over her face. Maria ran off, giggling. They would be fine.

Joan knew she didn't have long and walked briskly to the stables. 'Saddle Star for me please,' she called. 'Quick as you can, I need to make haste.'

Merek appeared from behind a large brown horse. A smudge of dirt streaked across his cheek, and the underarms of his tunic were stained with stale sweat. The smell of him made her step back.

'She's not here, my lady. You gave orders for her to go the forge.'

Damn. She'd forgotten that. Now the thought of seeing Annie was in her head, she was determined to go. 'What else is there for me to ride?'

Merek scratched his head. 'Only old Ted here, my lady. But you can't ride him; he's filthy muddy and no saddle.'

'Oh yes, I can. I'll ride without one. Fetch his bridle.'

Ted was a large powerful farm horse, more used to pulling wagons than being ridden. She tucked her skirts high, peasant-style, and giggled to herself at the look of surprise on Merek's face when he returned with the bridle.

Quickly, she fumbled in her purse for a coin and gave it to him. 'Not a word to anyone. Do you understand?' She would die of embarrassment if such a tale went around the village. 'Now, give me a leg up.'

As she rode out of the yard, she smiled at the astonished look on Merek's face as he stared at the coin in his hand. Goodness knows what she'd given him; a silver groat probably, more than he would earn in a week. That would certainly buy his silence.

She nudged Ted forward. The old horse shook his head and broke into a canter, his huge hooves thundering the ground. He was very wide in the back but surprisingly comfortable. She hadn't ridden like this since she was a little girl. If Sir John could see her now, he'd be so furious that his face would turn redder than a hawthorn berry, she thought, amused. It was quite a satisfying thought.

She reached the hill and let Ted walk. After all this, Annie had better be in. It would be so good to see her again. The last time she tried to make amends, that day when Annie came to see Richard about his cough, she'd been very stubborn. But that was a long time ago and now, with a few sorries from both of them and a hug, Joan was sure they would soon be as they used to be.

As she approached Ellyn's cottage, she saw Annie working in the garden and butterflies starting dancing in her tummy.

'Annie! I'm so glad you're in. I'll wager you've never seen me ride like this! Ted's the only horse to ride at the moment,' Joan blustered to cover her nerves.

Annie mouth gaped in surprise.

'My lady?' She dipped a curtsey and fiddled with the shovel in her hands.

'Is Ellyn in?'

'She's out, my lady. I'll tell her you called and wanted to see her.'

Not the open arms welcome she would have liked. Annie's tone was still that of a peasant to her lady. Joan suppressed a sigh. Annie could be so obstinate at times.

She slid off the horse and tied him to the fence. 'It was you I really wanted to see; I was just making sure you were alone. I've missed you, and I thought it was time we sorted things out between us,' she said, offering her hands in friendship.

Annie glanced down at Joan's outstretched hands and back up again. Her face was straight and she didn't move.

With a feeling of foreboding, Joan let her arms drop to her sides. 'Please, Annie, let's talk.'

Annie stiffened. 'I thought we said everything there was to say, my lady.'

'For God's sake, stop calling me that! Look, we both said hurtful things and I'm sorry, but it was a long time ago. We were such good friends once, and we've shared too much. Please, Annie, you still mean a lot to me. Can't we put it all behind us and be friends again?'

Annie remained rigid, lifted her chin and looked Joan straight in the eye. 'You made your position quite clear, my lady. Richard can't have two mothers and he's not my boy. That's what you said. Richard may be living with you, my lady, but he is still my son, and you were my best friend. You can't imagine how you hurt me. How would you feel if someone told you that you couldn't see Thomas again?' She lifted her chin a little higher. 'Over the years, I've learned to live with it. I know who I am: I'm just a peasant healer, and you are my lady. So, no, I don't think we can be friends again. Now, if you don't mind, I need to get this soil dug over.' Annie curtsied but held her stony gaze.

It wasn't what Joan had expected, and her cheeks flamed with embarrassment. She'd got it wrong. Annie's self-assurance made her feel rather small, and she was obviously determined to be stubborn. Well, Joan could be stubborn too, and she wasn't going to make any more of a fool of herself by pleading with her. If Annie wanted to play the peasant, let her!

Flustered and piqued, Joan stood on the stone trough, scrambled on to Ted's back and grabbed the reins. Sitting high on the horse's back, she looked down on Annie and deliberately used her 'Lady of the Manor' voice. 'I'm sorry you feel this way. Richard returns from school in two weeks. I thought you might like to know.'

Lifting her chin high, she turned Ted round and, with a sharp kick into the horse's sides, cantered away, biting back stupid and annoying tears. As much as she wanted to, she didn't look back.

How could she have got it so wrong? She'd been a cloth-head to think that just because she had no one to talk to, she could go and see Annie after all this time and make everything alright with just a few words. Now she had made things worse.

When she got to the top of the hill, she stopped and did look back. Annie was still standing exactly as she'd left her.

CHAPTER 62

Joan, along with everyone else, watched the lush green grass thicken and by June turn a golden yellow. When the seed heads opened and rustled in the breeze, she thanked God as the men picked up their scythes in high spirits and cut a bumper crop of hay. When they lay down their scythes for the last time, the first flash of lightning lit the sky and thunder boomed overhead. Her heart sank as dark clouds cloaked the moor and she felt the first thick drops of rain.

From the comfort of her hall, she sat watching the downpour outside. Holes in the yard filled with water and became puddles. Within days, puddles joined together and flooded the yard. Water poured down the lane and into the dairy. Maids, ankle-deep in water, furiously swept with besoms but were helpless against the flow.

When the storms stopped raging, Joan joined the workers in the fields, and together they stood in dismal silence. The sweet-smelling rows of hay were soggy black mounds, already turning musty with the smell of mould. The skies were ominously still; grey and heavy, promising even more rain. There was nothing she or anyone could do but pray for sunshine.

Their desperate prayers went unanswered, and it rained for the whole of June.

By July, the peasants gathered what hay they could, but little was worth saving. An atmosphere of gloom fell across the estate. It was the third wet summer in a row. Everyone prayed even harder for a good grain harvest. Without one, the winter looked very bleak indeed.

Joan paced up and down the hall, her clipped steps sharp in the silence. She didn't want the confrontation to come, but there was no avoiding it.

She stopped and listened. Definitely horse's hooves outside. Facing the door, she stood with her arms tightly crossed. She was ready.

The door opened and Sir John breezed in. 'What a long day! I'm exhausted. The speed that boy rides! We got out as far as —'

His eyes flicked in her direction. He had seen her and knew she was upset but was choosing to ignore her. That riled her even more. Like a hawk, she watched his every move. She waited until he had removed his boots, flung them across the floor and slumped into his favourite chair. Then, with slow deliberate steps, she approached and stopped two paces away and faced him.

'How could you?'

'How could I what?'

That innocent face didn't fool her. 'Thomas? Archery? This morning?' she prompted.

'Oh.' He shrugged. 'I forgot.'

'You promised. God knows it took me weeks to pin you down to go and watch him and then you forgot. Do you know, he was so excited, he was up before dawn?

He waited for you until midday. Simon brought him back.'

'I was busy. I can't remember everything, and I wanted Richard to see Grenfold Cleave and—' He was still slumped back, making light of it. She was sick of it all; sick of his excuses, sick of him ignoring Thomas, and sick at how dismissive he was.

'May I remind you that you have two sons. Or have you forgotten that as well?'

'I could say the same thing to you.'

The speed and venom of his retort hit her worse than an actual blow. It was true. She was as guilty as he was, and she had no one to blame but herself.

She knelt before him and looked deep into his eyes. 'I'm sorry. I did try, I still try with Richard and I know how you feel, but I feel the same about Thomas. He so desperately wanted to show you. He just wanted a little of your time,' she said, her voice breaking. 'He just wants his Papa to notice and be proud of him. Surely you can understand that.'

'Did you? Did you really try?' The derision in his voice was unmistakable. He seemed intent on punishing her, and she didn't know how much longer she could keep forgiving him, or even how much longer she wanted to. Those unrelenting eyes made her hard inside until she couldn't bear to look at him. She went over to the window and stared out.

'Richard is my heir,' Sir John said. 'I have to make sure that when the time comes, he's ready to take over. You know that. I've no time left for Thomas, and as I've said before, he's no better than a girl. He's useless and a weakling. He'll probably end up in a monastery as a scribe or something. He doesn't need me for that—'

'You want to shut Thomas away in a monastery and

be a scradlee!' She spun around and spat out the word. 'A scradlee, sitting in some cold room from dawn to dusk, straining his eyes and wearing his fingers to the bone copying texts? Is that truly what you intend?' Was he deliberately provoking her through Thomas? Her fury was back with a vengeance and she lashed out. 'You've never mentioned this before. And Thomas is not weak and sickly. He hasn't had an attack since Richard went away; I wonder why that is? You don't know it, because you don't take the trouble to know, but Thomas is a very bright and sensitive boy. He's far too clever to be a scradlee. I don't understand you. He could be a real asset to the estate – goodness knows, Richard hasn't got much sense –'

Sir John puffed out his chest. 'I'll have you know that Richard was top of his class in every subject!'

'Ah! I find that hard to believe –'

'Richard told me himself –'

'Richard is the biggest crooked-nose knave this side of Exeter!' Joan shouted.

Sir John threw himself out of his chair, his eyes blazing. 'How dare you call my son a liar! And you can tell your precious Thomas that I will watch his archery if and when I'm good and ready! Although I know it will be a waste of time, because I doubt he has the strength to draw the bow.' He stormed towards the door.

Standing totally still, Joan waited for the sound of the door slamming behind him. She didn't cry. She was beyond that.

Now she was certain. He didn't want her or her son and she didn't even like him. She daren't move, because if she did, she would break into millions of tiny pieces.

CHAPTER 63

Annie had timed it perfectly, but Cecily waylaid her in the village. It wasn't urgent, but she didn't like to refuse, and now she was late. She checked her basket. The little jar was still safely tucked between Isobel's lotion and John Forge's tincture. She quickened her steps. God willing, she might still catch sight of Richard before he went out with Sir John. It was all she had of him now, and they were moments to be treasured.

The manor was quiet and, stepping into the gloom of the cross-passage, she nearly tripped over Thomas standing in the shadows behind the doors. 'Thomas! You gave me a fright. What are you doing there?'

He scuffed his shoe across the stones. 'I want to play with my blocks, but they're arguing again and I'm afraid to go in. I hate it when they argue.'

His eyes were large and doleful, and Annie resisted the urge to gather him in her arms. Instead, she squatted to his level, tilting her head to one side as she listened. 'I hate it when people argue too, but I think they've stopped. Come in with me.' She held out her hand just as Joan's voice raged through the doors.

'May I remind you that you have two sons! Or have you forgotten that as well?'

'I could say the same thing to you!' Sir John shouted.

There was silence from the hall. Thomas continued to scrape his shoe backwards and forwards across the cobbles.

'Richard is my heir. I have to make sure that when the time comes, he's ready to take over. You know that. I've no time left for Thomas, and as I've said before, he's no better than a girl. He's useless and a weakling. He'll probably end up in a monastery as a scribe or something. He doesn't need me for that—'

Annie shut her eyes and felt every muscle tense. Thomas shouldn't be hearing this. Sir John and Joan had two lovely boys, one without a mother, the other without a father, and they didn't deserve either of them. God's teeth, how she wanted to knock some sense into them! What were they doing?

The angry voices from behind the doors continued to rage. Annie shouldn't have stopped with Cecily. She should have kept walking and told the silly woman she'd see her later. If she'd done that, she would never have heard this; but Thomas, poor little Thomas. He was staring at the ground, but his face was pale. His chin wobbled as he bit his lip to stop himself from crying. Pray God, Annie wanted to get hold of Joan and shake her hard, and then beat Sir John's stupid lordly chest with her fists.

But she couldn't. She was only the healer.

'And you can tell your precious Thomas that I will watch his archery if and when I'm good and ready. Although I know it will be a waste of time, because I doubt he has the strength to draw the bow.'

The door crashed back, Sir John casting a dark shadow as he disappeared into the light of the yard. For

393

a moment, Thomas didn't move. Then his face crumpled and a single tear trickled down his cheek.

'He didn't mean it, I'm sure he didn't mean it.' Annie reached to him but he stepped back.

'Yes, he did,' he said. Pushing her away, he ran outside.

She watched him go, her heart breaking for him, for Richard, and most of all, for herself. She wanted to run after him and make it all better, but they had heard it and neither of them would ever forget.

Hopelessly, she remained in the dark passage. What if, all those years ago, it had never happened? What if Thomas was now taking his place as the rightful heir and Richard was with her? Would Sir John and Lady Joan be content and happy together as they used to be? Would Thomas? And what sort of peasant might Richard be?

She would never know.

It wasn't her fault, so why did she still feel so guilty? At the time, she'd had no choice. There was nothing else she could have done. She must hold on to that belief, or she would go mad.

Annie picked up her basket, took out the little jar and left it beside the door.

CHAPTER 64

Joan wasn't looking forward to the coming evening. It wasn't the harvest festival; she usually enjoyed that occasion. It was just that there was so little to celebrate. The harvest had been poor again, Annie's friendship seemed a distant memory, and, try as she might, she could see no way back for her and Sir John.

She gritted her teeth as Agnes combed through her long thick hair. It wasn't all gloom. Richard was on his way back to school, and her apprehensions on his return for the summer had been unwarranted. He'd spent most of his time with Sir John, and when at home, he'd ignored both Thomas and the girls. He'd said little to her, other than when she asked, he'd said that he made a few friends at school, including Percy de Gravesmire, the Earl of Devonshire's son. He was still out of her reach, and despite her efforts to include him, he wasn't interested. Maybe he was growing out of such things and being at school had done him good, just as Carac said it would.

Overall, the summer had gone well. Richard had argued about going back to school, but Sir John had already paid the fees and insisted he return, which he eventually had with a lot of fuss and bad temper.

'Would you like some cloves or thyme in your hair, my lady?' Agnes had finished the braids.

'Cloves, but not too many.' Joan breathed in, relishing the pungent smell.

Had Carac solved the problem of the dyers guild? There seemed little point now. Her beautiful scarlet cloth had dried to a dull gritty brown. It had been a bitter blow but there was still the other red dye and the extra madder plants, thanks to him. She hadn't seen much of him lately, but then summer was his busiest time.

Agnes caught her hair and she flinched.

It had been a happy summer though, riding out with the girls and Thomas, having picnics by the river, then lifting her skirts and paddling in the ice-cold water looking for fish with Maria, who squealed saying they were going to bite. Thomas boasted that he could creep up-stream and tickle a trout on his belly. He said the fish went still and could be flipped out of the water, something he'd learned from Simon. He'd never managed to do it, but they'd all had fun while he tried.

Other times, she'd just sat back, enjoying the sun on her face as she watched the children jumping from boulder to boulder in an effort to cross the river without getting their feet wet. One strange thing was that Thomas had suddenly lost all interest in archery. He'd taken to accompanying Simon with his work on the estate and seemed to have made a friend in William, the smith's son. Sir John wouldn't approve, but Joan didn't see the harm, so she kept it quiet.

The wheat had grown tall and golden, promising a good harvest, but then God had seen fit to send the rains. As she'd ridden or walked the lanes, she'd despaired at the sight of the beautiful golden wheat lying smashed and brown on the ground. It was to be yet another hard year. When she prayed, she sometimes asked God what they'd done to make him so angry. He never answered.

Sir John was as distant as ever, and still had no time for Thomas or Maria. She'd given up hope of him changing towards her, but she had hoped for the children, who were so often disappointed. For once, she and Sir John both agreed that they would gladly dispense with the harvest celebrations but it was expected. Sir John said it would have to be simple with more dancing and less food and ale. He simply couldn't afford to do otherwise. There was no new kirtle or jewellery this year, but she didn't mind; it gave her the chance to wear her favourite yellow dress with her gold cross. She was not in a celebratory mood. Nobody was.

The corn dolly was presented as always and laid to watch over the Great Barn. The food was eaten, the empty platters cleared away and the trestles moved back to make space for the dancing.

Joan remembered to smile now and again as she sat at the high table. There were Annie and Ellyn with Peter and his family. She tried to catch Annie's eye, but they were laughing together over something and Annie pretended not to notice. How Joan missed her. And, close by were Geoffrey Miller, his wife Mary and their little daughter, Rose, snuggled on her father's lap. Among other families, children giggled and adults chatted.

Joan envied them. She couldn't remember the last time her family was all together, laughing and chatting like these. How could the peasants be so happy when they had so little?

She glanced sideways at Sir John sitting stiffly in his chair, his cold face staring into nothing across the hall. Now and then, he remembered to smile, but it didn't last long. He's still as handsome as ever, she thought, but the butterflies didn't dance.

Young, animated voices floated across the room to her, and she returned her gaze to the hall. Three little girls about the same age as Maria were playing tag, their cheeks rosy red and braids flying as they chased each other around the benches.

They made Joan smile. She turned to Eleanor on her left. Eleanor didn't look happy, sitting staring at her hands clasped in her lap, twisting her thumbs round and round. Maria looked bored as well; she was counting the beads on her bracelet. Finally, Joan's gaze fell on Thomas, where he was seated at the end. His mouth was turned down as he stared at his feet.

How can we be so miserable when we have so much?

The musicians picked up their instruments, and she watched with a pang of envy as Mary, Janet and little Rose joined hands and took their places in the circle of dancers. They waved to Geoffrey and Peter from across the floor with beaming smiles as they merrily waved back. Annie and William joined them and the dancing began.

Joan's foot tapped in rhythm to the music. The trouble was, her family was divided. There were Sir John and Richard on one side, and herself, Thomas, Maria and Eleanor on the other. Life had been so different before Richard was born. It was true she'd struggled with him, but then Thomas was born, and two years later, little Maria. Sir John had drifted away from them and taken Richard with him. It was so gradual, Joan hadn't noticed it at first, and by the time she had, it was too late. Goodness knows she'd tried to get things back as they were but she'd failed. And now she'd run out of ideas.

All her frustrations, the hurt, the disappointments, the years of condemnation in Sir John's cold eyes, had all been simmering inside for a long time, and now she could feel them bubbling their way to the surface. The situation was intolerable. He was making her life and her children's lives a misery, and she wouldn't put up with it for a moment longer.

She stood up and thrust out her hand to Eleanor. 'Let's dance,' she said.

'We're not allowed, J-Jay. Sir John says—'

'I don't care what John says. I am saying, let's dance. Thomas, Maria, you too.'

'Where are you going?' Sir John jolted back to the present.

'We're going to have some fun,' she said. 'We're dancing.'

'You can't dance with them. I forbid it.'

Her eyes defied him. She no longer cared about what he did or didn't forbid. Daring him to say more, she took a firm hold of Eleanor's hand and with a toss of her head, led them to the dance.

CHAPTER 65

Carac leaned back and rubbed his swollen fingers in the warmth of his hearth. Old age was a terrible thing. Thank the Lord for Simon, who was turning into a good bailiff. He hadn't wanted him to take over, particularly with Master Richard becoming the Lord one day. He'd wanted his son to go to university and have a better chance in life, but Simon didn't want to go. It was disappointing but it would have been futile to force the boy, and now that his joints ached, he was glad that he hadn't.

It was regrettable that he didn't enjoy Sir John's confidence as he once had. They'd shared so many ideas for the estate back then. He recalled their excitement at seeing the new waterwheel turn for the first time. They had stood together, leaning over the rails and watching each drop of water falling from the paddles as though they'd never seen such a sight before. They were like two excited boys. Those were good days.

That had changed when Richard was born. As soon as his son could walk, Sir John's world revolved around him, until it seemed that he lost sight of everyone and everything. Carac saw less and less of him and each time he did, Sir John seemed less of a friend and more of a lord. There was that business with the Knights Fees and the extra land. Carac had done his best to reason with the man, but he wouldn't listen.

Could he have done more? Sir John was still not confiding in him, and Carac had no real idea of what the situation was with the accounts. It was all deeply worrying. He'd heard rumours of the earl's affairs but nothing to act upon, and he doubted if Sir John would believe him in any case.

He sighed. It was very lamentable but all this looking back wouldn't do. He had to face it: he was getting old and tired. Things weren't what they used to be. He hated to admit it, but he had lost his enthusiasm and was only too willing to let a young and enthusiastic Simon take the reins.

A knock on the door broke his thoughts. Wearily, he rose from his chair and went to answer it.

'Hail! What a pleasant surprise.' The very sight of Joan lifted his spirits, but then she'd always had that effect on him. She looked tired. Her eyes were not quite as bright and her cheeks a little paler than usual. 'Come in, and welcome.'

'God keep you fair, Carac. It's been a while.'

Too long. He didn't see much of her these days and seeing her now rekindled his feelings for her.

'Indeed, and to what do I owe the pleasure? Not trouble, I hope.' Carac poured them some wine and settled back by the hearth.

'I need some advice.'

Carac had feared as much. There was gossip around the estate about the lord and lady always being at each other's throats, but affairs of the heart unsettled him.

He much preferred problems of a more logical nature, like figures. You knew where you were with figures.

'As always, I shall be of help if I can. Is it John or the red dyes?'

'Neither. I've come about Thomas, although I find John as onerous as ever. You weren't at the Harvest Festival, but you heard about it, I suppose?'

Indeed he had, and he had raised a glass to her indomitable spirit. 'I did hear something. You joined in the dancing and John didn't approve?'

'That's what they're saying, is it?' Joan fidgeted and brushed the folds of her skirts as though deciding whether or not to say more. Wisely, he let her take her time and sat back, content just to be near her again and hear her voice.

'You know what John's like and — I don't know, seeing the peasants so happy together, something inside me snapped. I'd had enough and needed to show him that. He was livid of course, still is, but I don't regret it.'

Carac had felt the same way for a long time. He studied her. Was there just a little of the sparkle missing from her eyes?

'And now?' he asked.

'You can imagine, we had a row and, despite all my resolve, I still have a small hope that we might at least get back to being civil to each other, for appearances, if nothing else.' She shook her head a little and sighed.

God's bones, what was he supposed to say? That Sir John was a hard, even a cruel man at times, who didn't deserve her? That's what Carac thought, but it wouldn't do to take sides.

'John's pride has been wounded. Give him time. Whilst not deliberately angering him, I've always found it best to stand firm. Not always an easy path to tread, in my experience.' He was totally out of his depth in such matters, but it was the best he could do. 'I hope that helps.'

Joan nodded and smiled, making his old heart flutter just as it always had. He'd better move on to safer ground. 'I'm afraid the only way I can see to join the dyers guild is for John to apply.'

'It doesn't seem fair that after all my efforts, John can join the guild and get the recognition when I can't. But it doesn't matter so much now. The scarlet cloth I showed you didn't work.'

'I am sorry.'

'I was so disappointed, but I shall keep trying, and the women are continuing with the other red dye. Anyway, I really came about Thomas. The thing is, he wants to go to school.'

Carac wasn't surprised. From what Simon had told him, the boy seemed troubled of late. He'd probably been working this out for a while. 'He's an intelligent boy. How old is he now? Six, seven summers?'

'He's seven birth dates. It was his idea and came as a complete shock to me. We were in the orchards yesterday, we both enjoy apple picking time, and I had a very interesting conversation with him...'

'I'm not the heir, am I, Mama? Richard will take over, even if he is riding in some battle being a knight in arms.'

The branches of the trees bowed low with fruit, some red for eating, others green for cider. Joan picked up two red ones from the ground and passed one to him. Taking a bite of the juicy crisp apple, she nodded in satisfaction. It was a good crop.

'No, you're not the heir, and we have to start thinking about what you are going to do,' she said.

They strolled on past the women and children, whose backs were bent double as they gathered fruit off the ground and carefully placed them in large willow baskets.

'I already have. I'm seven summers and old enough to go to school. Not Exeter where Richard is,' Thomas added quickly. 'Simon went to the monks in Tavistoke. He didn't like it much, but he says that was just him, and he wouldn't have liked school wherever he went, but he thinks it will suit me. It's quite small and, if you want to learn — and I do — the clever boys get a tutor all to themselves. I think I should like that. There's so much I want to know.'

He'd obviously thought about this, and the way he spoke belied his years, but then he'd always been like that.

Further down the rows, boys prodded and shook the boughs with long sticks, laughing and covering their heads with their hands as they jumped back to avoid the rain of apples.

Sir John would need persuading. She'd have to think carefully about that one. 'Why now? You've not mentioned it before.'

They were at the end of the row and he stood, shuffling one shoe through the grass, his fair hair flopping over his young face. 'I just do,' he said.

He wouldn't look her in the eye, and by the casual tone of his voice, there was more to it than that, but he could be very self-contained and Joan knew that this was all the answer she was going to get. She tossed her apple core aside and strolled on. They skirted past an ox waiting in his yoke as men heaved baskets piled high with apples on to the wagon.

'And after school, do you know what you want to do then?' She turned down the next row of trees.

'Oh, yes. I've thought about that too. I want to be a physician.'

'Do you indeed?'

'Yes, because you see, when I'm qualified, I can earn a lot of money as a private physician to the nobility. That way, I can help Richard, and I think he's going to need my help.'

'Whatever do you mean?' The things he came out with astounded her.

'Simon says that these days, you have to be very clever to run an estate and make it pay, and...well, Richard isn't very clever, is he?'

She hid a smile. No, Richard isn't very clever. 'That's very adult of you, Thomas.'

'I suppose I shall have to talk to Papa—'

'You leave him to me,' she said, although how and when she would do it she had no idea. They were hardly speaking.

Carac held his hands together, as though in prayer, his fingertips resting on his lips. 'And your problem is? It appears to me to be an excellent idea.'

Joan took a sip of wine. 'It's John. I'm certain he won't agree. He doesn't understand Thomas. He thinks he should be a scradlee shut away in some monastery. I can't let that happen. Thomas would hate it and I'd never see him again. You do see my problem, don't you?'

'Indeed. Thomas is a clever boy, and it seems to me that he is worthy of a more scholarly life. Why can't you just tell John what you've told me? I'm sure he'd see reason. He'd only have the best interests of his son at heart.'

Joan sighed. 'Oh, if only that were true! He'll tell me he can't afford it, I know he will. It's all he seems to say these days. If it was Richard —'

Carac nodded. He knew her dilemma only too well. If it was Richard, Sir John would agree to anything whether he could afford it or not.

'After our last row, he's hardly talking to me,' Joan added. 'You know what he's like.'

'Indeed I do, but as I said, all husbands and wives have quarrels. I'm sure you'll soon sort it out between you.' Carac doubted the words even as he spoke them; it was already far too late.

'I don't think so,' Joan said very quietly. 'Not this time.'

She looked so sad, sitting in his chair with her head down. He hoped she wasn't going to cry. He never knew what to do when women did that.

'If it's simply a question of the fees, I could —'

'No! If John found out — no. Thank you, but that isn't the way.'

'I understand. Then, as I see it, there is only one solution. You will have to talk to John and, if he refuses to pay for Thomas to go to school, you will have to pay the fees yourself.'

CHAPTER 66

Over the following days, Joan thought a lot about her conversation with Carac. If Thomas was to go to school in the New Year, she had to speak to Sir John soon and it wasn't going to be easy. She'd have to pick her time.

The time turned out to be the end of the week of the important October cloth markets. The sales had gone well, especially the sales of red cloth, she noted with quiet satisfaction. Sir John had never admitted that she'd been right or acknowledged her work, but then, she didn't do it for that.

On the last day of the sales, Sir John came home with a smile on his face. He even bade her good evening and, rubbing his hands together, spoke of the amount of money he'd made. By his slightly slurred speech, he'd had a few drinks, but he was in a good mood and now could be her chance.

Joan poured him a goblet of his favourite red wine and sat opposite so she could see his face. Slowly, she smoothed out the creases of her skirts and chose her words carefully. 'I've been thinking about Thomas. He's seven now and needs to do something more than be with Simon —'

'Whatever for?'

'He's clever, and I was thinking that maybe he should go to school.' She gauged his reaction like a cat watching a mouse.

There was no flicker of emotion as Sir John finished his wine and helped himself to another. 'I thought it was all decided that he would be a scradlee in a monastery. Until he's old enough, he can stay with Simon. And anyway, I can't afford the fees.'

It was exactly what Joan had expected. She breathed deeply, biting her nails into her hands. A confrontation wouldn't work; she had to keep calm. 'You've just told me how well the sales went, so surely you have enough. He wants to be a physician—'

'A what!' Sir John brushed the spilt wine off his tunic. 'The boy's mad! It would mean years at school and, later, the University of Oxford for his degree. It's out of the question!'

'Is it? Think: physicians are very well respected and needed in the highest society, particularly around the royal court...' Joan allowed the possibilities to play in his mind.

'True...' Sir John conceded.

'And with your position in society now and in the future with Richard's, of course, a physician could be very useful in such circles. Don't you think?' The cat had her prey within reach and was waiting patiently for the kill.

'It takes years to become a physician. I can't afford it—'

His response towards Thomas was always the same, and it made her want to scream. Joan could have said that a lot of the cloth sales were due to her red dye and hard work, but she bit her tongue. If they had another row, he'd only walk out as he always did.

'Think of the future. A Chiddleigh physician to the nobles, maybe even to the king himself. It could be a very good investment.'

Sir John frowned. 'A Chiddleigh physician in the royal court? Yes, well, it's a nice idea, but I need the coffer money to replace the sheep we lost during the previous poor years. Then there's Richard's school fees and Carac's corn driers. You don't understand; the expenses just go on and on. Maybe next year.'

He wasn't going to get away with that, and she wouldn't be dismissed on the excuse of costs. 'I know it was a poor harvest, but you've just said that the cloth sales were the best yet, and you tell me the warren is producing good profits. The coffers must be overflowing. Let's have a look in the chest and see...' She made to move.

'No! No, there's no need to go to all that bother!'

For a moment she sensed his panic but let it pass. 'It's no bother. Come on.'

Sir John ran his fingers through his hair and drew in an agitated breath. He was being evasive, but she wasn't going to give up now.

'No, there's no need...because, thinking about it, you're right. As you say, he's a clever boy, and a physician in high places could be very useful to Richard. I suppose I could buy a few less sheep, and Carac can wait for his corn driers.'

His voice was unnaturally bright, but his eyes wouldn't meet hers. Something was eluding her, something not quite right. She'd expected him to hold his ground, but surprisingly he hadn't. She pushed the feeling away. She had caught her prey, and Thomas was going to school. That was all that mattered.

CHAPTER 67

June 1344

Sir John held the message in his hands and read it again. He ran his fingers through his hair, poured a drink and tossed the letter to one side.

The previous four years hadn't been easy. Whilst still maintaining the outward appearance of a couple, he and Joan rarely saw each other, which suited him. He didn't know when he'd started to dislike her; he only knew that now he did. He'd put up with her sharp tongue and constant moans about Richard for years. Maybe that was what changed his feelings.

Either way, he no longer cared. Not content with the red dye, she'd taken it into her head to start breeding horses. She always had to be doing something. He'd never understood it. Still, it wasn't costing him anything, and it kept her amused. And he had to admit that she had a good eye for a horse and had bred some useful palfreys for the noble ladies.

Life was better when Richard was home from school, although the boy was always arguing that he wasn't going back. Somehow, Sir John had won each battle, but it had cost him the promise that, as soon as Richard was fourteen, he could go and stay with the Earl of Devonshire.

He'd always assumed that the boy would grow out of his fantasy of becoming a knight in arms. Regrettably, he never had, and the closer the time came, the more uneasy Sir John felt. Richard should be by his side and taking his rightful place, not going off playing at knights! His heir needed to be seen amongst his peasants and learn the ways of the estate for when his time came. It was just as well Richard had never realised how close he had come to getting his way over school, because the fees were getting harder and harder to find.

Sir John slumped into his chair and picked up the letter again. It was from the Earl of Devonshire, and wasn't so much an invitation as a summons to attend a banquet. There was no way out; they would have to go. Joan wouldn't want to, because her precious Thomas would be home from school. That was another expense he could well do without! With the wile of a witch, she'd tricked him into that.

Looking back, Sir John could see it all so easily. He should have taken his plans more slowly, listened to Carac and built his wretched corn driers to preserve what harvest was gleaned. He hadn't, and not just because of the money; it was also a question of pride. Carac was always right, and, for once, Sir John had wanted to prove himself.

Then there was the damn rabbit project! He shouldn't have made it so large, but all the rich landowners were doing it; he couldn't be seen not to. And all those lavish banquets he attended and gave, too many to remember—but he had to keep in with high society, it was expected. He didn't regret it all, exactly, but now he was literally paying for it.

He sighed crossly. They would have to go to the wretched banquet, and if Joan thought she would be getting a new kirtle, she was very much mistaken.

The banquet was as impressive as usual. The food was exquisite, and the servants kept the wine flowing freely. Even so, it didn't have the appeal it once did. Sir John glanced around at the gathering. Lord de Montif was strutting around as always, his belly too large, his voice too loud. The man was odious. How could he ever have wanted to aspire to that? Lord Falk was genuine on the outside, but he and the earl were thick as thieves and had done him no favours with the price of their rabbit stock. The same nobles who always attended these functions were parading their new clothes with their ladies by their sides, festooned with jewels. It was almost tedious.

The earl was making his way towards him. There was a time when Sir John would have felt honoured but now, as the earl sat next to him, he tensed. He wasn't sure why.

'News is that the French are fighting back. King Edward and his armies are having a tough time of it. I know—' the earl held up his hand— 'I'm as tired as you are with these demands for more funds and don't misunderstand me, the king has my full support, but—' he shook his finger— 'times are hard.'

Sir John doubted that the earl had ever known a hard time in his life.

Picking up his goblet, the earl continued. 'Sadly, such are the joys of rank and privilege. It is of no matter…'

He rearranged his face from dismay to acceptance and

shifted his chair closer. 'Have some more wine, and tell me, how is that son of yours?'

'Richard's still at Exeter and doing very well, as I knew he would. I was only saying the other day—'

'Didn't we talk about the lad coming to me to finish his education, so to speak?' The earl's sharp eyes never blinked as they held him in their stare. Sir John had never noticed before, but the man had mean little green eyes set too close together.

He shifted uneasily. This was a topic he would rather not discuss. 'Something was mentioned a while back, but Richard still has a year at school.'

The earl leaned back, his hands loosely clasped in his lap. 'A fine strong lad as I recall, and a very capable sportsman. Do you see him as a scholar? I mean to say unless he's likely to go to Oxford, what's the point? I can show him the ways of being a knight and introduce him to certain people. People who frequent the royal court...'

'You would introduce my son into the king's court?' Sir John's heart quickened. Could this be the invitation he had prayed for all these years?

'If the opportunity arose, certainly I would.' The earl nonchalantly studied his fingernails. 'Look, I've just had a thought. Instead of sending the boy back to Exeter in September, why don't you send him to me? Think of the money you'd save on the fees. It would cover this latest demand from the king.'

That was true. Maybe those eyes weren't quite so mean after all. And the king! King Edward III himself! How could he refuse such an opportunity? Richard would never forgive him if he did, but even so...

'It does make sense, but my plan is for Richard to

finish school and then run the estate alongside me. I don't want him to go to war, you understand?'

'My dear friend, I'm not suggesting any such thing.' The earl slapped him on the back and flashed a broad smile. 'I shall simply be furthering his and your interests. Nothing more, and in a year or two, I shall return Richard to you safe and sound, and maybe with an important invitation for you and your good lady.'

There it was. True, Sir John had debts, and maybe he had been a little careless with his spending now and again, but this was his reward. An invitation to the royal court! To sit at the king's table and eat his fare, to see and maybe even meet Queen Phillippa and her entourage dressed in rich clothes and wearing dazzling jewellery. And Richard being accepted and mixing with the highest in the land, maybe marrying into such a family. The possibilities were endless.

Sir John's insides churned at the prospect. It was all he could do to keep still in his seat, but it wouldn't do to look too eager. He bit back the broad smile that was fighting to stay on his face. 'Yes, you're right. It's an excellent suggestion.'

'Good! September it is, then. I look forward to seeing the boy.' The earl delicately touched each corner of his mouth. 'Now, I must have a word with Lord Whitcombe…'

Sir John didn't mention the earl's proposal to Joan. She would only find fault and spoil his moment. He couldn't think for the excitement of it. How should he address royalty? He would have to practise his bow and Joan her curtsey, and they would certainly need new clothes from the best tailors and seamstress in Exeter! Would Joan's jewellery be good enough? Best to make sure and buy one or two new pieces. He didn't want to be embarrassed for the sake of a coloured stone or two.

Now they were on their way home, and he had time to reflect. Had he done the right thing about Richard? Not everyone was chosen to attend the royal court, and the gleam in the earl's eyes troubled him. Could he trust the man? He'd had his doubts a time back, but the earl couldn't have known that the rabbit market would crash, could he? At least now there would be no more school fees, and Richard would be taking the Chiddleigh name into high places. Of course, he had done the right thing.

'Since when have you been so loyal to our king?' Joan broke his thoughts.

Sir John blinked. 'I don't know what you mean.'

'Don't give me that innocent look. You know exactly what I mean. Your friend, the Earl of Devonshire — sorry; Frederick — said he was most impressed with your generosity over the years to the king's funds.' She shot him a triumphant look.

Hell's fire, that woman had big ears! Now she'd have a go at him. 'And so he should be,' he muttered darkly.

'It's no laughing matter. All this time you've been saying that you can't afford this and you've no money for that while you've been handing bagfuls of the stuff to that old fox.'

'You don't like him, do you?'

Joan threw back her head and laughed in that annoying way of hers. 'Who does? I don't trust him, and neither should you. Just how much is left in the coffers? Be honest with me; how much?'

Damn. He didn't want to tell her but she'd only keep on about it until she wore him down, like the time she'd wanted money for Thomas to go to school.

'Now I know why you've been so secretive all these years. No wonder you didn't want Carac to know.'

She'd go running to Carac now, who would be all-knowing and superior. Sir John could hear his response now: if only you had taken my advice. He felt cornered. How dare she question his judgement and laugh at him? God's teeth, he was her lord and master. She was just like Carac, she had no vision. He would not be contrite, damn her.

'I am lord and entitled to spend as I see fit —'

'How much is left?' she demanded, staring at him.

He hated that look. It always made him feel like a schoolboy. 'Not a lot. Very little if you must know. But before you start, let me tell you it was all worth it. The earl and I have agreed that Richard is to leave school and stay with him. He has promised to introduce Richard to the royal court.'

Joan's jaw dropped and she reined Star to a halt. 'And you believe him? How can you be such a numbskull?'

Now she had on her superior face. God, she could be so demeaning when she wanted! 'Me, a numbskull? This is the opening I've been working for all these years. Think of it; we could be summoned to the royal court —'

'Oh yes, and while we're wining and dining with the highest in the land, there are no coins in the coffers and the estate is going to rack and ruin —'

'Well, at least it's good news, because in other ways things are going to get worse,' he snapped.

'What do you mean?'

'God's teeth, woman, you know the hay was poor again this year! Unless we have a miracle, the harvest won't be much! And you might as well know, since you'll find out soon enough, the rabbit market is finished. That's what I mean.' That wiped the smug look off her face.

'I thought the rabbits were very profitable. You've always said —'

'They were, but too many people got into it and now there are too many rabbits for sale. They aren't fashionable anymore. I can't give them away. The fur's not even worth having. The filthy things are costing me more to keep than I made from them in the whole of last year. I wish I'd never got into it.'

'The earl must be upset.' Joan nudged Star forward.

'Hardly. He sold off his stock last autumn.'

'And he didn't tell you?'

'He couldn't have known,' Sir John said.

'I bet he did. Who was the cloth-head who bought his stock?'

He cringed and looked away.

'Tell me it wasn't you.' She had that haughty tone in her voice and that annoying tilt to her head.

Well, he wasn't going to give her the satisfaction of admitting it. 'You're not being fair to Frederick. He's been very good to me.'

'Dear God, it was you! How could you have been such a fool? The earl must have been laughing at you. And now you're telling me that you're left with warrens full of rabbits that nobody wants and an empty coffer chest. At least we won't go hungry this winter. When I think of how you put off Carac's corn driers, which could have helped us through the bad years, and all the work I put in making a red dye to increase our cloth prices, when all the while you were secretly giving our money away. I can't believe it, John. Not even from you.'

Outwardly, she looked remarkably calm, but she was biting her lip. She must be seething underneath. He preferred it when she shouted; he could deal with that. When she was so controlled, she made him feel inadequate, but he was damned if he'd let her have the upper hand.

'I had to keep the king's fund a secret. You and Carac would never have understood. And I was right, because now Richard has the chance to walk with royalty. And no, I can't sell the rabbits, nobody wants them. If you're so worried about money, there is one thing I can do: I can stop Thomas from going to school.' Now who was in control?

Joan stopped her horse. With a smug feeling of satisfaction, Sir John watched her face fall and turn pale. 'You can't do that. He loves school and is doing brilliantly. Please, John, don't do this. There has to be another way.'

'If there is, I don't know what. Thomas is the least of my worries.' He moved Baron forward. 'Richard will soon have his place in high circles. He won't need Thomas.'

'You can't just throw Thomas aside!' Joan protested.

Sir John shrugged. 'I just have.'

CHAPTER 68

October 1345

Carac had a visitor. What a dejected-looking man he was, with his elbows on his knees and his head hung low. He was desperately thin, his hair and beard ragged and unkempt, and there were dark rings under his eyes. Carac hardly recognised him, but then, it had been a long time since he'd last sat in that chair.

'What am I going to do?' said Sir John, his head still in his hands.

'It's been many years since you've asked me that question.' Carac put a log on the fire, turned to the table and poured two goblets of wine.

Sir John slowly lifted his head as though it was too much effort, sighed deeply and gratefully took the drink. 'I know, and I'm truly sorry for that. How are you these days?'

'Feeling my years, I'm afraid. These old bones ache and some days, the pain is so bad I pray God to take me. I've tried chewing willow bark, but it made me sick to my stomach, and Annie gave me a potion made from the leaves, but with little result. So I bear it as best I can. I find jolts from a horse or wagon intolerable and rarely travel far from the house. Simon does all that, but we discuss things when he gets back. At least I've not gone mad yet.' Carac's wry smile slipped as he regarded his estranged friend. 'But you haven't come here to ask how I fare. Tell me what's brought you here.'

'You'd better read this.' Sir John held out a letter.

Carac recognised the red seal, raised an eyebrow and, with a feeling of foreboding, settled in the seat on the opposite side of the hearth.

October 1345

Sir John

At last! Our good King Edward III is back on English soil and prepares to return to France in the spring or early summer of next year with as large an army as he can muster. This is what so many of us have been waiting for. Needless to say, it falls on us, his loyal and faithful nobles to support him in his worthy cause.

You will be pleased to know that Richard is ready as a knight and can't wait to take up arms alongside the king and his heir, The Black Prince. Richard will require men on foot to go with him, a personal groom, full armour and weapons, and one, preferably two, good quality chargers. As a knight yourself, holding my knight's fees, I urge you to join us.

I know how proud you must be to think of your son carrying the Chiddleigh coat of arms into battle for his king and country.

Rest assured, such support from his loyal subjects will not go unrewarded.

Frederick de Gravesmire, Earl of Devonshire.

Carac read the letter twice more before carefully placing it on the table beside him. It was what he had feared all along.

'He promised me, you know,' Sir John said brokenly. 'Last year, when I agreed to send Richard to him, he promised. He said he would introduce Richard into the royal court and invitations for Joan and I would follow. He gave me his word that Richard would not be called to arms and he would return to me safe and sound. Those were his exact words. And now I get this. What am I going to do?'

'I take it you don't want to go to France?'

'Carac, do I look like a knight in arms? I wouldn't know which end to hold the mace.'

'And Richard?'

'Of course not. I never wanted him to go; the earl knows that. It was never what we agreed.' Sir John hung his head once more and addressed the floor. 'I don't know what I'd do if my boy goes to war. I don't think I could bear it.'

'He always wanted to be a knight riding into battle, ever since I can remember.' Carac poured more wine.

'A boy's fancies, that's all. He doesn't know the realities. He just sees the glory of sitting on his fine horse holding the Chiddleigh colours. You have to stop him.'

Carac wasn't sure that he could. 'The Earl of Devonshire granted you the Knights Fees lands, and that gives him a claim on you. He can call you to arms as a knight of war, and he will expect an army of men to come with you. You cannot refuse.' The earl was a tricky man to deal with, and Carac needed time to think. He held his hands together, as though in prayer, with his fingertips just brushing his lips. After a long silence, he looked up. 'How much do you owe?' he said.

'What?'

'I said, how much do you owe?'

'What's that got to with it?' Sir John stiffened.

'My dear friend, it has everything to do with it.'

421

Sir John sat up, his voice guarded. 'What makes you think I owe anything?'

'Don't take me for a fool, John. Years of lavish entertaining, expensive kirtles and jewellery for Lady Joan, hiring labour for building works, setting up the rabbit warren—'

'All necessary, you know that—'

'The estate is falling into disrepair due to neglect and lack of funds. I trust that your contributions to the king's fund have ceased?'

'Joan told you about that, then. I knew she would.' Sir John slumped back with his arms folded.

'Repairs are needed on the waterwheel for the cloth mill, for example, and—'

'Times were hard, still are, and we've had years of poor harvests. God's teeth, I couldn't have predicted those, could I?'

'No, you couldn't. But you could have built corn driers to save the wet grain, instead of leaving it to rot and go mouldy.'

'Yes, yes, you were right about that, and I admit, I do owe a little more than I would like, but—'

Sir John was getting defensive. He always did that when he felt uncomfortable. He was finding this difficult, which was understandable. It would be a severe blow to Sir John's pride to have to come to him for help after all these years. The situation was utterly regrettable. If only Sir John had confided in him earlier, maybe Carac could have done something. He wasn't enjoying this any more than John was, and as much as he felt like telling the man some more home truths, it wouldn't help.

Carac softened his voice. 'So, tell me. Have much do

you owe and to whom?'

The colour was rising to Sir John's cheeks. It reminded Carac of when he was waiting for an explanation from the little boy who had been found out in some mischief or other. Sir John fidgeted, uncrossed his legs, and then crossed them again.

'John, if you want my help, I need to know. Tell me, truthfully.'

So he did. When he finished, he hung his head in shame.

Carac raised an eyebrow and let out a long whistle. 'As much as that? Then it is worse than I thought.'

His knees creaking in protest, he got out of his chair and stood beside Sir John, placing a friendly hand on his shoulder. 'Let us take the air and we can talk as we go. These old joints of mine seize up if I sit for too long. Come, fetch me my stick and we'll take a turn around the grounds.' He smiled, offering his hand of friendship, which Sir John gratefully accepted.

They strolled through the orchards, making banal comments about the changing colours of the autumn leaves and the size of apples, but Carac's mind was elsewhere and only when his thoughts were clear, did he suggest they sit and rest.

'Are you aware that the Earl of Devonshire has acquired vast lands and estates across the entire kingdom over the past six years or so, all courtesy of the king?'

'I didn't know that.'

'Oh yes, he is now one of the most powerful men in the realm. Why do you think he was granted so many favours?' Carac scrutinised Sir John's blank expression. It was as he thought: the man had no idea. 'I shall tell you why. Men and money for the king's war in France. That's why.'

'I gave generously to the fund myself, I told you—'

'Yes, my friend, you did. But think; did you ever receive direct acknowledgement or lands for such loyalty? It is usual in such cases, I believe.'

'Well, no, but Frederick assured me the king was grateful and knew of my contribution. I was pleased just to get my name known in such circles.'

Carac shook his head. 'My dear man, you only had the earl's word for that. Why didn't you or any of the other — forgive me, John — minor nobles receive anything? Why was it only the earl who got the lands and titles?'

'I didn't know he had, and I don't understand what you're implying. What other nobles? And how do you know all this?'

Carac ignored the undertone of accusation. 'You're not the only aspiring rural knight the earl has befriended over the years, and Richard isn't the only son to further his education and learn the art of battle with him. We bailiffs make it our business to keep each other informed.'

'I never realised.'

Carac smiled at Sir John's naivety and waited, letting the implications of his words sink in. At last, Sir John's eyes widened incredulously.

'Are you saying that all the money I gave to the earl for the king's funds didn't go to the king in my name? That the earl never even mentioned my name to the king and took all the credit for himself? And that I wasn't the only one?' He ran his fingers through his hair. 'No, I don't believe it. You must have got it wrong.'

Carac waited. He could almost see Sir John's mind working.

'There was that business about the rabbit market,' Sir John continued. 'It was a bit of a coincidence that the earl was the only one not to lose a fortune. I wondered about that at the time, but I never believed it was deliberate. And I suppose I should have received something from the king. Are you sure? I mean, the earl wouldn't...would he?'

'I am as sure as I can be. He is not called the fox for no reason.'

'Why didn't you warn me?' Sir John demanded.

'As I recall, I did try, years ago. And, if you remember, I've always had my doubts regarding the earl, but it wasn't until very recently that I became acquainted with the facts. Until then, it was only rumoured. Even if I had said something, would you have listened?'

Carac watched with no pleasure as the colour drained from Sir John's face. 'I had no idea. I trusted the man. I believed he was my friend, and all the time he was laughing at me, playing me for the fool that I was. I didn't even get an invitation to the royal court as he promised.'

'Indeed. He will know your financial situation. You do realise that, don't you?'

'Will he?' Sir John's head shot up.

For a lord, he really was naive, Carac thought. 'I wouldn't be surprised. Knowledge is power, John. He will have made it his business to find out. He will not only know how much you owe but to whom.'

'Why? He already had my total trust, numbskull that I was.'

'Because with that knowledge, he knew exactly how much he could get from you for the king's funds, but, and this is the important point, he has the power and money to buy your debts. If he did, he could call them in at any time he chose and that gives him total control over you and everything you own.'

'Why would he want to do that? My lands are nothing compared to his—'

'John, this isn't about your lands. The earl enjoys manipulating people and having power over them. It's like a game of chess to him. He uses ambitious, low-ranking knights and gains their trust. He takes their money to give to the king's war efforts in his name, and in return, receives the king's favour and vast amounts of land. It is so simple, it's ingenious.'

'He wouldn't. He didn't.'

'I'm afraid he did.' Sir John had to be told, and Carac was the only one who could tell him. And now, watching his world crumble around him was one of the hardest things he had ever had to do.

'I'm sorry, Carac, but this is all too much. I'm finding it hard to believe, and I can't think straight. Why didn't I see it? I thought I was being so clever, that I was being accepted into high society and that all my ambitions for Richard and the Chiddleigh name were coming true. I believed him when he said Joan and I would get invitations to the royal court. And all the time, he was using and manipulating me like a puppet.' He buried his head in his hands.

'You did what you thought was best—'

'I could lose everything. My estate…all those dreams we had and achieved. Can you forgive me? But worst of all, I've sold my son. That's what I've done. By agreeing to let Richard go to the earl, I've lost him. How could I have been so stupid?' He lifted his forlorn eyes. 'Just tell me what to do.'

The poor man was at the end of his tether. All the frustrations and anger Carac had felt over the recent years changed to pity and regret. He only hoped he could help him now.

'It occurs to me that Richard knows nothing of this. If you refuse to let him go to France, he will never forgive you. In any case, the earl can call you to lead an army in his place. You would have no choice. The earl could simply buy your debts, call them in, and ruin you. I feel that Richard will go to war regardless.'

'Richard wouldn't—'

'Yes, he would. Richard is young, and this is what he's always wanted. If you try to stop him, you could lose him forever. And the earl is ruthless and doesn't like to be outwitted. As painful as it is, I believe you have no choice. You must let Richard go to France and be the knight at arms he wants to be, and pray to God that he is as good a knight as the earl says he is.'

That evening he watched Sir John drink himself into a stupor, and while he did, he assembled his plan. The following day, he refused Sir John any more wine, sent him to the trough to dunk his head and sober up.

Then he told him what he had to do.

CHAPTER 69

Joan dropped the pin on the floor and couldn't find it. She thought about leaving her veil behind, then thought better of it. Swearing under her breath, she went upstairs for another.

In the bedchamber, Sir John was bent over the coffer chest and on the floor beside him was a stack of silver plate. Her shadow fell across him and, as he turned, the shock — or was it guilt? — showed on his face. Frozen in mid-action, he held a fistful of her jewellery, the green and blue stones glinting innocently in the candlelight.

'What are you doing?' she asked.

'I'm sorting it.'

'Why?'

'Because I'm selling it.' He returned to his task, his arms deep inside the chest, her jewellery forming a pile of tangled colour unceremoniously dumped on the floor beside him.

'Are you going to tell me what's going on?' He pretended not to hear, probably hoping she would go away. 'John, I have a right to know. Are things so bad that you have to sell my jewels?'

He twisted round, his eyes cold and his jaw set firm. 'They will be if I don't.'

'John! What's happened? Tell me.' Joan touched her Mama's gold cross around her neck to reassure herself it was still there. No matter what happened, she'd never give that up.

'Richard is going to fight with the king in France. He needs men, weapons, armour... it all costs —'

'Why? He's just a boy. I thought he was never going into battle. That's what you've always said —'

'Yes, well, things change. The earl needs him and he's going. I don't have a choice, apparently, and I have to pay for it. So you'd better get Agnes to sort all your finest clothes; I'll have those too. We won't be entertaining for a while, so you won't need them.' Sir John turned his back, frantically turning things over and putting them on each allotted pile.

He still wasn't telling her the truth, and with growing unease she watched the piles grow. Dear God; Annie! Richard was going to war. She'd be devastated.

'Oh, and that looking glass I bought for you. That's worth a lot, so that can go too.'

He was serious. Joan stepped closer and peered over his shoulder into the vast empty cavern of the chest. 'Where are the coins?'

His face was just inches from hers, and in the dark lines she saw his worry, his fear but mostly in that frozen stare she had seen so many times before, she felt his enmity.

'Don't say it. There's nothing left and I haven't got time to explain.'

God, he was infuriating, but there was no point pursuing matters when he was in this mood. She bit her tongue. 'Are you happy about Richard going?'

'Of course I'm not happy, but there's nothing I can

do!' He stopped and rested his arms on the edge of the chest. 'When Richard leaves here, he will have the best armour, the best-equipped men and horses that I can buy. I can do that for him at least...' He tried to hide the pain in his face and the tremor in his voice, but she knew him too well. 'I want him to have the best chance. I want him to come back...' His voice was breaking, and, embarrassed, he turned away.

Joan put out her arm to console or comfort him perhaps, but he must have sensed it for he pulled away. Just a little, but enough.

She let her hand drop loosely to her side. There was nothing she could do.

CHAPTER 70

Joan took her time getting to Ellyn's cottage. Her stomach was twisting over, tight as a string on a lute. She hadn't felt like this since her wedding day. She didn't know what she was going to say, or how Annie would receive her. The news of Richard's departure to France would destroy her, but Joan hoped she could get close enough to help as a friend, and she still was a friend. She'd never thought of herself as anything else.

The cottage lay low on the top of the hill. It looked as though someone was sitting outside by the fence, but Joan couldn't be sure. She squinted in the morning light. Yes, there was definitely someone, but whether it was Ellyn or Annie, she couldn't tell. As she approached, she could see it was Annie, sitting on the ground, her knees up to her chin with her head resting on her arms.

'Annie.'

Annie looked up, her face ashen. Her wide eyes, usually so bright, were like dark pools of sorrow.

'So it's true,' she said, not moving. 'My boy's going to France.'

Joan slid from her horse and sat beside her. 'I'm so sorry. I had no idea, God's truth I didn't.' She went to put an arm around her but hesitated. 'How did you know? I only found out myself this morning.'

'One of the maids heard you and Sir John talking. Rumours spread like lice on a head, you know that.'

'God's teeth, and I got here as quickly as I could,' Joan lied. Sir John had been sorting her jewels at the time, and they'd talked about how much in debt they were. Lord, she wouldn't want that getting around too. The peasants might get restless and she'd never lift her head in the village again. 'Were folks saying anything else?'

'No, my lady. Just that Sir John was sending Richard with an army of men from the estate to fight in France.'

Thank God, the maid had probably rushed away with her piece of gossip. It was no time to be thinking of herself, but what a relief.

Annie's face puckered and she started to weep. Joan put an arm around her and drew her close.

'He'll be alright, Annie. I'm sure of it.' She wasn't sure that he would, but it was what Annie needed to hear.

'Will he? He's so young, and it's not fair. Sir John should be the one going, not my boy.'

'I know, but Richard's always wanted to be a knight. He wants to fight for his king and country. It's a very virtuous thing to do, and he's been learning the skills of battle with the Earl of Devonshire. The earl wouldn't let Richard go if he didn't think so highly of him.' Joan didn't think war at all virtuous, and she doubted the earl would care one way or the other how good Richard was, but she had to reassure Annie somehow.

'He will come back, won't he? I know I don't see much of him these days, but when I do catch a glimpse, it means everything. I couldn't bear it if he—you know.'

'Annie, as your friend, believe me, he'll be fine. You

know Richard. He's so confident and brash, he'll survive anything.'

Annie sniffed and wiped her nose with her sleeve. 'I suppose. Anyway, there's nothing I can do about it.'

'There's nothing any of us can do, and it won't help crying and worrying about it.' She would, they both would, but Joan didn't know what more she could say.

'Are we still friends?' Annie said quietly.

'Of course we are.' Joan pulled her close. 'We always have been, and I've missed you terribly.'

Annie smiled. 'I've missed you too. I suppose friends do quarrel sometimes, but I'm glad you're here now.'

'So am I. How are things? I've seen you out and about, busy as ever.'

'I'm rushed off my feet. Ellyn's showing her age and can't walk far, although on a good day she gets to the village. That's where she is now. In a way, I suppose we've swapped roles. She does most of the plant gathering and preparations while I do the visiting. I enjoy it though. It's nice to get out and meet folks. I just wish sometimes that I could help them more. I know some of our potions don't work that well, but folks like to think they do. And I keep trying to find new ways to heal.' Annie wiped her eyes. 'And you; how are you and Sir John?'

'We're fine.' Joan paused. It was good to be talking with Annie again. It felt just like old times. 'Actually, no. We're not fine. Swear you'll not tell a soul, but we live our own lives and just put on a show when we have to. He's not interested in me. I doubt he ever was. I don't think he even likes me. He only has two things in his life: Richard, and his growing status with high society.' And she wondered how long that would last now the coffers were empty.

'I'm sorry but not surprised. Rumours about your rows have been going around for years. I always thought he was a bit of a cold fish, and we all know what he thinks of the likes of us.'

'You're right, when his eyes are grey and staring with his jaw firm, he looks exactly like a herring.' Joan giggled.

'This feels like years ago when we sat on our log, sharing secrets and giggling, remember?' said Annie.

'I do, and I'm pleased we're friends again. We are, aren't we?'

Annie smiled. 'I will be if you will.'

'Come here and give me a hug.'

'We should celebrate and cheer ourselves up. We don't have wine, but Ellyn makes a mean elderflower drink.' Annie sprang to her feet. 'And then you can tell me about the dyes!'

CHAPTER 71

Joan stood at her window, watching the men below loading the wagons. Sir John's voice sliced through the air, sharp as the tip of Richard's lance. Was that the trunk holding his weapons? All that expense and for what? Sir John, after a flagon of wine too many, had admitted that the coffers were empty and until Michaelmas Day, they were penniless.

There he was again, his arm pointing this way and that like the spikes on a mace. How had it come to this? Joan still didn't understand why he was letting Richard go. There was something he wasn't telling her.

They were bringing out a second wagon, the one for Richard's supplies, his armour, and his shield. Richard's squire, who had been digging ditches and goading the oxen to the second ploughing until last week, fussed over the gleaming metal plate he had laboriously polished. He watched closely as the men loaded each heavy item of armour: two breastplates, four full-length leg protectors riveted at the knees, two shoulder protectors complete with leather straps, four full-length metal arm protectors and buckled straps, two helmets with over-the-shoulders chain-mail, two pairs of riveted metal gauntlets and metal over-shoes.

Would Richard really wear all that and still be able to sit on a horse and fight?

Four men pushed a barrel up two timber planks to the back of the wagon. They wiped their brows and cursed before loading two more barrels of vinegar. Somewhere in France, after Richard had survived the battlefield, his squire would help him out of his chain mail and armour and clean it, using a mix of the sand and vinegar. Joan felt as though she was living in one world whilst looking at another.

Richard was to make his way from the manor and through the village in a triumphant procession, gathering his band of men as he went. Sir John wanted his leaving to be a moment of glory and celebration.

Who was he fooling? He didn't want Richard to go any more than she or anyone else did, come to that. At least Thomas had been spared, but only after Joan had reminded her husband that, if Richard didn't come back, Thomas would be the only heir. That had sobered him up.

She didn't have a chance to say farewell last night, so she left her window and climbed the stairs to the other chamber where Richard was preparing to leave. She was genuinely sorry to see him go. Aggressive as he could be, she couldn't imagine him wielding a mace, swinging it high around his head and bringing it down on another's man's skull. Yet that was what he wanted to do; what he would do. The very thought sent a shudder down Joan's spine.

She tapped on the door and went in. Richard was dressed in his padded underclothes and chain mail and with a padded pourpoint jacket laced at the front. Over that, he wore a long surcoat in his favourite deep red and emblazoned with the Chiddleigh coat of arms across his chest and back.

The family coat of arms went back centuries to the days of King Richard I, according to Sir John. It featured four quadrants: a vert diagonal band for growth on argent for truth, an opposing azure band depicting loyalty, two wavy azure lines representing a river and a plain argent quadrant with four tenne lines signifying land and ambition. It represented an honourable, land-based family. Not one of aggression and war.

Joan wondered what Richard made of that, but whatever he thought of the coat of arms, he was still wearing it proudly. He looked much older than his fifteen summers. His shoulders were broad, like a man's, his arms muscular, and he had the countenance of a confident young man. Joan felt a lump rise to her throat and held out her arms to embrace him.

'It's a bit late for that, isn't it?' he snarled.

His words pierced her to the heart, and she stood awkwardly before him. 'I just thought I'd come and say farewell and God's speed. I might not see you for a while.'

Richard didn't move, his eyes never wavering. 'You never wanted to hug me before. I don't see why you should want to now.' He turned his back on her to gaze out of the window.

Joan was stunned, his words wounding her as surely as the sword by his side.

'I always knew you never wanted me,' Richard said. 'When I was little, I used to pray that one day you would, but you never did. You only had time for your precious Thomas.' His acerbic words burnt the air.

Dear God, he knew. All those years when she thought she had hidden it from him, he'd known. It was the one thing above all that she'd prayed God would never happen. And it had. Joan couldn't move, couldn't speak, couldn't even cry. She just stared at his back feeling shame and guilt.

Richard spun around and grabbed his shield so fast that she started.

'I love you, Mama,' he growled, as he brushed roughly past her on his way out the door.

Joan wanted to crawl away and die. For a moment she didn't move, then she shattered into a million pieces on the floor.

CHAPTER 72

In the village, small groups of peasants clustered in miserable huddles outside their homes and along the track. Annie was outside the forge with Peter and Janet. Peter's face was as dark as the thunderous sky above. Janet clung desperately to William, her hysterical wailing hurting her ears. The waiting was intolerable, for they knew that the procession was coming and would take him, and others like him, away from everything they had known to a brutal war they didn't understand.

Annie wanted to wail too, for she was part of this communal grief, but she couldn't show it, even though she was saying farewell to her son.

She heard solid wooden wheels rumbling on the track. Heads turned, and for just the briefest moment, the wailing stopped and a silent air of urgency rippled through the people. The relentless regular beats of hooves grew louder until they mingled with the jingle of harness and the snorts of the horses.

The village held its breath. The procession was almost upon them, and there wasn't much time.

A pair of horses crested the hill: Sir John on his black horse alongside Richard on his white charger. Steadily, they made their way down the slope, followed by a line of wagons stretching behind them. Behind the wagons, even though Annie couldn't see them, was a growing line of men and boys captured in their wake.

The horses were now walking along the main grass track through the village, and she could see Sir John's smile as he raised an eloquent hand to his people. No one smiled or waved back.

Richard sat astride a strong and handsome white horse, adorned with a red hood covering his ears and a large red and white sheet under the saddle which fell to below his knees. He held his chin high, his eyes shining. He looked magnificent in his red surcoat and metal chain mail. One hand clasped a long upright pole holding the Chiddleigh colours, a large flag bearing the family crest. From the height of his horse, he looked down on his people, proud and arrogant as ever.

Annie caught her breath with a flutter of pride. Her boy.

As the procession passed each cottage, mothers and wives clung to their loved ones in a last embrace as they, in their turn, tore themselves away and joined the straggle of dejected men ambling in the dust behind the wagons.

Janet held William tightly, and together they stood until the wagons trundled by and the very last man had scuffed his way passed the forge. It was his turn. For a moment they looked into each other's eyes. There were no words.

Annie looked on with a pang of envy. She wanted her boy and to be consoled with the other mothers, but all she could do was watch from the side. If only she could...

Fifteen-year-old William turned to his Pa and, with a few manly slaps on each other's backs and a curt nod to Annie, he stepped into the lane and went to war. He glanced back over his shoulder, his face pale with fearful tears brimming at the corners of his eyes.

He was scared, Annie could see that. When the time came, would Richard be scared? Nobody said it, but they were all thinking the same as her: that it may be the last time they saw their loved ones.

The procession stopped outside the inn. Rodin, the landlord, came out with two cups of ale for Sir John and Richard. Everyone waited in accusing silence while their lord and his son drank to the glory of the occasion. A few folks raised a weak cheer because it was expected, but the heavy atmosphere clung to their sour faces.

Annie understood their hatred, because she felt it too. Her resolve hardened. She would do it, pray God give her the courage, but there wasn't much time. She picked up her skirts and with a nod to Peter and Janet, quickly made her way through the bereft families to the edge of the village. Glancing over her shoulder, she saw that Sir John and Richard were giving their empty cups to Rodin and turning to their horses. If she hurried, she could still get there before they came.

Skitting across the ford, she rounded the bend and stopped. No one from the village could see her here. This was the place.

Her hands were sweating as she straightened her veil and smoothed her skirts. She took a deep breath and listened. The sound of the horses' hooves and the noise of wagon wheels resumed once more. The procession was moving on. He was coming. Her heart beat faster.

She stood on her toes straining for the first glimpse, her stomach twisting in knots. The wheels rumbled louder, and she could see the pair of horses, their black and white heads nodding in unison. Quickly she crossed to the opposite side where he would pass next to her.

Her heart pounded, the sound pumping through her ears. He was through the ford and coming closer. Holding her breath, she felt a trickle of sweat run down the back of her neck. She could do this. She could.

Now she could see his face. His eyes still shone, he was still smiling. Her hands were tight fists; she uncurled her fingers and wiped them on her skirts. The clouds of the horses' breath hung in the air, and Annie could hear the creak and taste the smell of the leather.

Her son was very close. Her mouth felt dry and she swallowed, her eyes never leaving him.

Now. It had to be now.

He was here, large above her with the smell of the horse and the chink of the bridle. Richard's leg passed so close that it brushed her, sending a shock tingling up the length of her arm.

Annie lifted her hand, but the words she'd practised stuck in her throat. She moved her hand towards him and opened her mouth, but she was too late; he had already passed.

Her hand stayed poised in mid-air as she watched his back, his horse's tail swishing gently from side to side. She had failed. Head down, she turned.

The sound of the hooves stopped. She glanced back. Richard was turning his horse. Annie couldn't move. He was coming towards her. She held her breath. He stopped just a pace in front of her, and she looked up into those beautiful brown eyes.

He was looking at her.

She trembled.

He was smiling at her!

She curtseyed.

She opened her hand and looked at the crumpled kerchief. The one Joan had given to her all those years ago and which had been kept safely at the bottom of a little casket with her most precious things until now.

Slowly, she held up her hand. 'For you, my lord. For luck.'

Richard raised an eyebrow just a little and tilted his head. He removed a gauntlet, his fingers just touching hers as he took her gift. He opened out the small pink square of stitched silk and gazed at it.

'I shall keep it close to my heart to guard me,' he said, before tucking it safely into his surcoat.

Did she imagine it, or were his eyes just a little moist?

With a final smile and nod, he turned away and, as Annie watched his back steadily disappear from view her heart swelled until she thought it would burst.

Her boy.

It was the best moment of her life.

CHAPTER 73

September 1346

Joan straightened her aching back and wiped the sweat from her brow with her sleeve. It was another scorching hot day, and she was glad of it. The wheat in the fields was tall with fat golden ears full of promise. It was harvest time, and it was going to be a good one. Everyone was at work cutting, raking and stacking the sheaves. It was a satisfying sight. She was parched and glanced toward the gate for the welcome sight of the maids bringing the midday meal. Disappointingly, the sun had only just moved out of the first quarter and there were no maids, but there was someone. He stared across the field, then strode toward her.

'So you're back,' Joan said, standing with one hand resting on her hip. She had dressed like a peasant with her brown kirtle tucked in high at the waist for working. She pushed her cap to the back of her head, the smell of honest sweat coming from her armpits.

Sir John looked her up and down, his expression changing from incredulity to scorn. 'What, may I ask, are you doing?'

'What does it look like? I'm gathering the wheat—'

'You're dressed like a peasant and smell like one.' Sir John wrinkled his nose in disgust.

Joan shrugged. 'What would you, my lord? That I work in my gown?'

'I would that you removed yourself from here, and dressed and behaved like the lady you are supposed to be. That is what I would, my lady.' His eyes bore into her, and his cheeks flamed.

'My lord, you have been away for three months and, as you can see, the corn is ripe for harvest.' Joan spoke slowly and clearly as though addressing a child. 'This weather may not hold, yet there are many more fields to reap, and since you have sent most of our men to France and we have no money to hire more, we need every hand to help or we shall all perish this winter. You may care to join us?'

Sir John's eyes widened in fury as she had known they would. She might be dressed and working like a peasant, but he wasn't going to treat her like one.

She'd coped very well these past months without him. The stables were neater and cleaner than they had ever been. She made a point of managing the peasants by involving them and not ruling by fear as he did, and as a result, they went about their business with renewed enthusiasm. She listened to what the reeves had to say, she discussed matters openly and they accepted her orders with a smile. Some peasants had done the work of two or three people, and they'd done it willingly. All it took was a little understanding. So how dare he turn up when he felt like it and assume he could interfere?

'Have you no pride in our position?' Sir John demanded.

Joan threw back her head and laughed. 'What position? In case you've forgotten, we are the lord and lady of an impoverished estate, most of which is owned by the Earls of Devonshire and Barcombe.' With a sense of confident superiority, she matched his stare as she called across to the reeve. 'Have the men finished cutting?'

The reeve nodded acknowledgement of his lord, but he addressed the Lady of the Manor. 'Yes, my lady. Should we move on?'

'Tell the men to take a short rest, and then yes. Hopefully, we'll get the next field cut and gathered by nightfall.' Joan turned back to Sir John. 'Sorry; you were saying?'

But Sir John was already striding away. Joan let out a long sigh. Life had been so much easier without him, and now he was back.

The moon was high by the time they finished the second field and every part of Joan screamed with exhaustion. She dropped her boots by the door. All she wanted to do was to get out of her filthy clothes, lie down on her mattress and sleep forever. Trailing her mantel behind her, she headed for the stairs.

'We must speak.'

Sir John's voice startled her. She hadn't noticed him sitting in the darkness. 'I'm too tired now, John. We'll talk after the harvest.'

'Look at you, working like a peasant. Your hands are red raw and cut. I don't understand you.'

Joan gave him a withering look. 'No, I doubt that you do.' She started to haul herself up the stairs to her bedchamber.

'No, you don't. I want to talk now.' He was beside her in two strides and grabbed her wrist.

'Don't you dare!'

His hold tightened, and he dragged her over to the

446

hearth and threw her into a chair. 'I do dare, because I am your lord and I want to talk, and you, my lady, are going to sit there and listen.'

His face was so close that the smell of wine on his breath made her gag and turn away. 'You've been drinking, and judging by the number of flagons on the floor, far too much. I'm not going to sit here and talk to a drunkard. I'll talk to you when you're sober.' She made to stand, but he pushed her back and gripped her shoulders so hard that she winced. He was towering over her, his stony eyes piercing through her.

'Yes, I've been drinking. I've been drinking a lot and do you know why? Because I finally get home after three months away and what do I find? The Lady of Manor working side-by-side with my peasants. Look at you! You're a disgrace to the Chiddleigh name.'

'Well, at least I'm doing something to try and keep the Chiddleigh name alive and not squandering our money on any cock-eyed idea that the Earl of Devonshire tells me to! And I'm not the one who sent your favourite son to his death on the battlefields of France!'

She didn't see it coming and the force of the blow threw her sideways. The sting of his strike spread across her cheek, and she glared at him with utter loathing. He glared back, his steely eyes never colder. Joan braced herself but then, as though suddenly spent, Sir John ran his fingers through his hair, shook his head, and slumped into his seat.

'Do what you like,' he said. 'I don't care anymore.'

CHAPTER 74

Joan took the latest panel of dyed cloth from the drying rack. Holding it out in front of her, she examined it closely, then bit her lip and shook her head. It was another disappointment. The colour was the brightest she'd made, but even after all her years of work, it still wasn't the brilliant red scarlet she was looking for.

'I hoped I'd find you here. I'm on my way home and dropped by to see the dyes.' Annie gazed round at the long lines of tun barrels with poles lined up ready for the maids to pummel the cloth and work the dyes with their feet. 'You've come a long way. What's that you've got?' she said, stepping around an array of pots and baskets full of white alum, murrey berries and tree bark.

'It's my latest effort. What do you think? It's nearly there, but I just can't quite get it right. I've tried everything, and I'm not sure what to do now.' Joan gazed at the cloth.

Annie put down her basket and stepped closer. She frowned and tilted her head first one way and then the other.

'I know what I would do,' she said, feeling the cloth between her fingers. 'There's a moss we use for sore skin. Ellyn calls it feather moss because it looks like the down of a young goose. It makes a wondrous green lotion that softens the skin. Isobel swears by it.'

'I'm sure she does, but what has it got to do with my dyes?'

'I'm coming to that. We grind the moss to a pulp and strain the juice—'

'And?'

'—and the juice is a bright, and I mean, a bright scarlet. I'm thinking that if you add some juice to your latest mix, it might just give you the right colour. And it really does make the skin soft.'

'So you think it might work and soften the cloth at the same time?' A slow smile spread across Joan's face. 'Annie, you're brilliant!'

'I know I am,' Annie said, smiling. 'The moss grows in the peat bogs on the high moor. I'll pick you some if you like.'

Joan's eyes lit up as she grabbed Annie in a tight hug. 'How I've missed you.'

'Let me go! You're squeezing the life out of me, and it's only an idea. It might not work.'

'What might not work?' Carac put his head around the door, smelt the urine and immediately reached for his kerchief.

Joan smiled with real delight. 'Carac! What a pleasure. I haven't seen you for a while.'

'Indeed. I find these warmer days ease my aching bones, and I like to get out when I can.'

'God pray they continue. I was just showing Annie my latest cloth, and she's got an idea to brighten the colour. Who knows? This time next year we could be selling the Chiddleigh scarlet cloth.' Joan's eyes glowed at the thought.

'After all your work, that would be most deserving and gratifying. I heard that Sir John was back. Is he home?'

'He came home three days ago. You'll find him in the hall, sitting in his chair surrounded by empty wine flagons.'

Carac raised an eyebrow. 'Indeed? Then I had better make haste. And well done with a good harvest,' he added over his shoulder.

'Is that true?' Annie asked. 'About Sir John, I mean. Is he really drinking?'

Joan sighed. 'Like a market sot. Sit down, Annie.'

Annie did as she was told. Joan sat quietly beside her, biting her lip and staring at her feet. 'You weren't in the field when John came home and found me reaping the harvest with my skirts around my hips, so you wouldn't have seen how furious he was. I suppose I should have taken more time to talk to him, but he made me so angry with his self-righteous manner. Anyway, by the time we'd finished reaping Park field, it was very late and I was so tired I could hardly stand. When I got in, he was waiting for me. He'd been drinking. We had a dreadful row. He said I was a disgrace, and I accused him of sending Richard to his death — I spoke in haste, and I'm sure it's not true,' she added quickly, seeing Annie's face fall. 'And then, for the first time, he struck me.'

'He struck you? Oh, Joan, what did you do?'

'Nothing; what could I do? He's never hit me before, and I was so shocked, But do you know, I feel glad he hit me, because it forced me to admit what I've known for a long time: that he is a cold, selfish and unfeeling man, and I hate him.'

Annie took hold of her hands. 'I'm sorry, but I've never understood how you ever liked him. What happened after he hit you?'

'We glared at each other for what seemed like an age, then he slumped back in his chair and told me to do what I liked because he didn't care anymore. So that's what I'm doing while he sits in his chair all day and night with a growing pile of empty cider jars and wine flagons at his feet. For which I am grateful, because I can't bear to even look at him, let alone have him to my bed.' She shuddered. 'God forgive me, but I wish he'd never come home —'

She broke off as a shadow cast across the floor. Pray God, Agnes or some maid wasn't listening. It was bad enough they knew of Sir John's state without gossip spreading of her own thoughts.

'Simon stopped me in the yard. He's just leaving with the wagon to go to the lime kilns and wants to know if you want any extra lime for the dyes?' Carac stepped inside.

Joan breathed a sigh of relief. 'Yes; tell him yes. Thank you.'

'Dear God, do you think he heard?' Annie whispered.

'I hope not, but I'd trust Carac completely. If he did, he won't say anything.' But Joan still bit her lip and frowned. She didn't want Carac to think ill of her.

'I'm sorry about you and Sir John. What are you going to do?'

She shrugged. 'What can I do? I shall continue as though he isn't here. I like managing the estate, having to plan and make decisions. And now I feel free, as though a heavy cloud has finally lifted. Every morning, I wake with my mind full of things to be done. And I'm pleased with the way the estate's running; the threshing is finished, the barns satisfyingly full of grain, the men are about to start the last ploughing of the year and the carp are breeding well in the ponds.' She smiled. 'And, thanks to you, I shall soon have my scarlet dye.'

CHAPTER 75

Carac was furious. How dare Sir John raise a hand to Joan, a wonderful woman whom he'd always adored? He wasn't surprised that it had happened or that Joan felt as she did, not after all the years of turmoil. Sir John was such a fool. He'd never appreciated how fortunate he was to have such a wonderful wife, and she certainly wasn't the sort of woman a husband could beat into submission. If he were younger, he'd throw down his hood and challenge Sir John, but he wasn't and Sir John was still his friend as well, albeit a difficult one.

Carac entered the hall with a sinking heart. Sir John was slumped low in his chair, his arms flopped over the sides and his legs sprawled wide. His head lolled to one side as though it was too heavy, his lips fluttering with every snore.

What was the man thinking? Carac tutted, stepped over the discarded empty flagons and jars strewn across the floor and shook him.

'What?' Sir John slowly opened his eyes. 'Oh, it's you. If you've come to moan about your figures, see Joan. She's running things now.' He waved an arm vaguely in the direction of the door and reached for his goblet, but Carac was there before him.

'I don't think you need any more of that. What do you think you're doing?'

'What's it look like? I'm getting drunk. It's what I do these days.'

Carac raised an eyebrow at Sir John's wine-stained tunic, his untrimmed beard and bloodshot eyes. He wouldn't get any sense out of him like this.

'The best thing for you is fresh air. Come on.' He hauled Sir John to his feet and trawled him to the door. 'We'll go to the orchards.'

He was getting too old for this, Carac thought. His shoulder ached and he missed his stick. After a few turns amongst the trees, he'd had enough. 'Is your head clearer now?'

'Pounding, if you must know. Why are you here? To talk about money, I suppose.'

'Let us sit awhile. I came to hear the tale of your journey with Richard. I confess the figures are of concern, but tell me, what has brought you to behave in such a manner?'

Sir John rubbed a hand over his head. 'Joan's taken over. Did you see her? Dressed as a peasant —' he spat the word — 'and working in the fields like one. It's easy for her with her feminine wile. As a lady, of course, the men and peasants fawn over her.' He wiped his hand over his face. 'She wouldn't listen, of course. We rowed, and do you know what she said? She said that I had sent Richard to his death. She had no right. God's teeth, I feel guilty enough; I don't need her telling me!'

'It was an unfortunate remark.'

'I told her she could get on with it and that I didn't care. And I don't. There's no point anymore.' Sir John picked a grass and sucked the end.

Carac had seen that evasive look before. Sir John was hiding something.

'Tell me about your journey with Richard. I imagine it was a proud moment when he set sail from Southampton.'

Sir John slid his foot through the grass, rubbed a hand over his face again and let out a long sigh. 'I didn't even get to Exeter. I expected Richard to be proud, acknowledging the peasants as we rode past; you know how he can be.'

Carac nodded. He knew exactly how arrogant the boy could be.

'But as soon as we left the village, he went quiet. I thought he might be a little sad at leaving, so I started to talk about all the things we would do on the estate when he returned. He let me talk, then he stopped his horse and looked me straight in the eye. I'm not coming home, he said. I'm a knight now and my oath is to fight the king's cause.

'I was shocked, of course, and blustered on about his inheritance, but he cut me short. You don't understand. I've lived in castles and mixed with the real high nobility. A remote sheep estate just isn't enough. It bores me, and in truth, I'm glad to be out of it.'

That would have cut Sir John to the quick, Carac knew. It seemed as though the boy was even more callous than his father. 'I'm sure he didn't mean it. He'll change his mind.'

'No, he won't.' Sir John discarded his grass and stared absently ahead.

'John, Richard spoke very harshly and with little regard to your feelings. He's pained you, but things will work out when he gets back —'

'Don't give me those platitudes. I know my son. He's ashamed of me. That's the truth. He didn't want me with him in front of his high-ranking friends in case I embarrassed him. He deliberately rode with the others, leaving me behind like some stray cur hound. He didn't even invite me to their evening camps. I could hear him and used to watch him in the shadows of the torches, making merry and guffawing over crude jests with the other knights sat around the fires. He's got what he wanted. He doesn't care a tinker's arse for me.'

And Sir John had given everything to that wretched boy, Carac thought. It was a pity the Earl of Devonshire got hold of him, but he'd expected nothing else from that old fox. 'What did you do?'

'A day out of Exeter, I'd had enough of being made the fool. I found Richard and told him I was turning back. I nearly didn't bother to tell him; he wouldn't have missed me. Probably for the best, he said. You'd be bored amongst us knights talking battles and things that you don't understand.' Sir John plucked a fresh blade of grass to chew.

If Richard had been Carac's son, he'd have dragged him by the scruff of the neck, given him a sharp tongue and taken his belt to him. It was what all boys needed from time to time, and Sir John should have done it years ago.

'So what did you do then?'

'I just rode and drank for weeks before coming back. I couldn't face going home. You can understand that, can't you?'

He could. Sir John's pride had been smashed by that ungracious devil of a son. If only Richard had been more like his understanding grandfather, old Sir James.

'Do you remember that time when you and Favian went out shooting arrows and accidentally hit the Earl of Barcombe's best ram?' he asked suddenly. 'You were afraid to face him, so you disappeared. It took me three whole days to find you hiding in the woods.'

'Favian, the Earl's nephew! That's a name I haven't heard in a long time. What's that got to do with Richard?'

'I'm simply saying that you can't run away. I'm sure Joan would have understood, and things will sort themselves out.' It wasn't the most convincing consolation, but it was the best that Carac could do.

'I doubt it. Anyway, by the time I got home, I'd faced the truth. Richard's right: I am nothing more than an impoverished lowly knight with a son who doesn't want me and a wife who doesn't need me. It would be funny if it wasn't so tragic.' Sir John shook his head, ran his fingers through his hair and stood up. 'So there's no point, and I really don't care anymore. And now I need a drink.'

Carac didn't try to stop him. He'd done his best, but he doubted it had been enough.

CHAPTER 76

Joan paused on the threshold and breathed in the warmth of the sun on her face. In the middle of the yard, Sir John was struggling to climb aboard Baron. He could hardly stand upright. He held the stirrup with his right hand but his left foot kept missing. She couldn't remember the last time he was sober. He disgusted her.

It was almost a year to the day since Richard had left for France. Ever since Sir John's return last autumn, Joan had watched him turn to drink while she continued running the estate. And she still enjoyed every moment.

Sir John was swaying in the saddle now, and Joan made a wager with herself that he would topple off somewhere between the yard and the village inn. It had happened before. He was a sad and pathetic shadow of his former self.

The midday bell was ringing. She was hungry and wiped her hands on the sides of her apron and shook off the horse hairs. The grey mare had produced another nice foal. She'd turn the pair of them out into the near fields in a day or two. There was something satisfying about seeing a foal like that and knowing that her price would cover Thomas's place at the University of Oxford. She was so proud of him.

Two men rode into the yard. Joan shielded her eyes against the sun. She didn't recognise them but, by the look of their smart clothes, the jewelled brooches on their shoulders and high leather boots, they appeared respectable. They sat on fine horses too, she noticed.

'Sires, be welcome. Do you require assistance?'

They removed their hats with a flourish. The one on the bay horse spoke but stayed mounted. 'Good morrow, my lady. We seek Sir John de Chiddleigh. Is this the manor of Court Barton?'

'It is, but Sir John's not here. I am Lady de Chiddleigh, you may speak to me.'

The man glanced over her dishevelled clothes, and Joan self-consciously brushed a stray hair from her face.

'My lady, we come from Exeter regarding business with Sir John. When might he return?'

How was she supposed to know? Probably when he couldn't drink anymore. When he did finally return, he'd be in no state to talk to these men of business. 'I'm not sure. Who shall I say called?'

'When he returns, be pleased to remind him of his contracts. He'll know what you mean. Tell him that the business must be concluded by the end of the year.'

'What business? What contracts?'

'Prithee, my lady, our business is with Sir John. Be pleased to tell him that if matters are not concluded satisfactorily, we shall have no choice but to return and take action.'

'What action? Who are you? I am the Lady of the Manor and demand to know your business here!'

They didn't answer and were already turning their horses. Well, really! Whatever business they had with

459

Sir John, it must be important for them to have come so far. The man said there were contracts. Joan didn't know of any contracts, although there had been that time when Sir John was always going to Exeter on business. Maybe that's what he meant. Joan had never found out what that business was, and what were these contracts he spoke of?

She picked up her skirts and hurried inside. Contracts would be in the form of sealed scrolls or folded parchment. Where would he keep them?

Joan gazed around the hall. Not in here; anyone might find them. If she had important papers, she'd keep them in the coffer chest. She hurried upstairs.

The chest sat in the far corner of the bedchamber. It was an enormous solid looking trunk, large enough for a man to lie down in, and made of thick oak, the corners and sides reinforced with several iron strips. On the front and set firmly in the centre was a sturdy round iron lock, but the key was missing, and in all the years they'd been married, Joan had never noticed where he kept it.

Her eyes swept around the room. It wouldn't be under the mattress, too easy to find. Not in his clothes trunk either; she and the maids often went there. She glanced up. That only left on top of the beams.

Dragging a stool over, she placed it beneath the first beam. Her fingertips just touched the top. She felt as far as she could, but there was no key. Moving her stool, she tried again but there was nothing.

Joan wiped the dust from her hands and moved to the next beam. At the end, where it joined with the slant of the roof, her fingers touched something. It was certainly heavy and smooth like iron. It felt cold and was longer than her hand. Excited, she wriggled it forward until it fell to the floor with a loud clunk. It was a large iron key with a ring at the top, a thick shank and a solid square of regular teeth at the bottom. It had to be the key to the chest.

She picked it up and inserted it into the lock. It was stiff and reluctant to turn. It must be the right one, though; what else would it be used for?

With both hands, she used all her strength and, with a begrudging grind, the key started to turn. The lock clicked a few times and then sprang open with a snap.

Joan inched open the lid and peered inside. There were no coins, and her jewellery had long been sold, but in the far corner, there was what looked like a roll of sacking. She'd never noticed it before, but Sir John was protective of his coffer chest and she'd only seen inside a few times. Her heart began to race and she reached in.

It was a long linen bag pulled tight by a drawstring at one end. Her fingers trembling, she fumbled with the twine. She slid her hand inside and touched parchment.

It had to be what she was looking for. She took it out, but there was more in the bag. Quickly, she tipped the contents into her lap. There were six rolled scrolls made of smooth, soft calfskin, the kind that only the most expensive parchment was made of. These documents were clearly important. Each scroll was neatly bound with two red silk laces, their long ends sealed together with an oval red wax seal.

Legal documents were sealed in such a manner. These must be the contracts the men had been referring to. The seals were still intact, and the same one had been used for each scroll, but she didn't recognise it. Whatever they were, and whoever they were from, Sir

John must have known, for he hadn't bothered to open them but simply stored them for safe-keeping.

Wasting no time, Joan picked one at random. Her insides tightening, she took her eating knife from her belt and broke the seal. Carefully, she unfurled the scroll.

It was written in a fair hand using black ink. She scanned to the bottom of the parchment. Robert Mockhampton. She'd never heard of him but it was his seal on the silk lace. She knew the other name though: Sir John de Chiddleigh.

Holding her breath, Joan sat back on her heels and started to read. Slowly at first, then more quickly. She got to the end and stared at the words dancing in front of her eyes.

It couldn't be true! She bit her lip and read it again to make sure. There was no mistake. She dropped her hands to her lap. Surely not. He couldn't have.

She took another scroll and read through. It was the same as the last. She picked up the next, and the next, until all six scrolls were scattered around her feet.

Dear God, what had he done?

CHAPTER 77

Whilst Joan sat in her chamber, stunned by what she had discovered, a motley looking group of men was walking down the hill towards Ashetyne.

They were too far away for Annie to recognise, but she didn't like the look of their bedraggled beards and tattered clothes. Whoever they were, they were heading for the village. She hurried back past the inn to the forge.

'Peter, you'd better come. There's a rough-looking group coming this way.'

Peter put a hand to the knife on his belt, picked up a rasp and followed her outside. Seven men were splashing their way across the ford, and a sorry-looking bunch they were too, as they dragged their feet with bowed heads. A tall one limped on one leg with the aid of a forked pole tucked under his right arm, and another's left sleeve dangled loosely over a stump of an arm.

'By the state of them, I'll wager they've been on the road a long while. They won't give any trouble.' Peter let go of his knife and relaxed his arm.

There was something, just something about the man with one arm. Annie looked again. Her eyes widened and she gasped.

It couldn't be! She checked again to make sure, and then crossed herself.

'By all the saints and praise the Lord,' she whispered. 'Peter!' She clutched his arm. 'Peter, I think it's William. Look!'

Peter stared at the figure. The rasp slipped through his fingers and he ran toward him, screaming his son's name at the top of his voice.

'Janet! Janet, make haste!' Annie rushed into the forge.

'Annie, in God's name, what is it?' Janet came through from the back, wiping her hands on her apron.

'It's William! They're back from France. Quick! He's coming down the lane with some others.'

Janet paled. 'My William? Are you sure?'

'Of course I'm sure! I saw him with my own eyes!'

'The Lord be praised.' Janet crossed herself, began fumbling with the ties of her apron and put her hands to her hair.

'Oh, you've no time for all that! Make haste!' Annie grabbed Janet's wrist and hauled her into the lane in a whirl of excitement. If William was back, then so was Richard.

Folks spilt out of their cottages and, as word spread, workers in the fields dropped their tools and came running. One of the men in the group waved and shouted, but Annie was too far away to hear. The rest of the group were waving too, in high sweeping movements above their heads. Anxiously, Annie searched their faces.

He wasn't there. Desperately, she looked again, then beyond them, but no proud knight was sitting on a white horse.

She had the most dreadful feeling in the pit of her stomach.

'Where's Master Richard?' she shouted, grabbing the nearest person's arm, but everyone was running and yelling and her words were lost. She ran with the crowd, swept up in the tide of bodies clamouring around the men. Like a sea rolling in, they moved towards the inn.

Annie was squeezed through the tiny doorway and found herself pushed up against the side and wedged between two bulky men. By the smell of them, they'd been spreading cow dung on the fields.

'Bryce wants a cider!' a voice called from the front.

'Then what are we waiting for?'

The room hushed as Rodin, the landlord, ceremoniously lined up seven ale cups on the dark oak trestle. He splayed his two arms, placing a hand firmly on either side of the row, and looked up. 'Now then, what's it to be; ale or cider?'

'Both!' said a voice in the crowd amidst hales of laughter.

Rodin filled cup after cup from his barrels, and not until every man held a cup did he pour the last cider for himself. 'Quiet! Quiet, everybody! They're going to tell their story. Leave the door open, it's that hot in here with so many!' he yelled above the din.

Annie strained to see. Mark, Joan's stableman, was holding a crutch under one arm. He'd lost a leg and dear God, William! The left sleeve of his tunic hung loosely at his side. Where was Janet? She searched the faces but it was impossible to see.

'Shouldn't we wait for the others?' a voice called from the midst of bodies.

Mark shifted his weight on the makeshift crutch.

'There are no others,' he said quietly.

'What about my Cedric?' A woman's voice came from the back.

'I'm sorry. We're the only ones left.'

No one moved or spoke, and then a sob came from somewhere in the room, followed by another and another spreading through the crowd as disbelieving voices mingled and rose to fill the room.

'What about Master Richard?' Annie shouted. 'Is he still fighting in France?'

The room fell silent. It was the way the men glanced awkwardly from one to the other that made her stomach lurch. Suddenly, she felt very sick and very cold.

'No, he isn't,' Mark answered at last. 'There was a big battle in a place called Crecy. When it was over, we found him on the side of the battlefield.'

Annie put her hands over her ears, trying to blot out what she already knew.

'We brought back his short sword and surcoat,' added Arthur.

The room started to swim around her. The crush of people was suffocating. She couldn't breathe; she had to get out. Pushing and swearing, she elbowed her way through the bodies to the door.

Once outside, she fell against the wall, her chest so tight she couldn't breathe.

We found him on the side of the battlefield.

No. No, it wasn't true. It couldn't be true. Mark must have made a mistake. Her boy was still somewhere in France, or maybe riding up Oakwolde hill at this very moment. Annie swallowed and looked up the lane towards the town, straining for the sound of hooves.

The only sound was a blackbird singing nearby. Her boy wasn't coming home and, deep down, she knew he never would be.

The picture she'd carried with her since the day he'd left was as clear as ever. Her beautiful boy, with his mop of thick black hair and long curling eyelashes, sitting on his fine horse and smiling at her as she handed up the kerchief. I shall keep it close to my heart to guard me, he had said. She could still feel the tingle of his touch.

A hot sting sprang to her eyes. Her knees buckled and, covering her face with her hands, she slid to the ground and sobbed until her heart was empty. Through tear-filled eyes, she raised her head and saw her hill. 'My boy,' she whispered. 'It's over.'

The hill was drawing her. Slowly, she got up, wiped her face with her sleeve, and started walking.

She nearly bumped into Sir John. He was staggering, his steps awkward as though his legs didn't know where to go. His head was down and, as she drew level, she saw it was buried in his hands. He looked at her through his fingers, his face contorted in an agony she understood only too well.

'My boy,' he said thickly. 'My boy is gone.'

'I know, my lord. I do know.'

CHAPTER 78

'Thank you for telling me.' Joan and Mark stood awkwardly in the yard, not knowing what to say. She tried not to stare at the pole tucked under his arm. 'You didn't walk from Ashetyne, did you?' she said.

'No, my lady. Borum gave me a ride on his wagon. I...have these.' Mark tucked his crutch high under his arm and held out a blood-stained piece of cloth with a short sword placed reverently across the top. 'They're Richard's; his short sword and the coat of arms from his surcoat...' His voice trailed off.

It was a sorry looking offering in exchange for a short life. Joan stifled a cry. She was still the lady. She must hold herself together. 'Thank you. I know these will mean a lot to Sir John. Do you know how he died?'

Mark hitched his crutch for better support and stared uneasily at the ground. 'After it was over, we found him at the edge of the battlefield. I didn't see much of him during the battle. Too busy fighting.' He tried a poor joke.

'I understand. At least he died bravely and with honour, fighting with his king as he always wanted. Knowing that makes me very proud.' Her voice trembled.

Mark averted his eyes. 'Yes, my lady.'

'I can't help noticing your leg. Were many of you were injured?'

'William from the smithy lost an arm; Arthur a couple of fingers; and, yes, I lost my leg.'

'I'm sorry. Truly I am. Of all the men who went, it could have been much worse, I suppose.' She wanted to flee, to have time to sort her feelings, but she needed to keep acting her part.

'Three out of seven, my lady. The rest died out there,' he said accusingly.

Joan's hand flew to her mouth. 'Dear Lord, I had no idea. Only seven? But over a hundred of you went. That's dreadful! All those men gone, and now their families are left to cope.'

She did feel truly shocked and guilty. Guilty for what might have been, for Richard and for Sir John. It was an uncomfortable moment, neither of them knowing what to say.

Feeling the cloth in her hands, it was surreal to think that it had been to France on Richard's back and when he went bravely into battle with his men.

'Well, it's good to have you back,' she said awkwardly, staring at the cloth 'I've missed you, and so have the horses. You must rest for a while and then we'll see. Maybe we can find you some lighter duties.' Good Lord, this was torment.

'I'll cope, my lady. I walked home from France. I'll manage here.'

Joan ended the conversation as quickly as she could, and as soon as he was out of sight, she fled to the orchards. It was the only place she was sure to be alone. Sitting under a favourite tree, she spread the remains of the surcoat over her lap.

469

Gently, she ran her fingers over it. This sad little piece of cloth was all that was left of Richard. She hoped he'd died quickly.

The memory of the last time they were together and the terrible truth he had spoken flooded back. Joan squeezed her eyes tight to block it out, but doing so hadn't worked then and it didn't now. In spite of everything she had done to him, he still wanted her.

I love you, Mama. Those were the last words he'd said, and they would haunt her for the rest of her life. It was all such a tragic waste.

When she returned to the hall, Sir John was slumped in his chair by the hearth, his legs outstretched with one arm dangling over the side. His tankard had slipped from his hand, spilling the last dregs of red wine on to the floor leaving a dark red stain. His mouth was open, his chest rising and falling in a heavy rhythm. Joan usually felt disgusted when she saw him like this, but now she felt only pity. The news would destroy him. She wouldn't wake him. Let him sleep off the drink in peace while he could.

She went upstairs and opened the coffer chest for the second time that day. There was no way she could discuss the scrolls with him now either. That would have to wait.

Reverently, she laid Richard's cloth and sword inside the chest. She would give them to Sir John later, after she'd told him. Before closing the lid, she softly ran her fingers over the cloth and touched the handle of the sword. She wanted to cry but couldn't; her guilt was too great. She thought she'd done her best at the time, but had she? Had she really? No matter that she wasn't his true moth—Annie! Good Lord, did Annie know?

Joan had to be the one to tell her. It would be awful if she heard it from anyone else. She ought to tell Sir John first, but she could hear from his snores that he wouldn't wake for hours. She had time.

Quickly, she crossed the yard, saddled Star and rode out to Ellyn's cottage. Crossing the river at the mill, she took the familiar path leading around the hill. As she approached the fork, the place where Richard had galloped off that day, she saw a sad little figure coming slowly down from the top of the hill, shoulders and head drooping.

Throwing herself off her horse, Joan ran towards her. 'Annie! I came to tell you—'

Annie slowly raised her head. Her eyes were red, her cheeks still wet. 'I heard,' she said simply. 'I had to go one last time, to say farewell.'

She looked so alone and vulnerable. Joan's heart melted with shared pity and remorse. Her eyes welled up, and she opened her arms. Annie slowly walked into them and laid her head on her shoulder.

'Don't say anything, Joan. Just...hold me and be my friend.'

CHAPTER 79

It was dark by the time Joan got home. She felt better. It was right that she and Annie had shared such a moment. The secret they had held and had wreaked havoc on their lives for so long was over. Now, she had to find the words to tell Sir John that his son was dead.

She took a deep breath and quietly entered the hall. As she expected, he was in his chair, bent over with his head in his hands. He turned vaguely towards her with vacant eyes then buried his head once more.

He knew.

He looked so fragile. She wanted to rush over, put her arms around him and tell him everything would be all right. But she didn't and they wouldn't. The last time she'd reached out to him, he'd pushed her away. Instead, she walked over and, kneeling in front of him, gently took his hands and held them.

The agony in his face cut through her. Her handsome Sir John looked old. His eyes were swollen with dark circles and his cheeks blotched with tears.

'I am so sorry,' she said softly.

He nodded and dropped his head. 'All I wanted for him was the best. Was that so wrong? In the end, I ruined everything. If I hadn't been so stupid, he would never have gone to France and he'd still be alive.' His voice cracked as he wept.

'That's not true. You did everything for him. He always wanted to be a knight. He would have gone some time. You mustn't blame yourself. You could have talked to me; I'd have understood.'

Would she, though? To her shame, she'd been so full of herself running the estate that all she noticed was his drinking, and she'd been contemptuous of that. She'd never bothered to ask why he was drinking, and she should have. She was his wife, no matter what she thought of him, and it was her duty to support him. As a mother and now as a wife, she had failed.

'I don't know why you never loved Richard, but when I saw that, I just wanted to save him from what I went through as a boy. I tried to love him for both of us, I suppose.'

'The way your mother never loved you?'

He nodded. 'My mother was a harlot,' he said, so quietly she wasn't sure she'd heard him right.

'I can't believe that. She was Lady de Chiddleigh—'

'I should have told you about my family years ago, but it's painful to think of it, and I was so ashamed.'

Joan shuffled a little nearer. She felt closer to him than she had in years. 'Will you tell me now?'

Sir John looked up at her, his eyes full of guilt and remorse. He nodded slowly. 'I owe you that. Papa, Sir James, was the High Sheriff of Devonshire. He was often away on Sheriff's business. One summer, when I was about four, I started seeing a lot of Uncle Boren. He was always with Mama. I was only little and thought what a kind uncle he was to look after her. I rarely saw Aunt Matilda, his wife, and I remember being sad about that because I liked her. She used to bring me honey cakes.' He smiled at the memory. 'Then, one morning, I found Mama and Uncle Boren together on the mattress where Papa usually slept. I didn't understand, but I knew by the look of horror and shame on my mother's face it was wrong.

'You have to understand that my Uncle Boren was the second son. He had no right to anything. I realise now that he was jealous of my father. Papa gave him a living and land on the estate, of course, but Boren wanted more. He was clever at making things, I remember. He made me a wooden rattle once. Not a baby's rattle; it had a handle and when I turned it quickly, the end spun, making a clacking noise. I loved that rattle. I think Boren wanted to use his skills around the estate, but Papa wouldn't let him. They were always arguing. I think Boren resented him.

'Anyway, when Papa came back in the autumn, he shouted a lot at Mama, and she was always crying. I remember being quite scared and thought it was my fault, though I didn't know why. One day Papa sat me down, wearing his serious face, and told me Mama wasn't very well and was going away for a while.' He sighed.

Joan waited and let him take his time.

'Not long after she'd gone, Papa and Uncle Boren had an awful row. They were in the hall, standing by the hearth and yelling at each other. I remember thinking that my Uncle Boren looked like a huge ferocious bear, with his long unkempt beard and wild hair halfway down his back. His voice was loud and rough. He scared me and I hid behind a large chest.

'I'd never seen my father so angry. His face was red,

and I thought, just for a moment, that he was the monster from the moor. Then, after more shouting, Papa, usually so calm and controlled, grabbed Uncle Boren by the front of his tunic and threw him out of the house, swearing and cursing at the top of his voice that he wasn't a Chiddleigh and he was never to darken his doors again.

'Papa banished him to the far side of the estate to a place called Combe Hide. It's a poor farmstead of one hundred acres of mostly wet grassland. I never found out if Aunt Matilda knew the truth, but she went with him.

'Papa was different after Mama and Uncle Boren had gone. He was irritable and stamped his boots across the hall. He always looked sad and didn't laugh anymore. I never understood why and thought I must have done something bad. I cried a lot.

'Then Carac became my tutor. Over the years, I saw less of Papa and more of Carac. He became my father figure. The following spring, Mama came home with a child in her arms. I was thrilled that I had a brother, but Papa started shouting again and Mama always seemed to be crying. I used to hide with my hands over my ears. Carac would take me for long rides to escape. I got to know the estate at a very early age.' He smiled wryly. 'Then one day, the shouting stopped, the baby disappeared, and Mama took to her room. Papa told me she wasn't well. The truth was that she was so ashamed, she became a recluse and spent the rest of her life on her knees praying for forgiveness. Not long after, Papa decided to move here, but she stayed at the old manor and died about two years later.'

It was such a sad story, it made Joan feel humble. She'd had such a happy childhood.

'What happened to her child?' she asked.

'Aunt Matilda and Uncle Boren took him to Combe Hide. They called him Aldred.'

Her jaw dropped. 'Aldred was your half-brother?'

'Yes, but at the time I never knew. I thought maybe the baby had died and that was why Mama was sad. I couldn't understand why she shut herself away from me, I thought it was my fault. It's a terrible thing for a child to think he's not worthy of his mother's affection. For years I lived with that.' He swallowed. 'When I saw how you were struggling with Richard, and particularly later when Thomas was born, I couldn't let Richard suffer as I did. You do see that?'

'Yes, I do, but I wish you'd told me. If I'd known, maybe things would have been better between us and between Richard.'

'I should have told you, but at the time, all I saw was history repeating itself. I was determined not to let that happen.'

She couldn't be angry with him — they were both hurting — but the silly, well-meaning man! If he had told her, history wouldn't have repeated itself. 'How did you find out what happened?'

'Papa swore Carac to secrecy, telling him only to tell me when he thought the time was right. Carac waited until Papa died and then told me. I was about ten, and I hated Aldred from that day on.'

Joan's heart was breaking for both of them now. 'It wasn't Aldred's fault. He was just the result of it.'

'Yes, but don't you see? If Mama hadn't had Aldred, Papa might have forgiven her. They might have been as they used to be, and we would all have been happy. Instead, because of him, our family was divided in two.'

Just as Richard had divided theirs, Joan thought.

Sir John shook his head and looked at her with eyes full of remorse. 'I never stopped hating Aldred, but it wasn't my fault. I didn't mean to —' he broke off.

Didn't mean to what? Joan didn't understand what he meant by that, but it was late, far too late.

CHAPTER 80

The candles guttered in the draught as Joan closed the hall door. She removed her boots and glanced over to Sir John's chair, hoping he wouldn't be there. She wasn't surprised that he was but, disappointed, she sighed and went over. The fire in the hearth was grey and the room was cold. She stirred a few embers and threw on a log.

It was December, six months since they'd heard the news of Richard's death. Six long months of Sir John sitting in his chair and drinking from sunrise to sunset. But that morning, he had surprised her when he'd got on Baron and said that he was going to check the coppice woods. It was the first sign he was coming back to himself, and she'd thanked God for it.

But when she'd ridden out to join him, the woods were silent. There were no men, no sounds of chopping axes, no piles of cut hazel poles and no Sir John.

Leaning over his chair, she removed the empty goblet from his limp hand, the smell of stale wine making her reel. His hair and beard, once so neatly trimmed, were unkempt and full of lice. There was a stain down the front of his tunic from spilt wine, and he stank. Empty jugs and flagons littered the floor. He was a pitiful and disgusting sight, and it made her want to scream and beat his stupid chest until it hurt. It had to stop.

'John! Wake up!' She shook him hard.

He blinked his eyes, slowly unfurled his legs and rubbed a hand through his hair and over his face. He reached for the flagon, but she picked it up before he could touch it. With resignation, he flopped back into his seat.

'Well?' he said.

'You can't go on like this. You'll drink yourself to death —'

'At least then your wonderful Thomas can take over. That would make you happy, wouldn't it?'

His words were vicious but she knew most of that was due to the drink. She knelt in front of him and took hold of his hands. 'Richard is dead. We can't bring him back. He always wanted to be a knight and go into battle with the king. You gave him that. Young as he was, he bravely led his men into battle and died honourably. He would have wanted it that way. You should be proud. I understand how you feel, but he wouldn't want to see you like this —'

Sir John slowly lifted his head, and his cold steely eyes found hers. In all the years she had endured that look, she had never seen such pain and hatred before. She didn't know this Sir John, and something inside her shrank away from him.

'What do you know, you stupid woman? You understand nothing.' He stood up, the sudden violence of the motion throwing her backward on to the floor. He stood over her, his jaw firm, his fists clenched tight.

Joan covered her face with her arms and cringed in fear. What had she done? She was only trying to help.

She squeezed her eyes tight, waiting for the blow.

It didn't come and, not daring to move, she listened to the staggered stamp of his boots across the hard stone floor and the bang as he slammed the door behind him.

She lay still for a long time. Only when she heard the clatter of hooves leaving the yard did she dare to open her eyes and breathe again. She was shaking and gripped hold of the chair to pull herself up enough to sit on it, fearful she'd fall. What had happened to him?

Joan felt like a drink herself and reached for the flagon. As she did, something moved under the sheepskin. She shifted her weight and felt underneath. It was a neatly folded parchment. Curious, she turned it over in her hands. She recognised the seal. It would be wrong to read it. She put it on the table next to her. What did this person want with Sir John?

She poured some wine and savoured the taste as the soothing liquid slid down her throat. Her eyes returned to the letter. She was running the estate and had a right to know what was going on. Hesitating, she reached forward but stopped. The letter was addressed to Sir John, but he was in no fit state to deal with anything and would never tell her its contents. She shouldn't — but if it was nothing, he would never know, and it could be something important.

Joan picked it up and tentatively opened it. The words leapt before her eyes, and when she finished reading, she flopped back into the chair, the letter still in her hand.

Now she understood. Finally, she understood.

CHAPTER 81

Joan wrung her hands and paced frantically up and down the hall. The slightest sound of boots outside or hooves on the cobbles sent her hurrying to the window in the hope it was Sir John, or least someone with news of him. No one had seen or heard of him since the day he'd walked out and she had found the letter.

That had been over a week ago.

Joan looked at the window in vain hope. The trees were bent over in the wind, and soon it would be dark. Had robbers waylaid him on the road? Was he now lying injured somewhere? If he was, he wouldn't last long in this freezing weather, and the men had searched all the roads. Maybe he was drinking his way from inn to inn across the shire? If so, he would be an easy target for pocket thieves or cutpurses. They had to find him, and soon.

There was also the matter of the scrolls to deal with. The two men had said they'd be back at the end of the year, and that was almost upon them. And there was the letter to deal with. She was powerless without him. She ground her nails into the palms of her hands. There was no point staying in and fretting; she had to do something.

Grabbing her warmest cloak, she smiled sardonically

as she saw its rabbit-fur lining. At least she'd got something out of that particular disaster. Bracing herself, Joan stepped outside into the fury of a cold northerly wind. Wrapping the cloak tightly around her and tying her hood under her chin, she shouted for a boy to fetch Star.

As she rode, she kept a wary eye on the sky. Low yellow clouds were gathering over the moor, a sure sign of snow. If she kept a good pace, she should get to Carac's house before the first snowflakes started to fall.

As soon as she arrived, Simon opened the door and welcomed her in. Holding her hands to the warmth of the fire, Joan glanced over at Carac, asleep in his chair. She hadn't seen him for a few months, and his appearance shocked her. His head was dropped on his chest. A few strands of thin grey hair parted at the centre of his head and hung limply to his shoulders. His cheeks were sunken and sallow, there were dark rings under his eyes and she could hear his laboured breathing.

'He sleeps a lot now but often talks of you. I know he'll be pleased to see you,' said Simon, offering her a hot spiced wine.

Joan sipped it gratefully, feeling the tingle as its warmth brought the colour back to her cheeks.

'Father?' Simon put a gentle hand on Carac's shoulder. 'Lady Joan is here to see you.'

Carac blinked and rubbed his eyes, a smile spreading across his mouth. 'Joan, how fare you?' He tried to stand. 'Forgive me,' he said, leaning back. 'It's difficult to move much these days. It's the old bones I'm afraid. They don't carry me as they used to.'

'But your mind is as sharp as ever,' said Simon.

'Forgive me, Carac,' Joan said. 'If I'd known you

were so poorly, I'd have come to see you before.'

'It's just old age, nothing more. It comes to us all. I think the good Lord will send for me soon.' Looking across at her, she saw that there was still a hint of light in his eyes. 'It is a blessing to see you now. Tell me, any news of John?'

'I wish there was, but no.' Joan leaned forward, her arms resting on her knees. 'It's my fault he's missing. He took Richard's death very badly and drank heavily. I could forgive him that, but Lord knows, I'd been understanding for so long and was at my wit's end. I thought that if I talked to him, reminded him how brave Richard was and that he wouldn't want to see him like that, I just thought it might help; snap him out of it, or something. I didn't know what else to do. I thought I was doing the right thing, but I only made matters worse. I've never seen him so angry—no, it was more than anger. It was hurt, self-loathing and desperation all at once. He stormed out, and no one's seen him since.' She didn't want to cry, but her eyes were filling up and she couldn't stop them. 'And there's this, you see.' She took the letter from her purse. 'I found it on John's chair the day he walked out. You'd better read it.'

Carac moved the candle closer and, with stiff fingers, unfolded the parchment and held it close to his eyes.

Sir John,

I am returned from the Siege of Calais and trust by now you will have heard the news of your son's death. It is my sad duty to inform you of the manner in which he died. At the height of the battle of Crecy, Richard was ordered to move forward. He disobeyed and was seen by many fleeing the scene of battle to the safety of trees to the left of the field. In the face of the enemy, he deserted his men and the king's army in the most cowardly way.

His actions brought disgrace not only to the name of Chiddleigh, but, because he was under my patronage, to my own house of Gravesmire as well.

The morning after the battle was won, Welsh spearmen found his body in the bushes. He had been brutally attacked and suffered numerous stab wounds. I find it curious that he was found in such a manner with part of his surcoat and short sword missing. I doubt the French killed him, for when the battle was won, they fled to their lines. Our losses were heavy, and maybe his own men sought revenge? We shall never know.

You must appreciate that I can no longer be associated with the house of Chiddleigh. I therefore rescind the three Knights Fees I formerly granted to you. I have notified the Earl of Barcombe, since I am under the belief that he, too, has associations with your title.

Frederick de Gravesmire, Earl of Devonshire.

'You can imagine how I felt when I read that, and poor John must have been devastated. And then, like a numbskull, I went on and on about how brave Richard was...' Joan bit her lip. 'How could I have known? I was only trying to help. And now he's disappeared with his mind in such torment. He could be anywhere, and if he's drinking, I fear for him. But I suppose it explains why he reacted the way he did.'

'Indeed it does. May I?' Carac passed the letter to Simon.

Simon stood behind Carac's chair and when he finished reading, neatly folded the letter back into its creases and solemnly handed it back to Joan. Reluctantly, she took out the six scrolls in her purse. 'And there are these. I found them months ago.'

Carac raised an eyebrow and started to read. When he had finished, he neatly re-rolled and tied each one and handed them back. 'The contracts add up to a very formidable amount of money. Did you know John was visiting a moneylender?'

Joan shook her head, burning with shame on Sir John's behalf. 'I had no idea. He called it business in Exeter. I can't believe he was borrowing for so many years and for what? For his obsession with status and the Earl of Devonshire's king's fund.' She spat out the words.

She was at a loss and, looking into Carac's wise old face with its lines and creases, had never felt more in need of his help in all her life. For a moment, if he had offered her his arms, she would have willingly fallen into them, but such behaviour would only embarrass him. 'What do I do?'

'You're well rid of that old rogue, and it won't hurt to lose the Knights Fees. My main concern is the Earl of Barcombe and whether he will follow suit,' said Carac, now sitting in his familiar pose with his hands together, as though in prayer.

'What do you mean?'

'If the Earl of Barcombe were to take back the Ashetyne lands, you'd have to leave Court Barton and head for the Chiddleigh estate in the north of Devonshire. The old house hasn't been lived in since Sir James moved down here years ago. I imagine it's in a very ruined state and the land up there is poor. If the Earl of Devonshire buys John's debts and calls them in, you'd have no way of paying him, and you'd lose everything. It's what I've always feared.'

'Would he do that?' Simon asked.

'I don't know,' Carac said heavily. 'He might.'

'But surely, the Earl of Barcombe won't take Ashetyne. The two families have been friends for generations.' The thought of losing Court Barton appalled Joan. She couldn't start again in a ruin of a house in the north of the shire!

'If it had been the earl's father, I'd have said no, but I've only a brief acquaintance with his son, and that was as a boy when he was growing up with John. In any case, John was better friends with the earl's cousin, Favian.'

It was her worst nightmare. They could lose everything. 'If the debts are called in and we lose Ashetyne, what could we do?' she asked.

'You'd have to sell the Chiddleigh lands to cover the debts. At least, Sir John would.'

'He'd never do that. It would be the end of generations of the Chiddleigh estate. It would finish him.'

Carac looked grim. He raised his eyebrows and slowly spread his hands on his lap. 'He may have no choice.'

They could never leave the manor, and with no estate, where would they go? Dear God, they'd be impoverished. Sir John would be no better than the peasants he despised. Papa might take them in, but the thought was abhorrent. The Lord and Lady of the Manor reduced to no better than beggars living on her parents' charity. There had to be a way.

'So what do I do now?' She swallowed her rising panic.

'We need to find him. Maybe he can plead with the Earl of Barcombe, but John holds the title of Lord and we can do nothing on our own.'

'The men are looking but have found nothing,' she said.

'Then the men must look harder. Simon, organise search parties to cover a wider area to set out at first light.' Carac paused, frowning a little. 'And there may be something I can do. I cannot promise it will come to anything and shall say no more, but rest assured I will do my best.' He laid a hand on her arm and smiled.

She returned his smile with little conviction. She could always rely on Carac. If anyone could find a way through this mess, he could.

Carac leaned forward and placed a hand over hers, his voice now so low she could barely hear it. 'It is nearly time to make my peace with God, and so I take the liberty to speak as I have never dared before. You are a fine woman who deserved better than Sir John. I have always held you in deep affection, more than a bailiff has the right to do.' He smiled at her, his eyes shining once again. 'No, I shall be true. I loved you and always have. There; it has taken me all these years to confess. It is one of the advantages of getting old: one can say more without fear of embarrassment. I haven't embarrassed you, have I?'

Joan looked deeply into his eyes. Such sincere eyes. 'You could never embarrass me, my dearest Carac. I don't know what I'd have done without you.'

'I wanted you to know. It was, and still is, my pleasure to help you in any way I can.' Carac held her eyes, and for a moment Joan wished he was younger.

She squeezed his hands, leaned forward and brushed his cheek with her lips.

Reaching the door, she swallowed the lump in her throat. As she rode away, she glanced back. Carac was leaning heavily against the door, smiling.

CHAPTER 82

Peter swung his arms and stamped his feet. He'd lost the feeling in his fingers and toes a long time ago.

He glanced around. The moors were turning from grey to night purple. He had no stomach for this. He pulled his woollen cloak close and shoved his hands inside. What was he doing up here in the freezing cold when he should have been working? Sir John was a drunken sot; why should he care where he was? And the chances of finding him were the same as catching a hare by its tail.

That afternoon, Simon had told his group to split up to cover more ground. Peter had jumped straight in and said he'd look along the high drover's road—a good track with rocks offering at least some shelter from the wind. Even so, he couldn't remember the last time he'd been so cold.

The bell tolled the third quarter. It was getting darker. His stomach groaned, and he could smell Janet's stew and feel the warm embers of the hearth waiting for him.

He'd never find Sir John now. He'd take the shortcut on one of the sheep trails down the hill and be home in half the time; no one would know.

He'd gone a short way when he saw a still dark shape

on the ground to his left. A thief? Alert now, Peter drew his knife and peered into the gloom. He couldn't make out any details, but any thief would have made his move by now.

He looked again. It could be a deer. There was a lot of meat on a deer. Silently, he crept towards it.

It didn't move. Slowly, he raised his arm and was inches from thrusting it into the flesh when it groaned — a man's groan. He leaped back, his knife still in his hand, his heart thumping out of his chest. Cautiously, he leaned in and saw Sir John lying on his side and curled into a ball like a baby.

What was he doing here like that? Sheathing his knife, Peter knelt and touched Sir John's cheek with a trembling hand.

The skin was cold. He snatched his hand away and crossed himself. Sir John had breathed his last.

The eyes flew open.

'God's balls!' Peter jumped back.

Sir John screwed up his face and clawed at Peter's sleeve. 'Help me. My leg,' he said, his voice strained.

Peter glanced down and gagged at the sight of the bone sticking out below Sir John's knee, shining white under the rising moon.

'Sir John? It's Peter from the forge. What happened?'

'Peter? Father Peter? Praise God. I prayed for you to come. Father, take my hands. My time is upon me, and I fear the flames of hell. Please, Father, I must confess.' Sir John gripped hold of Peter's arms, his glazed eyes fixed imploringly on Peter's face.

'Sir John, I'm not Father Peter. I'm Peter from the forge. Everyone's been looking for ye.'

Sir John pulled him close, his breath blowing hot air on

Peter's face as his voice rasped. 'Father, the flames are close, I can feel their heat. I beg you, I need absolution.' Desperately, he clawed at Peter, his face torn with anguish. 'I have lain here many a night, and I may not have long to live. Listen to me. Men — two, three, I don't know — dragged me from my horse. I tried to fight, but they were too many and armed with cudgels and knives. They beat me, searched me and took my purse. I dragged myself to the shelter of this rock, but I am afraid and weak. Father, are you listening?'

The man was delirious. Peter winced as Sir John dug his nails into his arm. He wasn't the priest, but Sir John thought he was, and he was desperate to confess. It would be wrong to hear any more, but he was curious.

'I'm listening,' he said.

'Thank you. Thank you, Father.' Sir John's eyes lost their fear and his grip relaxed as he held Peter's hands.

'It was the night of my wedding celebrations. It had been a long day, and I was bored with it. I was seated at the high table keeping a smile on my face but, in truth, waiting for the time to leave. My new lady sat to my right. She was a quiet little thing, although she didn't displease me. I was watching everyone enjoying themselves. A loud raucous laugh came from near the barrels. I looked over and there he was.' Sir John's eyes suddenly flared with hatred and he resumed his grip. 'He was a man now, but there was no mistaking him. He had no right to be there. He was deliberately goading me with his presence. I felt the fury rise to my throat and clenched my fists under the table to control my face. I couldn't do anything in front of my guests, but I watched his every move like a hawk. He was dancing and drinking with one of my kitchen maids.'

490

'Who was this man?' Peter asked, although he had a good idea.

'Aldred de Chiddleigh, Father.' Even in his weak state, Sir John spoke the name with venom. 'There is ill-feeling between his family and mine, and I can't tell you how much I have always hated him. I thought I should let the matter pass, but as I watched him, I could see that he was drunk. I feared he might cause a scene, challenge me, and speak of family matters. Matters that should not be known to others. I had to get him out, and I awaited my chance. I saw him stagger from the hall with the maid and went to follow him, but as I made my way through the crowd, I was waylaid by guests. I couldn't be seen to be anything other than courteous, but all the time I was anxious to end their idle chatter and find him. You must understand; I only wanted to speak with him and order him off my land.'

'And did ye?' said Peter.

'No. By the time I got outside, he was nowhere to be seen. I searched the yard and looked in the Great Barn but couldn't find him. I thought about returning to my guests and wished now that I had. Remember, Father, I was young and the new lord. I had to assert my position, and I was angry. I couldn't have him insulting me. I assumed he was going home and decided to find him. I took the path through the woods, leading to the river. It was dark. I remember I stood and listened many times. Once, I thought I heard a girl crying, but it was faint.'

Little Annie. Peter bit back his anger. 'So ye didn't try to find the girl to see if she needed help?'

'No, Father. I suppose I should have —'

'Yes, ye should.'

491

'I'm sorry, Father, but I had to find Aldred. Father, don't let go of my hands. Please, I was desperate.'

Peter couldn't bear to have him touch him, but Sir John was holding him so tightly that he couldn't pull away either.

'Go on,' he said.

'I kept on the path and reached the river. It was a little lighter there and, ahead of me, I saw two men fighting. I stood back in the trees. I was sure one of them was Aldred, and at first, I didn't know the other.'

'So what happened then?'

'They fought for some time, and then Aldred lay still. As the other man stood back, rubbing his hands, I recognised him. It was that numbskull, Peter, from the forge. He took to his heels and fled back through the woods. He didn't see me, but I saw the panic on his face. When Aldred didn't move, I thought he was dead.

'I approached carefully and stood over him. His chest was still, so I bent down to feel his mouth for breaths. Aldred roared like a raging bull and swung his bear-like arm at me. He took me off guard and hit me on my side, sending me sprawling. His huge bulk was swaying over me. He roared again and lunged. We wrestled, but he was much larger than me and pinned my arms to the ground. His face was evil and twisted with rage, and his ale-soaked breath suffocated me. He raised his arm, and I saw the glint of a blade. I was terrified and tried to move but he was too strong. I clawed the ground with my hands for a stone, a stick, anything to defend myself. I felt something. I didn't know what it was, but I grabbed it and with all my strength smashed it up to him. Once, twice, more I don't remember. He let out an ear-splitting howl and fell sideways. I got to my feet, shaken and breathless. He was clutching his side, rolling and moaning.

'That's when I saw the red stain growing through his clothes. I looked down at my hand. It was covered in blood and I was holding a knife. Stricken, I opened my fingers, let it drop, and staggered back. I stood there shaking and staring, as I heard him gasp violently and then lie still.

'Father, I didn't know what to do. I panicked and ran back through the woods as fast as I could. When I reached the yard, I was breathless and sweating. I went to the stables, out of sight. I was shaking so much I could hardly stand, and then I retched and brought up my wedding feast. I went into my horse's stable and threw my arms around his neck. I wanted to cry but squeezed my eyes tight, forcing myself not to.

'I couldn't stop trembling, and when I recovered my breath and stood back, Baron had blood on his neck and my hands were still red and sticky with it. I plunged my hands into Baron's water pail then wiped his neck and tried to wash away the blood spots on my clothes. With luck, they would pass for wine stains.

'I had no idea how long I'd been gone, but I had to get back to my guests and behave as though nothing had happened. I took a few deep breaths, straightened my belt and forced a smile on my face. What else could I do?

'As I entered the hall, my legs were trembling. I expect my face was white, but I kept that smile and took my place at the top table. I was shaking like a leaf and twisted inside with fear. I drank several goblets of wine and prayed I appeared no more than a little drunk.'

Sir John grasped Peter's hands harder. 'Believe me, Father, I didn't mean to kill him. It was an accident.'

The deathly silence of the moor stretched between them. Peter sat back, stunned by what he'd heard. Then, as the words shifted into sense, he felt the anger crawl from every part of him. He burned for revenge and leaned forward. Sir John flinched back.

'Ye killed him. All this time, it was ye,' Peter hissed. 'Ye sent me to gaol as a murderer and ye'd have let me swing on the gibbet—dear God, those tinkers. Knowin' they were innocent, ye let them hang in your place.'

'They were just tinkers and thieves; they would have swung in any case. Father, I beg of you, you must absolve me. It was an accident. I didn't mean—'

'I am not Father Peter!' Peter screeched just inches from his face. 'My God, you're more evil than I thought ye were.'

Sir John frowned. 'You're...not Father Peter?'

'No, I'm not. I told you, I'm Peter the blacksmith from the forge.' Peter watched with satisfaction as confusion, then truth changed Sir John's face from one fear to another.

'Dear God, you'll tell everyone! My peasants will hate me. They'll send for the sheriff. They'll gather at Gibbet Hill and cheer as they watch me hang from the rope. I'm your lord, I beg of you: don't do that to me.'

Peter's heart turned to stone as Sir John pleaded with him like a baby, clawing at his arms. Never in all his life had he felt so much contempt for one man. He wanted him to suffer and wondered if he dared to speak.

Then he looked at Sir John's pathetic face beseeching him and he knew what he was going to do.

'Now it's your turn to listen,' he said, 'because I've a

story to tell ye. I hope you're listening, Sir John.

'On the night of your wedding, the girl ye heard crying in the woods and didn't stop to help? That was my sister, Annie, the kitchen maid dancin' with Aldred. She was cryin' because he'd forced himself on her. That was why I sought him out. Ye were right, it was me ye saw fightin' with him.

'Later, it turns out that Annie's with child. Aldred's child. The news of that killed my Pa. In the New Year, Annie had a baby boy. A few weeks later, she was with the Lady Joan the night she gave birth. I believe Lady Joan's baby — your child — was born dead and, somehow, Annie's child was believed to be your son. The one ye called Richard. Because, strangely, the next day Annie no longer had her son. And I think Lady Joan knew. All those years, your kitchen maid and your lady were playing ye for a fool.'

'You lie. Joan wouldn't do that to me.' Sir John's voice was quiet.

'Wouldn't she? Richard didn't look like ye, did he? He was dark and stocky, just like Aldred, his father. As soon as I saw that, I got to thinkin'. I asked Annie once. She couldn't look me in the eye and deny it.

'Richard, your precious son, wasn't your son at all. His father was Aldred, and his mother was your kitchen maid. Richard was nothing more than a common bastard.' Peter leaned close to Sir John's ear and whispered. 'Do ye hear what I'm sayin'? Richard wasn't your son.'

Peter watched with twisted pleasure as Sir John paled, his face creasing in disbelief and his eyes closing in pain as his words tormented him.

'You're lying. Richard was my boy.'

495

'Was he? I don't think so.'

Peter stood and looked down on his lord, enjoying him suffer as he had made so many others suffer. 'You're not so high and mighty now, are ye my lord?'

Sir John regarded him and spoke quietly but with an underlying menace. 'I don't believe your madness, but if you swear to God that you'll say nothing of this night, I'll pardon you. You can fetch help. There's still time.'

'I might.' Peter paused. 'But then again, I might not.' He was toying with him, enjoying his power over him.

'I beg you. I can make you rich; give you money, land, anything you want. But in God's name, don't leave me here to die unabsolved or send me to the gallows. I'll burn in hell, you know I will.'

Peter stared down.

'Then go to hell,' he said quietly and walked away.

CHAPTER 83

Joan reached up and took the cloth from its drying rail. Her stomach churning, she glanced at Annie standing nearby. Annie was watching her every move, wringing her hands, her mouth tight with expectation. They waited silently, then Annie nodded.

Carefully, Joan laid it out, holding her breath and daring herself to look. She ran her hand reverently over the cloth.

How beautiful. The colour radiated. It was the most brilliant red scarlet she had ever seen and it was soft to the touch.

Warily, Annie reached forward. They looked at each other, each feeling the cloth.

'It worked. It actually worked.' Annie whispered.

Joan bit her lip as together they stared, disbelieving, at the cloth in front of them. After all the years of hard work, hopes and disappointments, this was the moment she had dreamed of. And now it was here, she couldn't believe her eyes.

A giggle rose into her throat, found its way around her tongue, and then burst out like a series of bubbles. Annie giggled too. Their giggles grew to laughter. She took Annie's hands and, together, they twirled around the dying shed, laughing and shouting at the tops of the voices. 'We've done it, we've done it!'

Annie's hair flew out behind her, as she threw back her head, her eyes bright and laughing. Joan was dancing on air as they spun around and around, faster and faster until the shed was a whirl of colours.

'Pardon, my lady, but they've found Sir John.' Mark's plaintive voice sliced the air and stopped them dead.

One look at his pallid face, his downcast eyes and the way he fiddled with his cap told her the worst.

'Who found him?' Joan's voice caught in her throat.

'Peter the blacksmith, my lady. This morning in the ling just off the drovers' road. He thought he'd fallen from his horse.' Mark shuffled, refusing to meet her eyes. 'I'm sorry, my lady, the Lord had already taken him. Peter said looked peaceful.' His voice trailed off.

Joan let go of Annie's hands and smoothed the front of her kirtle. 'Thank you for telling me, and thank Peter for me.'

She didn't cry. Her eyes didn't even water. What she felt was overwhelming sorrow and regret. For all his faults, Sir John deserved to be taken in a better way than to have slipped drunkenly from his horse. But that was the man he had become and the good Lord saw fit to take him.

CHAPTER 84

Peter, is that you? What are you doing up here on your own?' Annie put the gorse she'd been cutting into her basket and joined the huddled form sitting beside the rock.

'It's freezing up here. I should have thought you'd be nice and warm in the forge. It's the best job to have this time of year.' She tried to make light of it, for his eyes were heavy and his shoulders drooped as though he carried a millstone on his shoulders.

'What is it?' she asked. 'Is William alright? I thought he looked a little pale the last time I saw him and Janet—'

'I found Sir John.' Peter twisted around and pointed to the hill leading to the drover's road. 'Up there.'

'I heard. I was with Lady Joan when Mark brought the news. It must have been awful for you.'

Peter slowly raised his head and turned his ashen face towards her. She was shocked. He looked old and haggard with deep black rings under his eyes. It was a troubled face, and when he raised his eyes to meet hers, she felt an all-consuming dread. She knew what lay behind them. It was the burden of terrible sin.

'What have you done?' she asked in a hushed voice.

He buried his head in his hands and shook it slowly. 'He wasn't dead.'

Peter's voice was so low, Annie wasn't sure she'd heard him. 'What do you mean?'

His head shot up, every muscle in his face stretched tight as his eyes burned into hers.

'He wasn't dead!' he screamed. Then, shaking his head and in a quiet voice to himself, he said it again. 'He wasn't dead.'

Surely, he didn't mean he'd — Peter had never liked Sir John, but he couldn't have...

'But Mark said he'd fallen from his horse and the Lord had already taken him.'

'That's what I told them in the village.'

He was frightening her now. 'You didn't — I mean, I know you hated the man, but dear God, tell me you didn't kill him.'

Peter shook his head. 'It wasn't like that.'

'Then how was it? Tell me what happened.'

Peter looked at her with stricken eyes then stared at his boots. Then quietly, he told her the events of that night.

'Ye do understand, don't you? I was blind with rage. I had to revenge what he did to ye, to Pa, to all those men who died at Crecy and for William's lost arm. Sir John was a snivelling, grovelling coward, too afraid to face the gallows. He had blood on his hands, and he didn't care who swung for Aldred's death, just so long as it wasn't him.' He took her hands, his frightened eyes searching for hers, just as Sir John had done with him on that terrible night. 'Sir John was a murderer and didn't deserve my help. God will forgive me, won't he? He won't send my soul to purgatory to burn in the eternal flames?'

He was desperate for her reassurance, but she wasn't God, and she was still trying to take it all in. When she thought of her torment over Richard, and how Sir John had treated Joan and regarded all his people, she understood how Peter felt and, pray God forgive her, she was glad he did what he did.

'I think you were right. Even if you had gone for help, by the time you'd roused the village and returned in the dark, Sir John might have been dead anyway.'

'I was right about Richard, wasn't I?'

Annie sighed. 'Yes, you were.'

'And Lady Joan knew, didn't she?'

Anni nodded. 'It was our terrible secret. No one must know. That's what she said, and we made a vow that they never would.'

They held each other, and as Peter wept on her shoulder, Annie felt an overwhelming pity. Sir John, the man who had caused her own painful secret, had done the same thing to her brother. And, like her, he would have to find a way to live with it.

CHAPTER 85

Joan's slow steps crunched on the gravel path. She squeezed Maria's hand and just the feel of her young skin gave her comfort. Eleanor was unusually quiet, her feet dragging as she walked. Thomas's solemn face looked to neither right nor left at the people lining both sides of the path as they stood with their heads bowed, caps in hand, respectfully silent.

Sir John would have approved of that. As she passed, Annie gave her an encouraging smile. Dear Annie who'd stayed with her, soothing her guilt and letting her cry on her shoulder.

She could hear the gathering of people falling in step behind them. Annie with her brother, Peter, the one who found him. Joan would be forever grateful to him. If he hadn't resumed his search so early that morning, Sir John may never have been found. Ellyn told her that when the cold took hold, and it had been very cold, sleep took over.

Joan hoped she was right. She didn't like to think of Sir John suffering on his own.

Father Peter, in his usual black, stood by the church door. Upright and walking in a practised stately manner, he led the silent procession to the east side of the cemetery. Fixing her eyes on the back of his soft black cap, she followed behind.

The priest stopped at the head of a freshly dug grave, turned and opened a large leather-bound book, and waited. Thomas stood at the other end; Joan and the girls together along one side.

Not wanting to look into the empty hole, Joan stared at the corner of the grey stone church. The smell of woodsmoke hung in the air like a cloak. The bell began its solemn toll, then the sound of slow regular steps. They were bringing him now.

What had been his final thoughts? She wished she could have been with him and comforted him.

Six men came around the side of the church, carrying the coffin on their shoulders. She'd insisted that the coffin be made from the best oak on the estate. Peter had forged curled handles for each side, and John Forge etched a nameplate for the lid. Not that anyone could see it, for the Chiddleigh colours were draped majestically over its entire length.

Joan took a deep breath. She wouldn't weep. Sir John had always seen her as his lady, and she would not let him down, not this last time. He hadn't been perfect, but what man was? He'd been weak and gullible, and at times, cold and heartless. How many times had he infuriated her, making her so frustrated she'd wanted to scream and shout because he just wouldn't listen? Too many, that was how many, and sometimes she had. She smiled wryly. Sir John hadn't been a bad man, not really.

Father Peter began to read, his deep smooth voice carrying across the still morning. Joan bowed her head as the Latin words drifted over her. Four men stepped forward, picked up the ends of the leather straps and lowered the coffin into the depths in front of her. Thomas bent down and threw the first handful of soil into the grave. It landed with a scattering.

Such a sad and final sound, Joan thought, and threw in her own handful.

The priest shut his book and chanted a few last words. He nodded to Thomas, who, as the new Lord de Chiddleigh, led his family and people away from his father's grave.

It wasn't the right time to be proud of her son, but Joan couldn't help it. And she was sure that, despite everything, Sir John was looking down from heaven and feeling the same.

CHAPTER 86

August 1348

Four months later, Joan stared out of the hall window, her chin resting in her hand. She sighed. Understandably, Thomas had wanted to go back to school and she missed him. It was his last year before he would go to the University of Oxford to study to be a physician. Selfishly, she'd have preferred to have him with her, but he'd worked so hard with his studies and was so young to be the Lord of the Manor. That was assuming there would be an estate left for him to inherit. There were still Sir John's debts to deal with, and goodness knew how she was going to do that. She hadn't said anything to Thomas; there was no need to worry him.

She turned her gaze to the sheep grazing in the field. They didn't have a worry in the world. It must be nice to be a sheep.

It was odd. For months before Sir John's death, she had run things quite happily on her own. Yet now he was gone, she missed him, in a strange way. Annie said that time was a great healer, and she should know.

A smartly dressed man who looked to be in his mid-thirties rode sedately into the yard. He was very striking in well-cut clothes, with a large feather in his hat. He halted his horse but remained in the saddle and glanced around.

Joan watched, entranced, as he noted the manor house and the Great Barn, his expression giving nothing away. Casually throwing a leg over his horse's neck, he slid expertly to the ground. He had a certain presence about him. Was he one of the men from Exeter who had come for his debts? If so, handsome or not, he was out of luck.

A young stable lad darted across the passageway.

'You there! Come and see to my horse,' the visitor ordered.

The boy shyly stepped out of the shadows.

'Is your lord at home?'

Nervously, the boy shook his head.

'Then is Lady de Chiddleigh here?'

The boy nodded.

'Then fetch someone to tell her that Favian de Riddleham is here to see Sir John.'

Favian? Joan frowned. She didn't know any Favian. She turned from the window, smoothed her kirtle, patted her hair into place and stepped forward to greet him.

As Favian stood on the threshold, she couldn't help but catch her breath. He wasn't as tall as Sir John, but he carried himself with the same bearing of nobility. His dark hair was neatly trimmed to the shoulder and shone in the light of the doorway. He had the deepest brown eyes she had ever seen and a slight scar that ran from the end of his right eye and down his cheek. A fight perhaps, over a fair lady? Oh, now she was being ridiculous, but there was something about him that made it difficult to look away. An embarrassing blush flamed her cheeks. She hoped he hadn't noticed and lifted her chin.

'Good morrow, my lord. I am Lady de Chiddleigh. You wish to see me?'

He bowed and removed his hat, his eyes holding hers. 'Good morrow. Allow me to introduce myself: I am Lord Favian de Riddleham, nephew to the Earl of Barcombe.' A slight smile played around his lips.

Nephew to the Earl of Barcombe? This powerful man may hold her future in his hands. Cursing herself for feeling flustered, Joan fought to keep her voice steady. 'May I ask, what is your business here?'

'I wish to speak with Sir John, but I understand he's not at home.'

'You've obviously not heard, my lord. The good Lord took Sir John just before last Christmas. You may state your business to me.' He hadn't taken his eyes off her, which was flattering if a little disconcerting.

'I'm very surprised and sorry to hear that, my lady. John and I were boyhood friends.'

He held her gaze with a warmth that Joan had never felt from a man before. Her insides fluttered and, struggling to keep her composure, she led him to the chairs by the hearth.

'I'm pleased to meet you, my lord. I'm sure you'd like some wine and refreshments.' Her hand trembling a little, she poured some wine.

He swirled the goblet easily in his hand and took a sip. 'I congratulate you on your taste in wine, my lady,' he said, with a smile and slight tilt of his head.

She wished he wouldn't look at her under his eyebrows like that. It was both compelling and a little disarming. She returned the smile and demurely lowered her eyes.

Favian leaned back in his seat, looking totally at ease as they talked politely about the quality of last years' harvest, the recent dry spell and the state of the tracks. But he hadn't come all this way to discuss the weather, and those eyes were twisting her stomach in knots.

'You're probably wondering about the purpose of my visit,' he said, twirling his goblet and confidently crossing his legs.

Yes, she was.

'I bring both good and not so good news. Let us deal firstly with the not so good. My uncle, the Earl of Barcombe, received a letter from the Earl of Devonshire regarding events at the Battle of Crecy. I don't know if you are aware?'

Joan nodded. The old fox had said he'd written a letter to the earl.

'Then we are both aware of the unfortunate event, and I see no reason to dwell upon it. I'm sure you can appreciate that it leaves my uncle in a difficult position. The Riddleham and Chiddleigh houses have been connected for many generations. My grandfather and Sir James were particularly well acquainted, to the extent that our Ashetyne estate was granted to him. Given the, er, events in Crecy, you understand that my uncle has to maintain his position and keep favour with the king. He cannot be seen to continue his alliance with your family. As the Earl of Devonshire so succinctly put it, my uncle has no choice but to reclaim his lands from Sir John.'

So she was to lose the Ashetyne lands. But what about the rest of it? The palms of Joan's hands were clammy, and she felt uncomfortably hot.

'Of course I'm disappointed, but it is as I expected,' she said with fortitude. 'But what of your good news, my lord?'

He flashed a smile. 'A week after Christmas my uncle

received another letter. It was from Carac de Perceux.'

'Carac? God rest his soul.' Joan crossed herself. 'The good Lord took him a week after John. It was a terrible loss.' Just the mention of Carac's name made her feel empty inside.

Favian's voice mellowed. 'I'm truly sorry to hear that. I haven't seen Carac since I was a boy, and I'd like to have met him again. I thought, by his words, that he was a most astute and loyal friend to Sir John.'

'He was indeed, and I miss him deeply.' She couldn't explain just how deeply. Carac, with his dry smile and solid advice, had always been her friend and her rock, and now, when she needed him most, he wasn't there. Her eyes misted with tears, but she quickly blinked them away.

'My dear lady, I have no wish to upset you.' Favian's voice was velvet smooth. 'My lady?' He leaned forward and held out a silk kerchief.

Joan took it gratefully. It had his scent, and as she dabbed her eyes, the heat spread from her neck to her cheeks. She looked away. Lord, she was behaving like a young maid! What must he think of her?

'Carac was a dear friend. But pray continue.'

'In his letter, Carac explained the background of Sir John's acquaintance with Earl of Devonshire and the situation you are now facing.'

'Delicately put, my lord,' Joan said with a dry smile. 'Let us speak plainly: John accrued large debts over many years and has left me with no means of repaying.' She dared to look him in the eye.

'So I understand. My uncle has fond boyhood memories of when Carac and John were at the castle and would like to help, but as I explained, he is in a difficult position.' He flicked an imaginary speck of dirt from his hose. 'However, I am not. Also, I have a debt of honour to repay.' He finished the last of his wine, letting his words hang in the air.

'You intrigue me. Pray go on.'

Favian sat forward, his arms resting on his knees, his eyes never wavering from hers. 'As boys, my uncle, John and I spent many happy summers together. My uncle was a little older, and so it was John and me who formed a close friendship. One of our favourite pastimes was to swim in the river. That particular summer, we'd had a lot of rain, and the river was running high. I dared John to cross but he refused, saying the flow was too strong and he'd be swept away. I was a few years younger, always trying to prove myself, I suppose, and dived in. You can guess what happened.'

'John was right and you were swept away?'

'Exactly. The water was fierce and took me downstream. I tried to swim but the currents were too strong. I was terrified and screamed but couldn't hear above the roar of the water. I remember seeing the edge of the fall as I went over. It was the most frightening experience of my life. As the water crashed to the bottom, I was gasping, fighting for breath and believed I was going to drown. As I was floundering, my insides burning for air, two hands grabbed me and hauled me by the back of my tunic on to the bank. Quite simply, I owe John my life, and I should like to repay that debt, if I may?' He refilled their goblets and held hers out to her. As she took it, their fingers touched and Joan's heart skipped a beat.

She bit her lip. She must concentrate This man was about to reveal her future, and she was behaving like a tongue-tied dairymaid!

510

'One solution would be if I took this place off your hands and save your embarrassment.' He paused, studying her reaction.

Joan tried to keep the alarm from her face.

'To be honest, it is too small for my taste and the land insufficient,' Favian added. 'I have no use for it.'

Thank God for that. 'If my home is not to your liking, what do you propose, my lord?'

'Another obvious solution would be marriage.' He raised his eyebrows and tilted his head, still holding her gaze.

That was a thought—she shook herself. She was being ridiculous.

'What I propose is this: my uncle shall reclaim Ashetyne lands, and I shall personally buy the Chiddleigh estate from you at a value to enable you to clear your debts. As I said, I've no use for the land and am willing to grant you tenure, payable each Michaelmas. John's son—I take it he does have another son?'

'Thomas,' she said proudly.

'Thomas and his heirs shall retain the title of Lord de Chiddleigh, and no one outside of the two families need ever know the truth. In time, the Lord of the Manor may buy back the Chiddleigh lands, if he so wishes.'

It was a very generous offer and one she hadn't expected. It meant that she could keep her home and Thomas his title. Joan felt as though the weight of a millwheel had been lifted from her shoulders. She wanted to leap up and kiss him but instead allowed a discrete smile to spread across her face.

'I don't know what to say, my lord. You are too kind and have quite taken me by surprise.'

'I am only too pleased to help such an enchanting lady out of her difficulties.'

Damn, she was blushing again. 'I am indebted to you, my lord, and I know John would have appreciated your help. I thank you humbly and am pleased to accept your gracious offer.'

'Good! Then I shall hasten to Exeter and have the necessary papers drawn up. I shall return with due speed and look forward to enjoying your company again.' He smiled beneath those seductive eyes.

'And I, too, my lord.'

'Favian. And may I call you Joan?'

'Please do...Favian, and I await your return with pleasure.'

As she watched him leave, she smiled. The estate was safe, Thomas could go to Oxford and next year her coveted scarlet cloth would be selling well. And Favian — God had been kind. Everything looked set for a bright future.

As Favian rode out of the yard she wondered when she would see him again.

She hoped she wouldn't have to wait too long.